INTO THE FIRE

Susan Abel

Cover image – Fotolia Stock Image
Cover design by Cal Sharp, Caligraphics
Author photo by Katie Darby

ISBN: 9781091399556

DEDICATION

To my loving husband, Robb,
and daughters, Tara and Leah…
Without your encouragement and support,
my stories would never have become books.

To my inspirational parents who raised me
with the perseverance to overcome the many challenges
in my life and who lead by example that through hard work and
dedication your dreams can come true.

And, to the many horses that have graced my life
and taught me patience, forgiveness, how to trust again and the
wisdom of living life in the present.

Love you all…

ACKNOWLEDGEMENTS

Many thanks to Chris Hendell, Pam Ullrich and Carol Beers, for your countless hours of reading and critiquing. And thanks to my editor, Catherine J. Rourke, for applying your many years of experience and wisdom to my work.

Collectively, your honest and supportive feedback is guiding my progress to becoming a better writer.

What is life?

It is the flash of a firefly in the night. It is the breath of a buffalo in the wintertime.

It is the little shadow which runs across the grass and loses itself in the sunset...

~ Crowfoot - Blackfoot Chief

PART ONE

THE PLAN

1 – The Dream

Montana, 1994
Sunday

On a late-summer morning, Katherine Walker sat on the front porch of the rustic lodge she called home, eating breakfast as she peacefully enjoyed the view. Spots of sunlight danced off the rippling surface of Pine Island Lake, distorting the reflection of the surrounding mountains in a Monet-kind of way.

The illusion shattered when her husband blocked her view.

Steven Walker leaned against the porch rail, arms and legs crossed. "Still planning on leaving tomorrow?"

"I don't want to argue about this anymore, Steven."

Katherine set down her fork, having lost her appetite. For months, he had slipped into a routine of avoiding her until the past week. Suddenly, he sought her out at every opportunity.

"Don't go, then," he said.

Katherine took a deep breath. "We've gone over this a dozen times. How can you expect me to change my plans now? The show entries are paid."

"I don't feel good about you and Jessie out on the road… just you two women…" Steven paused, apparently grasping for another excuse. "And… I'll miss you."

She tried, but she couldn't resist. "Is that why you've been working so late every night… and most weekends… even when you don't have emergencies?"

Steven pushed off the rail, standing squarely, arms still crossed. A chill ran down her back as her husband's expression turned cold. "Well, someone has to pay for all your foolishness," he scoffed. "All that equipment—you paid more for that dressage saddle then you did for the horse!"

Katherine closed her jaw tight, struggling to restrain herself, but her patience had worn thin. "I can't believe you're going there again. We aren't poor, Steven. We could both retire today if we wanted to."

Between operating Steven's veterinarian practice and her riding school for the past nineteen years, they were debt-free with plenty in savings. What was he thinking?

She watched him shift his weight, struggling to come up with a rebuttal. Silence.

Katherine was on a roll and couldn't stop now. Questions that had been rattling around in her mind for months needed to be answered.

"I don't understand why you still work so many hours. You're rarely home anymore." Katherine paused until making eye contact. Did she dare ask? "Is there something you're not telling me?"

Steven stepped closer. "Oh, so you think I've been cheating on you? You're one to talk!"

Throwing up his arms, he stormed across the porch, mumbling something under his breath before reentering the lodge, accentuating his exit with a slam of the heavy front door.

Hoping to avoid her husband and another confrontation, Katherine left her plate and walked around the long L-shaped covered porch to the side stairs to escape to her sanctuary—the barn.

Walking down the drive, she tried to focus on the details of the trip, running through a mental list of what she needed to take. Soon her assistant trainer, Jessie Collins, would arrive to help pack and go over last-minute details in preparation for the road trip they were departing on in the morning. Traveling down the West Coast for nearly three months with a horse in tow took some planning. But no matter how hard she tried, she couldn't put Steven out of her mind.

Katherine kicked a pinecone from her path. Eighteen months ago, she and Steve were the happiest couple she knew.

What the hell happened?

As near as Katherine could recall, their problems had begun not long after she decided to return to competing on the national stage, hoping to qualify for the 1996 Olympics. At the age of twenty, she had abandoned her childhood and young-adult dream of winning a gold medal and retired one of the most gifted event horses on the East Coast to move West to take ownership of Two Ponies. The one-thousand-acre mountain estate had been left to her by her uncle, Joseph O'Reilly, in 1960. After managing her girl's summer equestrian camp for thirty-four years and raising two daughters, Katherine yearned to take on a new challenge or, in this case, resurrect an old one.

Anticipating an empty nest, it had seemed like the perfect time. Their eldest adopted daughter, Lisa, was attending Gallaudet University, a school for the deaf in Rochester, New York, where she planned to seek employment after graduation. Josephine, her and Steven's only child, was a sophomore in high school planning to attend college out of town. By the time Katherine had a horse ready to compete, they would both be out of the house. But even though the timing seemed right, all her planning didn't amount to anything more than a pipedream without a super-talented horse with the potential to go all the way.

Katherine soon learned a well-started prospect would cost more than she was willing to deduct from their retirement savings, even though Steven had been onboard in the beginning. So, she had begun to let the idea fade away. Then the most amazing thing happened—an off-the-track Thoroughbred purchased as a school horse turned into a legitimate prospect. Suddenly, her dream had a name—Major Command.

As Katherine approached the old barn on her way to the main one, she could see Major grazing at the back of his paddock. The old stables, built the same time as the massive century-old log-and-stone lodge, looked the same as the first time she saw it from the window of her uncle's Woody station wagon the summer of her first visit to Two Ponies as a child. Growing up in Boston, she had never seen buildings like these except in the Westerns she grew up watching with her father. She still felt humbled by their eternal presence, as unyielding as the region's rugged landscape.

Katherine glanced beyond the split-rail paddock to an opening in the woods, now grown over with ferns and vines. She smiled. There lay the remains of Baldy, the stubborn bald-faced buckskin gelding, and Flower, the sweet common-looking Paint mare that had ignited her love affair with horses so many years ago.

Major now shared the old barn, adjacent corral, and two-acre turnout with Cody, one of Katherine's retired school horses. The old chestnut Quarter Horse made a calm companion for the high-strung Thoroughbred. She couldn't trust Major, always the troublemaker, to be turned out with the rest of the herd for fear of him injuring himself.

Katherine walked up to the fence and whistled. On cue, Major galloped up to the gate all wide-eyed and nostrils flaring, followed by Cody at a slow trot.

The earthy scent of horse filled her senses. "Hi handsome," she said as the blood bay's brilliant scarlet coat glistened in the sunlight like a polished apple. It had taken Katherine years to move past the loss of her old eventing mount, Lady, and allow herself to become so emotionally attached to another horse. She reached over the fence and stroked his silky neck, but once Major realized she didn't have a treat for him, he pranced off wringing his neck and flagging his tail. Major wasn't as sweet as Lady, but he had a heart the size of the broad Montana sky and she loved his bravery and trust in her as she guided him over fences.

Katherine chuckled to herself. Yes, Major was brave, unless water was involved. She guessed he never had the opportunity to traverse a stream or swim in a lake, raised in fenced paddocks followed by a life on the track. It took months to get him to step calmly through a puddle without acting like it was boiling hot or a bottomless pit that would surely swallow him whole.

But water had not been their only challenge. The scary monster tree trunk along the lake trail came in a close second. The old bald log, with the engraving Steven had carved of a heart containing their names the night of her sixteenth birthday, stood shining white in the sunlight. Every time they approached it, Major would side-pass as far from the scary object as the path would allow. It seemed ironic for such a big and strong animal to be afraid of a log, but she understood how high-contrast items were difficult for horses to identify with their poor eyesight.

Katherine recalled Lady rarely shied and found herself frequently comparing the two Thoroughbreds. Lady had been bred for jumping and dressage and never raced, while Major had been bred to race and never jumped. But beyond their breeding and initial training, they were different sides of the same coin—both athletic and talented animals.

The big gelding stood taller and on heavier bone than her sweet girl, and Lady loved to perform and please, always giving her best effort, while Major continually tested her and challenged her to keep him engaged. Katherine found she needed to continually mix up their schooling routine to keep Major entertained and free of boredom.

Lady had been well started and proven in dressage and jumping prior to Katherine's ownership, whereas Major came to her knowing nothing more than how to let it rip down a backstretch. Yet, following two years of daily training and conditioning, she felt they were ready to test their abilities as a team in the eventing world. They would start on the West Coast regionally this fall and then if they qualified, head to the larger national competitions next year.

Since eventing bore a reputation as one of the most physically demanding equine sports for horse and rider, Katherine knew if she didn't pursue her dream now, it might never happen. Having not competed in decades, it would take years to reestablish herself before anyone would sponsor her. She hoped to qualify for Atlanta in 1996, so she wouldn't have the expense of traveling abroad.

Aware her dream was nearly impossible—giving her only two more years to complete the transformation of her ex-racehorse to a finished Level Three dressage horse and confident Grand-Prix jumper—she had to consider her age and Major's as well. Having raced for four years, she feared he might not have as many years to compete at this level compared to horses bred for this discipline.

While Katherine felt fit at fifty-four, a few old injuries were beginning to haunt her. She feared it was now or never. Why couldn't Steven understand that?

Just as she had anticipated, the timing couldn't have worked out better. Lisa had met a wonderful boy, Daniel Tyler, at school and following graduation the couple had married and moved to a nearby deaf community in New York.

Josephine would be leaving for college in two weeks where they would meet up with her between shows when she arrived in Los Angeles.

Both she and Steven would have preferred Josephine attend a school closer to home, but taking after her namesake, Katherine's stubborn Uncle Joe, she insisted on attending UCLA. Unlike her mother and great uncle, who chose the peace and beauty of a quiet life in the wilderness over Boston, Josephine couldn't wait to leave Flathead County for a big city. She wanted to be an actress and where better than LA?

Major returned to grazing as Katherine rested her head over crossed arms on the top rail and glanced toward the lodge. Would Steven really miss her? It was true they hadn't parted for more than a few days during their nineteen years of marriage, but things hadn't been hot and steamy between them for several months. In fact, she couldn't remember the last time they made love, with Steven coming home late and tired every night.

For that reason, Katherine suspected an affair, perhaps with his pretty and much younger brunette office manager, Sherri Sanderson. This was feasible. Steven had matured gracefully, looking more in his forties rather than his fifties, still fit and handsome. Only upon close inspection would anyone spot the gray peppering the temples of his full head of blond-streaked hair, or the mild age lines. When she had hinted at that very thing that morning, Steven automatically threw her past in her face.

Bringing up Billy Black was a low blow. That happened a long time ago, and she had made her choice. She chose Steven in the end and the three of them had put their turbulent past behind them and became best friends again—so what changed? Had he brought up Billy to somehow justify his own infidelity?

When she reached the main barn, Katherine walked past the entryway to the water tank just inside the front pasture. It was low. As she filled the large galvanized tank, she watched the horses grazing below, heads down, tails gently swaying in the breeze. Normally this sight would relax her and take her away from her worries, but not today. Steven's recent behavior nagged at her like a foot itch in her tall boots. Something just wasn't adding up.

He had always been the more devoted one, calling for no reason besides to tell her he loved her, wanting to cuddle, kiss, and hold hands—the hopeless romantic. She loved that about him.

She shook her head. It couldn't be an affair—not Steven. He had fallen in love with her from the first day they met as teenagers. It all came back to Major. Could he be jealous of the horse? She always had horses and he knew how much they meant to her. What was different this time?

Startled by the overflowing water running between her boots, Katherine jerked the hose out of the tank and rushed to turn off the hydrant. How was she supposed to focus on Major when she couldn't even focus on a water tank for five minutes? She tried to put Steven out of her mind by busying herself in the barn until Jessie arrived, checking each item off her packing list as she laid it on the barn floor: dressage bridle, jumping bridle, running martingale, splint boots, and bell boots. When she pulled her expensive dressage saddle from its rack, Steven invaded her thoughts again.

What baffled her most was Steven's sudden objection to the trip. She knew it didn't have anything to do with finances. Claiming to be concerned about her and Jessie traveling alone didn't add up either. He had plenty more reason to be worried about her getting injured from a fall on a cross-country course than anything happening out on the road. There had to be something else… something he wasn't telling her.

Jessie pulled up to the front of the barn in her new red Volkswagen Bug. Katherine smiled. She could use some of Jessie's cheerful, optimistic energy.

"Good morning!" she said, nearly skipping from her vehicle. "This is so exciting! How's the packing going?"

"Pretty good. I have everything laid out, so we just need to go over the list together and fill the trunks. Oh, and I could use help loading the hay."

"Where's Dr. Walker? You should take advantage of that big strong husband of yours more often." She raised her eyebrows twice, dimples punctuating her freckled checks.

"My goodness, Jessie, after all these years you still won't call him by his first name?"

"Sorry, he'll always be Dr. Walker to me," said Jessie, having worked as a vet tech for Steven during the off-season for years. She cocked her head and added, "You two still at odds about the trip?"

"Afraid so. I don't know, Jess. I'm having second thoughts about leaving right now."

"Really?" Jessie glanced around the barn floor. "Looks to me like you're ready to go."

Katherine took in a deep breath and exhaled, shrugging her shoulders. "I'm on the fence."

Jessie nodded, her usual cheerfulness turning to a deflated expression. "Well, we could wait until spring. Major would be further along in training by then."

Katherine shook her head. "No, our entry fees are paid, and we'll need at least two full years of competition to stand a chance of qualifying for Atlanta. It needs to be now. Grab my jumping saddle!"

Jessie's face lit up. "Yes, Ma'am!"

Katherine picked up her clipboard and checked off both

saddles.

Jessie set the saddle down next to the dressage saddle. "Say, I have an idea. Why don't you ask Steven to fly out for a visit between shows? There's nearly a weeklong break at the end of September."

"Great idea, Jess. We could rent a cabin in the mountains or something on the coast. We'll still be at the show grounds in Modesto that week. You wouldn't mind working Major for a couple of days, would you?"

"Of course not. Me and the big fella get along just dandy," she said, striding in the direction of the hay barn with the wheelbarrow, her carrot-red ponytail bouncing side-to-side. "How many bales? I still need to get back home and pack myself."

"Four," she yelled after her.

Katherine had already arranged for hay at each venue along with so many other details that took months of planning. How could she change her mind now? With Steven's approval or not, they were going!

2 – Phone Call

Steven sat at the desk in the library looking over his appointment schedule for the upcoming week. As he tried to put Katherine and the trip out of his mind, the phone rang.

"Hello."

"Hi Steve, Chief here. Got a few minutes?"

Chief Ken Taylor didn't have to identify himself; Steven recognized his deep gravelly voice immediately. Even though he no longer headed Elkhead's Police Department, Steven never questioned why he still went by Chief, figuring no one knew him by any other name after thirty years in that position.

The two men had become good friends about ten years ago. Steven's father and Chief had been close, but Steven never spent much time with him until Chief's old deputy, Mike Collins, took over as chief of police. Mike's son, Dane Collins, started dating Jessie, and Steven and Chief's paths began crossing at social events. The two avid hunters and fishermen naturally gravitated toward each other and began fishing Pine Island Lake together and leaving on week-long hunting trips each fall.

"Sure, what's up?" Steven asked, suddenly sitting at attention as some sort of inner alarm went off. Chief didn't normally make social calls on Sundays. He devoted the Sabbath to church and family; his wife of forty years, Flo; and their two sons and four grandchildren. Chief called for a reason and it wasn't to go fishing.

"Have some news on Werden," Chief said flatly.

Steven tightened his grip on the receiver. He knew which Werden; there was only one left.

The patriarch of the family, Jack Werden, died in prison from a heart attack at age sixty, only a few years following his incarceration. His parents were long gone, and his two sisters were married and living on the West Coast. His eldest boy, Kurt Werden, had died in a scuffle outside Rudy's Bar & Grill a while back. His wife, Cindy Werden, had run off with the family fortune and anything not nailed down shortly after her husband's sentencing, leaving their deaf daughter, Lisa Werden, a ward of the state. Later that year, after Steven and Katherine wed, they adopted Lisa, who had been a beloved student at Two Ponies.

That left only Ricky Werden, Lisa's much older brother, who along with his father had set fire to Katherine's barn full of horses to force her out of business. For generations, the neighboring Werden clan had desperately sought Two Ponies, with its eight-room lodge, adjacent acreage, and the other half of Pine Island Lake, to open an exclusive hunting and fishing ranch. Fortunately, their plans had been spoiled and the horses saved.

Both were charged and convicted of arson and, unfortunately for Jake and Ricky Werden, they were sentenced to the maximum term of twenty years. In a region that relied heavily on tourism including skiing, fly fishing, hunting, and Glacier National Park attractions, fires of any sort were taken seriously, especially in the late-summer dry season. If the barn fire had spread, it would have affected the area for years.

"He's out," said Chief, bringing Steven back from his thoughts.

Steven remained silent; no words could keep up with the thoughts racing through his mind about the possible consequences of this news. Ricky Werden—one of many unfortunate chapters of his wife's past, conveniently forgotten and swept under the rug—was back.

"I guess I lost track of the years," Steven finally said.

"Well, he did get out a year early, but there's something I need to tell you." Steven heard Chief swallow hard and take a deep breath. "I heard from a trusted source he might be planning to take revenge on Katherine."

"Why?" Steven's voice tightened. "What did she ever do to him?"

"Guess in his twisted mind, if it hadn't been for her, his brother and father would still be alive, and he wouldn't have lost the estate and his inheritance."

It took a moment for Steven to grasp that kind of perverse logic. "What do you know?"

"An old deputy of mine, now working at the pen in Billings, informed me that there was some chatter about Ricky and a plan involving your wife."

Steven could feel his heart picking up speed. "What kind of plan?"

"Don't have any details; only know he's been in contact with some of his old gang and that something's in the works." Chief sighed. "Katherine's been through enough… I'm so sorry to have to burden you both with this."

"What can the police do?"

"Not much, I'm afraid… until…"

"Until he does something," Steven interjected.

"We'll keep an eye open for him, but that's about all we can do for now. I just wanted to give you heads-up. Be careful, okay?"

"Will do. Katherine and Jessie are leaving with Major for California tomorrow."

"That's right. Good timing."

"Yeah, they'll be showing down the coast through the third week of November."

"Who else knows she's leaving and where she's going?" asked Chief.

"Probably all of Elkhead, between her students and their families."

"Dang, I guess their trainer trying to qualify for the Olympics is big news. Mike and Dane, along with the rest of the guys at the station, are on alert. If Ricky comes anywhere near Elkhead, we'll know about it."

"Thanks, Chief. Say hi to Flo and the boys for me."

"I will. Tell Katherine good luck with Major and keep us posted on their progress. You all take care."

Steven slowly set the receiver down and sat stunned. The news was a shock, yet it shouldn't have been. Of course, Ricky would blame Katherine. In his eyes, if she hadn't kissed an Indian in public, his brother's fatal stabbing would not have taken place. And, he could understand how Ricky might connect his father's heart attack to his imprisonment and the loss of their family fortune, all because Katherine wouldn't sell Two Ponies. Sick bastard! Like he and Katherine didn't have enough problems! Well actually, there was just one.

He had no qualms with Katherine returning to her show career, finally getting another nice horse of her own and pursuing her childhood dream. But shortly after she acquired Major from Billy Black—their friend, neighbor, and coincidently Katherine's old flame—their troubles began.

Billy had come across the retired racehorse, about to go to auction, while starting two-year-olds at a Thoroughbred farm in California two years earlier. Having witnessed the six-year-old jump out of his four-foot-high paddock nearly from a standstill, he purchased the bay gelding for close to nothing, hoping he would work out as an advanced lesson horse for

Katherine's riding program. When Major quickly progressed in his dressage schooling and Katherine discovered his talent for clearing fences, she began training him for herself.

Steven enjoyed seeing Katherine riding so much again and shared in her excitement over the horse's progress, but then she asked Billy to help train and condition Major, applying many of the techniques he picked up working alongside Thoroughbred trainers. Before long, Billy began spending more time with his wife than he did and when they were together, all she talked about was Billy this and Billy that.

After putting up with nearly two years of that nonsense, Katherine announced they were ready to compete. Steven relished the idea of wedging a few states between Billy and Katherine that fall. Then a little over a week ago, he learned Billy would be mirroring the woman's stops, once again working a string of farms along the coast. They planned to meet up whenever possible to monitor Major's condition. Why hadn't Katherine asked him to check in on Major? He would have flown down—he was the vet, after all!

Another argument that morning hadn't settled a thing. What did he expect after asking her to cancel her plans at the last minute? Why couldn't he just come out and ask her? Was she falling in love with Billy again? But he couldn't bring himself to accuse her without any evidence, although she had done nearly that very thing to him that morning. Perhaps she had good reason; he had been avoiding her. Things just seemed to be snowballing out of control. Now this business with Ricky.

Steven would need to tell Katherine the news before she left, but he wanted it to be when they were alone. Jessie would be arriving soon, and Josephine would be heading out to the barn for her morning trail ride, so he waited. He dreaded telling her about Ricky and dredging up the past, but more than that, he knew she would be scared. Now, she needed to leave and the sooner the better. And, perhaps having Billy around would be a good thing.

Ricky and his posse knew better than to mess with Billy Black. Despite the fact it was Billy who had killed Ricky's brother, Kurt Werden, in self-defense, the reputation stuck, not to mention all the subsequent brawls he managed to always come out on top of. Steven imagined Billy could have made a living as a professional bodyguard if he chose, being the equivalent of a black belt and more skilled with a knife than any man he knew. But the idea Billy would have ample opportunity to be alone with his wife still needled him like a burr in his seat pocket.

After Jessie left and Josephine rode by the lodge on her way out for her trail ride, Steven exited the side door for the barn. But the moment he reached the bottom step, he froze and drew a deep breath. Down the drive sat Billy's truck.

Billy was the last thing he needed. He stood staring at his old friend's new Chevy truck. He never could convince him to give a Ford a try. Steven shook his head. He didn't know how he felt about Billy anymore. Thirty years ago, the three of them became best friends, working and playing alongside one another the summer they constructed Two Ponies Equestrian Camp together. Then in an instant, everything turned upside down when he found Billy and Katherine together in the barn the night of her twenty-first birthday, which also happened to be the night of his first proposal.

It took him years to heal and forgive them both. Fifteen years later, he proposed a second time and Katherine accepted. They all put the past behind them until he saw Katherine light up like a fanned flame again just being in the same room with Billy. Sparks of jealousy rose from the ashes, recalling her similar behavior prior to her first betrayal. Had she fallen under his spell again?

As Steven approached the barn, he caught a glimpse of Katherine and Billy standing in the barn aisle together through the front window and open tack room door. He paused. They stood face to face and just as Steven began to walk on, feeling uncomfortable about spying on them, Katherine leaned in and gave Billy a lingering hug. Suddenly, the memory of that terrible night flashed before him… the two of them in the old stable, Katherine propped up on the feed bin with her dress hiked up to her waist, her legs wrapped tightly around his middle as they ravaged one another.

Steven lunged around the corner of the barn to confront them, nearly running into Billy.

"Hey Steve, how's it going?" said Billy, wearing his effortless smile. "I was going to stop by the lodge on my way out. You saved me the trip."

"Hey." Steven glanced quickly from Billy to Katherine, looking for any reason to suspect they had shared anything more than a goodbye hug. Katherine made eye contact, calming him. He turned to Billy. "Are you leaving tomorrow, too?"

"No, not until the weekend." The Blackfeet ran his hand through his long, still mostly black hair. A couple years older than Steven, he could pass for ten years younger. "Just checking in on Major and seeing Kat off. Pretty exciting, isn't it?"

"Sure," said Steven, lacking Billy's enthusiasm.

"Billy just showed me an easier way to wrap Major's legs with quilted squares and Polo wraps instead of the cotton batting and bandaging tape. He said that's what a lot of the barns are using now." Major stood in the cross-ties, legs wrapped, impatiently pawing the floor.

"Well, just be careful not to pull the wraps too tight," he

said, then shook his head. "But, if you leave them too loose, they might sag, and he could step on one and pull it loose, possibly tripping himself up in the trailer. Maybe for short rides, but I would keep with the cotton bandages for longer hauls."

"Good point; Doc knows best," said Billy, reaching out to pat Steven on the back. "See you in a few weeks, man. That's great you're coming out."

Steven cocked his head, peering at Katherine through narrow slits. This was news to him.

Katherine squirmed. "I told Billy I was hoping you'd make it down for a few days. We have a break the end of September."

Steven nodded. "Right." He should have been pleased, but it irked him that she had brought it up with Billy first. Was she acting out of guilt?

"Well, I'd better shove off," said Billy, turning to Katherine. "Safe travels and good luck this weekend. Take it easy your first course." He walked to Major, who instantly calmed with the stroke of Billy's hand on his neck. "And you, big fella, you take good care of our girl, okay?" Major tossed his head, appearing to agree.

Katherine laughed. "You be careful, too," she said to Billy, eyes sparkling. "Don't let any of those babies get the best of you."

"I'm not over the hill yet. At least I'm not jumping them over obstacles the size of my truck."

Katherine blushed. "Major flies over them like a deer."

Steven rolled his eyes. He couldn't take much more of their banter. Finally, Billy left, Katherine waving as he drove off. The moment his truck disappeared around the curve in the drive, Katherine's focus dropped to the ground. No doubt expecting more opposition from him, she rushed to slip Major into an empty stall. "I better pack some cotton and bandages," she said disappearing into the tack room.

Steven followed her. "I saw Jo take off."

"Yeah, she's trying to get as many rides in as she can before she leaves. Jessie and I got most everything packed."

"Yeah, I saw her leave."

"I'll be picking her up at seven. Thanks for keeping an eye on the herd while I'm gone. The girls will do most of it."

Steven watched her going back and forth between the storage locker in the tack room and her travel trunks, avoiding him.

"We need to talk," he said.

Katherine turned, putting her hand to her forehead. "Oh Steven, I don't want to leave angry at each other. It's too late to change my plans; entries are paid. Besides, Major and I are ready." She began packing again. "We've all worked so hard, it wouldn't be fair to any of us—Jessie, Billy, Major or me."

"I want you to go."

Katherine dropped what she was doing. "What? Now you want me to go?" She looked at him like he must be crazy.

Steven put his hands in his back pockets, staring at the plank floor. "I got a call from Chief."

"What's going on Steven? You're beginning to worry me. What's Chief got to do with anything? You two can't plan a trip while I'm gone." Katherine threw up her hands and resumed packing. "Sure, why not. It might do you some good. The girls can handle everything."

Steven walked to her and gently rested his hand on her shoulder. "Ricky is out."

Katherine froze. He could feel her take a deep breath and hold it. She turned to him, her hand to her mouth. "Where is he? What did Chief say?"

Steven led her into the office and sat her down on the

couch, taking a seat beside her. "They don't know where he is yet, but everyone on the force is going to take every precaution to keep you safe."

Katherine looked him square in the eyes. "Safe from what?"

"Chief said he might be looking to settle the score..."

"With me…" Katherine folded into his arms as if her last breath had been taken from her. Within seconds, their months of fighting became irrelevant. Steven felt foolish, having let his insecurities come between them. He pulled her close, resting his head upon hers and whispered. "Don't worry, Kat, I won't let anything happen to you."

Over my dead body!

3 – The Guardian

Sunday

Betsy White Cloud hadn't meant to eavesdrop; she had picked up the phone in the kitchen just as Steven answered the call in the library. But when she recognized Chief's voice, she had to stay on the line. The call may have come as a surprise to Steven, but not to her. Betsy had kept track of the years and feared Ricky might get out early. After all, it became her duty to keep Katherine safe after she promised Joseph O'Reilly on his deathbed that she would watch over his niece. But more than that, Katherine had become the child she had been denied. She would protect her to her last breath.

After cleaning up the kitchen, the seventy-nine-year-old Blackfeet hobbled on her cane back to her old bedroom behind the kitchen, forced to give up her favorite Paint room upstairs when her knees further deteriorated. Her room had served as Josephine's nursery and remained empty while Katherine and Steven tried for another child. When the couple gave up, Betsy moved back into the only bedroom on the ground floor besides the master suite to avoid the tall and tricky half-log staircase.

She missed the upstairs. Fond memories of sharing the second level with Lisa, Josephine, and Steven's father Doc fluttered through her mind, bringing a smile to her weathered face. She stopped just inside the door to study the portrait of herself astride her old Paint mare, Flower, which once hung in the Paint room upstairs. Her smile broadened, but only for an instant, recalling why she had stepped into her room.

Betsy sat on the edge of her bed next to the nightstand. , Setting down her cane, she opened the top drawer and leaned over to reach the back-left corner. Carefully, she pulled out a heavy object wrapped in a towel, laid it on the bed, and unfolded the cloth to expose the .357 Magnum Joseph had given her years ago. The revolver felt cool and heavy in her hands as she released the cylinder and spun it, confirming every chamber was loaded. She tilted the gun, locking the cylinder back into place.

Trying to remember the last time she had fired the six-shooter, Betsy just shook her head. Too many years had slipped by to recall. She would need to practice one day that week after Katherine left for the road and Steven for the office. Suddenly feeling exhausted, Betsy laid the gun down on the nightstand and stretched out on her bed for her midday nap.

A knock at the side door startled Betsy awake. It took her a moment to recall her sister-in-law, Kimi, mentioned she would stop by with some meat if the men had any luck hunting that morning. She wiped the sleep from her eyes and struggled to get up.

Unlike Betsy, her much younger twin brothers were given Blackfeet names by her stepfather. Mukki and Tahki and their families had moved from nearby Pikuni Blackfeet Reservation into the old Werden homestead following the Walkers' purchase of the adjoining property for back taxes. Shortly after the move, their wives began helping Betsy and Katherine with the housework every week. Unlike her identical brothers, their wives, Kimi and Nuna, couldn't look any more opposite—Nuna as thin and frail as a sapling blowing in the wind and Kimi, strong and round as a bear preparing for its winter nap.

Betsy placed the gun on her bed and covered it with her pillow, reached for her cane and started for the side door.

"Betsy, where are you?" Kimi called out.

By the time Betsy closed the bedroom door behind her and turned around, Kimi stood in the kitchen holding up a good size rabbit in each hand. "Steven let me in on his way out to the barn," she said, waving one of the limp hares in the direction of the side door. "Want some help with them?"

"Oh no, I can manage. It'll give me something to do this afternoon. Ever since Lisa moved out and we lost Doc last year, my days aren't as full as they used to be."

"I miss Doctor Walker. He was always hiding funny notes for us to find when we cleaned. I'll bet Steven misses him."

"We all do," said Betsy. "I sure miss cooking for him. Doc loved my rabbit stew. I'll make some tonight. Can you all join us?"

Kimi set the rabbits down in the sink. "Nope. The men are working in the shop, cleaning and doing repairs for the busy season. And, they have a few head of Wiggin's cattle waiting in the yard they need to get to before bow season opens next week."

Betsy chuckled under her breath. The "shop," as Kimi liked to call it, was a small meat processing plant in Elkhead owned by her brothers. They had begun working at Ed Porter's slaughterhouse as teens and remained faithful to Mrs. Porter after her husband died, running the business for the widow for over twenty years until she passed five years ago. The old bird shocked everyone in town when she left the business to a couple of Blackfeet instead of her out-of-town relatives.

"The boys helping out?" asked Betsy.

Kimi rolled her eyes. "Are you kidding? They don't like all the blood and guts. My Tanner started working a cattle ranch south of town and Nuna's two are riding broncs on the rodeo circuit again. They're gone almost every weekend."

"How about next weekend? I haven't seen my brothers in weeks. It'll be just Steven, Jo, and I, then Jo leaves the following week. We could use some company. It's going to get awfully quiet around here."

"I think Friday will work. The men are leaving Saturday hunting," said Kimi. "Say, will you still need us to clean every week this fall?"

"Probably not."

"We could start helping you with some of the cooking?"

"Oh no, I need to do something around here. A body is like leather; don't use it and it'll just rot. Let's start every other week after Jo leaves."

"Okay, let us know if you're having a bad day or need help in between."

"I will. I appreciate all you do." Betsy gave Kimi a hug and immediately backed away, making a sour face. "You smell like skunk!"

"Oh sorry, I shouldn't have come in. The dogs went off scent this morning and tangled with one of those devils; must have rubbed off on me." Kimi walked out onto the side porch, followed by Betsy. "See you Friday. I better get home and clean up," she said, turning to leave.

"Wait, sit with me a moment," said Betsy, tapping the top of the picnic table.

"What's up?" Kimi glanced down the drive. "Is it Katherine and Steven again? I see Billy's truck is here."

Betsy sat down. "Never mind that. There's something I need to tell you."

Kimi sat across from her and leaned in. "What?"

Betsy took a deep breath. "We got a call from Chief Taylor this morning. Ricky Werden is out of prison."

Following a few moments of silence, Kimi asked, "Will he come to the house?"

"I don't know. But, if he does show up, he'll be asking about Katherine. Chief said he might be looking to settle the score, so be careful."

"Settle the score?"

"He must blame her, somehow, for everything."

"That's terrible. Don't worry; no one gets anywhere near our place without Sky and Moose howling up a storm. Is she still leaving tomorrow?"

Just as Betsy opened her mouth to answer, Billy, Katherine, and Steven stepped out of the barn onto the drive together.

Kimi turned to follow Betsy's gaze. "Umm, that Billy!"

"Oh Kimi, nothing's going on."

"Steven seems to think so. A husband would know," whispered Kimi. "He doesn't want her to go."

"Well, now with the news of Ricky, I'm sure he'll feel differently. I'm glad Billy will be checking in on the women along the way. And yes, she's leaving in the morning."

Betsy didn't dare admit she had her own suspicions, trying to decide if she and Steven had reason to be concerned. She had noticed Katherine acting strange around Billy again, but chose to believe it was merely her excitement over Major's progress. Betsy found it hard to imagine something could be starting up all over again.

"Well, I think Steven has reason," Kimi whispered. "Especially, after what happened before."

"That was a long time ago. It's over; they're just good friends now. Katherine loves Steven; she never stopped. I watched them grow up together, best friends then teen sweethearts—it's always been Steven."

Kimi smirked. "Well, if that's true, why did she cheat on him back then? Did she love them both?"

"I don't think she knew what love was. Poor thing, growing up in the middle of her parent's disastrous marriage. She learned only what love wasn't."

Betsy thought back to the first day Katherine arrived at Two Ponies and how the girl craved love and approval. She could understand how earning the affection of a charming and exciting young man might validate her self-worth. She imagined after spending so much time with Steven all those summers, he seemed safer and more comfortable than charming and exciting.

"She was young and naïve," Betsy concluded.

Kimi turned once again, apparently studying the tall, handsome Blackfeet. "He is a charmer, that's for sure, and that smile." Kimi giggled. "I think I might have been tempted myself."

"Kimi!" Betsy gently smacked her sister-in-law's hand, but Kimi was right. Billy would capture any women's imagination, even now at his age. But still, after all these years, Betsy had difficulty understanding how Katherine could have thrown away ten years of Steven's devotion in the heat of a moment. "She knows better now," she said, trying to convince herself as much as Kimi.

"Well, I hope so. Steven's one in a million, to have forgiven them both like that."

Betsy nodded, but she knew Steven had made his share of mistakes, too. Even when Billy was presumed dead, thought to have drowned himself in Pine Island rather than go to prison for the murder of Kurt Werden, Steven couldn't bring himself to be there for Katherine. She begged him to forgive her with dozens of unanswered calls and letters. For fourteen years they didn't speak, Katherine withdrawing to a world of guilt and remorse, feeling responsible for losing them both, while Steven lost himself in his studies then later in his work.

"It took years, you know, for Steven to put that night behind them. He was devastated; swore to never forgive her."

"But, eventually he did."

Again, she just nodded. Betsy didn't like to think about the years they were estranged. Those were rough years for everyone. Not until Steven discovered Billy working on a road crew in Canada did everything get set straight. When Billy returned, Katherine realized her folly and finally made the right choice. Things couldn't possibly be unraveling again.

"Well, I think he's doubting her again," said Kimi. "Why doesn't he just confront her about it, instead of acting all pissed off. Men!"

"I know, it's so silly," said Betsy, shaking her head. "He's so afraid of losing her again. And, Kat isn't helping any."

Kimi stood up. "You should talk to them."

"They'll work it out for themselves. It's better that way."

Starting down the stairs, Kimi added, "Well, I hope so. They've been through a lot together."

Betsy waved goodbye and slowly made her way back to her room, Kimi's last words lingering in her thoughts. Sitting at her desk, she picked up a framed portrait of the Walker family she had taken years ago. Katherine and Steven stood in front of the paddock fence with Josephine and Lisa, at young ages, sitting on the top rail between them. Lisa, with her blonde hair and blue eyes, could pass for Steven's daughter, and Josephine couldn't be mistaken for anyone besides Katherine's offspring, mirroring her mother in every way with her auburn locks and captivating emerald green eyes.

Betsy's gaze focused on Katherine, with her arm cradling her tummy and glowing with pride as she showed off her baby bump, expecting their second child at the time. Remembering the loss of the baby boy only weeks later produced a single tear, leaving a trail down Betsy's plump bronze cheek.

Betsy recalled how, as newlyweds, Katherine and Steven dreamed of filling the six upstairs rooms with children. But, due to complications with her first birth and her age, Katherine seemed unable to go full-term again, and following two agonizing stillbirths, the couple stopped trying. The loss of the two babies traumatized Katherine to the point of having her tubes tied to ensure she didn't get pregnant again.

Even though Katherine had taken every precaution prior to and during her pregnancies, Betsy knew she felt somehow responsible and inadequate as a woman. Betsy knew this because she had shared the same feelings after being unnecessarily sterilized as a teenager at a federally funded clinic. This was during a time when it had become common practice across the United States to curb the American Indian population. Like Katherine, she had not been to blame, but the guilt and shame still followed.

After the last of the two little angels were buried alongside Joseph in the family plot, she imagined a part of Katherine's heart, like the spare rooms upstairs, felt empty and cold. As time passed, Katherine seemed to move through her sadness, putting all her energy into the two girls they were blessed with, her students, and always her horses. But Betsy feared a scar remained, embedded in Katherine's heart like a thorn waiting to fester. Was Billy the Band-Aid?

Betsy shook her head, pursing her lips, determined Katherine and Steven would work things out. They were meant to be together and always would be… period.

As soon as Billy left, Steven would tell her about Ricky. Maybe some good would come of this bad situation. She hoped the frightful news might bring the couple back together.

Ricky and that bunch of hoodlums would come for Katherine, Betsy was sure of it. But the timing couldn't have worked out better, with Katherine leaving, Lisa in New York, and Josephine flying out to LA soon. She figured Ricky would wait a few weeks until everyone's guard began to slip before making his move. It would be just her and Steven when he came.

This time, instead of tucking the gun away in the back corner, she folded the towel and laid it at the front of the drawer, placing the revolver on top of it with the grip facing out, easily within reach. She closed the drawer and sat with her eyes fixed on the nightstand. Ricky would come, and she would be ready for him.

When the side door creaked open and shut, she could hear soft voices moving slowly in the direction of the master bedroom. Betsy smiled.

4 – Goodbyes

Monday

Before daybreak, Katherine leaned over Steven, still in bed, and gave him a gentle kiss. "I'm packed and will be leaving soon."

He reached for her face and smiled. "You were amazing last night."

Katherine blushed. "You don't need to get up," she said.

Steven sat up in bed and wiped the sleep from his eyes. "Of course I do, silly."

Smiling, she brushed a few strands of straw-colored hair from his eyes. "Okay. I still need to load Major."

"Good, I'll take a quick shower."

"You better hurry; I need to hit the road."

Katherine exited the side door and walked briskly to the truck and trailer parked alongside the old barn, packed and ready to go. Major was finishing his hay, but the moment she entered the barn, his head shot up and he stood at attention. He had no doubt noticed the rig parked out front and was ready to go. She had been hauling him to Jessie's once a week over the summer to acquaint him with the trailer and get him accustomed to working away from Two Ponies. He had become a champ at both and looked forward to their gallops across Jessie's open fields.

He nearly put his halter on himself and led Katherine out of the barn to the back of the open trailer. She threw his lead over his neck and in he went.

The glorious smell of bacon and biscuits greeted Katherine

as she reentered the lodge. She found Betsy standing at the kitchen counter packing a breakfast-to-go.

"Good morning, Betz. Thanks for getting up to see me off."

Betsy handed her a warm paper sack. "There's a couple in there for Jessie, too," she said.

Katherine studied Betsy wiping down the range. Her dear friend had noticeably slowed over the past year and leaving her for a couple of months worried her. "I'll miss you," she said.

Betsy smiled and nodded. "Call us as soon as you arrive at the hotel tonight."

"I will. I said goodbye to Jo last night. I told her she didn't need to get up this morning."

"We'll all miss you."

Katherine caught Betsy trying to wipe her eyes unnoticed. "Oh Betz, don't cry."

"Silly me, can't control my emotions anymore. Besides, they're mostly happy tears."

Katherine studied her with a questioning expression.

"You and Steven. I was so worried. I'm so happy you straightened things out before you left. I was tempted to pull you both aside and give you a good talking to."

"I'm surprised you didn't." Katherine chuckled and gave the old matchmaker a hug. It was her plan all along for her and Steven to end up together. "We're good."

"Well, you better be on your way before this old woman gets all weepy again."

Katherine gave her a peck on the cheek. "Love you."

"Love you, too."

Betsy resumed cleaning the kitchen as Katherine searched out her husband. Steven emerged from their bedroom down the hall and they met in the great room. Katherine smiled into his sky-blue eyes and rested her head on his shoulder as he enveloped her. His masculine scent and radiating warmth summoned images of their lovemaking the previous night. She smiled.

"You'll do great!" he said. Katherine reluctantly pulled away from his warm embrace.

Suddenly, Jo came galloping down the stairs. "Bye, Mom!" she said, giving her a hug. "Good luck with Major."

"Thanks, sweetie." Katherine stood admiring her lovely creation. My, how the years had slipped by, her baby all grown up and leaving for college. "I'll see you in LA."

"Can't wait!" said Josephine, clasping her hands and rocking on her heels, kindling a fond memory of Josephine's first day of school as a child. She would always be her little girl.

The three of them joined Betsy now waiting at the side door. Major could be heard rattling around in the trailer.

"I better get going. Somebody's getting impatient." With one more hug from Betsy and Josephine, Steven escorted her out to her truck. Katherine slid behind the wheel and rolled down her window, resting her arm on the door. "I'll call you tonight."

"Good luck, honey." Steven placed his hand over hers and gently squeezed it. "I love you."

"I love you, too."

Betsy and Jo waived from the porch enthusiastically as Steven stood with his hands in his pockets, forcing a smile as she pulled away. Katherine wasn't surprised neither Betsy or Steven mentioned Ricky that morning. But she knew he had to be lurking in the back of their minds, each wondering as she was, when and where he would make his move.

The sun had not yet broken over the mountaintops as Katherine pulled into the Neals' spread with Major in tow.

Unlike Two Ponies, nestled between two mountain ranges, Jessie's family cattle ranch stretched along a good portion of the Flathead River basin. Jessie's house was on route to SR-15, which would take them south and around most of the mountains to connect with I-80 taking them to the West Coast.

Katherine parked out front of the weathered gray slat-board bunkhouse Jessie and Dane called home. It sat beside a matching hay barn that housed a few ranch horses, including Jessie's old black-and-white Paint, Oreo.

Observing Jessie's bags piled in a heap on the front porch and Dane's patrol car still parked out front, she guessed they were saying their goodbyes. Katherine honked her horn softly with a couple of abbreviated taps, hoping not to disturb Mr. and Mrs. Neal. The main house sat a little further down the drive nestled in an oasis of cottonwood trees, surrounded by miles of open pasture and hay fields stretching to the base of the surrounding foothills and bluffs. Moments later the couple emerged from the barn, holding hands. Apparently, Jessie needed to say goodbye to Oreo as well. When they reached her rig, Katherine stepped out of the truck.

"Seeing your lady off?" Katherine asked Dane.

"Here to see you both off." When Dane planted a long goodbye kiss squarely on Jessie's lips, Katherine blushed. It was times like this that her age smacked her square between the eyes. All her little girls—Lisa, Josephine, Jessie, and hundreds more—all grown, many with children of their own now, in what seemed like the blink of an eye.

She was pleased to see Jessie happily married, finally. For a while, Katherine feared she may have taken her advice long ago about taking things slow with the opposite sex a little too far, having remained single and living at home into her thirties. Relationships had come and gone, never lasting more than a year or so, until she met Dane at the clinic.

When he took over the police canine unit after entering the force, he had brought the dogs into Steven's clinic for their annual vaccinations. From what Steven said, they hit if off right away. Even then, it took five years for her to commit. Now five years into their marriage, they had no children. Katherine feared the misfortunes with her pregnancies at a late age might have discouraged the couple from trying.

"Good morning," said Jessie. "Dane told me that Ricky fella is out. Guess it's a good thing we're getting out of Dodge."

"Oh Jess, you're always so dramatic. We don't have anything to worry about, right Dane?"

Along with everyone else at home, she had played down the danger since receiving the news Sunday. The last thing Major needed was a nervous psychotic handling him. He had proven to be especially sensitive to her mood swings, which fluctuated like the wind as of late.

Dane pointed to the main house. "Better go say goodbye to your folks, honey." Jessie gave him a "you could have just told me you wanted to speak to Katherine privately" look before starting for the house.

The six-foot-two stout deputy turned to Katherine with his hands in his back pockets. "I wish there was a way I could join you ladies the first week or so, but my dad won't give me the time off. He says I'm needed here with all the rowdy hunters expected soon for bow then rifle deer-and-elk season."

"Mike's probably right." Katherine chuckled. "Hope none of them shoot themselves in the foot again this year!"

Dane looked up. "This is serious, Mrs. Walker."

"What is it with you two? Jess still won't call Steven by his first name and you won't call me by mine. We're all adults now, you know. Please call me Kat."

"Okay, Kat, but there is reason to be concerned. My dad told me about what happened years ago… the attack in the parking lot at Rudy's, then the fire years later. Who knows what he's capable of?"

"He just got out of prison," Katherine reasoned. "Why would he chance going back?"

"What's he got to lose at this point? His family is gone, his home, money. A whole lot of hate can build up over nearly twenty years in prison. Justified or not, he blames you."

"Are you trying to scare me, Dane? Because if you are, it's working."

"I'm sorry, I just want you to take this seriously. Did you tell Billy?"

"No, I guess I should have. I haven't seen him since Sunday morning. He's not leaving until this weekend."

"I'll call him when I get to the office. Are you carrying?"

Katherine's eyebrows shot up. "A gun?!"

"Yeah, a gun."

She shook her head.

"I thought not." Dane left for his car and returned with a leather case and handed it to her. "There's a loaded .38 Special and some ammo in there. It's registered in Jessie's name. You're always whipping our butts shooting skeet with a shotgun, but have you ever fired a handgun?"

"A few times, but it's been a while. Why not leave it with Jess? It is her gun, after all."

"She won't touch it. I bought it for her years ago—but can you believe it, the wife of a cop? Anyway, along the way, you stop and practice. Get comfortable with it. There's also a pen that's a sharp weapon and a can of mace. Always keep the pen on you and the spray in the truck within reach. Call often."

Katherine opened the case and picked up the pen and pulled it apart, gasping at the three-inch weapon resembling an ice pick, then put it in her pocket. The spray she placed in the console. "What about the gun? Glove box?"

"No, put it under your seat within reach."

"Good grief, Dane. Do you really think this is necessary?"

"Yes. Where are your first stops?"

"Tonight, we're staying at a horse hotel on the border of Nevada. Our first competition is a Region VI three-day event in Santa Rosa this weekend. We should arrive there Wednesday evening. Then we go on to Modesto for a dressage show and on to Show Jumping in Paso Robles. Then we have a ten-day break before our next event.

"I'm glad Billy will be spending some time with you ladies."

"Yeah, Steve is going to make a trip out, too."

"Great!"

Jessie walked up and threw her bags in the back seat. "I'm ready," she said to Katherine, then turned to her husband. "Done with the riot act?"

Dane shifted his weight and smirked. "Smart-ass. Gun under the seat, pen on Katherine, spray in the console. Call me—often."

"Yes, dear. Love you too," said Jessie, giving Dane a lingering hug.

"You guys kill it out there," said Dane.

"Poor choice of words, hon, considering."

"You know what I mean. Good luck!"

"Thanks!" Katherine smiled.

Major began pawing, producing loud banging noises in the trailer. "I think he expected another romp through the fields this morning. We better get him moving," said Katherine, climbing behind the wheel as Jessie jogged around the front of the vehicle to ride shotgun. Katherine rolled down her window. "Thanks, Dane, for everything."

Jessie leaned over the console. "Bye, baby."

"Be careful."

Major rumbled about getting his feet under him as Katherine circled the rig in the drive. Jessie waved out the window as they pulled out.

The two women smiled at each other and nodded. They were on their way. "California here we come!" said Jessie. "We've worked hard for this."

"We have. We're ready to kick butt!"

"Damn straight!"

Katherine laughed, her excitement and anticipation reborn. Maybe now she could put Ricky out of her mind and focus on Major.

As the sun dropped behind the mountains, Jessie napped while Katherine sang along to the oldies station, recalling a few of the same tunes that played on her drive West years ago.

An hour later, Jessie stirred in the passenger seat and stretched. "Where are we?" She glanced at the clock. "Gads, I didn't mean to doze off on ya."

"No worries, we're getting close to the border. We should reach the inn by dark as planned."

Jessie turned back toward the trailer. "How's the big boy doing?"

"He's been quiet, but we'll need to stop for gas soon."

"Those double tanks sure come in handy on long trips, don't they?"

"Yeah, this is the longest drive I've been on for years, since I moved West. I was just remembering that drive. I think this trip is nearly as exciting."

"Wow, I don't think I could have done what you did," said Jessie. "Picking up and leaving everything behind—family, friends, your home."

"I was glad to leave my mother, but I still feel bad about leaving my dad behind with that monster."

"Well, I'm glad I never met her and glad you made the move."

"Me too, and the best part was bringing Lady with me."

"She sure was a special girl."

Katherine smiled, glancing in the rearview mirror. "And, now I'm on the road with big boy."

"He's pretty special, too."

"He is." Katherine sighed. "What is it about horses? Major makes me so happy. I'm at peace when I'm with him, more than with Steven, Betz, or the girls. Is that a terrible thing to say?"

"No, I'm the same way with Oreo. I'd never admit it to Dane, but it's true."

After a moment of reflection, Katherine replied. "They're so simple, needing only the basics, no clutter or noise in their heads. Living purely in the moment and they take us there."

"Yeah, and a horse is a horse regardless of their breeding or in a fancy barn or out on the range. So pure," said Jessie, staring out the passenger window across the open range. "Think we'll be lucky enough to see some Mustangs?"

Katherine scanned the open prairie as far as the eye could see. "We might if we keep a look out."

"That would be fun," said Jessie. "We're just a couple of old horse-crazy gals, aren't we!"

"Old? Me maybe, but not you. How old are you now, thirty-five?"

"Thirty-seven."

Katherine couldn't help the temptation. "Still young enough to start a family, you know."

Jessie wrinkled up her nose. "Nope, too late."

"Not at all. It's becoming commonplace for women even in their forties." Did she dare bring it up? "I hope my troubles haven't swayed you and Dane."

Jessie turned in her seat. "Not at all. We tried a couple of times and it just didn't happen."

Katherine was relieved but sad for the couple. "Oh, Jess. I didn't know. I'm so sorry."

"Just wasn't meant to be, that's all. But I think I have Dane sold on getting a Paint mare and breeding her. I'll have my baby yet."

"That would be awesome." Katherine nodded in the direction of the exit sign. "Up ahead. Let's stop and get gas and something to eat."

"Sounds good; I'm starved."

"Oh Jess, you're always hungry."

5 – The Gang

Monday

Ricky Werden picked at his cigarette-stained teeth with a toothpick. "Good sandwich, Andy; better than any of that shit food in the pen, that's for sure."

Andy Ritter threw a blanket and pillow from the couch to the corner of the room, making space to sit down. "Guess the couch is working out; you slept 'til almost noon."

"Yeah, it's okay," said Ricky, getting up from the table across the room.

"When you gonna call Jake?" asked Andy.

Ricky sifted through a duffle bag on the floor containing his few remaining possessions. "Now," he said with a malicious sideways grin. "The sooner we get this show on the road the better. All these years planning… I can't wait to give her what she deserves… for Pa. And, we won't even have to lift a finger; she'll come running to us."

"And, what about him?"

"Oh, he'll come too. I have something special planned for that half-breed sack of shit… for Kurt. He should have stayed hiding like a coward in Canada. But oh no, he had to come back for her. Jake swears he saw them making out in the post office parking lot a couple years ago. When that pretty doctor of hers finds out what they've been up to, he won't care where they disappear to."

Ricky pulled a folded and tattered piece of paper from his bag. "Where's the phone?"

Andy pushed aside a pile of smelly dirty clothes and several empty potato chip bags from the end table, exposing the telephone.

Sliding in on the couch beside Andy, Ricky dialed the number. "Hey, Jake, it's Ricky. I'm out!"

Jake sounded nearly as excited as he was about being a free man again. They had been communicating about his plan the past two years and Jake was onboard one-hundred percent and ready to settle the score. Jake Schmitt and Ricky's older brother, Kurt, had been best friends all through school. Ricky liked to think he and Jake were best friends now. He felt he could count on Jake to do anything that needed to be done.

Jake and his younger brother Kyle—or "Tick" as Ricky liked to call him because of how he stuck to his older brother's side—had both been in on the fight the night Kurt died in his arms. He considered them the closest to family he would ever have again, glad to be rid of his good-for-nothing old lady and freak sister.

"I'm at Andy's place in Helena. He picked me up yesterday. We'll all head up to the cabin with the horses as soon as everything is done on your end. You call me every step of the way, okay?" Jake liked doing things his way sometimes and Ricky wanted to make sure it all went according to his plan.

"Andy says the ride back to the cabin isn't too bad, a little over an hour from where we'll be dropped off. Yes, we can trust this guy. He thinks we're just heading out for a hunting trip, but he got to know me and Andy well enough in the slammer not to cross either of us if anyone starts asking questions."

Jake asked about Andy again, too. "I told you he's cool; trust me. The cabin will be perfect."

Andy smiled at him from across the room. They had served five years in the pen together—Andy for burglary, getting out a year earlier. While living in the same cell for five years, they shared their deepest secrets and exploits. Andy was impressed by Ricky's stories of putting Injuns in their place. He had told him about his brother's stabbing, his dad dying in prison, and how he wanted to get even.

Andy's tales were tame compared to Ricky's admissions of rape and the mysterious disappearances of Blackfeet boys. One night, Andy told him about his grandfather's old hunting and fishing cabin he visited as a kid and teen. Andy inherited the old homesteaded property when his grandpa died while he was serving time and told Ricky he planned to go back as soon as he got out. The location of the cabin, near the Canadian border and accessible only by foot or horseback, became the foundation of Ricky's plan for revenge.

Andy, also without family, was all in, especially once he heard about the cash Ricky's dad had hidden in their barn. His father never mentioned it until he was on his deathbed in the prison hospital and didn't give an exact amount, only that it would be plenty to take care him for life.

"Well, you know what to do," Ricky continued over the phone to Jake. "Go to the house tonight. You remember where I told you to find the cash and guns? Good. You better not wake up any of those Injuns and make sure you leave the barn just the way you found it. Call me when you have everything. Then tomorrow morning, deliver the letter I sent you. It must be in person. It's very important no one else sees it. Let me know as soon as she has it." Ricky said goodbye and hung up the phone.

Andy stared at him, nodding. "Everything good?"

"Sure."

"How about the money? Can we trust him?"

"Don't worry, it'll be there. And, yes, I'd trust Jake with my life."

"Good. Should we start packing?"

"Yeah, we need to be ready to go. You have everything for the horses for a week or so?"

Andy glanced out the back window to where four horses stood grazing, tails swishing at flies. "I took hay up last trip, but we'll need to run to the feed store for grain."

"No 'you'll' run to the feed store. I'm going to hole up here until we're ready to go. Since I missed my parole appointment this morning, the State might already be looking for me." Ricky walked to the refrigerator and opened the door. "How about grub?"

"I stocked the cabin good over the summer. There's enough food for a month. We can pick up a few refrigerated things on the way. The creek next to the cabin runs year-around and it's ice cold. So long as we seal everything good and keep it submerged under water, it won't freeze, and the critters won't be able to smell it."

"Okay, sounds good." Ricky closed the refrigerator door and walked to a mirror hanging lopsided on the living room wall, studying his reflection. "Think I should change my looks? You know, just in case."

Andy just shrugged his shoulders.

Ricky felt the stubble on his face and ran his hand through his greasy brown hair. "Maybe I'll grow a beard and dye my hair too… what I have left of it! Can't wait for it to grow back again. What do you think, black or blond?"

"How about red to match that doctor's wife's hair? Still going to share her, right?" Andy began making lewd gestures with his hips.

"Oh man, am I ever ready for some of that. Been too long," said Ricky. "Yep, we'll all share her, just like the old days I told you about, Andy boy. Just like the old days!"

Jake Schmitt sat on the front porch of their dilapidated rental with his brother, Kyle, as the sun dipped below a distant mountain range. Jake held a beer in one hand and a cigarette in the other.

Kyle sipped on a bottle of Coke. "I'm a little nervous about tonight," he said. "We haven't done anything like this for a while."

"What, trespassing? That's nothing. All we're doing is getting what belongs to Ricky." Jake flicked an ash onto the floor board.

Kyle extinguished it with his boot. "What about this Andy fella? What do you make of him?"

"Ricky trusts him."

Kyle tipped his bottle, finishing the Cola. "I don't like it. Ricky just met this guy in prison, of all places. Why should we trust him?"

"Ricky's plan won't work without the cabin and the horses." Jake was getting annoyed with all the questions. Kyle always was a pussy, staying home and missing out on most of the fun growing up.

"This plan… it's crazy," said Kyle. "Why is he even bothering with her? I can see getting back at him, but why her?"

Jake gave his brother a long stare. "Don't you be going soft on us again. You know why."

"He wants her."

"That's right, in front of that red bastard. Seeing that will be worth all the trouble. Just because he grew up off the reservation, he thinks he's better than the rest of 'em."

"He's half-white you know."

"All the more reason to put him in his place, for good."

Kyle got up and stretched. "I like the idea of moving to a new place. Did Ricky mention the Canadian IDs?"

"No, but he said everything was done and ready to go months ago. Remember, we sent the photos to Andy last spring."

"Andy, again. Too much is relying on this guy."

"If Ricky trusts him, I trust him."

"Well, he better not back out of our deal. He promised we could keep two of the horses. I told him I wanted the roan with the bald face."

"You and your damn horses." Jake dropped his butt and snuffed it out with his heel before Kyle had a chance to. "Focus on tonight—okay?"

"When we leaving?"

"Around midnight. That'll put us there around one or so. Wear dark clothes."

Kyle opened the front screen door. "I know. I have everything packed from Ricky's list: hammer, flashlight, two pillowcases, and the two big duffle bags."

"I just hope we can carry everything in one trip."

"Yeah, me too."

Ricky paced the living room floor Tuesday morning while Andy sat on the couch watching cartoons.

"You getting cabin fever?" asked Andy. "You're more jittery than a hen on a chopping block."

"Yeah. Getting pretty sick of this place. It's like I'm back in prison."

"Hey, you're free to leave anytime. Shit, all you do is eat everything in sight."

"What else is there to do besides look at your ugly mug! I can't be seen. You know that."

"Then quit your bitching!" Andy changed channels. "Hey, come look at this."

Ricky joined Andy in front of the television. An aerial view of a forest fire north of the border in Canada filled the screen.

Ricky turned up the volume. The newscaster described the fire as fifty-percent contained about fifty-five miles north of the Montana border.

"That won't affect us," said Ricky. "See, it's burning to the east."

"So long as the wind doesn't change."

"They don't seem too concerned and, look, they're showing rain and snow for this week. No problem." Ricky returned to the window, anxiously peeking out the closed living room curtain. "Something happened. Jake hasn't called!"

"I just hope they got the money."

Ricky shot Andy a look that silenced him as he crossed the room. At least with Jake and Kyle, it wasn't just about the money. But what happened? Did something go wrong at his old homestead?

Ricky stared at the phone, willing it to ring. Surprising him when it did, Andy answered it. "It's Jake."

"Give it to me," demanded Ricky, grabbing the receiver as he slid onto the couch next to him. "What happened? You were supposed to call me as soon as you left. Did you get everything?"

Andy rubbed his thumb and index finger together nearly in Ricky's face. Ricky flung his hand away, picked up the desk phone and began pacing the room. "Shit! Never mind. You can tell me about it later. Go deliver the letter. Now! Call me as soon as she has it."

Ricky returned the receiver and slammed the phone down on the end table. "And, no they didn't get the money," he said before Andy had a chance to ask. "They parked in the trees and walked in after midnight like I told them to, and their stupid dogs started barking—howling, he said. Good thing they had them indoors. When the house lights came on, they hightailed it."

"When are they going back?"

"They aren't; we'll go. There's an old logging road that splits off the driveway and runs down to the lake a little west of the barn. That way we won't have to go near the house. Jake and Kyle would never find it in the dark. But we'll wait until the night before we leave, just in case something goes down. We'll be long gone before they put two-and-two together."

"Why didn't you think of this sooner?"

Ricky turned toward Andy. "How was I supposed to know they had dogs?"

"They all have dogs!" Andy smiled. "But I like this plan better anyway."

"I knew you would."

After Dane's call about Ricky getting out, Billy had felt on edge and needed some time to think and drove into town. When he returned home after dark, he found his wife, Sarah, waiting in the living room, sitting under her reading lamp with a book in her hands.

"Where have you been all day?" she asked.

"Met up with a few of the boys at Rudy's to play some pool after I got feed. Kind of lost track of time. How's the packing going?"

Sarah closed her book. "I don't see why we have to leave our home."

"I told you what Dane said. No way are you staying here alone at night. After what happened last time? You should have moved in with your folks then. I'm not making the same mistake twice."

"That was a long time ago."

"Oh, so you think those scumbags have changed?"

Just the thought of that gang getting their hands on his wife again or their teenage son, TJ, made him break out in a cold sweat. He wanted them gone, every last one of them.

"If Ricky's out for revenge, his plan will sure as hell include me. And, if he can't get to me, he'll go after you again, or TJ. I want you both at your folks on the Res by the weekend, before I leave."

Sarah gave him a grim look.

"I can't protect you when I'm gone." Billy wiped the perspiration from his forehead with his sleeve.

"Why are you still going, anyway?"

"You know we need the money," he spouted off. Billy grabbed his jacket from the coat rack by the door, pulling the whole thing to the floor, breaking it. "Shit!"

Sarah slammed her book down on the coffee table. "You're drunk again, aren't you?"

"I am not. I only had a couple beers."

"Well, at least you didn't get in a fight this time."

"How would you know!" he yelled, irritated with her endless questions.

"Let's see, your shirt isn't torn or dirty and your face is in one piece." Sarah stood up and walked across the room.

He didn't appreciate her tone or comments. Rarely did anyone leave a mark on him—only when he was really outnumbered—and they always ended up in far worse shape. "You don't know anything!" he shouted. "I need to unload the truck and I have some packing to do myself. Don't wait up."

Billy turned for the door, kicking the fallen coat rack against the wall to clear his path.

"What's going on, Billy? Were you even at Rudy's?" Now they were getting down to it. Billy turned to find a tear trailing down Sarah's cheek. Damn it, he didn't mean to make her cry. "No, Sarah. It's not what you think."

"You don't want to be with me anymore. What am I

supposed to think?"

"I'm not fooling around."

"Are you in love?"

"What?!"

"Billy, keep your voice down." Sarah approached him. "Is it Katherine again? Is that why you took those jobs, to be near her?"

Billy locked his jaw, turned, and stormed out of the house, leaving the door wide open behind him.

Halfway to the barn he stopped and lit a cigarette. He watched the door close and the living room go dark. Billy pitched the spent match to the ground and sent gravel flying with his boot. He'd be gone for two months and all she wanted to do was dredge up the past. No wonder they didn't have sex anymore.

When he reached his truck at the barn, Billy winced and flicked his partially smoked cigarette to the drive, taking his frustration out on the butt as he ground it into the dirt with his heel. What was going on with him? He felt restless again, like he did as a kid.

As he began unloading the fifty-pound bags of grain, he dared to honestly consider why he felt edgy. He hated to admit it, but he knew the answer. He threw the last sack down hard in frustration. Damn it! Sarah didn't deserve this shit. She was right… she was always right.

It was Katherine again! The way she looked at him, went out of her way to touch him… that day she pressed into him in the post office parking lot. The flame he had successfully suppressed for years flickered within him once more.

But for now, he needed to focus on Ricky and his gang. When the time came, he knew what had to be done. There would be plenty of time to figure out his feelings about Katherine… and hers for him… later.

6 – Best Friends

Tuesday

Josephine Walker pulled her buckskin, Bonanza, from his stall, their shadows running long down the barn aisle in the early morning sunlight. "Oh, come on, sleepyhead. Only one more week, then you can get fat and lazy with the rest of the horses for the winter."

She had named the gelding after one of hers and her mother's favorite television shows, having been raised on the reruns. Many times she and her mother and the rest of their riding party would line up abreast of each other in the back field and join in the "dun, dun-ta-dun…" intro song before galloping across the back field in unison. The series held a special place in her heart, having fallen in love with all the horses on the show, but especially Buck, Ben Cartright's Buckskin.

Bonanza stood quietly while Josephine pulled a bridle over his black-tipped ears. She walked the gelding to the pasture gate so she could mount him without having to trek down to the arena to use the mounting block. Her big boy stood just beyond her reach to mount him from the ground without a saddle. She loved riding bareback and when she wasn't, she rode western in opposition to her mother's preference of English.

Josephine enjoyed competing with Bonanza in speed and action events at local gymkhanas and rodeos with her friends from high school. Her mother had fought it in the beginning, instructing Josephine extensively in English growing up, but eventually gave in and supported her interest. She had hauled her and Bonanza to countless events, becoming the best show mom around—even though she looked as out of place as a leggy Thoroughbred running a cloverleaf with her Ariat Polo shirt, jean jodhpurs, and polished paddock boots among all the cowboy hats, silver buckles, and shit-kicking boots.

Wearing only jean cutoffs and a T-shirt, Josephine jogged Bonanza up the drive and through the opening in the fenced parking area leading to the lake trail. The cool morning breeze off the water might have given her a chill, but the gelding's twelve-hundred pounds of body heat kept her warm.

Once the trail leveled out, Josephine gripped with her knees and cued the Quarter Horse to strike off into a canter. She had to duck under a few low branches as they plowed through a bed of aspen leaves, the golden flecks flying up behind them like car exhaust. When she reached the open ridge overlooking Pine Island Lake, Josephine paused to take in the view as the scent of wet pine from the heavy morning dew filled her senses. No matter what time of year, the refection of the Continental Divide off the still morning water never failed to impress.

"I'm going to miss this, Bo Bo, and of course I'm going to miss you, big fella." She reached down and gave his generous neck a few pats. "But it'll be so exciting, living in a big city with big buildings and people from all over the world. Wish I could take you with me, but I'll be home for Thanksgiving before you know it." Josephine grabbed his black mane, clucked, and sent him trotting down the hill. They must hurry. She didn't want to be late.

At the stream, she waited. Before too long, she heard plopping noises in the stream gradually intensifying as a horse and rider drew near. She was ready, and the moment TJ and his brown-and-white Paint, Cisco, turned the bend into sight, she kicked Bonanza's flanks, sending him flying across the streambed and lunging up the opposite bank into a full gallop down the level path.

This was a game the two of them had played since they were kids. How far would she get this time before TJ tagged her? Could she break her record? The trail was open enough for two horses abreast, but she cut the corners to cover ground faster, challenging the teen to recall every low branch and sharp turn ahead.

The pound of Bonanza's strides was deafening, yet she could hear one more set of hoofs closing in on them. Another hundred yards sat the end of the clearing and her new record! The moment the trail straightened out, Josephine let the reins slide through her fingers and leaned over her mount, lengthening the gelding's strides. Suddenly she felt a tug on her ponytail, instead of the usual tap on her shoulder, just as she entered the stand of aspen.

Josephine sat back and drew up her reins. "I think I made it!"

"Not even close, Walker; maybe next time," said TJ, circling her like a war party around a covered wagon riding his spirited Medicine Hat horse. Tossing his head and almost cantering in place, the nearly all-white gelding bore the true Medicine Hat markings, with a cap of brown covering his poll and ears, a large patch on his chest and on each flank. TJ had proudly told the mythology of his magical horse more times than she could remember.

He explained a Medicine Hat horse, steeped in American Indian tradition and legend, was believed to have a magical ability to protect its rider from injury or death in battle with its protective shields of color. Already familiar with this story from when her mother had read her the Marguerite Henry book, *San Domingo, The Medicine Hat Stallion*, as a child, she never let on to TJ. She enjoyed listening to him tell the tale no matter how often he shared it.

Suddenly, TJ and Cisco became a blur. "Stop, you're making me dizzy!" she said. "And, I did so make it and, look, you pulled out my ponytail," Josephine whined, flipping her hair over her shoulder as she turned to face the Blackfeet teenager. "Theodore James Black Feather! Where's my hair band? Give it back to me right now."

"You can't tell me what to do. You're not my mother, you know." TJ pulled Cisco up next to her, holding the band out in a teasing fashion. "I like your hair down."

"Well, I like it up when I'm riding. Besides, I'll need to put it up when we go swimming later," she said, holding out her hand.

"The water is probably too cold now anyway. Winter is coming early."

Josephine reached out further.

Flashing his father's smile, he dropped the hair band onto her palm.

Then she noticed! "Your hair, you cut it!"

"Yeah, I think it makes me look older, more sophisticated, don't you?" he said in a low masculine voice, turning his head to give her a better view.

"No, I liked your hair long. It's always been long."

As the pair began walking side by side along the lake trail, Bonanza and Cisco breathing heavily in unison, Josephine sneaked peeks at TJ. The geeky and goofy neighbor boy she had played tag and hide-n-seek with since childhood did look different, more like a young man than an awkward teen. Even though he was six months her senior, she had always thought he looked younger than her… until now. Was it the shorter hair? For a moment, she might have even felt attracted to him.

Josephine shook her head, cracking a lopsided smile to herself. Enough silly thoughts.

"What did you bring us?" she asked, sliding her hair band over her wrist. For as long as they had gone on morning trail rides together, they took turns bringing breakfast.

TJ flipped a suede drawstring bag braided into Cisco's mane over the gelding's neck. "Ham biscuits, and they're still warm, but they won't be for long." TJ cued Cisco into a trot, leading the way down the trail toward the hunting cabin across the lake from the lodge.

When they reached the old log structure, built on stilts not far from shore, they slid from their mounts and tied them to a hitching post out front.

"Give me the sack and I'll set things up inside while you get us some water," Josephine instructed.

TJ gave her a smirk but didn't hesitate, grabbing the bucket off the front porch before heading to the pump out back. Josephine had always had the upper hand in their friendship.

He had never been shy about showing his feelings toward her. As far back as she could remember, he had a crush on her, kissing her as a toddler, long uncomfortable stares in puberty, and now looking for any excuse to touch her or be close to her, which had become a problem at school.

She didn't like the strange looks and rude comments made by her friends anytime he stopped to talk to her in the hall. "Why do you even bother with him?" they would say. Sometimes she pretended not to see him or would turn away and begin a conversation with someone else before he could reach her. She felt bad afterward, but TJ seemed to understand and never brought it up. She was glad she wouldn't have to choose between TJ and her friends at school any longer.

Next week she would be leaving for California! In no time at all, she would meet an older pre-law or pre-med student who struck her fancy. Aware of her beauty, having had her pick of boys through school, Josephine figured the possibilities would be endless at college.

Josephine slid a cassette into the battery-operated boom box setting on the counter. As she pulled plates and glasses from the shelf and tore a few paper towels off the roll that hung from a wire hanger above the water basin, she sang along to Garth Brooks' "Dance." Swaying to the melody, she set the table for two. When she opened TJ's sack, the glorious smell of ham and biscuits filled the room.

TJ soon joined her, set the water down and strutted straight to the radio. "Yuck, I don't know how you listen to this stuff." Within seconds, Garth was replaced by Chris Cornell belting out "Blackhole Sun."

"Well I don't know how you listen to that!"

"Are you kidding. Soundgarden is so rad!"

"Rad?"

"You know, radical, cool."

"That's not music?"

"Oh, you just like how those cowboys fill their tight jeans, is all."

"Theodore James!" Josephine scowled and turned off the boom box. "I think I'd rather have it quiet."

"Me too." He snapped back. Then they both laughed. This had become a ritual each visit to the cabin. "I really don't mind Garth that much, if you want to put him back in."

"No, I really would like some quiet. I want to tell you more about UCLA."

TJ rolled his eyes and filled their glasses before taking a seat across from her. Before she could take a bite of her biscuit, he leaned across the table and gently brushed a few loose hairs from her face. Josephine's tummy flipped like a pancake. What was that? Was she going to be ill? She pushed his hand away, sending her full glass of water flying.

"Geeze, Jo, I was only trying to keep your hair out of your food."

"Look at this mess, would you!"

"I'm sorry, you can have mine."

Josephine got up, took her plate to the basin to salvage her meal and grabbed the whole roll of paper towels. After wiping down the table and her seat, she got down on her hands and knees to dry the floor and wall. As she wiped up the corner, something brushed her hand. Stuck between the rough-cut baseboard and log wall was the corner of a Polaroid photograph. She pulled it out, got up off the floor and brushed the dust from it. She couldn't believe her eyes! "What is this?!" she shrieked.

Quick as a bear protecting its cub, TJ rushed to her side. Unlike the time he had pulled a sliver from her finger when they were kids, or when he helped her walk from the bus stop after she sprained her ankle playing softball, there wasn't anything he could do but stare at the photo alongside of her.

Her mother, appearing about her age, sat naked on the cabin couch, her long hair barely covering her breasts, with her arms around the bare chest of Mr. Black Feather, kissing him on the cheek as he held the camera. How much their parents resembled them at their age was unnerving. It was like looking at a photo of her and TJ undressed.

After glaring at the picture in disbelief, they looked into each other's eyes searching for answers.

"My dad and your mom?" questioned TJ.

Josephine pulled away, continuing to study the image as she paced the room. "We can't say a word about this to anyone, okay? My folks aren't getting along so great right now. This would really make a mess of things."

TJ nodded. "Mine too. But it looks like this happened a

long time ago, long before our parents got married or we were born."

Questions Josephine had thought about but never dared to ask suddenly took on new meaning. Why had her mother warned her not to get involved with any Blackfeet boys? Why did she act so silly around Mr. Black Feather sometimes, especially lately? She knew her father had noticed it, too.

"They already know," she said flatly, putting two and two together.

"Know what, who?"

"Your mom and my dad. They know—think about it. When did your parents start having problems?"

"About two years ago, but more so lately."

"Yeah, mine too. About the time your dad started helping my mom train Major. Soon they'll be spending time together in California. My dad and your mom must be worried they're getting back together."

TJ held Josephine by the arms to hold her in place. "You think there's really something going on?"

She wiggled away. "No. I don't think so. I don't know!"

"This is not good. I don't want my parents getting a divorce." Now TJ paced the room. "And, what if they married… then we would be like brother and sister!"

Josephine panicked hearing the "D" word. "What are we going to do?"

TJ took her by the hand and gently led her to the couch. "I don't think there's anything we can do."

Josephine nodded. She knew he was right. Tears pricked her eyes as fears of what the future might hold surfaced. In a moment of weakness, she leaned onto her best friend, resting her head on his shoulder. Immediately, he closed his arms around her, comforting her with a gentle stroke of her hair. They had hugged in the past, like when she made the varsity softball team and he earned his letter in wrestling, but this felt different—nicer.

After she calmed, she sat up to find TJ looking at her funny. Again, her stomach somersaulted. Suddenly, she sprang to her feet. The picture, the couch, their parents, she and TJ! Yuck!

"Let's head back." Josephine tucked the photo in her back pocket, put her hair back up in a ponytail and locked the cabin door behind them.

She tried not to think about the photo in her pocket, focusing instead on the image of her parents hugging yesterday morning before her mother left. Perhaps everything was fine now, back to normal, and there was nothing to worry about. She would destroy the picture when she got home, just to be on the safe side, but that image of the two of them together would be burned into her memory forever. She feared she would never be able to look at her mother or Mr. Black Feather the same again.

7 – First Move

Tuesday

Following a light breakfast for herself and Steven, Betsy busied herself in the kitchen. The house had become quieter with Katherine gone; next week Josephine would be leaving. She sighed, already looking forward to having everyone home for Thanksgiving. Just as she finished the dishes, she heard a large vehicle pull in the gravel drive followed by the honk of a horn.

By the time she dried her hands, retrieved her cane, and got to the side door, Steven stood on the porch conversing with a man standing out front of a large delivery truck. Oh no! It was one of Kurt's old gang, the taller of the two brothers who lived south of town. She couldn't think of their names. Betsy looked around for Ricky. *He's come for Katherine!*

Betsy hobbled to her bedroom dresser, her knees aching with each hurried stride. Thank goodness Josephine was out on her morning trail ride. She pulled the revolver from the drawer, cocked it, and rushed to the side door. Steven was now down on the drive talking with the man. She walked out onto the porch, .357 Magnum raised.

"Betsy, what are you doing?!" screamed Steven.

"I know who you are," she said to the man.

Steven walked toward her. "They have hay for sale. Jerry at the feed store told them Katherine was looking to stock up for the winter. Put the gun away."

Betsy stayed focused and aimed on the intruder. "Where's Ricky?" she yelled over Steven's head.

The man stepped behind Steven. "Ricky who? Are you crazy?"

"You know who I'm talking about. Ricky Werden. Steven, get away from him."

"He's in prison." The man turned to Steven. "Tell her to put that gun down."

Steven approached her on the porch. "What's going on, Betz?"

Not budging, Betsy whispered to Steven, "He's one of Kurt's old gang that attacked Beth and me at the hardware store years ago… and he was in on the fight at Rudy's that night. Something's up, Steven. Ricky's not far away."

Steven turned back to the man. "What's your name?"

"You're all crazy. I'm out of here." The man stomped around the cab of the truck, climbed in, turned the truck around and pulled out spinning gravel in every direction.

Betsy uncocked the revolver and lowered it to her side, locking eyes with Steven. "What did you tell him?"

Steven looked stunned. "I didn't know who he was. I told him there must be some mistake, that Katherine had already stocked up on hay and grain before she left for the coast. Shit, Betz, I just got an emergency call and was about to leave. I wasn't thinking."

"Did you tell him specifically where she was going?"

"No, just that she had left for a couple of months."

"I'll bet Ricky was in the back. I saw the other brother in the cab. Shoot, I can't remember their names."

"Chief will know."

Betsy sat down at the picnic table and set the revolver down while Steven called Chief.

It had begun.

Steven returned the handset to the library phone and found

Betsy still sitting out on the porch. "Their names are Jake and Kyle Schmitt."

"Yes, I remember now," said Betsy. "What about their story with the hay?"

"Their uncle owns a truck and they are known to buy and sell hay, among other things, and make deliveries. They rent a place south of town, like you said. Their parents haven't had anything to do with them for years… something about having stolen from them, and then there were the rumors about some nasty business with their younger sister. Their folks kicked them both out onto the street years ago."

"Sounds like friends of the Werdens, alright. Thank goodness we got Lisa away from those boys when we did."

"Well, they're grown men now, but I can't imagine they've changed much. Neither of them ever got married or had kids."

"Well, there's something we can all be thankful for!"

Steven chuckled, but only for an instant. He had to take Betsy's premise seriously and the possibility she was right about the brothers acting on Ricky's behalf. Hell, Ricky might have been inside that truck waiting to snatch Katherine up for all he knew. They must have been surprised to find him home. Normally, he would have left for the clinic hours ago.

"We need to warn Katherine," said Betsy, "and Billy."

"Yes. Katherine will call tonight, and I'll stop at Billy's on the way home. You and Jo going to be okay here until I get back?"

"Sure. She should be back from her ride soon. We'll lock all the doors and I'll keep my gun handy. What do I tell Josephine?"

"We've told her about the fire. No need telling her anything more."

"She needs to know the whole story sooner or later, Steven."

"Her mother needs to be the one to do that."

Betsy nodded in agreement.

Steven jogged down the stairs. "I'll be home as soon as I can," he called from his truck.

He hated leaving the women, but he needed to tend to one of his client's show horses that had torn its eyelid. It needed to be stitched as soon as possible. Then he would return to the clinic to go over his schedule with Sherri and reschedule his routine appointments and tend only to emergencies, so he could spend as much time at home as possible.

As he drove to the clinic, his mind darted between Katherine and Billy. How could he warn her without scaring her to death? How would his conversation go with Billy? My, how things had changed in twenty-four hours. Suddenly, he was glad she was gone. Now he wanted Billy to get out there as soon as he could and spend as much time with his wife as possible until he could break away.

First, he needed to get Josephine safely on her flight to LA. Maybe he would fly out with her and hook up with the women in LA. He would mention it to Katherine during their call that evening. Her local students could handle the horses and Betsy could stay with her brothers. Until then, it would be a stressful week, wondering when or where Ricky might make his next move.

After Steven left, Betsy returned the revolver to her dresser drawer and waited on the porch for Josephine to return. Just as she was about to doze off on the corner glider, she heard Bonanza's hoofs shuffle gravel across the parking area. Betsy looked up as Josephine waved on her way to the barn. She hated to burden the teen with this business about Ricky right before she left for school; this should be a happy and exciting time for her.

It wasn't long before Josephine trotted up the side stairs and approached her. "Hi Betz."

"Did you and TJ have a nice ride?"

"Sure," she said.

Betsy noticed her hair was dry. "You're back early and I see you didn't go for a swim today."

"Water's getting cold. TJ thinks winter is going to come early this year."

"I agree, the leaves are dropping weeks sooner than they normally do."

At that moment, a breeze off the lake blew a swirl of gold aspen leaves across the porch and between the teen's feet like confetti. "Shoot, I'm cold. I'm going to go take a hot shower and put on some jeans."

"Wait, come sit with me a moment, Jo. There's something I need to talk to you about."

Betsy was surprised by Josephine's sudden look of concern as if she expected bad news. The teen perched on the porch rail beside her and leaned in, all ears.

"Do you remember hearing about the barn fire here at Two Ponies before you were born?" Josephine nodded, looking relieved. What had she expected? Betsy pushed that thought aside for now. "Well, one of the men responsible for the fire is dead, Jack Werden. The other man, his son, Ricky Werden, just got out of prison. Chief thinks he might be dangerous. Do you know who I'm talking about?"

"Sure, I know who they are… Lisa's family. But what do you mean, dangerous?"

"He's a coward and blames your mother for everything bad that has happened to him and his family."

"You mean he's out to get even… to hurt Mom?"

"We don't know what he has planned, but some men came by earlier and I recognized them as old friends of Ricky's. They said they had hay inside their truck they wanted to show your mother, but I don't think that's what their visit was about. I think Ricky was behind it."

"They were looking for Mom?"

"Yes, so we're going to be extra careful until you leave next week."

"But, Mom's gone," Josephine said.

Betsy took a deep breath. No way to sugar coat it; Josephine wasn't a child any longer. But before she could explain further, Josephine made her own conclusion.

"Oh. Since Mom is gone, they might come after us." Josephine got up and slipped in next to Betsy on the glider and put her arm around her shoulders. "Don't worry, Betz, we'll be just fine. We can handle these goons."

Betsy had to smile. Josephine reminded her of Joseph in so many ways–stubborn and fearless. Betsy got to her feet. "Come with me," she said.

Josephine followed her through the lodge to her room where she showed her the revolver. "We'll take it out with us to feed later and practice a little, just in case."

Josephine's eyes widened. "I've always wanted to learn to shoot a handgun. I'll pick some cans out of the trash and we can line them up on the woodpile out back like they do in the movies. This will be fun! What's for dinner?"

Again, Betsy smiled, shaking her head. "I pulled out some chicken. I was going to grill it, but I think we'll stay in and fry it instead."

"Great, I love fried chicken."

And just like that, Josephine was off, sprinting up the stairs. Betsy laughed out loud. And she was worried about upsetting her. While Josephine got cleaned up, she unlocked the gun cabinet in the library and removed two cases of bullets, one box of low-grain for practice, and a case of hollow-points.

Again, Ricky hung by the phone waiting to hear from Jake. This time when it rang, he answered it himself. "Jake, what happened? What do you mean you couldn't deliver it?" He couldn't believe what he was hearing. "She's gone? You're kidding me."

Andy entered the living room and plopped down beside him on the couch to listen in. "What? That damn squaw! Getting all uppity, living with white folks for so long."

Andy tapped him with his leg and silently lipped, "What happened?"

Ricky kicked him back, scooted over and leaned forward, wanting his own space. "Where is she? Tell me word-for-word what he said." Ricky listened carefully. "Okay, go back to the feed store and see if Jerry knows where she's gone to, then come to Andy's. You still have the address? Good. It would be great to see you and we need to regroup." Ricky hung up the phone, ran his hand through his greasy hair, and turned to Andy.

Andy glared at him with a sour puss. "Doesn't sound like things are going according to plan."

Ricky gave him a quick rundown on what happened.

Andy punched the sofa. "Shit! I've got a lot on the line here if this doesn't work out. I quit my job. I've managed to string my landlord along for months, but I'm about to get evicted. I need that money. You wouldn't even have a plan if it weren't for me and the cabin."

"Don't worry, you'll get your cut once I get what I want."

"And what if you don't?"

"This is just a little setback, that's all. Once we find her and deliver the letter, everything will be set in motion."

When Steven finished at the clinic late afternoon, he headed to the Black Feathers. Sarah greeted him at the door with a smile as always, yet he felt there was something different… something unsettling in her eyes.

"Hi Steve, so good to see you… it's been a while."

Steven gave her a hug. "Been busy."

"How's the women making out with Major on the road?"

"Fine, they're making good time, stayed at a horse hotel last night and should arrive at the show grounds this evening. Major has been handling the travel just fine. I'm sure being an ex-racehorse and accustomed to being on the road has helped." Steven glanced at the Chevy truck parked in the drive. "I need to talk with Billy."

"He's down at the barn with TJ," she said. "You and Betsy should join us for dinner at my folks next week."

"That would be nice if I can pry Betz out of the kitchen. Thanks!" he said, starting toward the barn.

Steven found Billy holding a young sorrel gelding in the aisle, its eyes rimmed in white, nervously dancing in place. TJ slowly floated a colorful wool saddle blanket over the colt's neck, back, and haunches.

"Hi, Doctor Walker," said TJ, resting the blanket at his side.

"Looks like a pretty wild one," said Steven.

"Hey, Steve," said Billy. "Yeah, picked him up from the Mustang rescue last week—never been handled. He's coming along well, though, took to a halter and lead without too much trouble. He's smart."

"That can be a good or a bad thing."

TJ walked up to the colt and gently rubbed his neck. "Think it'll be good with this guy. He hasn't offered to bite or kick, just skittish."

"He's a looker for sure with all that chrome," said Steven, admiring the Mustang's white blaze down his face and four matching white stockings. "Got something I need to talk to you about."

"We're done for the day," Billy said to his son. "Go tell Mom I'll be up for supper soon."

"Yes, sir."

As soon as the boy was out of earshot, Billy turned to Steven. "What's up? You didn't stop by just to shoot the shit with your old buddy now, did ya?"

Steven sensed some trepidation on Billy's part. What did he expect? "Have some news about Ricky."

Looking a little relieved, Billy turned and silently led the colt into a nearby stall and began rubbing his neck until the colt settled down and quit resisting. He unclipped the lead and closed the stall door. Steven followed Billy out of the barn where he leaned against the wood pile and lit a cigarette. "I know, he's out. Dane called yesterday."

"There's more." Steven sat across from Billy on the corner of a picnic table and told him about the Schmitt brothers' visit. "When are you planning to leave?"

"Saturday. I'm expected to start at the first farm Monday. I was planning on visiting the women mid-week," said Billy.

"I'm going to fly out with Jo next week. I sure would feel better if you could meet up with the women sooner and spend as much time with Katherine as possible until I can get out there."

Billy flashed one of his smart-ass smiles. "Sure. Didn't expect to hear that coming from you."

Leave it to Billy to be blunt and to the point. Why should he be surprised? Billy knew him better than anyone besides Katherine… perhaps even better than Betsy. Steven guessed he had picked up on his suspicions, justified or not. Dang, was there something going on or was Billy just having a little fun at his expense? He wasn't about to confront Billy about it now;

he needed him with the women.

Steven got to his feet. "Well, how about it?"

"I have a few horses I'm scheduled to deliver Friday morning, but I could leave that afternoon, which should put me in Santa Rosa sometime Saturday if I drive straight through. Does Kat know?"

"Not about today yet. She'll be calling me when they arrive in Santa Rosa this evening. You should have Sarah and TJ stay with family."

"Already planned on it," said Billy.

"What about your livestock? Need me to feed?"

"TJ's going to drive over twice a day."

Steven got up to leave. "As soon as the police locate Ricky, they'll be keeping an eye on him."

Billy walked him to his truck. "Then what? And, for how long? We need to take things into our own hands if we get the chance. Betsy had the right idea!"

Steven chuckled, picturing Betsy waving the big revolver earlier. But he knew Billy wasn't joking. He was dead serious and perhaps he was right. He had thought the same thing—when would it end? The police department's hands were tied until something happened. He shook Billy's hand. 'We'll talk more when I meet up with you all next week."

As Steven drove home, a blanket of dread gripped him. His chest tightened with fear—the fear of once again losing his Kat. Would he lose her to Billy a second time, or worse yet, what if Ricky got to her? The possibilities were terrifying. He wondered what Billy had in mind. That was frightening, too, but something had to be done to end it once and for all.

When Ricky heard a vehicle pull up the drive, Andy met the brothers at the front door.

"Hey," said Andy. "We finally meet."

"I'm Jake, and this is my brother, Kyle."

Andy closed the door behind them.

Ricky shook Jake's hand and pulled him into a man-hug. "It's been a long time."

"No shit," said Jake, resting his hand on Ricky's shoulder. Jake had visited him a few years back but not since he started planning his revenge. No need in drawing attention to Jake with a visit in case things didn't play out as planned.

"Thanks. Find the place okay?"

"Yeah, just took longer than I remembered. Haven't been down this way for a while."

"How about a beer?" asked Ricky.

Jake sat down on the couch. "Sure." ,

"I'll take one too," said Kyle, sitting beside Jake.

"Of course, you will," laughed Ricky, nodding in the direction of the kitchen to Andy, before sitting across from the brothers.

Andy snarled at him but headed for the fridge.

"What did you find out at the mill?" asked Ricky.

Andy handed over the beers and sat at the table.

"Kyle almost blew it." Jake began, taking a gulp.

"What did Tick do this time?" Ricky asked.

"Man, that was years ago," yelped Kyle. "You ever gonna let that go? Ma and Pa would have found out eventually anyhow—right, Jake?"

Neither of them acknowledged Kyle's statement.

Jake pointed to Kyle. "Stupid here almost said too much to Jerry."

Kyle gave his brother a nasty look and sprang up off the couch and took a seat at the table across from Andy, studying the horses out the back window.

"California. She's heading to California."

"What?!"

"Yeah, she's on her way to some fancy horse show," said Jake.

"Eventing," Kyle corrected from across the room.

"Smart-ass!" Jake turned to Ricky. "Just because he reads all the time, he thinks he's so smart all of a sudden."

"So how do we find her?" asked Ricky.

"There's some association—here, I wrote it down." Jake began to search his pockets for the note.

"The USEA, United States Event Association, like in the Olympics," said Kyle. "They have a calendar of all of their recognized shows. It was my idea to contact them."

Ricky turned to Kyle. "When did you become such a horse expert?"

"I like horses. I read a lot of horse books and magazines. I've watched every Summer Olympics and..."

"We contacted them this morning," interrupted Jake. "There are two shows coming up this weekend, one in Stockton and one in Santa Rosa."

"How soon can you get out there?"

"Two days tops," said Jake.

"Do you have money for gas? I'll pay you back."

Jake nodded. "Sure."

"Go home and pack everything you want to keep and don't return to your place. It won't take long for the cops to figure out we might be involved when they disappear. Leave first thing in the morning and deliver the letter as soon as possible. You still onboard?"

"Oh yeah. Nothing here worth staying for," said Jake.

"Good. Call us when you find her."

8 – Santa Rosa

Tuesday – Saturday

Pleased they arrived at the show grounds in Santa Rosa before dark, Katherine would have the opportunity to let Major look around and feel settled in before bedding him down for the night. It would be important he got his rest. Once they located his stall, unloaded, and parked the trailer, they quickly removed his wraps so Katherine could tour the facility with Major in hand. The gelding looked relieved to see other horses, greeting them with a friendly nicker as they passed by. When they returned to his stall, he stood quietly awaiting his dinner, calm and content in his new surroundings.

On the way to their nearby hotel, they stopped at a gas station to fill up and stock up on drinks and munchies. By the time they pulled into the Best Western, it was dark. After checking in, they threw their bags on their beds and immediately took turns calling their men on the pay phone in the lobby.

Jessie left to make her call first while Katherine stocked the refrigerator. As she anxiously awaited talking with Steven, Katherine recalled their sweet lovemaking prior to her departure. It was grand feeling so close to him again. All doubts of his faithfulness had vanished. What had she been thinking, anyway? She filed away his strange behavior as feeling neglected. Katherine looked forward to his visit and a fresh start when she returned home in November.

She glanced at her watch when Jessie returned to their room. It would be nearly nine o'clock Mountain Time by the time she placed her call. She knew he would be waiting by the telephone. Just as suspected, Steven answered on the first ring.

"Hi hon, make it to Santa Rosa?"

"We're here. Just checked into the hotel."

"How did Major do on the road today? Got him bedded down for the night?"

"Yes, and he did great, even better than yesterday. I think he likes his new digs and he sure was happy to see the other horses. I just hope he'll focus on his work tomorrow. Glad we arrived early."

"I already miss you," he said, his voice suddenly sounding funny.

"What's wrong?" Silence. "Steven?"

"We had visitors today."

"Who?" Again, silence. What did he not want to tell her?

Steven cleared his throat. "Jake and Kyle Schmitt." Katherine nearly dropped the receiver, shuddering from head to toe. "You remember who they are?"

"Of course, I do. Wish I could forget them. What did they want?"

Katherine listened closely as Steven told her what happened, then he asked, "Did you talk to Jerry at the feed store about hay?"

"Yes, but that was over a month ago." Katherine gasped. "Oh Steven, when I stocked up on grain before we left, I told him I was leaving for a couple months, starting with a three-day event that weekend in California." Panic swelled in her chest to the point she could barely breathe.

"Don't worry, sweetie. Billy agreed to leave early. He should be there sometime Saturday."

Katherine exhaled. "Thank goodness."

"And, I'll be there next week. I'm rescheduling my routine appointments and referring emergencies to Dr. Hanley while

I'm gone."

"But, what about Jo this week, Betsy, and Billy's family? I know how Ricky works. He won't stop until he gets his revenge on us or someone we care about."

"Don't worry, sweetie. I'll arrange to be home this week. Sarah and TJ are staying with her family until Billy returns, and Betsy will stay with her brothers while I'm gone."

"How is Jo taking this?"

"She doesn't seem upset, but I don't think she truly understands the situation."

"That's for the best; I don't want her worrying. And soon she'll be safe at school."

"Billy…" Steven began.

Again, he sounded strange. "Steven?"

"Billy has the hotel address and, depending on the time of day he rolls in, he'll meet you there or at the show grounds."

"Okay."

Again silence. "What it is, Steven?"

"I love you."

"I love you too," she said. "No matter what happens, know that… okay?"

"Don't talk like that," he said. "Everything is going to be fine. What's your schedule for tomorrow?"

"I plan to school Major on the flat in the morning. We feared the show grounds might resemble a racetrack to him and he might think he's going to race again, but so far he's pretty calm."

"That's my girl. Just focus on Major."

"I can't wait to see you next week."

"Me too, sweetie."

"Goodnight."

Katherine sprang up in bed, sweaty and in a panic. It took

her a moment to recognize her surroundings. She was in a hotel room, with Jessie asleep in the bed beside her. She was in Santa Rosa. It was Wednesday morning. She vaguely recalled her nightmare, running full out and scared on Major down a narrow path, branches whipping her face as the thunder of the Thoroughbred's long strides pounded the earth beneath her. Whether she was being chased or chasing someone was unclear, but the fear lingered.

She knew she wouldn't fall back to sleep, so she quietly dressed and left Jessie a note saying she had left to feed Major and would be back in time for the complimentary breakfast the hotel offered. She would meet her there.

As she covered the short five-minute drive to the show grounds, her conversation with Steven the night before infiltrated her planning for the day. How would Ricky come for her? He might send his gang, but in the end, he would want it to be up close and personal. Suddenly jolted from her seat as the truck left the road onto a soft shoulder, Katherine turned the Ford sharply back onto the pavement, realizing she had passed the entrance to the barns. "Focus on Major!" she scolded herself, as she made a U-turn.

Yes, Major. She would school him dressage that morning and walk the cross-country course that afternoon. Thursday she would school him over the practice stadium and field fences the facility had set up. So far, he had been a good boy; she couldn't be more pleased.

Following each day's work, she would hand-graze Major as a reward. She wanted him tuned up but relaxed prior to the three-day event, starting with dressage on Friday, cross country on Saturday, and stadium jumping on Sunday.

After leaving the gelding blissfully enjoying his meal, she found Jessie at the breakfast buffet filling her plate full of scrambled eggs. The piquant scent of horses could be detected above the aroma of bacon as she sat amongst a room full of show patrons. Katherine recognized Jessie's jacket hanging off the back of a chair and took a seat opposite it. The room was teaming with riders, trainers, owners, and grooms, many of whom traveled great distances and arrived early as they had.

"Not as good as Betsy's cooking, but better than mine," said Jessie, taking her seat. "Aren't you going to eat?"

"I'm not hungry."

Digging into her eggs as if she hadn't eaten for weeks, Jessie glanced up at her. "You look like shit."

"Thanks." Katherine had to chuckle at her friend's brutal honesty. "I didn't sleep well."

"No wonder, with all this talk about the boogeyman coming to get you."

"It's no joke, Jess."

"Well, fretting about it isn't going to help."

"You're right, but we can't let our guard down either until Billy arrives."

Remembering Steven's words, "focus on Major," Katherine shook off those thoughts and changed the subject to all they had to do in the next two days in preparation for the weekend including bathing, grooming, braiding, and cleaning tack between Major's schooling.

Well, I think we'll be too busy to worry about anything with that schedule," said Jessie.

"That's the plan."

Yet, when they parked outside Barn B, she suddenly felt anxious. She reached under the seat feeling for the gun, checking to make sure it hadn't slid beyond her reach. Before exiting the truck, she opened the console and grabbed the pen-knife. Jessie glared at her with a "really?" expression, but Katherine slid it into her jacket pocket anyway, heeding Dane's advice.

"Bring both saddles and bridles, then you can do Major's stall while I ride."

"Will do," Jess said, striding toward their trailer.

"Thanks, Jess," she called out to her.

Katherine stood next to her vehicle, tightly clasping the weapon in her jacket pocket as she searched the bustling barn area. Everyone looked like they belonged. A shrill recognizable whinny followed by a few kicks let her know Major was done with his hay and ready to stretch his legs. Katherine jogged up the hill into the stable. Immediately Major recognized her, his finely shaped ears pricked in her direction. Katherine smiled as she approached his stall, releasing her grip on the fake pen to stroke the bay's silky neck. "Hello, Handsome!"

Her plan worked and there had been little time to dwell on Ricky or his posse that day. Following their chores, Katherine and Jessie strategized on how to get the most out of the green dressage horse on Friday. There was a good-size field of competitors in the Preliminary Division, so they determined they needed to place in the top ten in dressage to have a chance at placing in the ribbons following the stadium and XC portions of the three-phase event where the scores of all three phases were combined. Too low of a dressage score might be unsurpassable, even if they went clean both jumping courses.

On Friday their efforts payed off, earning a fifth place. She liked their chances of placing in the top three, considering many horses that excelled in dressage were not always as strong over fences. Major's flat work was coming along gradually, but jumping had come naturally to the fearless Thoroughbred, especially in the field where he could stretch his legs. He reminded her of a Pac Man on the cross-country course, gobbling up the fences in his path. Controlling his speed and strides had been the real challenge.

Billy had helped her prepare Major to compete by constructing practice courses at home with many similar jumps they expected to encounter that fall in the field and in the ring. They had schooled over much higher jumps at home than they would be jumping that day, hoping to move up two divisions by the end of the fall tour. But, since they were not allowed to ride either course prior to the show, she wondered how Major would react to the new obstacles on a foreign XC course and the bright and outlandishly designed stadium jumps.

There were so many unanswered questions. Was she prepared to guide him safely through these courses after having not competed for so many years? Was Major in good enough condition to complete the course strong? She would have her answers soon. Katherine would need to monitor herself and her horse closely. There would be no room for error or a tired horse over stationary fences.

Katherine didn't sleep well again Friday night, but this time it was a combination of excitement and nerves in prelude to their cross-country ride that day. After walking the course again Thursday afternoon, she felt confident about all the jumps except the water combination. Would Major's fear of water resurface in a new and strange place? Any thoughts of Ricky and his gang were pushed aside as she rehearsed their striding and approach to 10a, 10b, and 10c in her mind repeatedly while Major ate his breakfast.

Sitting in her truck, eating a light breakfast to go that morning, Katherine checked her watch and turned to Jessie. "Let's do this!"

Jessie grinned like a monkey as she jumped from the vehicle. "I'll start bringing up the tack."

Katherine entered the chaotic barn aisle, full of riders

preparing themselves and their horses to compete. Major looked possessed, his head turning in every direction, taking in all the sights and sounds as they got him tacked up. As soon as she gently placed herself in the saddle outside the barn, Major was ready to go. He didn't feel tense or fretful but more energetic and playful, amused by all the activity.

On their way to warm up, horses of every size, color, and breed passed them, many of which had already completed their course. A big chestnut gelding resembling Cody, his old buddy back home, captured Major's attention and Katherine had difficulty keeping her mount on track toward the warm-up area. The pair kept to the outskirts, trotting and cantering just enough to warm him up but not tire him out, as they waited their turn at the handful of practice jumps. Out of a division of twenty-five entrants, Katherine and Major had drawn the last ride.

Katherine's stomach tightened into a knot when their names were called over the loud speaker by the announcer. As they stood on deck, approximately two miles of nearly four-foot-high-and-wide obstacles, as well as substantial banks and ditches winding up and down hills and through water, lay before them. The time had come to test the pair's years of training and conditioning.

Not only did they need to navigate the grueling course cleanly to maintain or move up from fifth position, but it needed to be completed within the optimum time or they would receive a time penalty that could push them out of the ribbons. Katherine gazed up at the clear blue skies. Thankfully, it was a clear day and the course would be dry and fast.

As they waited their turn, Katherine managed to calm herself the way Betsy had taught her, breathing in and out slowly as she spoke to Major in a soothing voice, more for her benefit than for his. The off-the-track Thoroughbred seemed to be taking everything in stride.

"Next up, number thirty-one, Katherine Walker, onboard Major Command," said the announcer.

"Okay boy, here we go."

Major calmly walked into the start box. Again, her heart began beating overtime, her chest feeling as if it might burst through her safety vest. She fastened the chinstrap of her helmet and gripped her reins as the announcer counted down to her start. Ten, nine, eight… her finger on her stopwatch… five, four, three… deep breath… The whistle sounded! Off they galloped down the lane toward their first fence. Suddenly, her nervousness disappeared, concentrating only on Major and the challenges ahead.

"We've got this, boy!" she said to the big gelding. The wind in her face with Major's ears flicking back and forth between the terrain ahead and her cues prompted a vision from onboard Lady years ago.

Suddenly, the first jump lay before them. Major's ears pricked forward as he locked onto the fence, followed by the exhilaration of feeling him surge underneath her as they sailed over the obstacle. Again, his head bobbed in unison with the rhythmic sound of his long galloping strides as they approached the next jump.

Following a few relatively straightforward obstacles, more difficult questions tested their discipline and balance. They flew over large tables, though a keyhole and spanned ditches. Next came the challenging sequence through the water, with its steep bank down and tight turn between two narrow log jumps in a couple feet of water.

She could feel Major suck back and tense up. "It's good, boy; we're good. Nice and easy."

Into the murky water they plunged, water splashing her

hands and legs, churned up by dozens of horses that went before them. Major had no idea how deep it was or what lay beneath the surface, only his trust in Katherine carried them forward.

As soon as they cleared the first log and Major's head shot up questioning the second, the wet reins slipped through her grip. Major turned wide and by the time she gathered them back up, they were off-line and off-stride, coming into the second jump of the combination all wrong, but it was too late to pull up! Somehow the big athletic gelding rounded over the log but brushed the top and landed off-balance, nearly losing his footing. No sooner than they recovered, they were lunging up the bank to another jump. Once they returned to flat ground, Katherine scrutinized her mount's movement. Feeling assured by Major's square and balanced strides, she pressed on, but valuable seconds were lost.

The next obstacle, which appeared to be a straightforward jump the overcast afternoon before, glared ahead of them. The huge log appeared lit up from within, sunlight glistening off its polished finish. It was Steven's engraved log! Major hesitated, breaking stride and veering to the left, typical of most off-the-track Thoroughbreds with a dominant left lead. For that reason, Katherine always carried a crop in her left hand. Quickly, she showed him the tip of the bright blue crop and that's all it took to straighten him out.

"C'mon boy, get-up!" Katherine yelled, backing up her orders with her leg and seat. The pair sailed over the frightening obstacle, overjumping it and clearing it by what felt like nearly two feet. More seconds lost.

As they neared the end of the course, a familiar voice rang out above the crowd.

"Go, Katherine!" It was Billy!

There was no time to search him out, the crowd a blur as

they galloped by, nearing the finish. Was Major tiring? No, he felt good, a little winded, but good. Katherine checked her watch. She knew she needed to make up time, and the long stretch between them and the last jump and again to the finish would determine whether they placed or not.

Allowing the reins to slip through her fingers a measured amount, feeling she still maintained a handle on him, she leaned forward and felt Major respond with lengthened strides and a burst of speed. "C'mon boy, we're almost there!" The next challenge would be gathering him up in time before the last jump, which was a good-size table. She had rehearsed this very maneuver many times at home and at Jessie's, letting him go and pulling him back up, but would he respond here now?

A crowd lined the lane on both sides of the tape. She could feel Major's head wavering ever so slightly from right to left, distracted for the first time on course by the activity of the spectators crowded near the finish. Katherine found her spot, shifted her weight back in the saddle and squeezed the reins a few strides out to gather him up, but Major did not respond. Their take-off spot would be too long! All she could do was give him his head and trust in him this time. It seemed they were airborne forever!

"Wooo!" she exhaled as they landed. "C'mon boy, go!!"

With the crowd cheering them on, the retired racehorse jockeyed by the oldest contestant of the day crossed the finish line a fraction of a second within the optimum time!

"Good boy!" she praised, patting the bay's shoulder as Jessie came running up.

"You did it! Clean and no time penalty!" Jessie took hold of Major by the reins as she dismounted. "The lead horses didn't go clean; you're in first place!"

As out of breath as her mount, Katherine just smiled. It would be theirs to lose on Sunday.

"Any problems on course?" Jessie asked. "I lost sight of you after the keyhole until the final stretch."

"Just a couple," Katherine said, immediately looking over Major's legs. "I lost my grip on the reins in the water. Next time we're using the rubber-grip reins, rain or shine."

"You said a couple."

"He looked at the big log jump. I had to do a little convincing on that one."

"I don't know if I was more excited or scared watching you guys from the hilltop. He took that last jump huge."

"You should have seen the log!"

"And those bigger jumps, holy smokes!" said Jessie, referring to the jumps of the higher divisions.

"Next year!" she said. "Say, I heard Billy. Have you seen him?"

Jessie pointed. "Here he comes now."

Katherine handed Major over to Jessie, who immediately loosened his girth, took off his wet splint boots and began walking him.

Billy quickly caught up, surprising Katherine with a lingering hug. "I came as quick as I could," he whispered in her ear.

"We did it!" For a moment she lost herself in the excitement, melting into his embrace and rested her head on his shoulder, until she opened her eyes to Jessie's questioning stare. Katherine quickly broke away.

"Great job! Looks like you both made it in one piece," he said, glancing over her and Major. He turned to Jessie. "Hi Jess."

"Hi Billy," she said, still studying Katherine with a furrowed brow.

"Let's tend to Major," said Katherine, allowing Jessie to lead the way as she and Billy followed. On their way to the barn, Katherine ran through every detail of the course with him.

Once she finished, Billy asked the inevitable, "Have you seen anything suspicious?"

"We've been too busy to notice," said Katherine. "How long can you stay?"

"I put off my first job until Steven gets here."

"Thank you, Billy," she said, making eye contact. Shocked by his penetrating gaze, she halted mid-stride. "Has something else happened? I haven't spoken to Steven since last night. Is everyone okay?"

Once Jessie was beyond earshot, Billy took her by the shoulders and whispered, "Everyone is fine, but… we must end this, Kat. We can't go on like this, not knowing when or what Ricky's next move will be." The intensity in his eyes scared her. "When they come, I'm going to end it once and for all."

Katherine stepped back from him. "What are you saying, Billy?"

"You know what I'm saying."

"No, the authorities will handle it."

"Handle it? Sure, after it's too late. Who will "it" be, Kat… you, Betsy, Jo, Sarah, TJ?"

"Stop it, Billy!"

Katherine was suddenly aware Jessie had stopped ahead of them and stood glaring at them.

"We need to discuss this later."

Billy glanced at Jessie, then made lingering eye contact with Katherine again, nodding. "Sure. I'll go check in at the hotel and meet you at the restaurant for dinner."

"What time?"

"I could use a nap. I drove straight through. How about five o'clock?"

"Sounds good; we'll see you then."

Billy split off toward the public parking lot while Katherine hurried to catch up with Jessie who had resumed walking Major toward the barn.

As soon as she caught up, Jessie leaned in. "What was that all about? If I didn't know better…"

"It's not what you think," Katherine interrupted.

"I saw the way you two hugged. That wasn't any good old buddy, glad-to-see-you hug. And the way he looked at you!"

"He's just worried about me."

Jessie scowled at her.

"Okay, there's more."

"No kidding!"

"Let's get Major put up and we'll talk."

As they bathed, cooled and wrapped Major, Katherine couldn't help but dwell on Billy's statements. Could he really be planning on killing Ricky? He had killed before. This scared her, but the alternative did too—Ricky and his band on the loose and having to constantly look over their shoulder, worrying about the kid's safety for the rest of their lives. Katherine tried to shake off those thoughts and concentrate on her horse.

As soon as Major was settled in his stall, Jessie led the way to the truck. No sooner than Katherine sat down and closed her truck door, Jessie was on her. "Okay, let's have it."

"Not now. I want to get to the hotel and take a shower. I'm gross."

"Okay, but this better be good."

"You have no idea."

9 – The Story

Saturday

When Katherine stepped out of the bathroom with a towel on her head, she found Jessie waiting, perched on the end of her bed with her legs crossed under her, following her every move. Katherine propped a few pillows against her headboard and made herself comfortable. Jessie didn't say a word. Her expression said it all—tell me something soon or I'm going to drag it out of you!

"Okay, let me see… where should I begin?"

Katherine pulled the towel off her head and ran her fingers through her wet hair. She dreaded digging up the past, but Billy's behavior had left her no choice.

"How about you start with what's going on between you and Billy."

"It's not that simple. It's a long story."

"Well, start someplace and quick. I don't think I can wait much longer!"

"Do you remember the Indian ghost story you used to tell the girls at camp years ago?"

She chuckled. "Sure, I told that story every full moon before the girls went to sleep when I was a leader. Used to scare them to death. I heard it from one of the leaders when I first visited Two Ponies as a kid."

Jessie tilted her head, appearing deep in thought. "It was about an Indian who walked into Pine Island Lake to die rather than go on without his true love." Jessie paused. "I told the girls he would walk out onto the very shore below us every full moon searching for his lost love and when he didn't find her, he'd steal one of our souls and slip back into the lake to return the next full moon."

Jessie's eyes narrowed. "But what's that got to do with anything?"

Katherine took a deep breath. "Well, Billy was that Indian… and I was his lover."

Jessie's eyes opened wide as if she had seen a ghost. "What?! Seriously?!... How?... When?"

Katherine motioned with an open hand for Jessie to be patient. "Let me start at the beginning."

Jessie fluffed up her pillows and laid on her side facing Katherine, propped on her elbow as she hung on her every word.

"Well, as you know, Steven and I met during one of my summer visits to Two Ponies as kids, became best friends and later teenage sweethearts. When my parents bought Lady for my sixteenth birthday in Boston, I began seriously training and competing to someday qualify for the US Equestrian Team. For four years I didn't visit Two Ponies, not until my Uncle Joe died. I wish you could have met him, he..."

"Me too, but back to you and Billy, please." Jessie interrupted.

"When I returned for his funeral, that would have been the winter of 1960, Steven and I picked right up where we left off and when I learned I had inherited Two Ponies, that's when I decided to move to Montana with Lady and abandon my show career."

"How old were you?"

"Twenty. I waited to finish that semester, just in case I wanted to return to school later. Steven was a year ahead of me, attending CSU as you know, but his spring term ran two weeks later than mine. The day following my arrival, I met Billy."

Katherine got up off the bed and walked to the window, pulling the shear curtain open. She stared out beyond the parking lot across the Sonoma Valley stretching east to the Taylor Mountains in the distance. "He was magnificent then."

"He's not bad now," said Jessie.

Katherine turned to Jessie long enough to give her a look, before losing herself in the distant mountain range once again.

"He was everything Steven wasn't—mysterious, exciting, even dangerous. I found him breaking a colt in the lake." Katherine closed her eyes, the image still clear in her mind after thirty some years.

"He was nearly naked, wearing only jeans and a beaded choker, riding bareback on a beautiful gray mare as he led a sleek black colt in circles down by the beaver dam." Katherine chuckled. "He was so, you know… Billy—a mix of flirt, smartass, hardcase, and charm… and that smile." Katherine grinned picturing him then. "Needless to say, he swept me off my feet. I hired him on the spot to help construct the school before I had even secured the loan."

Katherine walked to the refrigerator and grabbed a water bottle. "Want anything?"

Jessie shook her head, emphatically. Katherine sat back down on her bed and took a drink.

"This is crazy. I can't picture you two together… well, until today," said Jessie. "How far did it go before Steven arrived?"

"Just flirting. He did hold me a couple of times, pulling me to the ground by surprise in tall grass to prove how vulnerable I was so he could give me self-defense lessons."

"Oh, the old 'let me hold you to show you how' trick."

"Yes, I was a sap. A naïve sap." Katherine's focus fell to her lap. "But I felt things, deep inside, I had never felt before…feelings I never experienced with Steven."

Jessie sprang up to a sitting position. "Wow, does Steven know about this?"

"I've never come out and said it, but I think he knew."

"Did Billy feel the same way about you?"

"I believe so. He had secretly left me shrines on the stump in the tack room for years, the day I arrived and on my birthday each summer visit, long before I even knew he existed."

"Oh my God, he had a crush on you for years?"

"Well, let me finish."

"Please do!"

"Steven moved into the lodge and Billy moved into the cabin across the lake for the summer while we all worked on the camp together. Billy was already with Sarah and got engaged about the time Steven arrived."

"Hmm… that was a bit of a coincidence. Any sex going on here?"

"Jessie!"

"Well, there must have been a bunch or hormones flying around."

"Steven and my relationship did become intimate that summer. It helped put Billy out of my mind… until…"

"Until what?"

"It was the night of my twenty-first birthday party. Steven proposed to me out of the blue, in front of all of our guests, before he returned to school the next week."

"He knew," said Jessie, scooting to the edge of bed.

"I think so. I just sat there in shock and took the ring from him. I never said yes. I felt faint and Steven helped me out onto the porch for some fresh air. When Steven left to say goodbye to my guests for me, I had to get away—somewhere I could think. I made a mad dash to the old barn. There sat

Billy on the stump waiting for me. That's when I learned he was my secret admirer. He had a gift wrapped in tissue paper he was going to leave for me, but he said it was time to stop playing silly children's games."

"What was it?"

"A chiseled wooden heart… with a gash across its center…"

"Oh boy. I think I know what happened next!"

"Yep, we made mad passionate love right there on the feed bin." Jessie's eyes were as big as dinner plates as she watched Katherine wipe a tear from her eye. "Then… Steven walked in on us."

Jessie put her hands to her face and gasped.

"I broke his heart, Jess. He swore to never forgive me."

Katherine paused, taking a few deep breaths hoping to compose herself. She hadn't thought about that night in a long time. How had she let that happen? How could she have done that to Steven? How did he ever forgive her and Billy?

Jessie encouraged her on, nodding her head. "Billy wouldn't leave Sarah because she was very sick, and he was the only one who could get her the medical treatment she needed. He was afraid if he told her about us, she wouldn't let him help. So, we waited. Steven left for Fort Collins without a word and we didn't speak again until the night Flower colicked. Remember? That was fourteen years later."

"Sure. Wow, there was a whole lot more to that story than you told me in the barn aisle that night."

"And, there's more." Katherine took a swig of water. "Billy stayed on and the two of us finished the inside of the barn and girls' cabins… and we continued to see each other… secretly." Jessie gave her look of shame. "I know, I was a rotten scoundrel. To this day, I feel badly about what we did—no, I did—to Steven and Sarah."

"What happened then?

"Sarah ended up needing surgery that winter and her recovery was slow. That spring we received the first of our deposits for the school and Billy and I went to Rudy's to celebrate. When Billy told me Sarah was feeling well enough to return to work soon and he planned to break things off that night, we kissed. That's when the Werden and Schmitt brothers walked in. They didn't like the idea of a Blackfeet with a white girl."

"The fight in the parking lot!" Jessie blurted out. "I never knew the whole story, only that Billy was attacked, and Kurt Werden ended up dead."

"We ran. Drove home and planned to ride across the border into Canada on horseback together."

"Wasn't it self-defense?"

"Sure, but things were different then, not that they're that much better now. But then an Indian didn't stand a chance when the death of a white man was involved. He would have been sentenced to life, which would have been the same as a death sentence."

"But you never made it."

Katherine shook her head. "I dropped Billy off at the bunkhouse to pack some things and drove to the lodge to get what I needed and the horses." Katherine rose to her feet and began pacing the room. "But when I reached the open ridge, I could see police cars pulling in next to the cabin across the lake, lights flashing. There was a full moon… I could see the surface of the water as clear as daylight… I watched Billy walk slowly into the lake until he disappeared beneath the surface."

Katherine collapsed onto her bed. "I thought he drowned… dead because of me. It was all wrong. Betsy warned me something might happen, but I didn't listen."

"Because Billy was Blackfeet?"

"Yes. You girls and the horses were all that kept me going those fourteen years."

Jessie got up and sat next to her, putting her arm around her shoulders. "When did you learn Billy was alive?"

"The day after Flower's colic, Steven found Billy in Canada working on a road crew and he brought him back to confront me. I was in a bad way then."

"You were about to lose Two Ponies because of the past-due loan."

"The school was all I had left." Katherine closed her eyes and took a deep breath. "I nearly…" Her eyes teared up, recollecting the night she almost walked into Pine Island Lake herself.

Jessie gasped. "Oh Kat, I had no idea… I wouldn't have left you."

Katherine squeezed her friend's hand. "When Billy learned I was still single and about to lose Two Ponies, he agreed to return that night. Steven brought Billy back for me."

"Wow, I think I'm falling in love with your husband."

Katherine managed a smile. "Oh Jess." She propped herself against the headboard. "Then there was the fire—those damn Werdens again. If it wasn't for Lisa and Betsy, I would have lost all the horses. And, if Steven hadn't shown up, Betsy and Stormy would have died in the fire."

"Steven was your knight in shining armor."

"Yes."

"He never stopped loving you."

"No, even after what I did. But Billy claimed to still love me, too. He told me he had done it for me, left me standing on the dock believing he had drowned so I would move on to a better life without him… with Steven. He said I deserved better than a life on the run with a half-breed and he didn't want to take me away from Two Ponies and Betsy. I don't think he ever felt he was good enough for me."

Jessie shook her head in disbelief. "But he risked getting caught coming back across the border to see you."

"He said he regretted leaving me that night and if I could only forgive him, we could start a new life together in Alberta."

She could see Jessie's eyes glistening. "Wow, how did you choose?"

"I wanted Billy back badly for so many years, but when he appeared like a ghost from the past, the choke hold he had on my heart let go. My despair turned to anger. How could he have left me? All those years I beat myself up over his presumed death." Katherine got to her feet.

Jessie stood up and met her eye to eye. "You choose Steven."

Breaking eye contact, she wiped her face. "It was the right choice. Let's get ready for dinner."

"Wait a minute!"

"What?"

"You know Billy still loves you, right?"

Katherine turned sharply. "No. He just still cares about me, that's all."

"No, he still loves you. And I think you might still love him."

"Jessie! Don't say such a thing. I love Steven!"

"I didn't say you don't." Jessie followed her to her suitcase. "You can douse a fire, but it doesn't take much to stir the ashes to bring back a flame. Now I know why Steven has been acting so weird. He's worried you and Billy are getting back together."

"He was just jealous of the time I was spending with Major."

"With Billy. He's not blind and neither am I. I saw the way

you two looked at each other… and when you hugged and rested your head on his shoulder… something was going on."

"There you go again, being all dramatic. I love only Steven."

"You trying to convince me or yourself? You loved them both then, why couldn't you now?"

"That's silly."

"Sure." Jessie cocked her head and smirked.

Katherine shook her head and walked into the bathroom. "I'll be just a few minutes, then it's all yours."

Katherine studied herself in the mirror as she dried her hair. What did Jessie see? Sure, she still felt a little something around Billy. It was only natural after what they had shared. That was normal… right? As she applied a little mascara, her hand began to shake. Could Jessie and Steven be right? Could they see something she refused to see? Was she falling under the spell of Billy Black again?!"

10 – The Letter

Saturday

Following dinner laden with stares from Jessie, Katherine drove the three of them to the showgrounds to care for Major. This time Katherine suggested Jessie hand-graze Major while she prepared his feed and stall for the night. Billy stayed close by, scrutinizing every person who walked through the barn. Katherine was glad he came, but since her talk with Jessie, she became very conscious of his behavior toward her, and hers toward him. At that moment, he seemed consumed by his duty as bodyguard.

As she picked the stall, Katherine's mind wandered, thinking back to the day she asked Billy to assist her with training Major. She had exited the post office after receiving her first USEA Omnibus containing a calendar of events, having decided to move forward with Major's training. She ran into Billy in the parking lot. When she told him the news, she had asked for his help.

They hugged, first joyfully, then it turned into something else when Billy surprised her with a tender kiss her on the top of her head. Beyond reason or shame she pressed into him, only for a moment, but long enough to get Billy's attention. It turned into an awkward moment, but they both laughed it off moving on to discussing building jumps and conditioning Major.

After that there had been the occasional hug in celebration of an achievement by Major, a new height or obstacle conquered or an improved dressage movement. She knew at the time their contact wasn't necessary, or particularly appropriate, but she had encouraged it anyway.

Being close to Billy made her feel like a young woman again. Was she going through some midlife crisis? She gasped to herself–had she been leading him on? She looked up from cleaning Major's stall and locked eyes with Billy. He gave her a reassuring nod, assuring her he was still on guard duty. Quickly, she looked away, resuming her picking. Damn, there were those feelings again! Why… how could he still have such an effect on her after all these years?

She shook off such thoughts. She needed to get her feelings under control, reminding herself she was in her fifties and married for nearly twenty years to a wonderful man with whom she shared a lovely family and home. And for Billy, he was just being Billy–the habitual flirt, always giving her looks and complimenting her, all innocent enough. That's all it's been. Move on.

"Would you mind breaking open a bag of shavings in his stall and pull that hose down the aisle to fill his bucket?" she asked. "It's a ton. I need to run a few things to the trailer?"

Billy flexed his right arm and smiled. "Sure, no problem."

Katherine smirked and shook her head. *See, there he goes again!*

She grabbed the dirty wraps and left for the trailer to swap them out for a clean set. As she unlocked the trailer, she had the strange sensation someone was watching her. She turned and looked in all directions, then gasped. Her truck, parked about thirty yards away, sat with the driver's door wide open.

Immediately, she turned to locate Jessie and Major. They were a good distance down the barn row grazing on a hillside. She reached into her pocket. Empty! Apparently, she hadn't thought to take the pen-knife with her or to lock her truck. With Billy there, she had become lax… or was it distracted?

Either way, it wasn't good.

She locked up the trailer and slowly walked toward her vehicle, her heart pounding, searching the barn area. A few girls hosed each other off in a wash rack beside barn B, but besides that it was quiet. Most of the horses had been fed and their caretakers gone for the night.

When she reached the truck, she peered inside. Her purse remained on the floor of the passenger side of the truck, right where she had left it. She slid in the truck and reached under the driver's seat. The gun was still there, too. Then she noticed it. An envelope had been slipped into a side compartment of her purse, barely protruding. Katherine quickly looked about again, searching the row of cypress running parallel to the parking lot for any movement. She must have just missed whoever left it, rushing to hide behind the trees when she exited the barn, leaving the truck door open in their wake.

Katherine sat in her truck, closed and locked the door, and opened the sealed envelope. There were two pieces of paper. The first was a short, handwritten note; the other, a map with directions. Immediately she looked to the bottom of the letter for a signature. All it said was, "Guess who?" Ricky! Lips moving, but without making a sound, she read the letter.

Hello there, Red Locks,

Follow my directions and no one will get hurt or disappear. Only share this with your Injun. I want you to make out with that half-breed piece of shit someplace public and make sure someone you know sees you. Better make it convincing. Then disappear before anyone can confront you about it. Leave a note to your husband that you two took off together. Tell him you'll be in touch in a few weeks. Then follow the map to the X on horseback and wait there by the river until we contact you. No cops or else!

Guess who?

Katherine stared at the piece of paper shaking in her hand. She jumped when startled by something moving in her side-view mirror. It was Billy striding up to her vehicle. She opened the door, still holding the letter. "Get in!"

Billy eyes grew narrow and his jaw locked, his face hardening. He must have recognized the fear in her eyes. Katherine glanced down the row of barns–Jessie and Major were out of sight. Billy jogged around the front of the truck and slid in next to her.

"Close the door," she said. Without another word, she passed the letter to him. As he read, she glanced at the map but couldn't make any sense of it.

"Here we go," he said, looking up from the letter with an intense gaze.

Katherine searched his dark brown eyes. "What are we going to do, Billy? Should we go to the police?"

"No. We're going to follow his instructions." Billy handed the letter back to her.

Katherine hung her head and took a deep breath. "When will this end?"

She felt Billy's hand gently clasp hers. "I'll end it, like I said I would earlier. You just need to help me get in position to do so. Can you do that?"

Katherine turned to Billy. "I don't know, Billy." She glanced back at the note, her eyes resting on the words *get hurt or disappear*. "Yes. If they followed us here, they're not going to stop. No one is safe."

"Where's the map?"

She handed it to him. "Are you familiar with this area?"

Billy nodded. "Yes. I know this country along the river well."

"Hurry, before Jessie returns. How are we going to get

caught fooling around?" This all seemed a bit ironic considering she was just thinking she needed to never allow any contact with Billy again.

"Do something to raise Jessie's suspicion before we head up to our rooms. Considering the looks she gave us at dinner, it shouldn't be too difficult. Pretend you're trying not to wake her, but make sure you do then slip out of the room to meet me in the parking lot."

"Yes, that will work. I'll park the truck under the light out front within view of our hotel window."

"Atta girl. Now you're catching on. After our little show, which is going to have to be a good one, go back to bed until you're sure she's asleep."

Katherine nodded, suddenly full of self-doubt. Already laden with guilt about what she had allowed to happen with Billy, could she do this? Should she do this? Her face felt hot just thinking about making out with Billy. No. Yes, she must! Billy's voice brought her back from her discussion with her conscience.

"Have the note ready for Steven. Then grab your bag and meet me in the parking lot. I'll be waiting. We'll take my truck and Jessie can haul Major home.

Without hesitation, before Billy could continue, Katherine said. "I'm taking Major."

"What? Are you crazy? You're going to take a Thoroughbred into the mountains?"

"He's fit, Billy; you know that better than anyone."

"Sure he is. Just hope he doesn't dump your ass when the first deer darts out of the woods."

"I can handle him." Katherine felt her eyes well up. "I'm not leaving him. This might be my last ride… I'm riding out on Major!"

"Good grief, Kat. You can't think like that. You'll be fine.

I promise. We're smarter than they are. I'll start planning tonight. Let me take the map."

"Okay, so we'll load Major and take my truck and trailer–then what? Where can we find you a horse?"

"Well, I'm not leaving my new pickup behind. What the hell! I'll drive back, too. We'll stop, drop off my truck and pick up Red. I'll leave a note, too. Sarah and TJ are staying with Sarah's family. By the time they find it, we'll be well on our way. Besides, that will play into our story perfectly."

"Running away together on horseback like we planned so many years ago."

Billy just grinned and nodded.

Katherine shook her head. "Hope it plays out better this time."

As Jessie hand-grazed Major, what Katherine had shared with her earlier rattled around in her brain like a pinball, setting off all kinds of bells and whistles following what she had witnessed between her and Billy earlier. She liked Steven a lot. They had formed a close bond, having worked so many years together and on so many difficult emergencies during that time, overcoming the odds in many cases with horses that seemed doomed. Steven never gave up on them, like he never gave up on Katherine. He was a true gem of a guy. How could Katherine have treated him so poorly years ago? Is she again?

Jessie never let on that she had a crush on Steven for years when she was younger. Perhaps that was why she stayed single for as long as she did and insisted on calling him Mr. Walker, trying to keep him at a distance emotionally. She had felt guilty about her feelings and fantasies. All the boys–and later, men–she dated paled in comparison to Steven, until she met Dane. His compassion for his dogs and his devotion to her captured her heart. She couldn't imagine doing anything that would hurt him.

She had grown up idolizing Katherine and, more than that, they had become best friends. She agonized over the fact her respect for her mentor may have been shaken. If something did happen between Katherine and Billy during this trip, she would be stuck in the middle having to choose between her loyalty to Katherine and her respect for Steven. What would she do?

Suddenly, she realized she had been gone longer than she meant to be. Katherine would surely have the stall done by now. Jessie directed the reluctant gelding away from the grass and along the row of stables to Barn B. As she had guessed, they were waiting to rewrap Major's legs. Immediately, she sensed something had changed. They were both acting strange–nervous, guilty, something. What had she missed?

"Sorry, I kept you waiting. Major was really enjoying the grass."

"No problem. Hold him right there and we'll get him wrapped for the night," said Katherine. It took longer than usual with the gelding impatiently moving about, more than ready for his late dinner. An uncomfortable silence fell among them as Katherine worked. When she was finished, Katherine threw a light sheet on the Thoroughbred and put him in his stall.

"Okay, he's good for the night. Let's get some sleep," said Katherine. "We've got another early start tomorrow."

Jessie just nodded and followed the couple to the parking lot in the twilight. They had driven over in Kat's vehicle, so Jessie climbed into the back seat of the crew-cab again while Katherine drove. Billy slid into the passenger seat. The air in the cab quickly became stifling as intense stares darted between Katherine and Billy like lasers. Just as Jessie turned to pop open the rear escape window for fresh air, she saw it out of the corner of her eye... Billy reaching toward Katherine slowly as if reassuring her about something, then slowly retracting his hand. The seat obstructed her view of where his hand rested, but the gaze between them confirmed it was intimate. Jessie squirmed in her seat. What the heck!

By the time they stopped to get gas and pulled into the hotel parking lot, it was dark. "I'll be right up, Jess. I want to go over tomorrow's schedule with Billy," said Katherine when they parked.

Jessie eagerly exited the truck and headed for their room on the second floor. Why hadn't she done that earlier when they were waiting for her in the barn? As soon as she got to their room, she rushed to the window. Carefully she pulled the curtain open just a sliver. They were both outside the truck conversing, then Katherine glanced toward the window. Jessie froze. Then she watched in disbelief as they held hands for a moment before parting for their respective rooms.

Quickly she undressed and slid into bed, forgoing brushing her teeth, and closed her eyes. Katherine entered the dark room and quietly went into the bathroom with her purse for what seemed like an hour. What could she be doing in there? When she finally exited, Jessie could see she was still dressed as she laid down on top of her bed. Jessie didn't dare move; she could feel Katherine looking in her direction. This went on for nearly an hour. Jessie fought off sleep; she needed to know what was going on.

Guessing Katherine felt confident she had fallen asleep, she slowly sat up, checked one more time in her direction, then quietly stood up and padded her way to the door. The dead bolt clacked as she released it. Katherine froze in the doorway watching to see if she moved. Jessie held her breath. Carefully, Katherine closed the door behind her.

Jessie waited a few minutes, then darted to the window.

Through a crack in the drapes she peered down to the parking lot below. The flood light encompassed Katherine's truck and as soon as Katherine entered its radius, Billy emerged from the shadows. She leaned against the truck as Billy stood within inches of her. Jessie gasped as Billy pressed Katherine against the side of her truck with his lower torso and kissed her passionately.

Katherine must have said something, because suddenly they froze and looked up toward the window. Billy stepped a short distance away. Through Katherine's hand gestures and body language, it appeared they were disagreeing about something. Then Katherine became still as Billy approached her again, cradling her face in his hands as he kissed her affectionately. Katherine reached for a squeeze of his hand as they parted and disappeared back into the darkness.

Jessie's heart raced, rushing to climb back into bed and resume the same sleeping position. She listened as Katherine quietly entered, undressed and slid into bed.

Ricky wiped the sleep from his eyes and yawned, wincing at the smell of his own breath. He sat up on the couch where he had fallen asleep waiting for Jake's call. He could hear the TV on in Andy's bedroom and checked his watch. It was nine o'clock. Why hadn't they called?

Jake and Kyle had arrived in California two days ago, but had no luck finding the O'Reilly woman at the Stockton show the first day, but located her in Santa Rosa yesterday and were waiting for the right opportunity to deliver the letter. That was nearly twenty-four hours ago.

Suddenly the phone rang, startling him. "Hello," he answered tentatively. "Yeah, it's me. Give me some good news, bro."

"Done," said Jake. "We're almost to the border of Idaho

already."

"Shit! Why didn't you call me sooner? I've been sitting here waiting to hear from you. We still have to go for the money and guns."

"You said come straight back. I couldn't find a working pay phone at our first gas stop."

Ricky shook his head. "Okay, okay, how did it go down?"

"Dumb bitch left her truck door open. I put the letter right in her purse and watched her open it. The Injun was there too."

"Perfect! When will you get here?"

"Early morning. We should be at least twelve hours ahead of them."

Andy entered the living room and stood over him listening intently. Ricky knew what was on his mind. "We'll get the money and guns tonight," he told Jake.

Andy smiled, nodded and walked into the kitchen.

"I'll call Bobby with the trailer and let him know we want to leave first thing tomorrow morning. Come straight here. Andy and I will have everything ready to go."

When Ricky got off the phone, he found Andy leaning into the refrigerator. He pulled out a beer, opened it and took a swig.

"See Andy, everything's back on schedule and according to plan."

Andy smirked. "When do we leave? It'll be about a three-hour drive."

"Let's take off around ten-thirty."

"I'm ready!"

11 – The Raid

Saturday – Sunday

Kimi sat out on the screened-in back porch, sipping a cup of tea with Nuna as long shadows of the Continental Divide inched across Pine Island Lake. The last of the Canadian geese announced their departure south with a medley of honks overhead.

Nuna clasped her mug with both hands as a cold breeze blew off the water. "Wonder if the men will see snow in the high country?"

"I hope so… easier to track," said Kimi.

Elk bow season opened the next day and their husbands had left that morning to set up camp with the horses. Their plan was to bag an elk first thing in the morning and return to the shop before customers started arriving with their kills to be processed.

"Wouldn't it be nice if they both got one this year?" said Nuna.

"Sure would be."

"And, two more during rifle season, then we could fill both freezers and have meat left over to trade."

"So long as there aren't any fires again this year, they should be able to bag at least two," said Kimi. "But it sure has been a dry summer."

Nuna got up from her seat. "I'm cold; I'm going in."

"It's beautiful out."

"Oh Kimi, you never get cold."

Kimi laughed. "Yeah, I do have an extra layer, don't I? I'm going to stay and finish my tea. I'll be in shortly."

"Well, good night then," said Nuna, holding the door open for the dogs. "We should head to the shop early, just in case some lucky hunters show up."

"Yep, good idea. See you in the morning."

Kimi stared out over the dark water. She felt too unsettled with everything going on with Ricky Werden getting out of prison and wanting to harm Katherine. Their families, the Walkers and White Clouds, had become close over the years, sharing Two Ponies and every triumph and sorrow that had come along.

She pulled a chair around and rested her tired feet upon it. Silently, as dusk turned to darkness, she mulled over every detail Betsy had shared with her about the two men's visit. This whole thing seemed like something out of a mystery novel. She sat pondering what might happen next, praying there would be a happy ending.

Ricky checked his watch again. Finally, the hands read ten-thirty. "Let's head over."

Andy turned off the TV. "Great, the Jeep is full and I'm ready to go."

The men drove from Helena to the old Werden estate, void of much conversation besides the occasional "turn right or turn left up there" instructions by Ricky.

"Slow down," said Ricky as they approached the driveway. "Here we are. Go real slow so we don't miss the old two-track. We don't go too far before it splits off to the right."

Andy leaned forward over the steering wheel, studying the woods for the opening.

"Wait!" yelled Ricky. "I think we just passed it."

"I didn't see anything," said Andy as he braked and put the

Jeep in reverse.

"There," Ricky said, pointing to a path. "Doesn't look like they've used it in a while."

"It's pretty grown over, but I think we can get through." Andy turned onto the bumpy road, branches slapping the Jeep's canvas top and scraping its sides like nails on a chalkboard. "Damn it, Ricky! My Jeep is getting the shit scratched out of it!"

Suddenly, Andy braked. A section of the two-track appeared washed out.

"Can we make it?" asked Ricky.

"I think so," said Andy. "Good thing we have a four-wheel drive."

The Jeep pitched to-and-throw, groaning like an old man and spinning gravel, as they navigated the deep ruts cutting across the drive, but they made it through without bottoming out. As they climbed upward again, cresting a hill, Andy once again slammed on the brakes. "Shit! Guess this is the end of the road," he said, staring at the large fallen tree crossing their path.

"We'll have to hike in from here," said Ricky. "It's not much further."

The men grabbed the pillowcases and duffle bags from the backseat, climbed over the tree, and started their trek down the drive toward the lake. Ten minutes later they emerged from the woods with the barn in clear view ahead of them, the lake down the hill below and the house about fifty yards uphill. At least sixty feet of open yard lay between them and their bounty. They studied the homestead.

"House looks dark," whispered Andy.

Ricky continued to study his old home, looking for any movement, particularly for any dogs. It was a clear night, but only a sliver of a moon dimly lit the yard. The house sat in the open except for one cottonwood, which shadowed the back of the house.

"Okay, let's get in and out as quick as possible. I see only one vehicle; they might not even be home."

Andy traced Ricky's every step toward the old pole barn. Ricky felt relieved once they made it behind the structure, but they would need to enter from the front, facing the house. Again, Ricky led the way, both men slipping quietly into the barn undetected. But, much to their surprise, a few disturbed chickens began clucking above them in the hay loft.

"We're done for," said Andy.

"Shhhh, hurry—over here," said Ricky, pointing to the floor of the feed room. He pulled the flashlight and hammer from one of the bags, handed the light to Andy and began prying the old boards loose with the hammer claw as quickly as possible. Ricky cringed when a squeal from a rusty nail sliced the still night air. More chickens became restless. "Check the house."

Andy cracked open the barn door. "All is quiet."

"Shine that light down here," said Ricky as he slid down into the hidden cellar. "Hand me the pillowcases."

Even in the shadows, Ricky could make out a broad grin stretching across his accomplice's face, squatting beside the opening, as he shined the light into the metal box full of cash.

"That sure is a purdy sight!" said Andy.

"Shut up, will ya?" Ricky filled the pillowcases with one-hundred-dollar bills and handed them up to Andy. Next, he found two large ammunition boxes full of firearms. He handed up two rifles, a shotgun, and several handguns.

"Any ammo?" whispered Andy.

"Yeah, we'll take as much as we can carry." Ricky began stuffing his hunting jacket pockets with boxes of shells and bullets. "Here," he said, setting a box on the floor above him.

"Load that .38 just in case."

Kimi woke up on the porch where she had fallen asleep. She got up and let both dogs back onto the porch. She always put them out to do their business before locking up for the night. Immediately, Sky and Moose stood at attention, looking in the direction of the barn. Kimi squinted to see through the shadows as she strained to hear the muffled sound of distressed chickens.

"Something must be after the hens again," she said to the huskies. "We might have us a fox or coyote, boys." Every year before winter hit, carnivorous critters became a little bolder, desperate to build a good lair of fat beneath their coats before the snow flew.

Kimi picked up the flashlight they kept at the back door for such occasions and let herself, Sky, and Moose out the back door. The dogs ran toward the barn, tails wagging as they frantically picked up some sort of scent leading to the door of the stable.

Just as she gripped the barn door handle, Sky startled her with a sudden outburst of howling. When Moose raised his hackles and began growling, Kimi froze in place. That was no fox or coyote scent they had picked up! Could it be a bear?

As she leaned an ear against the door to take a listen, the door flew open hitting her in the head. Everything went black.

Ricky held tightly to the "Oh Shit" handle above his door as Andy stepped on the gas when they hit the pavement, the Jeep's tires screeching. Ricky studied Andy's bare leg covered in blood with the flashlight. The bottom half of the right leg of his jeans had been ripped off in the attack. He could identify at least three deep bite wounds.

"Looks like they've stopped bleeding. Sure you don't want

me to drive?"

"Hurts like hell, but I can still use my leg," said Andy. "How bad is it? Do you think I need stitches?"

"Can't go to an ER. They'll be looking for dog-bite victims at all the hospitals and clinics as soon as they find the dog and the bloody leg of your jeans. Damn if I couldn't find it in the dark."

"What are we going to do?"

"As soon as we get home, I'll clean it up and then we'll decide."

"Shit!" Andy pointed down the road ahead of them. "Now, we're really done for!" Flashing lights could be seen in the distance heading their way.

"Pull down that drive, now!" shouted Ricky, motioning to the right.

Tires squealing, Andy turned off the paved road onto a dirt road. Gravel flying, they came to an abrupt halt about fifty yards down a dark tunnel of trees and turned off the Jeep lights. They turned and watched three police cars fly by.

Andy faced Ricky. "That was close. I thought you said they wouldn't be coming from this direction?"

"I thought they'd take the highway."

"Well, you were wrong. What else you gonna be wrong about?"

"What are you saying?"

"The 'plan.' What else isn't going to go according to plan? Piece of cake, you said."

"We got the guns and money, didn't we? It was a success as far as I'm concerned."

Andy pulled back out onto the main road. "You calling my leg a success?!"

"You know what I mean."

Andy gave him a nasty stare. "You don't give a rat's ass

about anything but getting even with that bitch and that Injun of hers."

"Like you give a shit about anything besides the money!" Ricky snapped back. "You knew all this going in. We talked about the risk. So, stop your bitching. We'll take care of your damn leg, okay?"

"Okay. I just don't want any more surprises. I just want my money and the fresh start you promised."

Ricky reached down and patted the full pillowcases at his feet. "Don't you worry. This time next week we'll all be riding off into the sunset."

Kimi woke up to Nuna's frantic screams, her head pounding.

"Kimi, where are you?"

Kimi tried to identify where she was. It was black as tar, cold and damp. The last thing she remembered was standing at the barn door. "I'm here!" she screamed. As far as she could tell she was in a hole in the ground. When she tried to stand up, she hit her head on a board ceiling. She began clawing at the wood above as she yelled to Nuna. Kimi heard footsteps above her. "I'm down here!"

"Are you okay?"

"Yes, where am I?"

"You're under the feed room floor."

Kimi could see light from a flashlight through the floor boards above her. "Get me out of here!"

She heard Nuna grunt and grown as she labored to pry the floor boards up. Kimi pushed on the planks from below and soon there was an opening, but she couldn't pull herself out of the shoulder high hole. Nuna disappeared and reappeared with a five-gallon bucket and handed it to her. Carefully, she balanced on the bottom of the pail and managed to pull herself onto her tummy, then with Nuna's help, up and out of the cellar.

As soon as she was on her feet, Nuna wrapped her arms around her. "Thank goodness you're all right," she said flashing the light at her face. "Oh no, your head! You have a big bump on your forehead. What happened?"

Kimi reached up and felt the bump that was throbbing. "I came out to check on the chickens, they were fussing. The dogs started barking and growling when we reached the barn. I was standing in front of the door… that's the last thing I remember."

"I heard gunshots, grabbed the shotgun and came running! But hurry, it's Moose. I think he's been shot!"

Nuna led her outside where Moose lay just outside the door. He raised his head but couldn't get up.

"Where's Sky?!" asked Kimi.

"I don't know," cried Nuna. "I've been calling for him."

"Run to the house, call the police, and call Steven," ordered Kimi.

Nuna nodded and rushed off to the house. Kimi cupped her hands around her mouth and called for Sky repeatedly, scanning the surrounding woods. She squatted down beside Moose, stroking the top of his head. In the dark, even with the flashlight, she couldn't make out how badly he got hit and was afraid to move him. She took off her jacket and covered his trembling frame. "You'll be okay, boy. Steven's on his way and he'll fix you right up." Kimi pushed back her own tears; someone had to remain calm and in control.

Questions raced through Kimi's mind as she waited and comforted Moose. Where was Sky? Who did this? Was it that Werden man? Would he come back? What was he after? Could this somehow be related to Katherine?

Soon, Nuna rejoined her and she began calling for Sky again. Kimi feared the worst knowing Sky would have come when called if he could.

"Should one of us go looking for Sky?" asked Nuna.

"No. Whoever did this is might still be out there. Better we wait here for the police. They'll bring their hounds."

It didn't take long before Steven drove up in his truck aiming his headlights toward them. He lurched from the vehicle with a flashlight.

"I came as quick as I could. How's he doing?"

Kimi stepped aside. "He can't get up."

Luna began crying again. "Oh, poor Moose."

After a quick examination, Steven ran to his truck and opened the passenger door. Then he took off his coat and laid it down beside the injured dog and carefully slid him onto it.

"I think he was hit in the shoulder and hip. I don't think any vital organs were hit, but I can't say for sure until I get him to the hospital, clean his wounds and take X-rays." As Steven carried the dog to the truck, Kimi and Luna followed in his shadow. "Any sign of Sky?" he asked.

"No," said Kimi. "We've been calling for him."

Steven gently set Moose down on the floor of the cab. "He might have chased whoever it was. I need to get Moose to the clinic fast. He's lost a lot of blood. Go in the house and lock up. Arm yourselves. The police will be here soon. I'll call you as soon as I have some news."

"Thank you, Steven, we'll do the same." Kimi stroked Moose on the head, then grabbed the shotgun and Nuna by the arm and headed for the house as Steven sped off into the dark.

12 – The News

Sunday

The next thing Jessie knew it was daylight. She turned to find Katherine's bed empty and her friend's suitcase gone. She rushed to the window and ripped open the curtains. Her worst fears realized, both trucks were gone. On Katherine's bed lay a piece of paper and an envelope. The envelope was addressed to Steven, the note to her. She read the note out loud in disbelief:

Jess, I will miss you dear friend. You were right. Billy and I have fallen back in love. I believe we were always meant to be together. We have taken Major with us. On the bathroom counter, you'll find one of my credit cards. Get yourself a flight home. Please call Steven and tell him I'll be in touch with him soon and please deliver the envelope to him. I just can't face anyone right now. I fear I would weaken. Don't try to find us. Forgive me.
Love, Kat

Jessie tossed the note back on the bed and stared at it. This couldn't be happening. Steven, Jo, Major, her dream of qualifying for the Olympics? She'd gone insane! Her focus shifted to the envelope. At least Katherine saved her from having to choose between her loyalty to her and Steven. But how would she tell him? She picked up the hotel envelope… it wasn't sealed. She could only assume Katherine expected her to read it. Jessie sat on the bed and pulled the single sheet of hotel stationary from the envelope and read it to herself:

My dearest Steven,
It kills me to hurt you again, but it would hurt you more if I stayed and continued to pretend. We would only be putting off the inevitable. I tried, but I can no longer deny my feelings for Billy. You deserve more. I love you, I always have, and I always will. I don't expect you to ever forgive me this time. I don't deserve it. I will be in touch soon, but I just can't face anyone now, least of all you. Please tell Jo and Betsy I love them, and I'll be in contact with them soon, too. I'm so sorry. Please don't try to find us.
Love, Kat

Jessie sat on the bed holding the letter for the longest time. Her body had gone numb, unable to feel the sheet of paper in her hand. Would her legs support her? She tested them on a short walk back to the window, gazing at the empty parking spots. She slowly packed her things and walked down to the lobby to check out. As suspected, Katherine had taken care of the bill. Jessie stared at the pay phone. *Damn it, Kat!* She would have plenty to say to her the next time she saw her, or would she see her again? Jessie called Dane first. He would still be home.

"Hi honey," she said, sheepishly.

"What happened?"

"It's a long story, but I'm coming home."

"What? Is Kat okay?"

"Kat is fine, physically anyway, but I think she's lost her mind. She ran off with Billy and they took Major with them. She left me a note." Silence. "Dane, are you there?"

"I know you said the Walkers have been having some marital issues, but this doesn't make any sense. Why couldn't they have just waited until following the show circuit, if indeed they are running off together? Something's not adding up."

"Oh, honey, not everything is a case that needs to be solved. You didn't see them together. I did. I spied on them in the parking lot last night. You should have seen how they kissed."

"When did Billy arrive?"

"Yesterday."

"Had you seen anything… anyone that didn't belong. Did Kat mention anything?"

"No. There's no mystery to it, honey. They used to be lovers, you know, years ago. Kat told me all about it last night."

"How are you getting home?"

"Kat left me a credit card. I'll take a taxi to the airport and call you before I board my flight. But I have to call Steven first. Can you believe it? She left it up to me to call him. I thought I knew her better than this."

"You make your call and get on that plane. I'm going to go to the office to tell Dad. Something's not right. I'm going to find Ricky."

For the second time that week, Steven sat at his desk in a daze still holding the receiver in his hand. He had insisted Jessie read him the letter twice. His and Katherine's last evening and morning together played repeatedly in his mind as the words "continue to pretend" bore a hole through his heart.

She seemed so happy, they seemed so close. It was the best sex they'd had in a long time. Her last words to him, "I love you, too. No matter what happens, know that… okay?" suddenly took on new meaning. Had she planned this all along?

"What the hell!" Steven slammed the receiver down. Did Billy have that strong of an influence over her? He picked up a portrait of Katherine and the girls from the corner of the desk and studied it.

"No!" His Kat was no longer the young naïve twenty-one-year-old Billy could put under his spell. Nearly twenty years of marriage, the joys of raising Lisa and Josephine, and the sorrow of losing two babies had cemented their relationship, a bond that could not be broken, even by Billy.

He rose from the desk and began pacing the library. But then his doubts returned, recalling the way Katherine had been acting around Billy for months, and he couldn't forget the near-admission by Billy at the barn the other night, suspecting a confrontation. What happened? Was Ricky involved? Too many questions and not enough answers—hell, no answers! He called Chief.

"Hi Steve, expected I'd be hearing from you. Jessie called Dane; he just filled us in."

"It's all so insane!"

He could hear Chief take a deep breath. "Could it be true? Katherine and Billy again?"

"I don't know. She'd been acting strange for months, we hadn't been getting along. But, with the news about Ricky, we seemed to have put that all behind us before she left."

"Dane thinks it's linked to Ricky somehow. That he might have gotten to her, to both of them, threatened them with the safety of their families."

"That entered my mind, too. I just don't know what to think."

"I'm sorry, Steve. You both are in our prayers, I just don't know which scenario to pray for."

"I know, they're both bad." Steven took a deep breath and settled back into his chair. "She's either left me, or she's in danger. I don't know if I want to get my hands more on Ricky or Billy."

"If it's Ricky, I'm glad she's with Billy," said Chief.

"Yeah. I agree. What next?"

"Mike has assigned Dane to finding Ricky. We'll want to see the letters from Katherine. And, if you think of anything or hear from Katherine again, take good notes and share everything with Dane. She might try to relay something indirectly if she's being held captive."

"Sure, I can do that."

"You need to stay with Jo and Betz, then see Jo safely off to school. We'll keep you posted."

"Chief…" Steven began, then paused. "Things really were good before she left."

"I believe you."

"Has anyone spoken with Sarah?" asked Steven. "I wonder if Billy contacted her."

"I don't know. Dane may have."

"I'll call and go see her right away."

"Good," said Chief. "Let her know what we suspect. Tell her to do the same if she hears from Billy."

"Damn it, Chief, I thought this was all behind us years ago. When is it ever going to end?"

"We'll find her, Steve. I'll contact my buddy at the pen and see if he's heard anything more. He might be able to get one of the inmates to talk."

"That would be great. What about the Schmitts?"

"We're trying to locate them, too," said Chief. "They've disappeared."

"Well, that tells us something right there."

"I thought the same thing… too much of a coincidence."

"Thanks, Chief."

When Steven set the receiver down and glanced up, he found Betsy standing in the doorway leaning on her cane. The old Blackfeet woman appeared to have aged beyond her nearly eighty years in an instant, her dark mahogany eyes shrinking into her weathered face, the corners of her perpetual smile turned downward. He met her halfway with a hug. He could feel her trembling.

"I came to let you know I had breakfast ready," she said, her voice cracking. "I heard… I..."

"It'll be okay, Betz. We'll find them."

Betsy held him at arm's length. "She didn't run off with Billy. I feel it in my bones."

"The alternative isn't much better."

"Yes… it is. She'll be safe with Billy. He won't let anything happen to her."

"You're right. You're always right, Betz."

"What about Jo?" she asked.

"I'll talk to her. She needs to know the whole story and now she'll have to hear it from me."

Jessie sat gazing out the plane window on the tarmac on the opposite side of the same mountain range they viewed from their hotel room the day before. Overnight her world had exploded. Suddenly, her future became unclear. Would she ever see her best friend again? Could they remain friends? What would happen with the riding school? What would happen with Major? The only thing she guessed wouldn't change would be her employment at the clinic, which brought her thoughts back to Steven.

The call was short. After she read both letters to him, twice, he barely said a word. Her eyes began tearing up again just thinking about it. His voice, faltering and breaking like a schoolboy, sounded as if he had just been plowed into and survived a hideous crash… stunned and in shock. All he said was how they had made up before she left and how he thought things were great between them again.

As the plane approached the runway, Dane's words played

over in her head. What if they hadn't run off together? What if her lifelong friend was in danger? She gripped the armrests as she was thrust back in her seat, the jet soaring off the runway. As soon as they settled in at cruising altitude, Jessie pulled a notepad and pen from her purse and began to jaunt down everything Billy and Katherine said and did, to the best of her recollection. She knew she could count on Dane wanting to know every detail. She would be prepared.

Josephine was greeted by her father when she came downstairs for breakfast. She wasn't happy with him putting an end to her morning rides with TJ all because of this Ricky guy. Now he had that look which meant a lecture about something was imminent.

"Good morning, Jo."

Josephine gave him a fake smile and opened the refrigerator. "What's for breakfast… where's Betsy?"

"She's not feeling well and laid back down. We need to talk."

The teen grabbed the milk and cereal and poured herself a glass of orange juice and headed for the dining room. Her father followed and sat across from her.

"What did I do this time… leave a gate unlatched, not put something away?"

"It's nothing like that."

Her father was acting and sounding stranger than usual. About to pour her milk, she set the carton down and braced herself. "What is it, Dad?"

"We got a call from Jessie this morning."

"Is Mom okay? Did she take a fall?"

"She's okay… I think."

"You think?" Something bad happened, she knew it. "What is it, Dad? Just tell me."

"Your mother left during the night with Mr. Black Feather. She left a note."

Josephine's heart missed a few beats. "What did it say?"

"It said they were running off together. But I want you to know I'm not buying it. We may not have been getting along that well lately, but your mother loves us and would never leave us. We think Ricky Werden and his gang have something to do with it."

Josephine felt her face turn hot. She should have shared the photo she found with her dad. Maybe he hadn't known they were once in love. She sprang from her chair recalling she had forgotten to throw the photo in the trash. It must still be in her jean pocket in the laundry hamper.

"I'll be right back."

When she returned, he hadn't moved an inch. "What is it Jo? Are you okay?"

She sat next to him, still questioning if this was the right thing to do. "I have something. I don't think Mom is in danger; I think they really did run away together," she said in a breathless tumble. She set the photo on the table in front of her father, afraid of what his reaction might be.

He calmly took the photo and studied it a moment, then set it back down.

"Where did you find this?"

"In the cabin."

"This was a long time ago, sweetie."

"You knew?"

"Yes, I knew. Everyone knew."

"What about now? They've been spending an awful lot of time together. Is it possible they fell back in love?"

"Think about it, sweetie. All the work she put into Major. They could have waited until after show season. None of it makes any sense. That's why we think there might be something else going on. Of course, we don't know for sure."

Josephine didn't know how to react. She was relieved her parents might not be getting a divorce but frightened of the alternative.

Before she could respond, her father continued. "And, there are some things your mother was planning on telling you at some point that will shed some light on the situation, but now you're going to have to hear it from me. Josephine silently listened.

Steven had planned on telling her the whole story, but he ended up skirting the more sensitive parts, like finding her mother and Billy together the night of his first proposal. Nothing would be gained and possibly her respect for her mother tarnished. He told her Katherine had been dating them both and chose Billy the first time. Steven shared a few details about the night of Kurt Werden's death, Billy's presumed death and how he found Billy years later and when given the choice between them again, she chose him.

Steven was surprised by how few questions she asked and how well she took the news about the letter and what he shared about the past. She was no longer his little girl but Steven still felt the need to protect her by not telling her any more than necessary… only enough so she could get a grasp of what was happening and why.

When he explained more about the alternative reason she may have left, he told her as little as possible about what Ricky and his buddies might be capable of. For her benefit, and perhaps his own, he tried to remain optimistic regardless of which scenario might be playing out.

They agreed that if there were bad people after Mom, they were glad she was with Mr. Black Feather. Josephine had grown up knowing Billy like an uncle and trusted him.

"He won't let anything happen to Mom," she said. That seemed to be the consensus, he just prayed they were right.

"Does, Mrs. Black Feather know?"

"Yes, but I'm heading to see her now."

"I want to come with you. I want to see TJ."

"No, you need to stay here and keep an eye on Betsy for us."

"Okay, but you'll let me know what she says?"

"When I get back. Eat your breakfast and don't worry. The police will find these men and your Mom soon."

Josephine gave him a hug. "I hope so, Daddy."

At that moment, she still seemed like his little girl. He planted a delicate kiss on the top of her head. "I won't be gone long."

Steven's conversation earlier with Sarah over the phone had been brief. She had not heard from Billy, but Dane had called and given her the news. Still, he wanted to talk with her in person. He was anxious to hear what Sarah would have to say. Perhaps she might have more insight into what has been going on between his wife and her husband.

When he pulled up to her parents' home, Sarah was waiting on the porch. Her family still lived in the same house Sarah was born in, a small two-bedroom wood-slat house on the reservation.

"Hi Sarah, I came a soon as I could."

"Let's go for a walk," she said sharply, leading the way out to the street. He knew Sarah nearly as well as he knew Billy, and in thirty-four years he had never witnessed her this upset.

"I can't believe it. Here we are again!" she spat.

Her comment and attitude came as a shock. "Where are we again, Sarah? Is it Katherine and Billy again, or is it the Werdens again?"

"You really think they're in danger? Have you gone blind?"

"No, I haven't been blind to them flirting again. I started getting suspicious, too, but the more I thought about it, the more I'm convinced this is not what their disappearance is about. I sincerely don't believe they would leave us, not after everything we've all been through together, all our years of marriage, the kids, our friendship."

Sarah just gave him a "you've got to be kidding" look. That was not the reaction Steven was hoping for.

"Okay, like I said, I had my doubts, and my first reaction was anger, too, when Jessie called. But, what about all the work they put into Major? They could have waited until after show season. It just doesn't figure."

Sarah stopped walking and turned to him. "I want to believe you, but if you're right, why didn't they just go to the police?"

"Of all people, Sarah, you should know the answer to that question."

Katherine had shared with him years ago that back in 1956, before either of them knew Billy and Sarah, the Werden and Schmitt brothers had gang-raped Sarah when Billy was serving jail time for an altercation involving the brothers.

Sarah shook her head. "Times have changed."

"Have they? You really think Ricky has changed, locked up for nineteen years?"

Suddenly, Sarah's demeanor changed. "No, probably not," she said with tears in her voice, no longer on the defensive.

Steven pulled her into a consoling hug. "I know, part of me wanted to believe they ran off at first too, rather than the alternative. We love them so much we'd rather lose them again and be safe than consider the possibility they're in real danger."

"Oh, Steven. I don't know what to think. What's going to happen?"

Steven held her at arm's length. "I don't know, but I do know there's a lot of good folks working really hard to find Ricky. We have to do all we can to help them, because when we find him, we'll find Kat and Billy."

Sarah nodded, wiping her face with her sleeve. "Okay, but what can we do?"

"Have you heard from Billy yet?"

"No, not a word."

"If you do, and it's a letter, get it to the police. If he calls, take notes. It could be important."

"What do I tell TJ? He's been asking questions all day. He knows something's happened."

"I just talked with Jo. They need to know the truth… well, most of it anyway. I spared Josephine some of the more sensitive details."

"You're right. I'll talk with him now."

Reaching their house, Sarah casually asked, "Do you ever think about what might have happened if we'd had that dinner together years ago as planned, before you found Billy?"

Steven couldn't help but grin. "We would have had a lovely meal recalling old times together," he said. He knew Sarah was hinting at the possibility they might have sought comfort together that night, considering Billy was presumed dead and Katherine had rejected him yet again the night of Flower's colic. And, he admitted the question had crossed his mind a time or two over the years.

"You're probably right," she said, giving him a hug.

They wished each other good night and Steven left the reservation with more questions and fewer answers then when he arrived.

Courage is not the absence of fear
but rather the judgment that something else
is more important than fear...

~ Ambrose Redmoon

PART TWO

THE RIDE

13 – Prelude

Sunday – Monday

From a crack in the living room drapes, a laser of early morning sunlight abruptly split the room in two as the sun broke over the horizon. Stretched out on the couch, Andy locked his jaw and gripped a cushion as Ricky cleaned his wounds. The pain pills he had taken, leftover from an injury to his hand earlier that summer, had helped him rest comfortably the past few hours, but any contact was excruciating. He glanced over to his coat hanging on a chair at the dining room table, the right sleeve torn in a few places. If he hadn't been wearing it, his arm might have been in worse shape than his leg.

"I think I'm going to need a new coat," said Andy, wincing.

"Hell, that's nothing some duct tape can't fix," said Ricky.

Andy scowled. "Duct tape!" Expecting Jake and Kyle any minute and Bobby with the trailer within the hour, he knew there wasn't time to shop for a new coat, but he felt like complaining about it anyway. He loved that fleece-lined jean jacket. "When this is over, you owe me a new one."

"Sure, just hold still."

" Shit, that hurts!"

"I'm almost done."

He watched as Ricky applied an ample amount of first-aid cream over his wounds. Only one worried him. It looked rather deep. He still thought it needed stitches, but Ricky insisted it would heal fine without them. They both knew the police would still be looking into any dog bites or leg injuries at every hospital or Doc-in-a-Box within a two-hundred-mile radius.

Ricky placed a gauze pad over the wound. "Hold this while I wrap it."

Andy grimaced as Ricky wrapped his leg with vet wrap from the barn. He wouldn't admit it, but Ricky was doing a good job cleaning and patching him up. When he was done, it was a tight fit into a clean pair of jeans, but he managed to slip them on over the bandage.

While Ricky impatiently waited for Jake and Kyle at the window, Andy gimped to his bedroom to finish packing. As he tossed some clothes into a duffle bag, he felt grateful the bites were on the outside of his leg and that they were riding back to the cabin from the trailhead instead of hiking in, as he normally did. No way would he have been able to walk that distance with a bum leg but riding in would be no picnic either. He emptied the medicine cabinet of every pain pill regardless of their expiration date and stashed them in his ditty bag.

Andy felt proud of how well he had prepared for their stay, stocking the cabin with canned goods, beer, a few bales of hay and a couple decks of cards during his visits over the summer. Borrowing a four-wheeler from a friend at the tire store where he worked made is easy. Also, during his last stay, he cut down a few small dead trees and chopped them up for the potbelly stove and constructed a small corral from samplings in an aspen grove out back of the cabin.

Ricky had come through with the cash as promised to reimburse him for all the supplies and horses. And when this was over, they would be splitting the remaining booty four ways. He was shocked to learn there was over two-hundred grand stashed away in that barn. He would start a new life in Canada, buy a little place, and settle down. Approximately fifty-grand would last him a while. He never thought he would see that much money in his lifetime, but a bigger cut sure would be nice, or all of it when the time was right. But for now, he was ready to do whatever it took for crazy Ricky to get his revenge!

Jake pulled the overhead metal door of the storage unit shut with a loud bang and slid into the torn driver's seat of their rusty 1979 Dodge Ram pickup. It would be no great loss leaving it behind. "Got everything? Ricky is waiting."

His brother just glanced at him and nodded. Everything they chose to keep fit into four bags thrown in the bed of the truck. Ricky had asked them to pack light.

Kyle remained silent on the drive from the storage unit to Andy's. Jake knew Kyle wasn't one-hundred percent onboard with Ricky's plan. He didn't want any harm coming to the redhead. He guessed Kyle had a soft spot for her as a horsewoman. Jake didn't care one way or the other about her or where they ended up afterward, only that they would be finally getting even with the prick who took the life of his best friend. The woman would be just a little frosting on the cake.

Moving to a new country with a new identity excited him as well. With some cash in hand, he would surely attract some good-looking chick to cook, clean, and lay whenever he wanted. And, he and Ricky discussed starting a new gang to pull off some small jobs occasionally for fun and to keep a little cash flowing.

Jake wondered if Ricky would invite Andy along. He wasn't too crazy about this newcomer but realized they needed him to make Ricky's plan work. Jake scratched his chin. Maybe afterward, Andy would need to have a little accident.

Eventually, Ricky took a seat on the couch as he waited for Jake and Kyle to arrive. Through the dirty back window, he watched Andy filling hay bags beside the shed while the horses stood at the fence pawing, ready for their breakfast. It occurred to him he hadn't ridden a horse in years, and he could count on getting sore following their jaunt to the cabin. He walked to the kitchen counter and added Advil to his shopping list just below rope.

Ricky smiled. Soon he would have his revenge. He imagined them both tied up and at his mercy… but there would be none. After they had their way with her in front of him, they would strangle them both and dump their bodies on one of the cabin beds with a lit cigarette. It would appear to be an accidental fire, no questions asked.

His plan was going well so far, but they needed to stay on schedule. He glanced at the stove clock. Damn it! Bobby would be pulling in soon with the trailer and Jake and Kyle hadn't arrived yet. They needed an early start to stay ahead of their guests. With a four-hour drive and the ride in ahead of them, he wanted to get to the cabin with enough daylight to get settled in and scout the rendezvous location. There, Jake and Kyle would wait to take the couple hostage then escort them to the cabin.

No sooner than Jake and Kyle arrived, Bobby pulled in with his truck and stock trailer. Following a chaotic thirty minutes of loading horses, feed, and supplies, the two-vehicle and trailer caravan left for the cabin. Anything that didn't fit was left behind. Ricky instructed Jake to park his truck behind the barn, out of sight. Andy would disappear just as Jake and Kyle had, without a trace.

Ricky and Andy led the way in the Jeep packed so full Andy had a hard time seeing out the rearview window, followed by Jake and Kyle riding with Bobby in his rig. Their only stop: a roadside convenience store and gas station on the way.

After only a few hours of sleep, Steven drove to the clinic to check on Moose before his meeting with Chief, Mike, and Dane at the station. The Husky was resting quietly and seemed to be out of danger. Sadly, he learned from Dane that Sky had not been as fortunate, found by the police dogs on the old lumber road shot dead, but not before taking a good piece out of someone.

The moment Steven stepped from his truck in front of the Elkhead Police Station, Dane pulled up alongside in his canine unit truck. "Hi Steve," he said, leading a Shepherd and hound out of the back. "We found plenty this morning. We'll get these guys."

"Guys?" questioned Steven, following Dane and the dogs in the front door.

"Yep, found two sets of men's boot prints."

Chief was already seated in Mike's office. Steven slid a chair from the corner to join him. "Where's Mike?"

"Getting us some coffee and donuts, of course," said Chief with a chuckle.

Mike walked into the room with a bakery box and a drink holder carrying four steaming cups of black coffee balanced on top. "Here you go, fellas." Each of them quickly grabbed a cup before he dumped everything.

Dane joined them, having dispensed of the dogs in the kennel out back. "Just what I need," he said, swinging another chair around with one hand while scarfing down a glazed donut with the other. "We were up all night at the crime scene."

Mike sat at his desk blowing on his java. "Okay, here's what we have so far. Correct me, Dane, if I miss anything."

Dane nodded between bites of a second donut.

"There were two perpetrators," Mike explained. "One was bitten pretty badly from the amount of blood we found where their vehicle was parked. Had to be some sort of four-wheel drive to have gotten in as far as they did down that two-track. We also found some jean material, no doubt torn from one of the perps' pant leg."

"Any reports of dog bites at the hospitals?" asked Chief. "Any labs back yet?"

"Not yet…" said Mike.

"But we found a flashlight… with prints!" interrupted Dane, enthusiastically.

"We're running the prints and blood now," said Mike. "If we have clear prints and they've got a record, we'll be able to identify them immediately."

"They'll be Ricky's and one of his buddy's," said Dane. "They left a couple of hundred-dollar bills and some ammunition in that secret cellar. Only Ricky would have known about it."

"That makes perfect sense," said Chief. "And now we know they're armed."

Steven shifted uneasily in his chair. "Any luck finding Ricky, or who picked him up?"

Chief turned to Steven. "Security cameras at the pen show him being picked up by someone in a black Jeep."

"Bingo, a four-wheel drive!" said Dane.

"No one got out of the vehicle and the cameras got only a partial plate number. Another car pulled in behind them," Chief continued. "And, he didn't show for his parole meeting Monday."

"No surprise. Hopefully, we'll be able to identify the owner of the Jeep by the prints or plates," said Mike.

"How about the Schmitt brothers?" asked Steven.

Dane set his coffee down and crammed the last bite of his third donut in his mouth. "Nowhere to be found. They vacated the rental in a hurry, leaving a lot of personal items behind."

Steven tapped the top of Mike's desk. "They left for Santa Rosa once they learned Katherine was there. It had to be them. Ricky couldn't be in two places at once."

"But they'll be looking to hook back up with Ricky at some point to get paid," said Dane.

Mike made eye contact with Steven. "Between the prints, the labs, and the plate, we'll have an ID on someone soon."

Steven nodded as Chief placed a hand on his shoulder. "How did it go with Sarah last night?"

"Okay. No word from Billy yet. She has her doubts they ran off together but isn't totally buying into the hostage situation either." Steven turned to Dane. "I told her to let you know if she hears from Billy."

"Good," said Dane.

"I'll be here at the office if you need me," said Mike. "As soon as I hear anything from the lab, I'll let you all know. We're running that tag, too. Narrowing it down to a black Jeep will help. I'll keep checking the hospitals.

"Steve, let Dane know if you hear from Katherine." He nodded. "Chief, would you mind paying a visit to the penitentiary today? See if anybody knows who might have picked up Ricky." Chief nodded. "Dane, start with the Schmitts' buddy at the feed store, then their family."

Dane stood up. "Will do."

Mike tipped his cup, finishing his coffee. "Let's meet here again tomorrow, same time."

Steven shook Mike's hand. "Thank you."

"We'll find her, Steve."

Each of the men went his separate way on assignment.

Steven tried to remain optimistic, but all he could picture was Katherine and Billy being held at gunpoint or worse. Normally not a praying man, he found himself asking for a miracle as he drove home. *Please let us find them alive!*

Dane hurried to make it to the feed store before lunch break. Hopefully, Jerry would be working that morning.

When he arrived, he found Jerry loading a truck out back. The expression on the round middle-aged man's face as they made eye contact left little doubt he knew something. Dane tilted his head in the direction of his cruiser parked in an adjacent lot. Jerry nodded in response and hurried to load the last of the feed bags before uneasily approaching the police car.

"Get in; I have a few questions for you," he said, pointing to the back seat. Dane hoped questioning Jerry in his unit might intimidate him and scare a little more information out of him.

Jerry wiped his perspiring lip and hesitantly slid into the seat behind Dane, glaring at him through the metal grate divider.

"Close the door," ordered Dane. Slowly, he closed his door.

Dane locked the doors. Immediately, Jerry's complexion turned from cherry red to pasty gray. "I know you were buddies with the Werden boys and still are with the Schmitt brothers. You might have even been in on some of their nasty business years ago."

"No, not me," he said, shaking his head.

"We're trying to locate these boys. Do you know their whereabouts?"

Jerry wiggled in his seat. "Well, Jake and Kyle live just south of town…"

"Not anymore, but I have a feeling you already knew that," Dane interrupted. "We know Jake and Kyle spoke to you recently about Katherine Walker, Ricky's old neighbor out on

Pine Island Lake."

"Yeah, she was mentioned in conversation."

"Go ahead."

"Well, the first time, they stopped by about a month or so ago. Jake said they had some good hay for sale and asked if I knew of anyone that might be interested. I mentioned Mrs. Walker."

"And after that?"

Jerry eyes widened, sweat forming on his brow. Jerry had slipped up.

"You said that was the first time."

"I just told them what I'd heard. A lot of folks knew she was leaving for the West Coast," said Jerry in one hurried breath."

Dane had him on the ropes. "How about Ricky? Did they mention him?"

"Nope, and I haven't seen him since he got out of prison." Again, Jerry stuck his foot in his mouth, sweat running down his face.

"How do you know he's out?"

Jerry swallowed hard. "They must have mentioned it."

"So, they had heard from Ricky then?"

"I suppose so."

Dane turned in his seat, facing Jerry. "Either they had, or hadn't—which is it?"

"They didn't say, but I guess they must have to know he was out."

Dane slid his card through a hole in the grate. "You call me if you hear from them again."

"Yes, sir, I will."

"You better because if something goes down, you could be considered a conspirator."

Jerry nodded. "Are we done?"

"For now." Dane unlocked the doors.

Jerry scooted out of the vehicle and walked briskly to his truck, glancing over his shoulder a few times on route. Dane sat and watched him until he drove off, probably to get a burger. Shaking his head, he started his vehicle, slung it in gear, and headed for the Schmitt family residence. Dane guessed Jerry wasn't involved, but he had confirmed their suspicions that the Schmitt brothers were acting on Ricky's behalf, if not working with him directly. It was a start. Hopefully, he would learn more from their family.

An hour later, Dane pulled out of the Schmitt driveway with no new information. The parents weren't even aware their sons had moved out of the rental and hadn't spoken to them in nearly a year. Next, he visited the uncle with the commercial moving truck the brothers had borrowed, but he turned out to be no help either. Only the sister remained, and he feared she would be a dead end, too.

When he pulled in the drive, there were no cars parked out front. Dane knew her husband, Matt Butler, who managed a gas station and repair shop down the road. And, he was aware the couple had two teenage boys who had gotten into their share of trouble over the past couple of years, but he couldn't recall ever meeting Mrs. Butler.

After getting no answer at the door, he parked and waited. It was a long shot, but about thirty minutes later, an old green Plymouth sedan pulled in. Dane exited his vehicle. A small, frail woman stepped out of the car and approached him.

"Can I help you?" she asked.

"Are you Tammy Butler?"

"Yes, what is this about? What did the boys do this time?"

"I'd appreciate a few minutes of your time, Ma'am. It's regarding your brothers."

She studied him tentatively. "I suppose I have a few

minutes." She pointed to the porch.

The middle-aged woman sat on the stairs, studying him. She wore her dirty blonde hair up and hid behind a massive amount of makeup. He leaned against the rail opposite her. "Do you know where they are?"

"No, why?" Unlike the parents and uncle who automatically directed him to the rental house, Tammy knew they were no longer there.

"When was the last time you saw either of them or heard from them?"

"I don't remember."

Another evasive yet telling answer. "A week, a month, six months?"

"It's been so long I don't remember, really… a year, I think." Tammy broke eye contact, blankly starring out across the yard. "I can't help you, officer. We aren't a close family."

What Chief had mentioned about some nasty business between her and her brothers came to mind. Dane handed her his card. "Thank you for your time. If you hear from either of them, I'd appreciate a call—doesn't matter what time of day. My home number is on the back. It's important; a women's safety is involved."

Tammy glanced toward him for a fleeting moment, her lips parting as if about to say something, then dropped her focus and nodded.

"Good day, Mrs. Butler." By the time he reached his car door she had disappeared into the house. Frustrated, Dane left for the office to care for the dogs. For a moment, he thought he might have reached her. He suspected she knew more than she was saying but wasn't talking out of fear for her own safety or that of her family. If anyone, she knew what her brothers were capable of.

The high afternoon sun nearly blinded Andy as he searched the road ahead for the sign to the trailhead. Just as he was about to signal Bobby to turn around, certain they had missed it, a small green sign appeared ahead. Squinting, Andy read "Snake Canyon Trail" and pulled off the highway onto the narrow dirt road, with Bobby following.

Andy nudged Ricky with his elbow. "We're here."

Ricky sprang up in his seat and checked his watch. "It took longer than you said."

"I normally drive faster, but every time I tried to speed up, Bobby would fall behind."

"How far does this go?"

"There's a parking area about a mile in," said Andy. "That's as far as the truck and trailer can go."

A cloud of dust followed them, so thick at times they lost sight of Bobby's rig behind them.

"Slow down," ordered Ricky.

"Okay; you're the one who said we're in a hurry to get up there." Andy was getting tired of him being so bossy. He would be glad when he had his money and could go his own way, but for now, Ricky could play the head dick. Ever since Ricky mentioned the money in the pen, Andy was content playing the dummy. Only a few more days!

Kyle glanced back at the trailer. "Do you have to drive so close?" The horses are taking in all that dust."

"Yeah, you're driving up their ass. What's the rush?" said Jake. "I don't give a shit about the damn horses, but that dust is starting to get in the cab, too."

Bobby gave some lame excuse he didn't want to lose the Jeep. Kyle turned away and smiled, like they could lose their mile-long dust trail. And people thought he was slow. But Kyle could tell Bobby was a real cowboy and he admired him for that.

"How many horses do you own?" asked Kyle.

Bobby smiled. "Ten, I think."

"Wow, that's a lot. What breed?"

"Quarter Horses, cutting horses. I have a real purdy Palomino stallion I compete on, a couple geldings in training, and a few mares and babies. How about you?"

"Just one. The roan in the back is mine," said Kyle, proudly. "But she's just a trail horse."

"She's solid, good bone, and I'll bet she's a smooth ride… nice sloping shoulder and long fetlocks set at a good angle. She'd make a nice ranch horse."

"Thanks! I like her kind, wide-set eyes."

His brother jabbed him with his elbow. "Enough of that horse shit. I can't understand half of what you're saying."

"Well, if you'd ever pick up anything besides a 'Playboy' you might learn something." Jake gave him one of his "who do you think you're talking to" looks.

Kyle turned and looked out the back window. Maybe he would teach Strawberry to work cattle. His dream was to get a small spread with a few steers. He strained to see his horse in the front of the stock trailer, but a film of dust covered the small window.

Turning, Kyle caught a glimpse of the black Jeep ahead through the dust. That Ricky. He wasn't happy about this whole business of Ricky getting even with the horsewoman. Why couldn't he just be happy to be out of prison and get on with his life? But no, Ricky had to have his revenge, which was nothing more than an excuse to have that redhead he had always wanted.

And, bringing Billy Black into it? He was wicked good with a knife and never lost a fight. Kyle rubbed his crotch. He never was the same down there after Billy laid him out cold the night

Kurt died. He was dangerous, and Kyle didn't want any part of him. Ricky was asking for trouble messing with that Indian.

He decided then he wasn't going to let Ricky hurt the woman or anyone else again. He would finally stand up to him and Jake, too. All those years of teasing and belittling him, all the terrible things he watched them do and got blamed for. He would come up with his own plan for revenge. He'd show 'em he wasn't so dumb after all!

On Monday afternoon, Katherine pulled into a gas station behind Billy outside Salt Lake City, their final stop before the last eight-hour stretch home.

Katherine checked on Major while Billy filled both vehicles. He was antsy, wanting out of the box he had been confined to for over twelve hours. They had agreed to drive straight through, with short stops along the way to rest Major's legs. Katherine had covered the trailer floor extra deep with shavings, but she still checked his legs every stop for any sign of heat or swelling.

When she offered him water, he playfully splashed her in the face. Billy turned when he heard her laughing.

"Did he get you again?"

"Of course," she said, wiping her face with her sleeve. "Let's pull off on one of those dirt roads over there. I need to clean the floor again."

"Well, if you would quit feeding him so damn much hay, he wouldn't keep filling the trailer with manure!"

"He's bored out of his mind. He needs something to do in there," she explained.

"You spoil that horse rotten."

Just then, Major screamed in her ear with a deafening whinny, as if protesting Billy's comment. They laughed, and once again she felt herself slipping under the spell of those dark eyes and captivating smile.

As she picked around Major's feet in the trailer, she gave her feelings about Billy some honest and objective thought. Why was she afraid to admit to herself she still loved him? Loving Billy came as naturally as taking her next breath. He was a force of nature. She loved Steven as her husband, and she loved Billy—well, as Billy. She had been able to separate and manage the two for years until working so close with Billy again had upset the balance. Even then, up until their convincing display for Jessie in the hotel parking lot, she had kept her feelings for him in check.

But since then, tremors of the yearning that shook her to her core as Billy pressed her against the truck continued to haunt her like aftershocks following an earthquake. She had felt the earth move! It was all wrong but had felt so right. She found herself closing her eyes and picturing being with Steven, like the old days, welcoming the flood of guilt to extinguish the flame.

Billy must have felt it too that night because a slight look of triumph and satisfaction could be detected whenever they looked at each other. He knew he had gotten to her and she hated that he knew. Even though it was supposed to be an act, they both knew it didn't turn out that way—not entirely, anyway. Katherine felt ashamed, as if she had cheated on Steven. Had she? Did feelings count?

Katherine shook her head, closed the trailer door and slid back behind the wheel. Thank goodness they were driving separate vehicles. Surely by the time they arrived at Billy's, she would get a grip. Then, what healthy woman wouldn't have reacted the same, especially with a man like Billy? All normal. It would pass.

14 – Mount Up

Monday – Tuesday

Happy to finally come to the end of the dusty, winding road, Ricky told Andy to park at the far end of the parking area to leave room for Bobby to turn his rig around. Ricky felt relieved there were no other vehicles.

Andy pointed down a ravine off to the right. "I found the perfect spot to hide the Jeep around that bend," he said.

"Great! Let's get Bobby on his way first," said Ricky.

The men converged in the parking area.

"When do you want me to pick you and horses up?" asked Bobby.

"We'll let you know, probably in a few weeks after rifle season. One of us can drive to a phone with the Jeep."

"Great, I'll help you unload the horses and once I get paid, I'll be on my way," said Bobby.

"Let's take care of that now," said Ricky, settling his debt.

Once Bobby left, they wasted nearly an hour of precious riding time unloading and deciding what to take this trip and what they could leave behind in the Jeep for later. Kyle watered the horses, one at a time, down at the creek while the rest of them covered the Jeep with pine boughs.

When it was time to mount up, Kyle immediately claimed the lightest colored horse, its coat a mixture of red-and-white hairs. Andy would ride his big spotted horse, Nugget, so that left a brown and a black horse, which had been recent purchases along with two saddles for this ride.

Ricky looked at the remaining nags. "Which one is the smoothest?" he asked Andy. Jake gave him a look as if to say he'd like the smoothest, too. Neither of them had ridden in years.

"It won't matter; we're going to be walking in. The going gets rough and the horses are pretty weighted down," said Andy. "But, the black," he noted, "has a nice forward walk."

Ricky walked up to the black horse, untied him and mounted. "This saddle is a piece of shit, Andy! I feel like I'm sitting on a rock."

"I bought what I could with the money I had," he answered.

"And the stirrups are too long."

"Get off; I'll fix them for you," said Kyle. Well, at least the pervert was good for something. "Thanks, Tick." Ricky laughed when Kyle shot him a pissed-off look. While Kyle adjusted his stirrups, Andy and Jake mounted their horses.

Once he and Kyle were seated, they were underway. Andy led the single-file group down the trail along Snake Canyon Creek, followed by Jake and himself, with Kyle bringing up the rear on the dirty-looking horse he named Strawberry.

Thirty minutes into their ride he already felt sore and the stupid horse he was riding kept trying to brush him off on every damn tree along the edge of the trail. He would be lucky if he was able to sit or walk by the time they reached the cabin. Ricky had to remind himself why crossing the border on horseback remained their best option, avoiding the border patrol. Soon he would have his revenge and disappear into Alberta, no one the wiser.

At nightfall, Katherine followed Billy's truck down his drive and pulled up to the barn. TJ had already been there to feed and gone. Major frolicked in the round pen while they packed their supplies. At first, they considered taking a pack animal, but Billy said they could carry everything they needed on their mounts if she rode western. It took a little convincing, but

Katherine eventually gave up her English saddle.

They packed a picket line to tie the horses, a rope, ground cloth and tarp, two light-weight goose-down sleeping bags, two blankets, a change of clothes, some canned goods, jerky, matches, a hatchet, compass, two slickers and flasks of water. Also, Katherine scooped a few days rations of grain into a bag for the horses. Billy felt there would be enough grass along the way to graze the horses a couple hours a day to sustain them.

As they packed their saddlebags on the back porch, Katherine had to ask. "Do you think Steven and Sarah really believe we ran off together?"

"Sarah might; I can't speak for Steven," he said, not taking his focus away from the clothes he was stuffing into his bag.

Obviously, things had not been going well at the Black Feather household either. "What about Mike, Dane or Chief?" she asked.

"They might have their doubts, but they have no way of knowing."

"Do you still think we made the right decision… not contacting them?"

"Yes. Ricky hasn't done anything that would put him away for long and he'd just be out again. Then we'd be right back where we started, never knowing when he might make a move on one of us. This way we have some control and the opportunity to get to Ricky."

Up to this point, they hadn't had a chance to discuss their escape or attack strategy in detail, driving separate vehicles, but Billy promised to fill her in on his plan that night when they made camp.

Katherine still had her doubts about just the two of them taking on Ricky and his band of misfits, but what Billy said about ending it themselves made sense. Only they knew what these men were capable of and only they would be in a position to end it. She had to trust Billy on this one.

As she watched him pack, including several knives, a box of box-cutter blades, and his twelve-gauge shotgun, Billy described their course. They would follow the stream up to the base of the Big Bear Mountain range, ride up and over the range down to the Eagle Crest River and follow it north. Ricky's map marked the meeting spot at the junction of the river and a creek about ten miles south of the border. Billy said he was familiar with this area and identified the location of the meeting spot right away. Considering both animals were in good condition, he felt they could make it in three days.

Once they had everything stowed away, they headed to the barn to saddle the horses. Billy would take his personal mount, Red, a big chestnut Mustang accustomed to mountain terrain and the cold. Billy attempted once again to convince her to take one of his hunting horses, but she wouldn't budge. Major might not be as sure-footed or bomb-proof, but she felt confident they could handle anything as a team.

Katherine dug out her waterproof quarter sheet from her trunk to help protect her thin-skinned, satin-coated Thoroughbred from the cold temperatures and the expected rain and snow in a couple days. Billy packed most of their supplies on Red but that still left a front-and-rear saddlebag and bedroll. Major turned to smell the new and unusual objects as Katherine secured them in place. Just as they were about to mount up, Billy left for the house unexpectedly.

"Figured I'd better leave Sarah a note," he said when he returned. "I wrote the same message you did to Steven, pretty much. I told her not to try to find us and that I would be in touch soon."

"Hopefully, that will be the case," she said, cynically.

Billy clasped her firmly by the shoulders. "We'll be fine."

The confidence in his dark russet eyes nearly convinced

her, but there was no turning back now anyway. She nodded. "Let's ride."

Billy taped a flashlight to the barrel of his shotgun and, resting it over the pommel of his saddle, lit their path along the stream. Katherine kept alert for any red eyes in the dark along the way.

As they followed the stream, it didn't take long for Major to make Billy's point about taking an off-the-track Thoroughbred in place of an experienced trail horse. The western saddle felt strange to him, so much heavier and bulkier than his English saddles. Add the noisy gear and bedroll bouncing on his rump, he felt obliged to throw in a few crow-hops and bucks along the way. Sometimes he wouldn't even kick out but just bounce up and down like a pogo stick on his back end.

Katherine was thankful Billy had convinced her to ride western. The security of the saddle horn and deep seat came in handy during his spontaneous airs above the ground.

Riding along the stream through the valley had been easygoing, with only the occasional fallen tree to step over or ride around. They had walked in the dark for about four hours before making camp around one in the morning. Katherine made a soft bed of pine needles and laid out their ground cloth and sleeping bags while Billy left with a hatchet to collect firewood. They didn't bother making a lean-to that night, with clear skies and no precipitation expected.

While Billy chopped, she cared for the horses. Major stood quietly tied next to Red as she groomed him. The two boys continued to hit it off. She guessed it didn't hurt that Red resembled his good buddy, Cody. Considering Major still had his summer coat, she threw one of their blankets over him for the night.

After Billy returned with his arms full of wood, he left again with his shotgun. "I disturbed a rabbit back there. I'll see if I can find him again."

"Don't we have enough to eat for tonight?"

"We need to conserve our canned goods. You never know if or when we'll come across any game."

Katherine waved him away and began making a fire. Ten minutes later she heard a single shot. Then she sprang to her feet. Billy was calling for her to bring rope and a blanket. *What in hell blazes?!* She quickly located the rope and borrowed Major's blanket and ran in the direction of the flickering light. There sat a large dog with its paw caught in a trap.

"I just came across him," said Billy. "It's an old bear trap, made for a much larger animal, so I don't think his leg is broken."

"What's he doing out here?"

"He might have been with some hunters and got lost."

The dog tried to get up but whimpered with any movement of the trapped leg. When Billy slowly approached him, his hackles raised as he growled and bared his teeth. "Well, maybe I was wrong; he might be feral."

"Or just frightened."

Billy took the rope and made a lasso, tossing it over the dog's head. Then he gently tightened the noose. The dog began to resist.

"You're going to choke him."

"I won't let it get that tight. Take that stick and see if you can release the trap and I'll keep him off you."

The dog continued to fight the rope. "He's just going to hurt himself worse. Let me try."

"Don't, Kat; he might take a piece out of you!" Billy warned.

Katherine ignored him and slowly approached the trapped animal while Billy focused the light on the dog and trap. "He might be part wolf; he looks a lot like Shane," she said.

"You're right. Look at the size of his feet and he has yellow eyes. But his ears are smaller, Malamute or Husky-cross, I'll bet. Be careful."

"It's okay, boy. I'm not going to hurt you," she said in a soothing voice as she slowly walked toward the scared animal. "How about we call you Ladd, after Allan Ladd. Laddy, yeah, I like that even better. Do you like that, Laddy? Now you need to let me help you, boy."

The canine stopped growling but watched her closely. Katherine moved her hand toward him slowly, stopping every few inches, waiting for his reaction. He had moved as far back as he could with his trapped leg extended. "Easy, Laddy, easy boy..." With a quick movement she pressed hard on the trap release and it sprang open.

Billy relaxed the rope and Laddy wiggled out of the noose and darted to the tree line with a slight limp. Before disappearing into the woods, he turned toward them and paused for a moment.

"You're welcome," said Katherine.

"You know you'll never see him again," Billy said, leading the way back to camp as he gathered up his rope.

"Maybe, maybe not. Who knows, he might return the favor someday like in the fable about the lion and the thorn."

"Right. You know how crazy that was, getting your hand that close?"

"I wasn't afraid of him. He knew I was trying to help. I could see it in his eyes."

Billy stopped to face her. "There's a thin line between brave and stupid. You let me take the risks from now on, okay?"

Katherine had to chuckle, considering their plans. "It's a little late for that, don't you think?"

"I suppose you've got a point. Speaking of which..." Billy walked to his pack and returned with a handle full of box-cutter blades. Katherine had been curious about their use when she noticed him packing them.

"Here's how I see it going down," he began. "Ricky's too much of a pussy to confront me himself before I'm restrained. Two of his buddies will meet us at the river and take us hostage. They'll frisk us for any weapons, then put us back up on our horses with our hands tied behind our back while we're led to Ricky."

Billy went on to suggest what Ricky had in mind after that. What he described astonished Katherine at first, but after the shock wore off, she knew he was right, remembering how Ricky would stare at her in town, undressing her with his eyes. He planned to rape her in front of Billy.

"First thing in the morning, I'm going hide a single-edge blade in the cantle of our saddles. Just a little cut in the leather at the back under the lip will do just fine and shouldn't get noticed. Then I'm going to tape one to the inside of my belt, in the back, as backup. Your belt is too narrow. Then all we have to do is weaken the rope and when the time is right, break free. Preferably this will take place while we're being escorted to Ricky on horseback."

They were both aware of the frightening alternative. If Billy couldn't get to one of the blades during their ride and take Ricky out when they first saw him, there might not be another opportunity until Ricky and the others were distracted by their attack on her. This point went unmentioned. No need in stating the obvious.

Then Katherine considered what Billy's next move would be. "Then what? You won't have a weapon."

Billy pulled his knife from its sheath and sprang to his feet. "Over here," he said pointing to his saddle. After checking the rabbit, she joined him.

Billy turned over his Big Horn saddle. "Here, in addition to the box-cutter blades, I'll rig a knife under the tree of the saddle with the handle just within reach through the grip hole." He placed the knife just so. "It'll be a little tricky, but we should be able to feed it out the front without too much trouble."

"We?"

"I'll rig one on your saddle too, just in case," he said. "And, even if I don't get to a knife, I have other weapons."

"Right," she said, recalling his display of the martial arts at Rudy's.

"But, hopefully, one of us can get to a knife."

The thought of using a knife on a human being—even Ricky or one of his thugs—rattled her. Could she, would she, be able to defend herself if she needed to? "I don't know, Billy, I've never hurt any living thing before. I get squirmy just thinking about blood. I won't even step on a worm!"

Billy chuckled, then his face hardened. "You will if it's his life or yours, or just think of the kids—whatever it takes for you to dig deep and find enough courage." Billy gripped the handle of his straight blade and quicker than she could blink, planted it center of a tree trunk about forty feet away.

Katherine jumped! "Good grief, Billy!"

After retrieving his knife, he returned to her side facing the tree. "You can do this, Kat. It'll help if you feel confident using one. I can teach you."

"Okay," she whispered.

"You hold the handle in this position," he illustrated. "Keep your eye on your target and throw it like this, keeping your arm straight, eye on the tree… just like throwing a baseball, and I know you can throw a baseball. No different; it's all about the follow-through. Here, let me show you."

A smile crept across her face, recalling his self-defense lessons the summer they met. "Billy Black, are you pulling your 'let me show you how' trick on me again?"

Billy laughed out loud. "Maybe."

"Well, it's not going to work this time," she chuckled.

Suddenly, straight-faced, he answered, "This is no game this time, Kat. I'm dead serious."

Katherine locked her jaw. The mention of the word "dead" sobered her on the spot.

"If something happens to me, you need to know…"

"Okay, okay; show me."

Billy handed her the knife and walked her halfway to the tree. Holding it how he showed her, he guided her arm in slow motion. "Cock your arm back like this, blade toward you, handle toward the sky, keeping it straight, then release it pointing the tip at your target." He stepped away. "Try it."

Katherine studied the tree, took a deep breath, and wheeled the knife through the air. It hit a little low but struck the trunk. "I hit it!"

"Good start," he said, retrieving the knife. "Okay, now throw it harder this time."

Putting a little more muscle behind it, the knife hit its mark dead center of the tree, chest-level. "Okay, I think I've got this."

"You sure do. You're a natural. Now start adding a little more distance each time. You have to learn to gauge the rotations according to your distance."

Katherine turned to Billy. "Thanks." Suddenly, the realization of what they might be riding into gripped her. She fought off the tears, but Billy knew her too well. He took her in his arms.

"I'm sorry, I didn't mean to scare you. I just…"

"I know." Katherine rested her head on his shoulder,

allowing the warmth and strength of her old friend to comfort her. The aroused feelings she felt earlier were replaced by genuine affection.

Pulling away, he brushed a tear from her cheek and raised her chin. "We can do this—together."

Offering a weak smile, Katherine wiped her face with her sleeve, nodding.

"Well, I'm starved—let's eat!" Only Billy could move on from a tender moment to food in an instant.

While Billy dressed the rabbit, Katherine opened a can of beans and heated it on a rock beside the fire and constructed a spit over the coals using one of Billy's knifes and some green branches.

Billy glanced over to check on her progress. "Not bad for an old city girl."

"That was a long time ago."

"Yes, it was. Hand me that," he said, pointing to one of the branches she had cut. "Can you believe it's been over thirty years?" Billy sharpened one end of the skewer with his knife, then ran the stick through the carcass, placing it in the spit over the coals.

Katherine caught a glimpse of Billy's nostalgic expression in the firelight. "That was some year," she said, "the year I moved to Two Ponies."

She was so young and naïve, moving from Boston to the wilds of Montana on her own at the age of twenty. Billy Black had captured her imagination, so handsome and charming yet dangerous and mysterious. He was a wild one, but that had attracted her even more. She blushed recalling their uninhibited sex.

"Do you ever wonder where we would be today if we hadn't gone to Rudy's that night?" he asked.

"Oh Billy, how can you think about such things at a time

like this?"

"I think about it all the time."

Billy must have read the panic on her face. He reached over and clasped her hand. "I know you still care, too. You won't admit it, but I see it in your eyes, and I feel it when we touch." He released her hand, but his dark russet eyes still held her captive. "I never stopped loving you, you know?" he said casually, as if discussing the weather.

Katherine wanted to run and hide. This was exactly what she didn't need to hear. She took a deep breath as she considered her response. "Yes, I still care, but not like you think. There's a lot of different kinds of love."

"You don't need to explain. I just wanted you to know how I felt, that's all."

She knew what he meant; he wanted to get it out in the open tonight in case he didn't get the chance to tell her later. She tried not to think about it, the real possibility that one or neither of them might make it through this alive. But she knew Billy would—somehow, someway—make sure he took Ricky with him. Knowing Billy would die to protect her and the kids made her even more vulnerable.

Billy rose to his feet to retrieve something else from his pack, then sat beside her, again focused on an object in his hand. Katherine was stunned when he handed her the chiseled wooden heart he had given her the night of her twenty-first birthday.

"Do you remember?"

Images of that night raced through her mind. How could she ever forget the night Steven first proposed, the night she learned Billy was her secret admirer, the night she and Billy first made love and Steven found them together! She swallowed hard but couldn't find her voice.

"You left it when you ran to catch Steve," he said.

Katherine studied the wooden heart with a deep gash running across its center. Why had he held onto it all these years, but more importantly, why was he giving it to her now? Did Billy think it might have the same effect on her tonight?

Suddenly she found her voice. "I always wondered what happened to it, but it won't work a second time, you know." She reached to hand it back to him.

"I want to you have it."

Katherine slipped the token into her pocket, once again at a loss for words. Their attention was drawn back to dinner as juice from the rabbit crackled in the fire.

"Sounds done," he said.

"Good. I'm pretty hungry myself."

Billy stuck his knife into the rabbit and placed it on a nearby rock to cut it up. Katherine ate a few bites of beans and handed the can and spoon to Billy. They ate the pork and beans in silence while the meat cooled.

Katherine's mind wandered back to the wooden heart in her pocket. Little did Billy know, she still had one of the stones of his first offering to her on the tack room stump as her secret admirer when they were kids. The nearly clear, streambed-polished stone with a hint of pink lay someplace at the bottom of her jewelry box.

"Here, be careful; it's hot," he said, handing her a leg.

"It's good. I haven't had rabbit in a while. It was Uncle Joe's favorite," she said. "What would he have done in this situation, I wonder?"

"If it was you and Betsy in danger and it was him they wanted, he'd be doing the same thing."

"Yes, I believe he would," she said, making eye contact once again.

Unexpectedly, a branch broke behind them. Billy reached for the shotgun and Katherine grabbed the knife still setting beside her. "Don't think it's a bear; the horses would have let us know. But stay close to the fire just in case." Billy stood up, poised and ready to shoot.

"There!" shouted Katherine, pointing toward the brush. "I saw something."

Billy swung the barrel around.

"No, don't shoot!" she yelled. Two yellow eyes reflecting the firelight approached them. "It's Laddy. He's come back."

Billy lowered the shotgun. "He must be hungry. Who knows how long he was caught in that trap. The rabbit must smell pretty good to him."

"See, I told you he'd be back." Katherine picked up a piece of meat and walked toward him, his front legs splayed, head down, looking more like a wolf than a dog as he studied her every move. She broke off a piece and tossed it to him.

"He must not be totally wild. He still associates food with people," said Billy.

Laddy slowly picked up the morsel and swallowed it without chewing. Katherine threw him a bigger piece where he had to come closer. Carefully, he moved within reach of the meat. The next piece she placed only a couple of yards away. Laddy froze, not ready to venture that close. Katherine stepped back and allowed him to retrieve the handout.

"That's good for tonight. I'll have him eating out of my hand in no time."

"We'll see, if he sticks around that long."

"Good night, Laddy," she said as he disappeared back into the shadows. She smiled, remembering her old companion, Shane, always at her side. In all the years he had been gone, she hadn't felt ready to invest her feelings in another dog. The saying goodbye was just too painful. But now with Laddy, she regretted having waited so long. Katherine hoped he would stay so she might have the opportunity to gain his trust and earn his loyalty. For now, she could use a distraction—anything besides Billy Black!

While Billy threw another log on the fire, Katherine left to check on Major. She was amazed by how well he had adapted to his new role. Katherine wrapped her arms around his neck, breathing in his earthy scent. A tear ran down her cheek, knowing Major would be there for her no matter what she asked of him—whether it be as a lesson horse, working hard to please her as an eventing mount, or even now as a sure-footed trail and pack horse—and tomorrow he would be carrying her in battle as her warhorse. *God, horses are amazing!*

When Katherine gave Red a pat, Major gave her a nudge. "Don't worry, handsome, you're still my main man. You rest up, boy. Tomorrow we're heading up that mountain." Katherine glanced at the outline of the range silhouetted by the starry sky. "Good night, sweetie."

Billy was already in his bag when she returned to their camp, his cowboy hat resting over his eyes and his shotgun within reach. Katherine felt bad and a little embarrassed she had jumped to the conclusion he was trying to bed her.

Katherine slipped out of her bra before sliding into her sleeping bag. She lay on her back studying the hypnotic treetops gently swaying in the breeze until her eyelids became heavy.

The moment TJ turned the last corner in their drive, he saw his father's truck parked out front of their house. He rushed into the house through the front door, calling for his dad. With no answer, he ran out the back door. There sat Mrs. Walker's truck and trailer beside the barn! TJ searched the structure, finding no one, but he did notice Red and his dad's and mother's saddles missing. When he returned to the house, he found a note sitting on the kitchen table written in his father's handwriting to his mother.

I'm sorry, Sarah. You were right. Please don't try to find us. I will be in touch soon. Billy

TJ stared at the piece of paper, recalling what his mother had told him about his father and Mrs. Walker possibly being in danger. If that was the case, the glaring words "don't try to find us" might imply no cops. TJ paced the room. Okay, they left from here on horseback, but for where and why?

Taking a quick inventory of what was missing from the house and barn, it became clear they rode into the mountains. After quickly feeding the horses, TJ followed fresh hoof tracks leading to the stream. They would traverse the streambed as far as the waterfall and rapids a few miles down, then they would need to travel on land. He could pick up their tracks there.

He stood, trying to decide what to do. Should he call his mother? No, she would insist he return to his grandparents immediately and she would notify the police. For some reason, he felt certain his father didn't want them involved. There was a good chance of snow any moment and all tracks and chance of finding them would be lost. He knew what he had to do. TJ ran to the house and dialed the Walkers.

Luckily, Josephine answered the phone. "Are you alone?"

"Yes, I'm in the library reading. Betsy is in the kitchen and my dad is on an emergency call. You sound funny. What's wrong?"

"I'm at our house. My dad and your mom were here."

"What! When?"

"Sometime last night. They left here on horseback, heading north up the stream. I'm going to follow them. If they're in trouble, I might be able to help."

"That's crazy, TJ. We need to report this. Let the police handle it."

"My dad left a note saying not to try to find them. I think he means the police. They'll figure it out soon enough once they find their trucks and the note and realize I'm gone. I just want a head start. Besides, it could snow up there any minute and their tracks would be lost and then no one could find them. I need to leave now. Promise not to tell anyone, okay?"

"Okay."

"I'll mark my trail like we used to when we were kids, remember?"

"Sure, with broken branches."

"Then they'll be able to track me even in the snow. Bye, Jo. I might not see you before you leave."

"TJ… I'm scared. Why is this happening to us?"

"I have to pack and get going. I'll miss you."

Before she could reply, TJ hung up the phone. He knew she would only try to talk him out of going.

TJ packed a bed roll, some jerky, a water flask, his hunting compass, binoculars, and enough grain for Cisco for a few days along with his shotgun and knife. He considered himself nearly as skilled as his dad with both weapons. As he started down the stream, a breeze out of the west gusted, flipping Cisco's mane and nearly blowing off his hat, confirming his fears of a front blowing in. He prayed to the spirits of his ancestors that the rain and snow would hold off long enough to find his father and Mrs. Walker safe.

It took Josephine a few minutes to process what TJ had told her, finally setting down the receiver. Should she tell Betsy and her dad? She had never broken a promise to TJ before. Besides, like he said, they would figure it all out soon enough anyway. Then a crazy fleeting thought breezed through her mind. Maybe she could be of help, too.

Yes, she would join TJ. Maybe if she hurried, she could catch him before he left. She didn't leave for school until next week. If they didn't find them in two days, she would turn back.

Josephine hid the book she had just started reading in the bottom drawer of the desk and joined Betsy in the kitchen. "I'm going for a ride. It's such a pretty day… don't worry, I'll stay in the arena."

Betsy dried her hands at the sink. "Okay, dear."

Josephine nodded. "Say, I want to start reading that old book, the one with you on the cover. It's one of mother's favorites, but I couldn't find it in the library."

"*The Fellowship*. I think I know where it is."

While Betsy searched the library at the opposite end of the lodge, Josephine quickly pilfered the pantry, tossing cans of beans and tuna fish into a sack along with some jerky. For good measure, she snatched a couple of biscuits cooling on the stove. Quietly, she grabbed her coat and dug out a sleeping bag from the back of the closet before Betsy returned. Down the drive she ran, safely making her escape to the barn.

Bonanza stood finishing his breakfast in his stall, taking quick notice of her before returning to picking through the shavings for the last few pieces of hay. By the time she packed her saddlebags and pulled his tack out, the gelding stood waiting, anticipating a ride.

"Hi, Bo Bo! It's going to be a long one this time. We're going to find Mom," she said, whispering into his ear as she bridled him. Tacking in record time, she attached her saddlebags and hoisted herself onto the big Buckskin and trotted down the drive hoping Betsy wouldn't notice. As soon as they hit the lake trail, they set off at a canter for the stream.

15 – The Search

Tuesday

Dane woke up to the bedroom phone ringing a little after six o'clock in the morning. Jessie rolled over in bed beside him, squinting, as he reached for the receiver on the nightstand.

"Who would be calling at this hour?" she asked, sounding annoyed, then swiftly sprang up in bed. "Maybe it's Kat!"

"Hello."

"This is Tammy Butler. Is this Officer Collins?" the woman whispered.

Dane slid his legs over the side of the bed and sat up. "Hello, Mrs. Butler. Yes, this in Officer Collins."

Jessie scooted next to him, resting her head on his shoulder, trying to listen in on the call.

"I'm sorry I'm calling so early, but I had a bad dream… about Kyle… you must think I'm crazy. Have you found him? Is Kyle okay?"

Dane wiped the sleep from his eyes. "Thank you for calling, Mrs. Butler. I'd be happy to talk with you in person at the station in about thirty minutes." Silence. "Or, I can come to your residence."

"Make it after seven; that's when my husband leaves for work."

Before he could reply, the call went dead. "She hung up."

"What did she say?" asked Jessie. "I couldn't hear."

"Something about a bad dream and she wanted to know if we had found her brother." Dane got up and ran his hand through his hair. "I'm meeting her at her house a little after seven. I need to take a shower. Go back to sleep."

"Are you kidding? I've barely been able to sleep the past couple of nights without a word from Kat."

Dane took a towel from the top of the laundry basket. "We're doing all we can, sweetie."

"I know," she said, quickly throwing the bed together. "Think I'll go out and spend some time with Oreo, maybe take him for a spin before work. I don't know how Doc is doing it… going about his day-to-day routine, not knowing. He planned to spend more time at home, but I think it gives him too much time to think. He'd rather keep busy at the clinic."

"I would do the same if I was him," said Dane, laying out a clean shirt and jeans on the bed. "The waiting and not knowing is the worst."

Jessie slipped into her jeans. "I'll be at the clinic after eight. You'll call me with any news?"

"Sure will."

Jessie caught him just before stepping into the shower and gave him a peck on the cheek. "Love you."

"Love you, too."

On his drive into town, Dane thought about what Tammy had said. It was obvious she cared about Kyle and just as obvious she didn't give a rat's ass about Jake, not even mentioning him. He hoped she knew something that would point them in the right direction—any direction for that matter. He had become stressed out, too. They hadn't turned up a plate number yet, but the lab results were due back today. He was ready to make things right again around here. His wife was a wreck, and everyone was on edge.

When he pulled up to the Butler house, Tammy sat on the front porch.

"Good morning, Ma'am."

Tammy only nodded. She looked like hell, barely

resembling the woman he met his first visit—no makeup, her hair a mess, and clothing wrinkled. The bags under her eyes told how little sleep she had gotten.

Dane sat down across from her on the porch rail.

"What did Jake do this time to get Kyle in trouble?" she asked.

"We believe your brothers are involved in some plan of Ricky Werden's to take revenge on Katherine Walker and Billy Black Feather. Do you know who they are?"

"Sure. Who doesn't around here? Heard they were back at it again."

"What do you mean?"

"You know, fooling around. I don't know why she would want anything more than that handsome doctor of hers. Some women are never satisfied."

Damn, this was news! Could they really have just run off together? Dane tried to conceal his surprise. "How do you know this?"

"Jake saw them together a year or so ago, outside the post office."

"Doing what?"

"Hugging, kissing, I think. Kyle told me about it."

"I see." Dane didn't know what to make of that piece of information. "Do you know if Ricky Werden has been in touch with your brothers since he got out of prison?"

"Sure, him and Jake are like brothers."

"Did they say anything about a plan?"

"I don't talk to Jake, only Kyle. But no, to answer your question. I wouldn't put it past Jake. He has a terrible hate for that half-breed."

"Billy Black Feather?"

"I thought he went by Billy Black."

"He does, but his legal name is Black Feather."

"Right. Well, whatever his name is, Jake could hurt him bad. The woman, maybe, or just teach her a lesson."

"What about Kyle?"

"Kyle wouldn't hurt a flea. He's a good man, just a little slow, if you know what I mean. Kyle's never been able to hold down a job; he had no place else to go. So, he just goes along with whatever Jake says…" Tammy hesitated. "Unless someone he cares about is involved."

"Like when?"

Tammy's focus dropped to her lap. "When I was twelve, Jake started…" Nervously, Tammy ran the hem of her blouse through her fingers. "He told me how pretty I was and that he would love me more if I… you know, let him touch me."

When Tammy looked up, a tear ran down her pale cheek. "I didn't know better. It started out innocent enough, but it didn't take long before he wanted more. He threatened to tell all my friends at school if I told on him. Kyle was only a kid, but he knew it wasn't right, and when Jake started getting rough and bringing the Werden brothers into it, Kyle told our folks."

"I'm sorry, Mrs. Butler. I know this isn't easy, but what you told me might help keep Kyle safe. We'll do all we can."

"Do you know where they are?"

"No, not yet, but we have a couple of leads we're working."

Tammy shook her head. "Now, I'm even more worried."

"Why?"

"Kyle likes that Walker woman; she's a horsewoman you know. Kyle loves horses… has since he was a kid." A smile softened her ragged face for a moment before turning cold again. "If Ricky tries to hurt her, Kyle's going to try to stop him."

"Did Kyle tell you where they were going?"

"Just that they were leaving on a hunting trip to a cabin in the mountains. He was all excited about getting to ride some horse. He did mention the cabin belonged to some friend of Ricky's. Then he hugged me, like he was never going to see me again." Tammy wiped her eyes. "That was over a week ago and I haven't heard from him since."

"Thanks, Mrs. Butler, you've been very helpful."

"Please find Kyle before he gets hurt."

"We will do our best. Please let me know if you hear from Kyle or if you think of anything else that might be helpful."

Just as Dane got up to leave, Tammy said, "There is one thing."

"What?"

"My brothers don't hunt."

Following his meeting with Tammy, Dane drove straight to the station just in time for their update meeting. Chief and Steve were already seated in his dad's office.

"Where have you been?" asked Mike.

"I just met with Tammy Butler. She called me at six this morning, wanting to talk."

"Great, what did you learn?" asked Steven.

Dane repeated their conversation except for the part about Steve's wife and Billy making out. "We need to find out if any of Ricky's buddies from the pen own a hunting cabin."

"That might help narrow things down," said Mike. "We have several matches on the partial plate for a Black Jeep; now we can cross reference them with ex-cons and owners of mountain property."

"Great!" said Dane. "What about the labs?"

"I was just telling Chief and Steve the blood on the jeans is O-positive, not Ricky's."

"Dang, that's the most common blood type out there,"

said Dane.

"Yeah, and the only clear prints we found were Luna's and Kimi's," Mike added.

"So, we're looking for an owner of a Black Jeep who owns a mountain cabin, has O-positive blood, and was most likely an inmate at the Billings pen, right? How hard can that be?" asked Steven.

"The plates are our best shot," said Mike. "As soon as we narrow it down and have an address, Dane will get right on it."

Steven got to his feet. "Are you looking for Billy's and Kat's trucks?"

"Yes, statewide APB," said Mike.

After Steve left, Chief stood up. "Can't imagine what he's going through. Just terrible business, all of it. I'll leave for Billings now. Let me know if there's anything else I can do."

"Will do," said Mike.

As soon as Chief left, Dane turned to his dad. "There's more."

"What, from the Butler woman?"

"Affirmative." Dane shook his head. "Apparently, Kat and Billy were seen making out in town."

"When? By who?"

"A year or two ago. Jake had seen them."

He could see his dad was weighing his response. "I don't know if we can bank on anything that derelict says."

"Makes you think, though, doesn't it? Maybe they did just run off."

"Not likely," said Mike. "We still have the Schmitts' visit with the truck and Ricky needing cash and weapons."

"Coincidence, maybe. It makes sense he'd go straight for the cash after he got out of the pen." Dane stood up. "I may not have told you all the details of what Jessie saw in Santa

Rosa. Sounded pretty racy between the two of them. She sure was convinced at the time."

"Well, either way, we need to proceed as planned. Ricky is still wanted for questioning regarding the assault on the women and dogs."

While Dane waited for the lab and research results, he gave Jessie a call to fill her in and fed and exercised the dogs. Jessie wasn't surprised by what Tammy had said, and they discussed the possibility of them running off together again. There were solid cases both ways; only time would tell. Unfortunately, if Ricky was involved in their disappearance, time might be running out. But he kept his fears to himself.

Within the hour, Mike and Chief both came up with the same name and a Helena address for Andy Ritter, one of Ricky's cell mates with O-positive who drove a black Jeep and happened to own a hunting cabin near the Canadian border. It had to be him. Hopefully, he would lead them to Ricky who would lead them to Katherine and Billy.

Dane sped home, lights flashing, to swap his patrol car for his pickup so he could survey the residence undetected. As he drove toward Helena, he recalled a few instances where Katherine had acted a little strange in Billy's company. He hadn't thought much of it at the time. The Walkers and the Black Feathers seemed happily married and he knew they all had been close friends for years. He just hadn't known how close until now.

He slowly approached the address, a duplex in a seedy part of town. Immediately, he noticed a handwritten for-rent sign in the front window. He pulled in the drive and dialed the number on his new mobile car phone. He still marveled at the new technology, even though its range was limited, but this close to the city would be no problem. A man with a heavy German accent answered. After identifying himself, Dane confirmed Andy had been a tenant about six months prior, but he left no forwarding address. He ended the called, disappointed.

Shit, this was their only lead. The cabin didn't have an address, which was common for homesteaded land back in the early 1900s. Andy's grandfather had willed the hunting cabin to his grandson. All they had was the county, Glacier, one of the largest in the state, and a few landmarks east of the Big Bear Mountain Range and Eagle Crest River, south of the border and with access off Highway 89.

Still sitting in the driveway, Dane got on the radio to call the office. He hated to inform his dad their only lead was a dead end. Then abruptly, he disconnected the call. "Damn it!" Why hadn't he thought to ask the landlord if he had heard from anyone for a reference?

Dane redialed the landlord. "Hello, this is Officer Collins again. Say, has anyone contacted you as a refence for Andy Ritter?"

"Yeah, the week he moved out."

"You don't happen to have a name or phone number do you.?"

"Maybe," he said. "Let me see; I keep files." After a few minutes of silence, he came back on the line and gave him a phone number.

Dane quickly dialed the number. A gruff-sounding man answered. Again, he introduced himself and explained the situation. The man confirmed Andy was renting a little farmhouse north of town, then asked if he was in some sort of trouble, informing him Andy was behind on rent. Dane explained he had just a few questions regarding a case they were investigating. He jotted down the address and disconnected the call. Smacking the steering wheel in victory, he backed out the drive and drove north out of Helena.

As he sped toward the farmhouse, he radioed Mike. They agreed he would just pass by to see if the Jeep was there. If it was, he would radio for backup before going in. Mike said he would call the Helena Police and the County Sheriff's office to give them a heads-up.

Again, Dane felt a sinking feeling in the pit of his stomach as he passed by the farmhouse. He saw no vehicles in the drive by the house or out front of the barn. The screen door swung open in the breeze, and bags of clothes and personal items lay dumped along the drive. They had already cleared out. Dane pulled in and parked, drew his gun and approached the front door. It was unlocked. Inside, the house looked the same, with items strewn about and the kitchen rifled through.

Out the back door, Dane found day-old horse manure and truck-and-trailer tire tracks where a rig had circled. They took horses with them. Things began to fall into place—Kyle looking forward to riding a horse, he and Jake heading to a cabin, not to hunt but with easy access to the border carrying cash and guns. He didn't like the way things were beginning to add up.

Then he found a Dodge truck hidden behind the barn. He immediately called in the plates, feeling certain the vehicle would be owned by one of the Schmitts.

As he approached the house again to take a closer look, he heard his mobile phone ringing. He swung open the truck door and grabbed the handset, hoping to catch the call-in time.

"Hello, Dane here."

"It's Steve—have some news."

"What's up?"

"Billy and Katherine were at Billy's."

"When?"

"Sometime last night."

"Let me guess—they rode out on horseback."

"Well, yeah, how did you know?"

Before Dane could explain, Steven continued. "But there's more. The kids took off after them."

"Are you kidding me?"

"TJ must have found their tracks and called Jo. Sarah called when TJ didn't return from feeding this morning. We drove out to their spread together. His horse was gone, and a few camping supplies. Then Jo disappeared on Bonanza. Betsy said she had taken some food."

"This is not good, Steve. I'm sure my dad filled you in on Andy Ritter. I'm north of Helena at his rental now. He's gone; left with horses for the cabin. He wasn't alone. I'm seeing four different sets of hoof prints and an abandoned truck I suspect belongs to the Schmitts."

"Oh my God! Kat and Billy are riding to meet them, and the kids could end up in the middle of it all."

"Calm down, Steve. I'm calling Mike now. We'll get a chopper in the air as soon as possible."

"I'm riding in. If I hurry, I might be able to catch up to the kids before dark."

"I'll come with you."

"No, I can't wait for you. I'm already packed.

"Are you armed?"

"Yes, I'll be heading north upstream toward the Big Bear Mountain range. The cabin is located between the range and Highway 89, right?"

"Yes, Be careful. I pray you find them. We'll be looking for you. Godspeed."

16 – High Country

Tuesday

As Billy led the way up the range that stood between them and the river, Katherine could feel the temperature drop. Heavy clouds hung so close she felt she could reach up and touch them. They rode into a strengthening wind that came at them from all directions, whipping Red's crimson tail ahead of her in circles like a lasso.

Earlier in the day, she caught glimpses of Laddy traveling parallel to them in the woods, but it had been some time since her last sighting. She hoped he hadn't parted ways, avoiding the higher altitudes and colder temps.

Major handled the steep grade and unsure footing nearly as well as Billy's surefooted Mustang and seemed to be thoroughly enjoying the adventure, his finely shaped ears flicking back and forth. Katherine stroked his shoulder. She was astonished by how fuzzy he had gotten overnight. Even with the blanket thrown over his back, his coat had lost its luster.

"Major's coat is growing before my eyes," she yelled to Billy, attempting to be heard above the crunch of leaves and the wind howling down the face of the mountain.

Billy turned his head. "What?"

"Major's coat is growing before my eyes," she yelled again.

"He'll adapt. Horses are good at that. He's doing great."

"I knew he would," Katherine gloated.

Billy just threw back one of his smart-ass smiles before resuming a serpentine track up the mountain between stands of aspen and pine. She felt grateful how familiar he was with the area and their destination.

Katherine pulled her thoughts away from what awaited them, focusing on Major and the beautiful view of the valley below and snow-covered peaks of the Continental Divide in the distance, reminding her they could get snow at this elevation any moment. Just the thought triggered her to zip up her jacket to her neck.

She sat relaxed in the saddle, her hips swaying side to side to the rhythm of Major's ground-covering strides, feeling as comfortable astride her trusted steed as on her living room sofa, perhaps even more so. For a moment she closed her eyes, allowing Major to follow Red without any guidance.

Remembering one of Betsy's lessons as a child, she focused on the scents and sounds surrounding her to clear her mind… the familiar scent of horse, which always had a relaxing effect on her, mixed with pine and the earthy smell of the Montana landscape. Barely audible was the distant chatter of squirrels and jays, warning their neighbors of the strangers and possible danger passing through.

The sound of Major's rhythmic four-beat gait rustling through a bed of leaves took her back to her childhood rides with Betsy through the aspen groves of Two Ponies. Where had the years gone? As they rode in silence the remainder of the morning, Katherine reflected on her life.

She concluded she had enjoyed a good go of it, having spent a considerable portion of it working with horses and riders, living her dream. She had been worshipped by her father, loved by two wonderful men, blessed with two lovely daughters, and earned the respect and affection of hundreds of students. Sure, there had been the bad—her unhappy childhood, the years she had thrown away living in the past and punishing herself to no avail, and the loss of her two little angels.

But, overall, she had lived a rich and full life. If it came to choosing between her life and the safety of her family, she would not hesitate. But she wasn't about to go out without a fight, and she knew neither was Billy.

Katherine studied her escort's broad shoulders ahead of her, his trained eye choosing the best path for the horses and guessed he must be having similar thoughts. She knew he loved Sarah and adored TJ and would do whatever it took to put Ricky and his hate behind them. She prayed she could provide enough of a distraction for Billy to do what needed to be done. She imaged that would be a knife to Ricky's heart.

Over the next rise, the trail opened to a field that stretched for miles scattered with a series of small ponds. The smell of sulfur reached her senses. *Mineral springs! Maybe even hot springs!* A soak in one of those pools sounded mighty fine having spent so many hours in the saddle.

When she cued Major for a trot to catch up with Billy, the cross-country mount came to attention, head raised and nostrils flaring, seeing the open field. "No boy, it's not time to hand-gallop."

"Mineral springs, right?" she asked. Billy nodded, riding beside her. "Know of any fresh water nearby for the horses?"

"There's a creek just inside the tree line over there," he said, pointing ahead. "Let's graze the horses while we stretch our legs and eat. I'm hungry."

"Sounds good." Steam could be seen rising from the surface of the pools. "How hot are those springs? I could use a bath."

Billy turned to her with a devilish grin. "What a brilliant idea!"

"Don't get any ideas, buster. We'll take turns grazing and bathing."

He laughed out loud. "Sure, whatever you say. Nothing I haven't already seen."

Katherine snickered, "I suppose you're right, but I'd still appreciate a little privacy."

"Well, let's see if we can even get in. Their temperatures are changing all the time. Don't want to cook."

Billy trotted to the first pond, dismounted, and led Red to its bank. "Ouch, this one's too hot." "This one's better, but still too hot." Katherine followed, becoming discouraged. When he reached the third and largest pool, he just smiled and nodded.

"I feel like Goldilocks," she laughed. "Me first."

"Okay, let's untack here."

Once Billy was a distance away watering the horses, Katherine threw a blanket over a nearby bush for good measure and undressed. She put her hair up and quickly stepped into the waist high pool. It was not scalding but hot enough it took a few minutes to gradually sink in above her shoulders. It felt like heaven on her aching body.

Billy couldn't resist and from above Major's tall back he caught a glimpse of Katherine as she approached the pool and slowly sank into it. God, she was still as beautiful as he remembered. Becoming aroused, he wondered if he still had a chance with her. He loved Sarah, but it was never the same as with Katherine. He questioned if she might feel the same way about Steven. What they had years ago was so hot, so out of control. But more than the sex, he had never felt so accepted or respected by a white and, without a doubt, she had loved him.

Katherine was such a mystery, sending so many mixed signals over the past two years he didn't know what to think. Working so close with her for all those months had been torture, his desires growing with every lingering stare, every unnecessary touch. Then the other night in the parking lot—how much was an act and what wasn't? Tonight, they would huddle to keep warm on the mountaintop with the uncertainty of what the next few days might hold. Could something develop? He needed to know, but he would be the gentleman she needed him to be… unless she made the first move.

Needing a distraction, he watched the horses peacefully grazing.

"Your turn."

Billy turned to find Katherine standing behind him, dressed. "That water is great. My skin is so soft," she said.

That was all he needed to hear, but he masked his impure thoughts with a joke. "It's the minerals. We should come back sometime and bottle it. We'd make a fortune!"

"Not a bad idea!"

"The horses didn't drink much… might want to try again," he said, and began stripping on the spot.

"Billy Black Feather!"

"Nothin' you haven't seen before, either," he hooted, stopping at his skivvies and boots. "Shit its cold!" Billy searched out his towel and hurried toward the pool.

Katherine couldn't help but chuckle at the comical sight of the near-naked cowboy strutting up the hill wearing only his hat, briefs, and boots. Then something occurred to her—the absence of the beaded medicine necklace Sarah had given him years ago.

"Hmmm." She wondered if he had just left it home, so it didn't get lost, or if this was some sort of message to her as it had been in the past. Katherine shook her head and decided she was reading too much into it and turned to lead Major and Red back to the creek.

The big bay took a deep drink, then began pawing at the

water playfully, splashing her and Red. "You goofball, and you used to be afraid of water, remember? Guess it's just fine on your terms, ha?"

As he took a second draw of sparkling spring water, she noticed he had dropped a little weight. It was no wonder. Major had never put in so many hours under saddle or traversed such terrain. She smiled, watching the two geldings nuzzling each other. Her boy had quickly bonded with Red. Wherever he went, Major followed, yet she didn't trust him to graze free. But his attachment came in handy, like now, and standing tied quietly all night beside Red. She was so proud of how well-behaved he had been.

Then startling her, Major suddenly reared, nearly pulling the lead from Katherine's grasp. Her hands burned to hold on as the gelding circled her. When Red struck off at a gallop toward Billy, there was no holding him. Major raced off after his friend.

Dread crept up the back of her spine as something big moved through the brush across the stream only a few yards away. She held her breath as the deep-throated pulsing sound of a grizzly echoed across the open field. Katherine wanted to run, but she somehow remembered her Uncle Joe's warning from years ago and froze in her tracks.

"If you ever confront a bear, don't run; stand your ground and look it straight in the eyes," he had told her. "Running only triggers their hunting instincts and there's no outrunning a bear. If it acts aggressively, make yourself look as big as possible, threaten it with an object, stomp your feet, and scream."

The pounding of her heart was deafening. Her body felt numb. She didn't know if she could move if she tried. The grizzly rose to a standing position, sizing her up, then wrung his neck with short open-mouthed snarls, letting her know he meant business. It would take only a matter of seconds for him to reach her. Glancing down at her feet, she noticed a large branch. She bent over and snatched it, raising it over her head.

The bear bellowed and pawed the air, then it suddenly turned. Laddy appeared on the streambed, lunging toward the grizzly fearlessly with his teeth bared and hackles raised. The bear, now on all fours, glanced between her and its new adversary. Immediately, Katherine took advantage of its confusion and shook the branch above her head, yelling at the top of her voice and making sounds barely recognizable as human. The grizzly retreated into the forest at a gallop.

Katherine slowly stepped back without taking her eyes off the woods, half expecting the bear to come charging. "Come here, boy," she called to Laddy, who took a few cautious steps in her direction. "You can trust me. I'm not going to hurt you."

Laddy came within a few feet, carefully studying her as she slowly knelt to his level. "Thank you, boy. You may have just saved my life. We're even now."

She reached out her hand. Stretching his neck, Laddy smelled her fingers then backed away.

"Well, that's a start."

Suddenly, she heard something running up on her from behind. Katherine spun around to find Billy wearing only his hat and boots, carrying his shotgun. "I heard a bear!"

Katherine's face flushed red-hot, taking in a full-frontal view before turning away. "He's gone. Laddy and I scared him off. But, if we hadn't, you surely would have," she snickered.

Billy glanced down at himself and covered his manhood with his hat.

"You grabbed your hat to save my life?"

"I never took it off. Glad the mutt came to the rescue. I'm

freezing," he said, already heading for his clothes.

When Katherine turned, Laddy had already disappeared.

"Let's get going. We'll just eat some jerky for now. I want to make it to the top before dark," Billy shouted back to her.

Katherine couldn't help but let her gaze rest on Billy's well-formed buttock as he tracked up the hill, but she allowed herself the pleasure only for an instant before collecting Major and Red, who were grazing without a care, and began saddling them.

Josephine halted Bonanza, carefully studying a thick stand of aspen before her. TJ had marked his path clearly with dangling branches at eye level up until now. She rode each way around the grove, searching for tracks or any sign horses had passed through, but couldn't find a clue. The ground was rocky and lacking TJ's tracking talent, she returned to his last marker and once again faced the grove. Left, or right? She couldn't guess and get herself lost; she must turn back. She felt like crying having come this far, but more than that, she needed to find her mother. She wiped a tear from her eye and turned Bonanza back down the mountain, feeling defeated.

Suddenly, a horse whinnied a distance beyond the aspen grove behind her. Bo's sides heaved and vibrated as he replied to the call. "Is that Cisco, boy?" She pivoted and started back up the hill. Sure enough, TJ appeared from the right side of the grove on his Paint.

"What are you doing here?!" he demanded.

Josephine was so glad to see him she just rode up beside him and gave him a hug. Besides, wasn't it obvious what she was doing? She answered anyway. "I came to help."

TJ did not look pleased. "You're crazy! You're not helping. Now they'll send out the Marines."

This was not the welcome she had envisioned. "But you

said they would come looking for you anyway."

"Not as fast. Did you tell anyone?"

"Of course not."

"Leave a note?"

"No." Now Josephine was in full-out tears. "I had to come."

"Okay, okay; don't cry. I just didn't expect you to show up like this. And, you shouldn't be riding out here alone. There's bear, mountain lion, and wolves, or Bo might have spooked, and you could have taken a fall."

Josephine wiped her face with her sleeve. She felt better knowing TJ was just worried about her. "I'm glad I caught up with you, I was about to turn back. I couldn't tell which way you went around the aspen. How fresh are their tracks? Do you think we can catch them before nightfall?"

"Slow down. We? I should send you back right now."

Josephine could see him weighing his options, realizing she wouldn't make it home before dark on her own and whether he should escort her home. The expression on his face told her he realized if he continued, he was stuck with her.

"Okay, let's get moving," he said. "I figure we're still at least half a day behind them."

Josephine smiled. "I brought biscuits."

TJ laughed. "Sounds good. Betsy's are the best. But let's try to top this ridge first." After marking their path around the aspen with another broken branch, TJ led the way up the steep grade.

"We'll find them safe, TJ. I know we will."

TJ wasn't as optimistic. The freshness of the occasional manure pile told him how far ahead they were and each one he found confirmed they were losing ground. Precious minutes were lost each time he stopped to confirm their path by looking for overturned leaves, misplaced rocks, bent grass, snapped branches, and the occasion hoof print left in the parched soil. But the lightest snowfall would take it all away. The only encouraging thing seemed they were traveling on a straight northeast course. If it snowed, they would continue the same course until they could pick up their tracks in the snow. Thank goodness he thought to bring his compass.

TJ leaned over, spotting another clue. A fresh silver scrape on a rock left by a horse shoe confirmed they were still on track. He knew they were still following their parents' trail, having found a clean hoof print left by Major. In the mud surrounding a spring earlier, he identified the popular eventing shoe studded with plugs.

Glancing back, he watched Jo carefully guiding her horse along behind him. Still a bit angry with her for having struck out after him uninvited, it was also nice to have her along. He didn't know when he would get to see her again after she left for California. And, who knew what guys she would meet at school. He wished she never had to leave. He would enjoy their time together, and perhaps this might be an opportunity to win her over before she left—impressing her with his tracking skills and maybe even saving their parents' lives. If that didn't impress her, nothing would. Josephine looked up to meet his gaze. TJ nodded to her, earning her radiant smile.

Just as he was about to turn his focus back up the steep grade, Bonanza slid on some loose rocks. Attempting to regain his footing, the big gelding overstepped and caught the heel of a front shoe with a rear toe. He nearly fell over, but with the help of Josephine's counterbalancing and strong hands and seat, she managed to keep him on his feet.

"Are you okay?"

"Yes, but something's wrong." Josephine dismounted Bonanza to examine him. "He pulled a front shoe! I can't ride him like this on these rocks. What are we going to do?"

Aware of the gelding's terrible feet requiring special shoes and pads, he dismounted and inspected the horse's foot. "At least it came off pretty clean," he said, setting the gelding's bare foot down. He knew as well as Josephine a horse carries most of its weight on its front end and riding in this country without both front shoes would be asking for a stone bruise or abscess, not to mention he would be off balance less the shoe and pad on one side and more likely to strain something.

"You're right. You can't ride him like this. Let's lead the horses to the top of this ridge where we can redistribute our gear. You'll have to ride double with me on Cisco."

Josephine knew riding double was their only option, but she felt a little uncomfortable about it. They used to ride double as kids all the time, but now?

When they reached a level spot, TJ transferred items to Bonanza to make room for Josephine to sit behind him while Josephine slipped off the gelding's bridle and secured it to her saddle. She was thankful she left Bonanza's halter on under his bridle with a lead rope tied in a cavalry knot as her mother had taught her. They easily undid the knot to lead Bo like a pack animal.

Once they had everything in place, TJ mounted Cisco, followed by Josephine riding as close behind him and the saddle as possible to keep off the gelding's kidneys.

"I'm sorry, TJ," she said, feeling like a real burden now. No way would they be able to go as long or at as quick a pace, putting extra stress on Cisco riding double.

"Accidents happen."

She tried to keep her arms at her side, but as soon as they started uphill again, she had to wrap her arms tightly around TJ's middle to keep from sliding off the Paint's rump.

Immediately, she felt her face get hot and her lower regions come to life as her bosom pressed against TJ's back. She wasn't a kid anymore. She knew what she was feeling. She had felt this way with other boys, when they fondled her breasts or ran their hand between her legs. But that was as far as she had allowed it to go.

She was proud of the fact she remained a virgin, even though she had kept it a secret from all her girlfriends who weren't. They were certain she had done it with at least one of her many boyfriends. Little did they know that was why she had had so many. When they didn't get what they wanted, they moved on. Josephine was waiting for true love, and none of the boys at school had come close.

But now it was TJ making her feel this way. She wasn't sure how she felt about it, but after a few more hours, all she cared about was stopping for the night.

"You okay back there?" he asked, turning his head so she could hear him above the wind and leaves.

"Just fine," she lied. Her arms were killing her, not to mention her bottom. But at least she kept warm between Cisco's body heat and snuggled behind TJ. "Feels like the temperature dropped thirty degrees the past hour," she added.

Josephine wiggled closer and held tight while they maneuvered up a steep turn. As TJ neck-reined his gelding along the best footing, he placed his free hand over hers, clasping it tightly as Cisco surged up another steep incline with Bonanza in tow. Josephine closed her eyes and placed her chin on TJ's broad shoulder. When their path leveled out again, she whispered in his ear, "What are we going to find when we catch up with them, TJ? Is it possible they ran off together?"

"My mom thinks they might have. But I believe they're in trouble. That's why I'm here."

"Me too."

TJ patted his shotgun resting in the scabbard on Cisco's shoulder. "I'm prepared to do whatever it takes to keep them and us safe."

Josephine had to know. "Could you shoot a man dead if you had to?"

"Sure. My dad killed a man. If he can, I can."

"Yeah, my dad told me what happened. It was the brother of this Ricky guy. It all seems so crazy, like out of a movie, what happened then and what's happening now—this whole revenge thing."

"I know. I wish things could be back to the way they were."

"Me too."

"Except one thing."

"What's that, TJ?"

"I wish you weren't still leaving."

Josephine didn't reply. She now had mixed feeling about leaving for school. She turned her head and rested it against his warm strong back. The events of the past few days had brought them closer, if that was possible. They were in this together, sharing the same feelings of fear and rejection and needing to know the truth and that their parents were safe. The thought that she could be falling for her lifelong friend, the little boy next door who had always adored her, frightened her. This was not part of her well-laid plans.

Steven rode his stocky gray Quarter Horse, Dandy, hard and heavy hoping to gain ground on the kids. Immediately, he noticed the deliberately bent over branches marking their way. He felt a little reassured knowing they intended on someone following them. He hadn't decided what he would do when he caught up with the kids. He understood TJ's logic on following them while their tracks were fresh, but it didn't make sense taking Josephine along with him. He would be torn between being angry or commending them on their bravery, but either way he would send them home.

After hearing the news that Katherine's and Billy's trucks were parked at the Black Feathers, Mike cancelled the APB on their vehicles. He considered this good news since they were not yet in the hands of Ricky and his gang. But equally disturbing was their ride into the mountains, which very well might be at Ricky's request. Then, there's Jo and TJ, riding after them—stupid kids! But he couldn't blame them under the circumstances.

His next call was to Flathead County Sheriff's Department to request a Search and Rescue air team to try to find the kids before trouble found them. Unfortunately, Mike soon learned Search and Rescue would not dispatch a chopper team without confirmation someone was lost or injured. They just couldn't justify sending out a team on the chance a verified emergency call came in, especially during hunting season and with a forest fire raging across the border. Mike called Chief.

"I know of a fellow who owns a bird that might help," said Chief. "I agree, this could turn bad quick if those kids ride into a hostage situation. And, this might be our only chance of locating Katherine and Billy. His name is Roy Higgins, he's an actor from LA who has a cattle ranch outside Great Falls."

"Roy Higgins, I've seen him in movies—Westerns, right?"

"Yeah, that's him. He started as a stunt double then got several supporting roles, which eventually led to leading roles. He mostly directs now."

"At least they didn't need a stunt double for him."

"Right." Chief chuckled. "I'll give him a call and explain everything. Hopefully, he's in town and willing to help."

"How did you two meet?"

"We're both members of the Montana Cattlemen

Association. Nice fellow. I'll let you know as soon as I reach him."

"Thanks, Chief."

Mike sat sipping his coffee waiting for Chief's return call when Dane returned from Helena and rushed into his office. "I just contacted the weather service and thunderstorms are expected this afternoon and this evening."

"Damn, we've been praying for rain all summer and it has to come now. Well, hopefully it'll help with the fire."

"No such luck there. Doesn't sound like the front is reaching that far north." Dane sat down and scooted his chair up to his desk. "How soon can we get in the air?"

Mike explained they didn't have a chopper, not yet anyway, and that hopefully Chief's friend would come through. "I heard the fire is fifty-percent contained and, unless the wind changes, should stay north of us and not be a concern."

"Good, but there's a good chance of snow by morning in the high country," said Dane. "We have no way of knowing how prepared the kids are for that kind of weather, not to mention Steven would lose their tracks." Dane shook his head. "Sure hope we can get in the air, and soon. Steven said they were heading up the stream and we know the general location of the cabin, so that will give us some parameters to search."

Mike chuckled. "Sure, that should narrow it down to about a thousand square miles. It'll be like finding a needle in a haystack, I'm afraid. Not to mention most of that area is wooded."

"Steven is riding his gray and the kids are riding a nearly all-white horse and a Buckskin, all light-colored animals."

"That might help if we're lucky enough to get in the air."

Dane sprang to his feet when the phone rang. Mike answered.

"Hi Chief, what's the word?" Mike nodded to his son. "Great, we'll be ready."

"We got it?" asked Dane.

Yes, he can pick us up at Glacier Park International Airport in two hours, Hangar Twenty-three. We'll have to hustle. That will only give us a couple of hours of daylight, that's if the storm holds off."

"It's better than nothing," said Dane. "Let's go!"

17 – Rain

Tuesday

The pungent scent of pine filled Katherine's senses as a light rain began to fall. Major followed Red step for step as she rested her reins over the horn of her saddle while she zipped up her jacket and tilted her cowboy hat down over her face. When the rain began to pick up, Katherine trotted up alongside of Billy. "Should we stop and pull out our slickers?"

"Up there is a good spot," he said, pointing up ahead.

When they reached level ground under a canopy of thick pine, they dismounted. Katherine's legs nearly gave out under her when she touched the ground. Billy gave her a sideways smirk.

"I'm sore too," he said, "It's a bitch getting old. I remember the last time I rode up here just a few years ago… no problem."

Each of them placed their hat over their saddle horn as they slipped into their rain poncho, pulling the hood up over their head before placing their hat back on.

"It feels cold enough to snow," she said.

"It will tonight. I can smell it."

"What about the horses—should we graze them before the snowfall?"

"Let's go a little further. If I remember correctly, there's an open field with more grass ahead."

When they reached the grassy field, they loosened the horse's cinches and let them graze.

"I don't know how you know where we are or where we're

going," said Katherine. "It all looks the same to me."

"Each peak of this range has distinct features. We've been riding a pretty straight northeast track from my place to between two peaks."

"But we can't even see the mountains in this haze."

"I got my bearings before we rode up into the clouds," he said. "We're cutting across the lowest point of this range to get to the river, which we'll have to cross to hook up with the trail on the map."

"Why didn't we just drive to the trailhead like on Ricky's map?"

"You're asking me this now?"

"I trust your judgement… just curious, that's all."

"Remember, we're smarter than Ricky. If we had parked our rig at the trailhead, park rangers might have called in our plates. If Steve and Dane are doing their job, which I'm sure they are, they issued a bulletin on our trucks. This was the best way to follow Ricky's instructions and not alert the police. To end this the way it needs to be ended, we don't want the law involved."

"Do you think anyone will try following us?"

"Not if our display for Jessie was convincing enough. Even if they did, they'd be at least half a day behind. If things go according to plan, Ricky will be history by the time they catch up with us."

He shot her a glance as cold as her hands. She just nodded.

Billy left to hunt for dinner while she stayed with the livestock. About thirty minutes later, he approached carrying his shotgun in one hand and a large snowshoe rabbit in the other.

Surprising them both, Red and Major abruptly took a few quick steps and stopped all eyes and ears, looking in the direction of the tree line where Billy had just exited. Four wolves trotted out into the open.

"That's odd," said Billy. "During the daylight."

Katherine became concerned when the lead wolf continued in their direction even though the rest of the pack hung back. The horses stood between them and the predator.

Billy moved slowly into position to give him a clear shot and raised his gun. Katherine heard him load the chamber.

"No, don't shoot!" she screamed, recognizing the canine as her new friend. "It's Laddy!"

"What the hell—he's running with wolves?"

"That must be how he's survived." Katherine walked past the horses and took a piece of jerky from her pocket. Laddy stopped and watched her closely. "Here boy," she said, kneeling, and extending the meat.

Laddy cautiously approached her then sat down as if to say that's a far as I go. Katherine turned her back on him and began walking away, curious to see what he would do. Laddy began to shadow her, step for step. Again, she turned and offered him the food. This time, to Katherine's delight, he slowly took the meat from her outreached hand, stepped back, and ate it.

"See," she yelled to Billy who was tying the hare to his saddle. "Eating out of my hand!"

Billy just smiled and nodded.

When she glanced back to the tree line, the pack was gone. "C'mon, boy, you can stay with us now. I'll take care of you." Laddy stayed back as she approached Billy.

"We need to get moving," he said. "This could turn to snow anytime."

"Okay. I think he's here to stay this time."

"Great, just what we need—another mouth to feed."

"He saved my life, remember?"

"Okay, he's earned a meal or two." Billy jostled dinner

against Red's shoulder. "Glad I found this big guy hiding in the tall grass."

"But I didn't hear a shot."

"Saving ammo. I followed his movement in the grass until there was an opening." Billy motioned throwing his knife.

"Impressive. He's a lot bigger than the cottontail."

"Good thing since we'll be having a guest tonight." Billy turned to Laddy. "I think he might have watched me make my kill and decided to join us."

Katherine laughed. "Maybe, he's a smart one."

"Let's mount up. We might be able to find a cave along those rock shelves up ahead." Billy pointed down a canyon. "It'll be a little out of our way, but hopefully we'll find shelter for the night. We'll have to backtrack and pick up from here in the morning."

"Sounds like a plan."

The temperature continued to drop as Josephine and TJ climbed higher as evening approached. When they topped what they thought to be the peak, they got their first view of their surroundings in hours and realized the top remained at least another half-day's ride across an open field and up a fair distance of rocky terrain scattered with pine at the tree line. On each side of them the mountains rose up to snow-covered peaks.

Josephine sighed. "What should we do? Ride on or stop here for the night?"

TJ studied the sky then turned to her. "It'll be a gamble whether we make it across before dark or dry with the looks of those clouds building, but it would be nice to gain a couple more hours on them before we make camp for the night."

"Let's go for it," she said.

"Okay. I think it'll be fine for Bonanza to trot, maybe even lope a little in this tall grass."

Just as TJ asked Cisco for a trot, thunder could be heard in the distance. They followed their parents' clear path across the field, marked by toppled seed-head stalks, as the mountain tops quickly disappeared in a fog of clouds. When it thundered again, Josephine held tight as TJ made a kissing sound. Cisco responded to the cue, lunging into a canter with Bonanza keeping pace alongside.

Later Tuesday afternoon, Steven came across a thrown shoe, recognizing it as one of Bonanza's, no mistaking the clips and pad. Certain that Josephine knew better than to continue riding Bonanza, he imagined they doubled up on Cisco and were using Bo to pack. This would slow the kids down considerably and give him a better chance of catching up with them before dark. Steven kicked Dandy's flanks, picking up a trot as he looked ahead for the next bent branch.

Steven pulled Dandy to a halt as the distant groan of a helicopter approached. He turned his mount and hurried toward the nearest clearing, just a small opening in the middle of dense forest. But it was too late; they had already flown by. They made a few more passes but still didn't notice him waving his jacket. It had to be Mike and Dane searching for the kids. He just hoped they located them before dark if he didn't. He backtracked and resumed following their trail.

Gazing out across the vast expanse, their goal became blurry as the freezing wind brought tears to Josephine's eyes. The sky had darkened, but she could still make out steam rising from what had to be hot springs feeding small ponds scattered along the way.

The wind began carrying small freezing droplets that stung her face. "I don't think we're going to make it," she yelled.

"Listen!" said TJ, bringing Cisco and Bonanza to an abrupt halt, causing Josephine to slam into TJ's back. She strained to hear what he observed above the howling wind.

"It's a chopper! I'll bet they're looking for us." TJ immediately cued the horses back into a canter.

Josephine sheltered her eyes, trying to locate the helicopter, but the visibility was too poor. A flash of lightning struck a tree at the edge of the field a few hundred yards away, causing her to flinch. She turned her head behind TJ's back, closed her eyes and prayed they didn't get struck next. She could feel Cisco's strides lengthen to a gallop as huge raindrops began pelting them. More distance grew between them and the sound of the aircraft until there was only the sound of wind whistling in her ears as they cut through the storm.

Billy held the hood of his poncho in place against the wind and rain with one hand while he neck-reined his Mustang with the other. Red and Major groaned and Laddy panted as they climbed the steep rocky floor of the canyon at dusk. Each step of their horses' shod hooves echoed through the narrow gorge. The rain came down in sheets, but thankfully their long slickers covered their bed rolls and saddle bags. Laddy shook, spooking Major with his spray, but only briefly as the exhausted gelding quickly fell back in step behind Red.

"There!" Billy called out, pointing to a large jetting rock formation creating a canopy. "That will do."

Immediately, Laddy sought shelter under the rock ceiling with barely enough room for the horses to stand beneath it. They stood with their heads held low, both geldings too tired to mind the small space.

"I'll give them just a half ration tonight after they cool down. We have only enough feed for one more day," said Katherine, sounding concerned.

"That's all we'll need. We should reach the meeting spot tomorrow afternoon."

"Then what will they eat?"

Billy smiled. Just like Kat to be more concerned about the welfare of the horses than her own. "One day at a time, but to keep you from worrying all night, there should be plenty of grass along the river still."

"Of course," she said, still looking worried as she rubbed Major down with a towel.

Billy first strung up the tarp to block the wind and rain blowing in from the west. Next, he found his hatchet at the bottom of his supply bag. "I'm going to get some wood for a fire. I saw a fallen tree back there that still looked partially dry."

"Great. I'll try to collect some dry pine needles to cushion our bed rolls."

"We'll need them to start a fire, too," he said, as he lumbered back down the canyon, stiff from so many hours in the saddle.

As he chopped the dead tree, he thought about his family. He told himself Sarah and TJ would be okay without him if things didn't go according to plan. They could move in with Sarah's parents and live off what they get for their farm. She was a good woman, having stood by him through all his nonsense over the years. He felt bad about having left on bad terms, but she would forgive him like she always did, especially once she learned it was to protect her and TJ.

Returning with his arms full of wood, he found their bed rolls laid out on a bed of pine needles and a collection of branches and pine cones piled out of the rain and ready for a fire. Billy carefully placed the logs in teepee fashion over the kindling and pulled a dry pack of matches out of his jacket pocket. It took a few tries, but eventually he got a fire started. Laddy didn't waste any time curling up beside the fire to thaw and dry out.

When he slipped the matches back into his pocket, he felt an open box of Marlboros. He hadn't smoked a single cigarette since he arrived in California. He knew Katherine didn't approve of him smoking, and it had been so dry, he feared a dropped hot ash could start a fire. But with the rain, maybe he would light one up after she fell asleep. He could use a smoke.

Katherine stood between the horses, patting, and talking to them like children. Her love of horses rivaled his own passion for the simple creatures they both chose to make their life's work. If only humans could be as honorable. Remarkable animals, really, never ceasing to amaze him; honest, trusting, and forgiving. Katherine understood this as well.

Billy walked up beside her and pat Red on his damp shoulder, pulling a couple peppermints from his stash in his jacket pocket.

He fed Red one, then reached out to Katherine. "Here," he said, dropping the other in her hand. He was rewarded with a warm heartfelt smile. God, even looking like a drowned rat, she was beautiful.

"Thanks, Major deserves a treat; he's been such a trooper. I'm so proud of him." She extended her open palm and stroked his neck as he patiently accepted his treat. "What a good boy."

In the close confines between the horses, he could feel her penetrating warmth clear to his core. Billy imagined taking her in his arms and kissing her. When she turned, her jade eyes searching his, he thought she might be sharing the same feelings, but reminded himself "only if she makes the first move."

"We've always shared our love of horses," she said, turning her attention back to Major.

Those weren't the feelings he was hoping for, but it was a start. "Yes, from day one," he replied, and dared to say what he was thinking. "We would have made a good team, you and me."

She only offered a thin smile and returned to the fire beside Laddy to heat the last can of beans. "This will hold us until the meat is done," she said.

Setting his idealistic romantic intentions aside, Billy joined in preparing their meal. Laddy followed his every move as he cut strips of meat from the hare. He draped the pieces over a green branch above the coals so the meat would cook faster this time. They needed their rest and he wanted to get an early start in the morning.

After the three of them ate their fill in silence, Katherine slipped into her sleeping bag snug against the rock wall, leaving room for his bag between her and the fire. Billy stared into the flames, stealing fleeting glances at Katherine's lovely features outlined by the dancing yellow-orange light.

"At least the storm has let up," she said.

Billy nodded. The weather was the last thing on his mind.

"Good night, Billy," she whispered, then with his last comment apparently still on her mind, she added, "I believe things ended up the way they were meant to be, me with Steven and you with Sarah."

Did he dare say it? "Remember, you made that choice for both of us."

Katherine's expression of shock surprised him. Hadn't she ever thought of it that way? She turned and propped her head on her hand. "Aren't you happy?" she said. "You have a wife who loves you beyond words, a son who worships you, a beautiful home, and you're getting to do what you love every day. Isn't that enough?"

Billy poked at the fire. "Most of the time."

"Most of the time?"

He turned to her. "Except when I'm with you," he said, coming clean. "Are you happy, Kat?"

"Yes, Billy, I'm happy." Turning away, she laid back down, pulling her bag over her head. "We better get some rest."

"Good idea." Billy laid his bed roll beside hers and slid in, leaving a small space between them.

As Katherine fell asleep, her shallow breaths and the crackling fire the only sound, Billy's mind would not rest. Lying on his back, he followed the sparks from the fire dance into the heavens until they died and disappeared. Katherine was right; he did have a lot to be thankful for. Why couldn't he be happy with what he had? Why had he always felt he needed more… that he needed Katherine's love and acceptance.

He studied Laddy, curled in a ball beside the fire. They weren't much different, both half-breeds, uncertain of where they fit it. Like Laddy, he shared a wild side, the urge to run with the wolves. Then came Katherine, who tamed them both.

As the fire settled, a burst of embers resembling fireflies drifted off into the night. Billy laid there, contemplating life and how it paralleled a spark, conceived in the heat of a moment, then set free to go its own way in the wind, only to disappear in what seemed like an instant. He sat up and pulled the Marlboros from his pocket, glanced at Katherine, and returned the box to his pocket.

TJ aimed for a tight cluster of lodgepole pine, alongside a creek, which would provide shelter from the pelting rain and water for the horses. Josephine clung to him, her head resting against his back, trusting him to take care of her. He felt foolish to have continued on with her, especially after Bonanza threw his shoe. He should have turned back and escorted her home safely. Instead, they were soaked to the bone in near freezing temperatures and about to spend the night on the side of a mountain where it could snow any second. Neither of them thought to bring gloves or rain gear, but he did think to grab the tarp off the wood pile on a whim before he left. Now it could very well save their lives. He had to get Jo dry and warm as quick as possible, fearing hypothermia.

When the rain turned to a light mist the last half mile or so, he brought the horses down to a walk to cool them down slowly. He halted under the heaviest canopy of pine boughs and turned back to Josephine. "Let's make camp here before it starts coming down hard again."

She seemed to be frozen in place, her hands locked around his middle. He reached down and clasped her ice-cold hands and squeezed them. "Jo, let's make camp."

Slowly she slid down off Cisco, nearly stumbling to the ground on stiff legs and numb feet. He quickly dismounted to aide her. Immediately, he located the tarp.

"Help me, Jo. We need to make a lean-to."

Josephine seemed to be coming out of her stupor, studying the tarp. "Yes, we'll need a rope to throw it over and something to tie the corners."

"We can use the tie line," said TJ. "We'll tie the horses by their lead ropes for tonight."

Josephine looked at the drenched and exhausted animals and smiled. "They look like they'll stand just fine." Both horses stood head down and breathing steam into the cold night air. "And, I'll tear strips from one of the towels."

Within minutes they had shelter, but Josephine was shivering. He pulled their sleeping bags out, surprised to find they were dry on the inside. He laid one down under the tarp, had her slip off her wet coat and wrapped the other bag around her. "Climb under there out of the wind. I'll be right back." He said. "We need a fire to get you warmed up."

Josephine nodded and sought shelter. He managed to find some dry pine needles and pinecones but most of the branches were damp. Luckily, his matches had kept dry and he was able to get a meager fire started. He prayed he could keep it going.

TJ rifled through their supplies, locating a can of soup. He leaned into the shelter. "How about something hot to eat?"

"That sounds great," she answered, her teeth chattering as she peeked out at him.

"You need to get out of those wet clothes," he said. Josephine gave him a look. "Seriously, I won't look. Strip, then climb in your bag. Just let me know when you're ready to hand them to me. I'll drape them over some branches beside the fire to dry them." Thankfully, the fire began to burn better once the branches dried out from the heat of the burning needles and pinecones.

"Okay," she said. Following several minutes, the garments finally appeared out the opening for him to take. "Here you go."

Trying to be a gentleman, he turned his head as he grabbed her rolled up clothes. When he unrolled them to hang, to his disbelief, her bra and panties fell out and right into the fire. "Shit!" He tried to pick them out, but it was too late.

"What happened?" she called, burrowed deep within her sleeping bag.

"Did you pack any extra underwear?" he asked, timidly.

Josephine stuck her head out and gasped at the sight of her burning undergarments. "TJ, what did you do?"

"It was an accident, I swear! You have more, right?"

"No, I had to hurry and sneak out, so Betsy didn't see me!"

Now he'd done it. "I'm really sorry, Jo. They just fell out. I didn't know they were tucked away in there."

She glared at him. "Guess I'll just have to do without them." Suddenly, she started laughing, apparently finding humor in the situation or perhaps hypothermia had set in and she was delusional. "I've never gone commando before!"

He joined her in a good laugh. "Are you warming up?"

"Yes, I am. You were right. I needed to get out of the wet clothes."

He stirred the soup heating beside the fire which was now blazing thanks to Jo's underwear. "Did you bring any other clothes?" he asked.

"For the fire?" she teased.

"No, to change into."

"No, did you?"

"No." They began laughing again, this time at their stupidity.

"That wasn't too bright of us was it?" she said, still giggling.

"No, it wasn't." TJ looked toward Cisco and Bonanza. "I'm going to lead the horses to the creek. Keep warm, the soup is almost hot. I'll be right back."

Josephine shook her head, still surprised by her lack of foresight. She should have known there would be a chance of rain or snow and thought to bring at least one change of clothes, but the excitement of catching up with TJ to find their parents had rendered her brainless. She just hoped they had enough wood to keep the fire going all night, or at least until their clothes dried.

But she was even more surprised by TJs blunder. Having made numerous hunting trips into the mountains with his dad, he should have been better prepared. They may have made light of the situation, but she imagined TJ knew as well as she did or more so, how serious this situation could turn any moment.

TJ returned with their saddles and pads. Setting the saddles on end next to each other, he formed a wall at the back of the shelter. He then covered the remaining hole at the back with pine boughs. Bonanza's pad made a functional makeshift door at the front, sealing off that end.

"How is Bo's foot?" she asked, peeking out.

"A few small chips, but nothing to worry about. He's fine. They're enjoying their grain."

Josephine wasn't sure if what she heard was rain coming down or just droplets blowing from the trees onto the tarp. "Is it raining again?" she asked, concerned about the fire and her clothes.

"No, seems to have stopped for now. Sure is cold, though." TJ looked down at himself. "I'm going to need to dry my clothes, too, Jo," he said. "Turn around."

"You're shy?" she teased.

"Just trying to be a gentleman, but..." TJ began stripping in front of her, starting with his shirt.

"Theodore James!"

"You can turn away… if you want to… or not."

"In your dreams," she snapped back. Pulling her sleeping bag over her head and curling in a ball, she tried to erase the image of TJ's manly russet-colored bare chest and his jeans resting low on his hips exposing his chiseled eight-pack. When she finally came to her senses, she realized she had both bedrolls in with her.

She yelled out to him. "TJ, you're going to freeze to death out there."

"I unfolded my saddle blanket; it's mostly dry."

"Good. I don't need my guide coming down with pneumonia," she joked.

"Thanks, glad you're so concerned." He said, sarcastically.

Josephine scooted over to the opening to peer out at TJ

who sat on a log watching over their clothes and the fire, wearing his hat, boots, jacket, and Cisco's Navajo saddle blanket wrapped around his middle.

"Seriously, I don't know what I would have done out here without you," she said in a more serious tone.

TJ nodded, giving her a sideways smirk.

"Soup hot?" she asked.

He stirred the Campbell's can and carefully tested the chicken noodle soup with a spoon on his Swiss Army knife contraption. "Dinner is served!" He handed her the can wrapped in what was left of the towel she shredded along with his knife sticking out of it.

Starved, she eagerly ate half the can. "Yum, good and hot."

TJ looked at her funny.

"What? I'll leave you some; don't worry."

"No, eat all you want." TJ shook his head. "I'm sorry, Jo. I should have escorted you home today."

"I'm okay—warm, dry, and fed."

TJ patted her clothes and turned them over to dry the other side. "We don't have much food left. I'll need to hunt tomorrow. And, if it snows…"

"We'll worry about that, if and when…"

TJ interrupted her. "Even if it doesn't snow, we don't have enough dry wood to keep a fire going all night."

"We're in this together, TJ. You and me. We'll be fine."

TJ stared into the fire. "Not to mention we'll most likely lose their tracks and even if we do manage to locate them again, who knows what we'll find or what we'll be riding into."

"Geez, Mr. Gloom and Doom here." She handed him the bottom half of the soup which he scarfed down.

"I'm just worried about you."

"Don't be. I'm fine, and I'm not sorry I came. No regrets, except I wish I'd grabbed some extra clothes and underwear," she snickered. "I'm sorry I didn't come better prepared."

"Yeah, me too." TJ smiled and nodded toward the back of the lean-to. "You need your rest; get some sleep."

"What about you?"

"I'm going keep the fire going as long as I can. Here, your clothes are mostly dry. Stuff them into the bottom of your sleeping bag, climb in and zip it up with only a small hole to breathe. And, hand me my bag."

Josephine followed his instructions and handed him his sleeping bag. "Good night, TJ."

"Good night, Jo."

18 – Snow

Wednesday

Josephine woke up in the middle of the night shivering. When she peeked out of the shelter, she was shocked to find a powdering of snow covering everything, including a lump next to the dead fire! "TJ!" she screamed, "Are you okay?"

Much to her relief the lump moved. TJ peeked out of his bag. "Shit!"

"I'm cold, TJ." Her speech slurred as she shook uncontrollably.

"Me too," he answered, his teeth chattering.

Large snowflakes fell in slow motion, illuminating the night nearly as bright as a full moon. It was beautiful but frightening at the same time. "What are we going to do, TJ? Are we going to die out here?"

TJ got up, having put his jeans back on, and shook the snow from his bag. "Get dressed, Jo, and come out."

Normally the one giving the orders in their relationship, it felt strange having TJ take control. But she had to admit, she liked it. Josephine quickly dressed into her warm clothes which felt wonderful, but once she stepped out of the shelter and into the wind, the chills returned.

"It's below freezing now and it's only going to get colder by daybreak," he said. "We need to consolidate our body heat. I'm going to zip our sleeping bags together."

It took a second for what he said to sink in. "We're going to sleep together?" she asked.

"Yes."

"Okay," she said warily. It made sense, but she felt anxious at the thought of sleeping nearly naked together. "I'm going check on the horses," she told TJ, when she needed to pee. She made quick work of that task, brushed the snow off the horses and led them to the creek for a drink. Her hands stung and nearly froze to the wet lead ropes as she led them back and tied them off again. She hastily patted Bonanza's neck and quickly returned to the shelter where she found TJ waiting for her inside.

Josephine slipped into their makeshift teepee, closing the saddle pad door behind her and removed her boots.

Her eyes were immediately drawn to his damp jeans lying on top of their combined bags. She could see he still wore his shirt and hoped he still had his drawers on under there.

Josephine slipped off her coat and rolled it up, inside out, to use as a pillow as TJ had. "Turn around," she said. "Thanks to a pyromaniac, I don't have anything on under these jeans." TJ smiled and turned away.

Again, following his lead, Josephine pulled off her damp jeans and laid them out over the bed to dry. Nervously, she scooted in beside him wearing only her shirt, leaving as much space between them as the bags would allow and zipped up her side. Immediately, she began to feel warmer in the close confines of the shared space.

For the longest time, they just laid on their backs in the dark. staring at the snow collecting on the tarp above.

Eventually, TJ broke the silence. "The snow will help insulate us," he said, releasing puffs of vapor into the frigid night air.

"TJ?"

"Yeah?"

"You know you're my best friend, right?"

TJ turned his head to within inches of her face. "Sure. And,

I think you know how I feel about you."

Josephine smiled. "Yes, TJ, I know. The whole world knows."

TJ turned away, once again facing the ceiling. "Can you ever be serious? Everything doesn't need to be a joke."

"I'm sorry, TJ. I didn't mean to make fun of you. You're right. I think sometimes when I'm afraid of something, I make a joke about it instead. Like now." Josephine turned to face him. "I'm scared… I'm scared we won't wake up in the morning… and if we do, I'm scared we'll get lost. And if we do find our parents, I'm scared of what we'll find."

TJ turned to face her. "No matter what happens, I'll take care of you, Jo. I promise."

"I know you will." Josephine tried to fight it but gave into the urge to lean in and give him a peck on the cheek, warming her from the inside.

Smiling, he gently swept some loose hairs from her face, but this time she liked it and found his hand and clasped it. He squeezed back, reassuring her. Being close to TJ felt different. In place of the butterflies she felt earlier, she now felt a yearning to get closer to TJ, in an intimate way. She slid beside him… so close she could feel the warmth of his breath on her face and the heat of his body beside her. In the dim light, she could just make out the questioning expression in his dark brown eyes.

Josephine parted her lips and nodded invitingly. TJ didn't hesitate, cradling her face in his hands as he slowly brushed his lips against hers. Like a tuning fork, electric sensations reverberated through her body. TJ must have felt it too because he suddenly kissed her passionately, igniting desires she didn't know existed. Needing to slow things down, Josephine rolled back onto her back and realized she knew everything there was to know about TJ except one thing.

"Have you ever… you know?" she asked.

TJ hesitated. "No."

"Really?" She thought all boys had sex in high school.

"I know, it's pretty lame."

"No, TJ, it's sweet."

TJ's eyes smiled. "And you?"

"Me neither."

"Really, all those boyfriends?"

"I was waiting for it to feel right. I wanted it to be special, with someone special… like you, TJ."

TJ couldn't believe what he was hearing. A million prayers had been answered in four words, "someone special like you." Covered in snow, on top of a mountain in the freezing cold, he finally got to kiss the love of his life, and she wanted more.

He kissed her again, this time exploring her mouth with his tongue, as he cautiously caressed her breast, ready to retreat at her slightest hesitation. His heart sank when she pulled away and sat up.

TJ watched in amazement as Josephine slowly unbuttoned her blouse and slipped it off her shoulders, her nipples standing erect in the cold night air. She was lovelier than he could have imagined.

"You're beautiful," he whispered.

She began unbuttoning his shirt, but TJ couldn't wait and finished the job himself, then stuffed both their shirts into the sleeping bag to keep them warm.

"It's still cold," Josephine giggled, slipping back into the sleeping bag. After his briefs joined their other garments at the bottom of their warm cocoon, he held the woman of his dreams lying naked beside him.

Time stood still for Josephine as TJ delicately traced the

outline of her face with his fingertips. She closed her eyes, listening to the unspoken language of love in his touch. It told her all she needed to know. When she opened her eyes and looked into his, she saw her beauty in his mahogany pools. One tender kiss set off a spontaneous flurry of kisses, each wetter and deeper than the last, until they lost all inhibition and bravely explored each other's secret places.

Josephine clasped her hands around TJ's neck and drew him to her as he hovered over her. As he took her, she yelped in pain but only for an instant. The excitement and ecstasy that followed turned the discomfort to a vague memory. Every fiber of her being lost its distinction as they meshed into one. She was certain nothing had been or ever would be as perfect again. TJ fulfilled her in every way. This had to be love!

Suddenly, TJ rolled off her. "No, don't stop," she moaned between rapid breaths.

"I have to," he said.

It took her a moment to understand his meaning. "Of course," she said. Again, TJ was looking after her, taking the necessary precautions. "Hold me, TJ. Never let me go."

Without another word, Josephine rested her head on his chest, safe and warm in his arms, listening to the rhythmic beats of his pure heart. She felt at peace and prayed they would survive this ordeal. Now there was so much more to live for… to be with TJ forever.

Billy woke up in the middle of the night to find their fire smoldering beneath a fresh powdering of snow that had blown in on them. He slid out of his bag, pulled on his boots, and went to collect more wood. When he returned, Katherine was awake and rekindling the fire with her reserve of dry pine needles and cones she had collected and wisely stashed in a crevice out of the elements.

"You were right," she said. "You do have a nose for snow."

"Unfortunately." He hoped they wouldn't get too many more inches.

"Have you seen Laddy?"

"No, he's probably curled up with a she-wolf someplace."

Billy dragged the dead sapling near the fire and began chopping it into pieces, tossing the first two on the fire.

"Did you get any sleep?" she asked.

"A bit—how about you?"

"I passed out and only woke up because I got cold after you got up."

"Sorry about that."

Billy took a seat next to Katherine beside the fire. They sat quietly with their own thoughts for several minutes before she surprised him with a question, no doubt a remnant of their brief conversation earlier.

"The kiss and hug in the post office parking lot… what was that all about?" she asked, studying him hard. "Be honest."

"Testing the waters, I suppose."

Katherine chuckled. "You're such a scoundrel."

"Yep, that's me, alright—once a scoundrel, always a scoundrel." Billy figured he had nothing to lose at this point and decided to put it all out there. "When you wanted to spend that much time together, I'll admit I thought maybe…?

"What, that we'd have an affair… again?

"Okay, now it's your turn to be honest. Tell me you didn't feel something that day at the post office?"

"That was years ago," she stalled. Katherine's focus dropped to her lap. Of all nights, of all situations, he deserved to know the truth tonight. She looked into his questioning eyes. "Yeah, I felt something. I'm still a woman, you know. I don't have one foot in the grave yet."

"Oh, I know that for a fact."

Katherine shook her head. "I'm sorry, I didn't mean to lead you on. I never intended on anything happening. I knew we'd make a great team training Major. And, I will admit, I do enjoy the flirting and attention."

Billy's eyes glistened in the firelight. "How about in the parking lot the other night?"

Katherine stood up, but there was nowhere to run, nowhere to hide. She fiddled with her hair, curling it around her finger like she did as a girl, and nervously brushed off her jeans. Just thinking about their kiss and Billy's groin pressing hard against her made her face hot, even in the freezing temperatures. She didn't dare answer him honestly this time and she didn't want to lie to him either. Following a nervous lap around the fire, she sat back down without a word.

Billy wrapped his arm around her and whispered in her ear. "I knew the answer. I just wanted to hear you say it, but I guess you did by not saying anything."

Katherine turned to face him. "You could have sex with me right now, couldn't you, without so much as an ounce of guilt?"

"Why should I feel guilty? My feelings are true. I don't just want to have sex with you, Kat. It's always been more than that. God, you should know that by now, but if that's all I can get, I'll take it."

"That's not how it is for me, Billy—not anymore. Yes, you can arouse me. I'm a mess right now trying to control my desires."

"Why, life is too short, and it seems to be feeling shorter every minute lately."

"It's not happening."

He took her by the hand. "Okay, I give up. Then just lay

with me one last time, Kat. No funny business, I promise. I'll keep you warm."

Katherine smiled. It seemed harmless enough since they were both clothed and they now knew where each other stood. She could give him that much after having flirted and led him on for months just to satisfy her own selfish ego and to feel young again, not to mention the guilt that lingered following his comment about her making the choice for them both.

"Okay," she whispered.

The expression in Billy eyes nearly made her cry. He opened his sleeping bag to make room for her. With only enough space to lay on her side, she slid in front of him facing the fire. Katherine closed her eyes as Billy gently closed his arms around her.

For a moment it was 1960 again and she pictured them lying on the floor of the old cabin together, drained from having spent every ounce of energy in their lovemaking. Even though she had tried to deny it to herself for years, they had been very much in love and perhaps they still were. But she believed with all her heart what she had told Billy—that she belonged with Steven, she always had and always would.

As she began to douse off, Laddy approached them from out of the shadows, cold and damp. She guessed he needed some comfort and warmth, too. Shocking her, he curled up at their feet. Katherine drifted off to sleep, warm and safe, the dangers that tomorrow held put to rest for the night. For the first time in days, she felt at peace.

19 – Reflection

Wednesday – Thursday

Steven woke up at daybreak in his small one-person tent covered with a dusting of snow. The skies had cleared, but he could see the higher elevations had received more snow overnight, and he worried for Josephine and TJ. He had packed well, prepared for the worst weather, and brought extra provisions for the kids, knowing they were most likely not as equipped.

Steven didn't take time to eat. He quickly mounted Dandy, who had grazed all night, and resumed following their trail while eating a biscuit and elk jerky as he rode. He made up time trotting when the footing allowed and cantered across open fields. He felt confident he had gained ground on them. Thankfully, he could still follow their signs.

He searched the skies and listened for the chopper. Steven wished he could communicate with Mike and Dane to let them know their course. He prayed he would be seen and get the opportunity to point them in the right direction, a steady northeast course.

As he rode, he had plenty of time to dwell on the events of the past few days and the current possibilities. He felt confident his wife and best friend hadn't run off together, but they had been thrust into an extremely stressful situation where the opportunity to seek comfort in each other's arms would be tempting. Had they made love these past few nights together?

If that wasn't enough, there were the kids. He was worried

sick about his little girl on the mountain in the rain and snow without shelter. She had never shown any interest in camping or going on hunting trips and would be unprepared for such a situation. Thank goodness she was with TJ. Then he got to thinking about those possibilities. He knew TJ has had a crush on Jo forever. She had never returned his sentiments but, again, under these circumstances, who knew what might develop.

Katherine had discouraged Josephine from dating Blackfeet boys, for obvious reasons, and Jo had never shown any interest in doing so anyway. She hung with the popular white kids, none of whom had anything to do with Blackfeet students at school. He had seen firsthand how segregated the student body was at school events and competitions. He didn't like it, yet it was most likely for the best considering Josephine's safety.

Two decades following the night at Rudy's, relations between the two races appeared to have improved, but the abhorrence could still be heard, felt, and seen. Chief kept him abreast of the continuing random hate crimes perpetrated against both races. He wondered if it would ever change or end. But, so long as the hatred continued, he would worry for his daughter. A beautiful girl from what most would consider a rich family, by Blackfeet standards, made her a prime target.

TJ had looked after his daughter her whole life and he was thankful for that, but he hoped they remained only friends, nothing more. Katherine felt even stronger about it after what she had been through, all the direct result of a white girl and a Blackfeet boy kissing in public. Perhaps someday people of all colors and race might accept each other and their differences, but that day hadn't come yet—not in Montana anyway. He would try not to dwell on the possibilities; their safety came first.

When the wooded area opened to a large field, Steven got his first glance of the forest-fire smoke billowing in the distance and detected the slightest scent of smoke. Steven cued Dandy for a canter and followed the well-beaten path through the tall grass.

As Roy navigated the helicopter north along the stream running from Two Ponies toward Glacier, Mike could see the forest-fire smoke plume on the horizon across the border. "Sure hope they get it under control soon."

"I heard they lost some ground with the stronger winds," said Roy, as he fought to keep the aircraft steady.

Dane studied the wall of smoke. "Looks big. We couldn't see a thing yesterday with all the cloud cover."

"Okay, get your glasses out. We're close to where we turned back yesterday when the storm hit," said Roy.

Dane pulled his binoculars from their case. "They got snow last night."

Mike studied the range from the front of the chopper, seated beside Roy. He knew the kids might be in trouble and wondered if Search and Rescue might get involved now that it snowed. He would give them another try later if they didn't find the kids today. If only they could locate Steve, he might be able to narrow their search.

"Roy, let's focus on the open areas and make two passes over each. If Steve's in the area, he'll try his best to make himself visible so he can let us know which way they're headed."

Roy turned the chopper toward the first opening he saw. "Good idea. We have only three hours of fuel before we'll need to return and refuel. Let's make every minute count."

Billy had woken Katherine up at daybreak to get an early start down the mountain. Already, the snow was melting from the sun and made for slick and unsure footing. To avoid any injury to the horses, he took a gentle serpentine path on their descent. By noon, about halfway down, they had ridden out of the snow altogether and the skies had cleared revealing a wall of smoke on the horizon to the north. They had heard about the fire over the radio on their drive from California, but at that time it had been reported mostly contained. For the first time the slightest smell of smoke could be detected. Billy wasn't worried, yet. Several times over the years smoke had reached them from fires that never threatened the region.

When they came upon a good observation point with a clear view of the valley and river below, Billy stopped to rest. He pulled out his binoculars and searched the river basin from the south, looking northward for a creek emptying into it from the east beside a ridge.

"Come here, Kat."

Katherine rode up beside him and he handed her the field glasses. Billy pointed a distance north of them. "Follow the river up the valley. Do you see the first line of brush running perpendicular to the river?"

"Yes," she said.

"That's our creek. That's our meeting spot."

"How long a ride, do you think?"

"We'll camp at the base of the mountain tonight then cross the river first thing in the morning. We'll want to be fresh and have our wits about us."

Katherine just nodded.

Billy could see the fear returning to her eyes. "We've got this."

Katherine patted Major's neck for more reassurance. As she followed Billy's path, she began talking to her horse. It had always helped to calm her nerves on course at events and it seemed to help now as they rode toward danger. As Katherine shared her thoughts with Major, she kept pace with Red but far back enough so Billy couldn't hear. She told Major about her first visit to Two Ponies, how she came to love her Uncle Joe and Betsy, the life lessons they had taught her, and best of all, learning to ride on Flower.

Around noon they stopped to graze the horses and eat a little lunch. Katherine hardly ate, having little appetite. They shared the last can of tuna fish in silence. She imagined this was how soldiers felt the day before combat. They were going into battle—a war waged against them because of race and indifferences and consequences out of their control. The more she thought about it, the more insane it all seemed. She just wanted it to be over and to return home.

Josephine woke up to the chatter of a Canadian Jay. Lying naked beside TJ, she remained still for a few minutes, just enjoying his warm breath on the nape of her neck and his masculine scent. She wanted to wake him and make love again, but she knew they needed their strength for whatever lay ahead. She was happy to see the sun filtering through the hole at the back of their shelter and that she could no longer see her breath. She felt certain combining the sleeping bags had saved their lives, thanks to TJ.

Slowly, she turned to face him. "Hey, sleepyhead," she whispered. "It's morning and the sun is out."

TJ smiled. "God, you're beautiful."

Josephine returned his smile. "You were magnificent last night."

"Wow, magnificent?"

Josephine blushed. "I think I'm falling in love with you, TJ."

"If you're falling, I crashed and shattered into a million pieces years ago." TJ kissed her. "I've loved you for as long as I can remember."

Josephine cocked her head. "What do you think our parents will say?"

"Do we have to tell them?"

"I tell my mom everything. And, why not? We didn't do anything wrong. We're legal consenting adults."

"You're too funny. They're not going to approve, and you know it. Neither will your friends."

"I don't care about my friends. And, our folks… will it matter?"

"No."

"Well, it's settled then. We'll tell them."

"Okay, but we have to find them first. Let's get up and get going." TJ reached to the bottom of the bag and pulled out their clothes.

"It's going to be cold."

"Not as cold as last night."

They both dressed quickly and put their coats and boots on before opening the front of the lean-to.

"The sun feels good," said Josephine. "Look, the snow is melting."

TJ took his watch from his pocket. "Shoot, Jo, we slept until almost ten!"

"What? We better get moving. We have some jerky left. Will that be enough for you this morning?"

"Guess it'll have to be."

Bonanza, nickered. "We need to graze the horses, TJ."

"Give them the last of the grain this morning, and we'll graze them this afternoon. I'm anxious to find their tracks."

After they had everything packed, Josephine slid on behind TJ, Cisco once again leading the way with Bonanza close behind. They were delighted to come across their parents' tracks about an hour later and even more thrilled to find they were easier to follow in the muddy footing, saving valuable time.

That afternoon, they stopped at a grassy area beside a small stream and let the horses graze while TJ hunted. Josephine stood running her fingers through Bonanza's tail that had collected a few burrs and small branches. As she worked at a knot, she fantasized about marrying TJ someday, after school perhaps. But then she got to thinking about where they would live.

To become an actress, she needed to live in LA. She tried to picture TJ living in a big city and just shook her head and started in on Bonanza's mane that had curled into dreads in the wind. She concluded if TJ loved her as much as he said he did, he would follow her anywhere.

She heard two shots fired and shortly afterward, TJ showed up proudly carrying his kill—two scrawny squirrels. Josephine gave him a pathetic look.

"That's all I could find, they're good eating and they'll cook quick," he said, defending his role as provider. "Look at what else I found!" TJ set the squirrels down and pulled a rolled-up piece of aspen bark from his pocket. "Follow me."

Josephine traced his steps to Cisco where TJ unrolled the thin piece of bark, revealing red and cooper colored pastes. "I found the last of some berries and a mineral deposit by the creek." With his finger he painted a red circle around Cisco's right eye. "This will give us alert vision," he said, then he ran two brown squiggly lines across his rump. "Power and speed." Mixing the remainder of the paint he coated his hand and made orange imprints on his horse's shoulders. "These represent the enemy we will conquer." TJ stepped back to admire his work. "Now we're ready to ride into battle!"

TJ tied his kill together by their tails and hung them over Cisco's withers in front of the saddle, mounted and pulled out his compass. "Let's go," he said, helping her climb aboard.

As they resumed their northeast trajectory, Josephine tried not to look at the poor little creatures bouncing on Cisco's shoulders as they trotted along. She had always found excuses to not join her parents on fishing or hunting trips; she just didn't have the heart for it. Again, the idea of TJ adapting to city life seemed doubtful. She pictured entertaining guests with TJ cooking squirrel on the grill.

They made good time all morning until they lost their parents' trail again when the footing turned to mostly surface rock.

"Now what, TJ?"

"We'll keep heading the same direction. Hopefully, we'll pick them up again."

When Jake and Kyle rode up emptyhanded for lunch, Ricky ran out to meet them at the coral. "No sign of them?"

Jake shook his head and dismounted.

Kyle sat on his almighty horse with a stupid smirk on his face. "What are you grinning about, Tick?"

"Maybe they're not coming," said Kyle. "Maybe they really did just run off together."

Ricky sneered at the dimwit. "They know better. They'll show up." Ricky turned and noticed Andy had joined them.

"How long are we going to wait?" asked Andy. "They should have been here yesterday. I think we should just divvy up the money and head for the border in the Jeep. I started smelling smoke last night. We don't know how far off the fire is now." Andy pointed to the range beyond. "And look, it snowed up there last night. It could snow in the valley any time."

"You sound like a bunch of old women. We're not going anywhere. They'll show; I guarantee it. Besides, if the fire gets closer or we get a lot of snow, like you said, we have the Jeep if we need it."

Kyle slung his leg over his horse and slid off. "I'm not leaving Strawberry!"

"Fine, you can ride out if you want, Tick. You and that nag of yours can roast or freeze for all I care. But, if any of you want your split, you'll hold tight." Ricky turned back to Jake. "Ride back out after lunch and plan on staying until just before dark."

"Sure, as soon as I get some chow," said Jake, leaning his shotgun against the fence before leading the way to the cabin door. Ricky patted his friend on the back. He knew he could count on Jake.

That afternoon Katherine picked up where she left off, sharing her life story with Major, his ears flicking back and forth as she spoke, now at more of a whisper. She reminisced about showing Lady and her adventure moving West, skimming over the year she fell in love with the two amazing men in her life and the pain and tragedy that followed. Katherine moved on to telling stories about her favorite school horses over the years, including how she found Stormy, about Texas and his tricks, and how little Dusty saved all the horses from the barn fire.

By late afternoon, she barely had a voice, but felt driven to complete her story. Hearing it out loud somehow made it all more real. Sometimes much of her past seemed lifetimes ago, almost like it happened to someone else. As she tired, she eventually included some of her painful memories, many of the recollections bringing tears to her eyes. She recalled her Uncle Joe's funeral, the night Steven found her and Billy together, the night she watched Billy walk into Pine Island Lake, and the loss of her two beautiful babies.

To lift herself back up, she returned to the rich and happy times of her life, which brought happy tears. She smiled recalling the first day she met Steven and their swim in the lake and the day she found Billy breaking the black colt by the dam, and later her wedding day and the birth of their perfect little girl. By the time they reached the river, she felt exhausted, as much from the emotional roller coaster ride as she did from traversing the mountain.

Billy looked as spent as she felt, guessing he had been doing a lot of thinking, too. What else was there to do? The horses grazed and Laddy rested in the shade as they made camp for the night at the base of the range not far from the river. Billy easily speared a couple of exhausted Kokanee Salmon as they fought their way upstream to spawn and cooked them in foil over the fire. They were delicious and Laddy seemed particularly fond of their pink flesh as well. The horses feasted on the abundant sweet grass and clover along the river bank.

For a moment Katherine set their mission aside and allowed herself to admire the stunning view laid out before her. Highlighted by the amber slanted rays of the low-setting sun, the still vibrant green valley, sprinkled with fall blue-and-gold wildflowers, converged on the wavering river which seemed undecided whether it should rush or take its time finding its way to the sea. A patchwork of golden aspen interspersed with stands of Ponderosa pine framed the gorge in the shadow of snow-covered peaks. If she survived this ordeal, she would love to return to this spot with Steven and Josephine one summer, if she could get her daughter to agree to camp for a few nights. She smiled at the thought of it.

With no sign of rain, they placed their bags on the open ground beside the fire and climbed into them for the night.

Laddy laid beside her and for the first time he allowed her to pet him for more than an instant. While Katherine ran her fingers through his thick coat, she studied the heavens sparkling above, pointing out the North Star and the Big Dipper to Billy.

"Do you believe in heaven?" she asked him.

He didn't answer right away. "You mean, do I believe in God?"

"Something after this."

"Yes, I believe in a spirit world. I am half-Blackfeet, remember."

"Your mom was a Christian, and your parents were married in a church."

"That was my dad's concession to earn my mother's hand." Billy rolled onto his side to face her. "In all the years we've known each other, this is the first time we've had this conversation."

"About time, don't you think?"

"Yeah, of all times, you picked a good one." Billy studied her. "How about you?"

"Yes, I believe there's a heaven where everyone you've loved and lost are waiting for you, all your pets, too."

"Now there, we're in agreement. I believe all creatures great and small—the sacred *naahks*, as the Blackfeet call them—cross over to the spirit world. Animals have a pure spirit; it's man who must prove his worthiness. I was taught that we're all children of the creator, designed to serve one another in this world and in the next."

"That's lovely, Billy," she said, smiling. "I can just picture Flower, Lady, and Shane running to greet me and my Uncle Joe and my Dad will be waiting for me. I know my Dad has been watching over me."

"That is a nice thought to hold onto," he said.

"No, I really believe it. I don't know if I ever told you, but the night you returned with Steven, when you saw me on the dock, I was so depressed and ready to give up on my life until something brushed over my head. It felt like when my dad used to stroke my hair before kissing me on the top of my head as a child. I believe it was him, reaching out to save me that night."

"You never mentioned that part before," said Billy, still sounding guilt-ridden after thirty years for having left her at the dock that night. "I talk to my dad sometimes," he said.

"Me too, and my Uncle Joe."

In the firelight Katherine could make out a tear running down Billy's cheek.

"What is it Billy?"

"If there is a heaven or a spirit world," he whispered, "I don't think they'll be letting me in after what I did."

"Oh, Billy, that was in self-defense."

"Not Kurt… my first son, William, Jr.," he whispered. "If I hadn't been using drugs, he would be alive today."

Katherine leaned on her elbow cradling her head. She could see Billy's eyes glistening in the firelight "You don't know that. Babies die of SIDS for no reason at all. You're a good man, Billy, and a great father to TJ."

"Not so great in the husband department, though, ha?"

"I have no room to talk," she said. "We're both blessed to have such loving and forgiving partners."

As Billy leaned over to place another log on the fire, something reflected the firelight around his neck. It was the beaded choker Sarah had given him.

Katherine gleamed. "Good night, Billy."

"Good night, Kat."

Sleep did not come as easy that night for Katherine with the unknown future looming over them larger than the star-studded sky above. Just before she closed her eyes, a shooting star darted across the heavens. She recalled the night after the barn raising, lying on a pile of shingle bags between Steven and Billy and making a wish upon a fallen star. She had wished the three of them would remain best friends forever. It took years for her wish to eventually become true again. Tonight, she wished for their safe return to their families. *Take care of us, Daddy.*

Following their late start, TJ didn't stop for a break all morning. After topping the mountain, they were able to pick up their parents' tracks again. When they stopped at a clearing to graze the horses, he searched the river basin below with his binoculars for any sign of their parents but had no luck. He did notice the growing smoke flume to the north. "Can you smell smoke?" he asked Josephine.

"Yeah, a little."

"Look," he said, pointing north.

Josephine joined him. "Hope it doesn't come this way," she said.

"Me too."

Riding nonstop again that afternoon, TJ finally stopped at dusk to make camp in a stand of pine. "Do you want to combine the bags again tonight?" he asked, hoping Josephine would say yes. "As clear as it is, it'll get even colder than last night."

"Sure. I'd like that."

He smiled and pointed. "There's a good spot. While you make our bed, I'll find some wood for a fire so we can cook the squirrels. I'm starved."

"Me too," she said. "I could eat a porcupine."

TJ laughed. "Maybe tomorrow."

When he returned, Josephine had run a line for the horses,

made their bed under the trees and gathered a pile of kindling ready for the fire. "Good job!"

"I'm getting the hang of this wilderness stuff," she said, yet when it came time for dressing the squirrels, she quickly disappeared to water the horses.

TJ had done plenty of thinking about their future together over the course of the day and ended up with more questions than answers. Neither of them had brought up her leaving for school again. Would she ask him to move out there with her? Would he, if she asked?

He had never been to California or seen the ocean. It seemed like it would be fun place to visit, but he couldn't see himself living there. His dad always came home with stories about the terrible traffic, smog, and the characters he met with blue hair, tattoos, and body piercings. Sounded more like a different planet than just a different state. The more he thought about it, the more impossible it seemed.

Jo would most likely leave, meet some rich, educated guy, and it would be over. No way could he ever compete with that. He considered ending it then, but he wasn't ready to give up on his dream just yet. TJ loved her more than life itself. For tonight, he would cherish what might be their final hours together. He felt certain they would catch up with their parents the next day.

When Kyle returned with Jake at dusk following another uneventful day waiting by the river, he cleaned Strawberry's hooves and brushed her pink coat until it shined like a polished gem. He was glad he had thought to pack some grooming supplies before they left Andy's. He had become very attached to the mare in just a few days. After all, Strawberry was a dream come true. His parents and later Jake never allowed him to have a single pet, let alone his own horse because of the cost to maintain them. But now he was about to acquire more money than he ever thought possible. He would have as many animals as he wanted.

He didn't like their chatter about leaving the horses and taking off with the Jeep. Kyle would not leave Strawberry or the other horses to die in the fire or starve over the winter. He might not be the sharpest tool in the shed, as Jake always liked to say, but he had come up with his own plans to ensure no harm came to Katherine or the horses, even to her Indian friend, if they ever did show up.

Kyle hoped they had run off together. That would be the easier of his two plans. When Ricky finally gave up on them showing up, Kyle would sneak out before daylight with all the money, turn all the horses loose and lead them across the border with him riding Strawberry. Ricky, Jake, and Andy would be left with nothing and no way to chase him.

If the couple did show up, he would help them escape. They would ride off home and again he would leave with all the money and horses. He was brilliant! He would get back at Ricky and Jake and save everyone at the same time. He would be a real hero like in the Westerns he loved to watch.

"What you smiling about, Tick?" asked Ricky, who had sneaked up behind him in the dark. "Dinner's ready. Leave that damn horse alone; it won't have any hair left by the time you're done with it."

Kyle followed Ricky into the cabin, still smiling.

It was late by the time Dane rolled up to his house after dropping Roy off at Chief's. The lights were still on and he knew Jessie would be waiting up to hear the latest.

His wife met him at the door. "Any luck?"

"Nope. They got snow in the high country last night."

"I hope the kids are okay. I know Billy and Katherine were

prepared."

"We'll go out again first thing in the morning. We're expanding our search zone north toward the border."

Jessie brought Dane a plate of leftover lasagna. "Here, eat. Tomorrow's going to be the day, isn't it?"

"By our best estimate, Kat and Billy should be meeting up with Ricky and his partners sometime tomorrow."

"What on earth were they thinking? At first, I was relieved they didn't run off together. Then when I began to think about the alternative, I wish they had."

Dane inhaled his dinner, having eaten only the sandwich she had packed him all day. "I just hope the kids have lost their tracks and don't catch up with them."

"Me too. Here Kat and Billy are risking their lives for the safety of their families and the kids could be riding right into trouble along with them. It's all so crazy."

Downing his last bite, Dane moved to the couch and opened a beer Jessie had set down for him. "My dad said there's a good chance Search and Rescue will send their chopper out tomorrow, too."

Jessie sat beside him and rested her head on his shoulder. "About time."

Dane wrapped his arm around her. "They do good work, hon. They're mostly volunteers and they can't send a team out unless they know someone is in danger or injured."

"I suppose. They just don't know all we know about the situation."

"That's what my dad is trying to do—fill them in to help sway them."

Jessie tuned the television to the news. "The fires were still pretty far north of that region, the last I heard," she said.

The couple waited for an update and were shocked to learn the wind had shifted and the fire now reached just northeast of Glacier National Park and was burning south east.

Dane slammed his beer down, spraying the table. "Shit, just when you think things couldn't get any worse!"

Chief sat with Roy in his family room switching between the news and weather channels, monitoring the fire. "If the fire continues to spread south, can we still take the chopper out?"

"Depends on the direction of the plume," said Roy.

"I'll bet Mike isn't having any luck getting Search and Rescue to join in the hunt, not now. They'll need to keep their choppers and men available in case that fire reaches the border tomorrow."

"You're probably right."

"Dang, they all could be riding into an inferno." Chief got up and walked to his liquor cabinet that appeared to be an old wood whiskey barrel until he opened it. "I need a drink. Care to join me for a brandy?"

"Don't mind if I do."

Chief removed a decanter and poured two glasses. "I'm going to see what I can do from the ground tomorrow. There are several trails leading into that area off Highway 89. Maybe I can locate that black Jeep. My truck has a radio."

"Great, we can keep in touch. Let's pick a channel now."

"Let's use frequency fifty-five," said Chief.

"Got it. If this fire does move south, I might be joining you. I feel I have an investment in their safe return now," said Roy. "Tell me more about this couple and the two families."

"How late you want to stay up? It's a doozy of a story!"

"I've been so geared up I haven't been sleeping well anyway."

"Me too." Chief began at the beginning, the night at Rudy's and, an hour or so later, wrapped up with Ricky getting out of prison and his plan to take revenge on Katherine and Billy.

"Wow, that is quite a story," said Roy. "I hope it'll have a happy ending."

"Me too. These folks are like family."

Josephine woke to TJ whispering in her ear. "Get up, Jo. We need to get an early start."

She found herself lying on her side, her head resting on TJ's bare chest, their legs intertwined. She didn't want to leave the warmth and safety of his arms. The sensation of their lovemaking the night before still lingered.

She rested on her elbow, studying his smiling eyes, then raised her eyebrows and gave him a mischievous grin.

TJ shook his head. "No, we need to get up and get going so we can gain some ground."

Josephine pouted for a moment, wondering when they would have the opportunity to be together again. That thought was immediately pushed aside when TJ mentioned he was certain they would catch up with their parents that day.

"Okay," she said, settling for a kiss.

The horses had been individually line-tied during the night and able to graze. They had no more grain for them. Following a drink from a nearby spring, they packed and mounted and began their remaining trek down the mountain before daybreak.

Josephine closed her eyes and leaned her head against TJ's back as they swayed in unison to the horse's slow four-beat gait as they carefully descended in the early morning haze. She listened to the forest awakening around her—the dew dripping from the tree bows, the early morning chatter of jays, and the bustling of squirrels preparing for winter.

She checked on Bonanza regularly, keeping pace behind them. She would have enjoyed riding her boy the duration of their search but snuggling with TJ was nice, too. If the circumstances were different, she would be thoroughly enjoying their adventure, besides nearly freezing to death. She now regretted declining all the invitations by her parents to join them on camping and hunting trips. Now she just prayed she would get the opportunity to join them someday, maybe even return to this mountain and the beautiful river valley below.

California seemed so distant to her now. She recalled how exciting their visit to the campus had been last year, seeing the ocean for the first time and visiting the attractions in Hollywood —Universal Studios, the Chinese Theatre, and Walk of Fame. But now her excitement and anticipation had dulled. For the first time she realized how much she would miss her family, Two Ponies, Bonanza, and now TJ, more than ever. Doubts about leaving and becoming an actress crept into her mind and heart. She needed her mom and one of their heart-to-heart talks. A tear escaped as she wondered if she would see her again.

20 – The River

Thursday

Katherine woke up to a warm sensation on her face. Peering through the small opening in her mummy bag, she found Laddy hovering over her trying to lick her through the hole.

"Good morning, boy." Sitting up, expecting to find Billy lying across from her, she was surprised to find the space bare. He must be packed up already, she thought.

Laddy whined and nuzzled her. "What boy? You hungry?" When she turned and found Red and Billy's saddle gone, she jumped to her feet in a panic. He wouldn't have left without her, would he?

Katherine ran for the river, catching Billy just before reaching the river bank. "Billy! What are you doing?" she yelled.

Billy just kept walking without acknowledging her presence.

"Stop, Billy!"

When he halted, he turned and locked eyes with her. "I'm going on without you."

"Katherine shook her head. "No, we're in this together, remember. This wasn't our plan!"

"It was never my plan to take you in."

Katherine was so angry she could barely see straight. "You said our best chance of getting to Ricky was with me as a decoy," she shrieked. "They're going to be waiting for you, Billy. If you show up without me, they'll just shoot you on the spot. Ricky wants me and only for you to watch. That means they'd keep us both alive until…"

"Until what, Kat? Until he rapes you?!" said Billy. "What if I didn't get an opportunity to break free, or what if they got trigger-happy and killed me right off anyway? I'm going to take them one by one, my way." Billy shook his head. "I overslept. I was supposed be long gone before you woke up."

"So, you've been lying to me this whole time? How dare you treat me like a child!" Katherine walked in front of him, the pieces beginning to fall into place. "Oh, I see. Was it also your plan from the beginning to try to take advantage of me in a weakened state?"

Billy reined Red around her to the bank of the river.

"You are a dirty rotten scoundrel, Billy Black!" she screamed.

"Go back to camp; wait for me there."

"No, you can't make me! I'm coming," she said, stomping off to get Major.

"No, you won't. Major won't cross. He was my insurance. Bye, Kat."

Billy kicked Red and off they leaped into the fast-moving river.

Katherine stood watching him cross the turbulent waters without turning back.

"No, he's not going to do this to me again! Leave me with all the guilt!" she told herself.

Katherine ran back to camp, saddled and bridled Major, leaving most of their supplies, and slung onto his back. By the time she returned to the river, Billy was out of sight.

Grimacing, she knew Billy had a point. Just standing near shore, Major felt on edge, obviously uncomfortable with the noise and movement of the raging water. "Well, let's see if we can prove him wrong, boy," she said, reining Major toward the bank. The big bay baulked and spun away at every effort.

"Oh, come on, boy. Red's over there. Don't you want to find your buddy?"

Then her focus switched to her canine companion, standing only feet away. If she could get Major to cross, would Laddy try to follow? Would he get swept away in the current? And, if they did make it across and Ricky or his gang spotted him—or worse yet, Laddy tried to protect her—they would shoot him for sure.

Katherine swallowed hard. She knew what she had to do.

She dismounted, picked up a rock and threw it at Laddy. "Go! Go away! Get out of here!" she screamed, flaying her arms.

Laddy just froze with a confused expression. She picked up two more rocks and through blurred vision flung them at him. The first one missed, but the second hit him on the rump. Laddy retreated a few strides, then turned and stopped, facing her again with a wounded expression, his tail between his legs. Tears rolled down her cheeks as she picked up more rocks and hurled them at him, ordering him to go. Finally, Laddy scooted off into the woods.

Katherine gathered herself and remounted; she must ford the river and catch up with Billy before the meeting spot. Again, Katherine prodded and pleaded with Major but he refused to step into the river. Determined, she kicked him harder than she ever had before. Major reared, nearly flipping over on her. She had only succeeded at stressing her horse to the point of panic.

She began desperately searching along the river for a better crossing point. Downriver about a half mile, the surface looked calmer; it had to be either deeper or shallower with fewer boulders. She would find out soon enough. It would cause her to fall behind Billy further, but it might be her only chance at getting the gelding across.

Major became more relaxed as she rode along shore, becoming accustomed to the sound of the fast rushing water.

As they got closer, it became obvious the river was shallower with a relatively level floor, like a water obstacle. Perfect!

"C'mon boy, piece of cake… you can do it!" she urged with her leg and seat. Major, placed one foot into the water, only to spin away again. Now he was just testing her.

Recalling how she got him to walk through his first puddle, she broke off a branch and returned to the best crossing point. As an ex-racehorse, Major understood and respected a crop. Katherine held him square between her legs and, with the crop in her left hand, she urged him forward with taps on his rump. Major planted all four feet, shook his head, and leaped into the water, nearly leaving Katherine behind. He hopped across the river like a stone skipping across the surface, until they reached the opposite shore. Again, she was thankful for that saddle horn.

"Good boy," she praised, patting him on the neck. Katherine pointed Major north and struck off at a canter after Billy.

Ricky had set his alarm and woke up Jake and Kyle before dawn to head to the meeting spot, feeling certain their guests would arrive that morning. Once they left, he peeked in on Andy who appeared sound asleep, so he went back to bed. They had all stayed up late drinking and playing cards the night before.

An hour later, Ricky woke up to take a piss, regretting he hadn't earlier when he saw the brothers off. Just as he rounded the back of the cabin, Ricky stopped and ducked behind the corner. Andy stood at the corral saddling his horse beside a pile of packed supplies. Ricky guessed he must have planned his little exit yesterday, remembering it was his idea to break out the cards and beer, guessing they would all be sleeping in.

Ricky tiptoed back into the cabin and checked the moneybags under his bed. Sure enough the cash was gone, and Andy had stuffed his bedroll on his cot to appear he was still asleep. Ricky tucked his eight-round Colt 1911 pistol under the back waistband of his jeans, covered it with his shirt and confronted Andy.

"Watcha doing, Andy?" he asked, shocking him. "I heard some noise; and thought I'd check on the horses."

"Sorry, Ricky, I didn't mean to wake you."

"I'm sure you didn't."

Andy gave him a questioning look. "I'm just riding out to check on the Jeep—make sure it's still covered and start it up. It's been sitting for days. We may need it."

"Is that a fact?" he said, slowly moving in Andy's direction.

Andy stood beside his horse now saddled but not fully packed. Nervously, he glanced down at his shotgun scabbard lying beside his saddlebags on the ground. "Yeah, you want to join me? Nice morning for a ride."

"And I suppose you'd want me to lead the way?" asked Ricky.

"If you wanted to." Andy stepped closer to the butt of his gun.

Ricky stopped about ten feet away. "Heck, we could take off and split the money just between the two of us. Kyle might be right; maybe they aren't coming."

"Now you're talking," said Andy, sounding revived. "Go get the money and I'll have your horse ready to go by the time you get back."

"But you already have the money, don't you, Andy?"

Andy threw himself to the ground and scrambled for his gun, but Ricky had his drawn and barreled down on him before he could position the shotgun to fire it.

"Real disappointed, Andy. I trusted you. Thought we were friends."

Two shots echoed through the valley.

Kyle jumped to his feet from his post on the ridge and yelled down to Jake hidden in the bushes. "Where did those shots come from?"

Jake appeared out of the brush. "Hard to tell."

"Might be some hunters."

"It's bow season, dummy. Come on down," his brother called to him.

Kyle carefully climbed from his observation point.

"They might have come from the cabin. Let's go check it out," said Jake.

"Ricky will be pissed if it's nothing and we left our posts."

Jake just strode past him toward the horses staked out upriver. Kyle followed him, hoping the shots were fired between Ricky and Andy. Maybe Ricky shot Andy, catching him running off with the money, or Andy shot Ricky and took off with the money and the Jeep. Kyle smiled at the thought of the latter. He didn't care as much about the money as he did the horses, and no harm would come to the woman.

But it was Ricky who exited the cabin to meet them.

"We heard shots," said Jake.

"That Andy, he was aiming to run out off with all the money," said Ricky, pointing to the rear of the cabin. "He's out back. Bury him in the cellar, so the animals don't dig him up, then head back down to the river."

Jake laughed. "That's awesome; we didn't need him anymore anyway. One less split. You heard him, Kyle; I think I saw a shovel in the cellar."

Kyle opened the two solid, heavy double doors leading to

the cellar on the back side of the cabin. Jake helped him drag the corpse in, instructed him where to dig and left. Kyle jammed the shovel into the floor of the cellar and stood looking at Andy's face that was beyond recognition. Perhaps he would take just his share and the horses.

When Billy heard gunshots, he estimated they were only miles away, perhaps close to the meeting place. It could be a hunter, but he also considered the possibility of anarchy amongst Ricky's gang. Billy guessed the same boys who showed up at Two Ponies most likely drove out to California and sure as hell didn't do it as a favor. There was money involved. He had no idea where the money came from, but if enough was involved, members might be looking to decrease the split. This would certainly help his cause—fewer men to go through to get to Ricky. Billy hung close to the tree line, hiding in the shadows as he tracked north.

He felt certain Katherine wouldn't get Major to cross the river, but if she did, he planned one more stop to protect that stubborn redhead. He had pointed out the wrong creek and meeting place to her, a good distance before the actual spot illustrated on Ricky's map where the next creek met the river beside a high ridge. That's where he would find one of the lookout men positioned with a perfect view of any approach. He would take him hostage to draw out the others and get them to tell him where to find Ricky. This had been his plan all along.

Taking Katherine was mostly out of necessity. Ricky needed to believe his little scheme was working. He probably had someone back in Elkhead—that busybody Jerry at the feed store, no doubt—to monitor things. If they didn't show up at the meeting place and Katherine resurfaced in town, Ricky would have given up on his plan and the opportunity to get to him would have been lost. Then, who knew what Ricky might try next.

But he had to admit Katherine wasn't entirely wrong. The opportunity to have her to himself for a few nights had crossed his mind. He needed to know if any of her signals were legit, which she made clear the other night were nothing more than enjoying his attention. He had expected as much but knowing for certain where they stood cleared his mind and his purpose. He would end this today at all costs.

Katherine came to an abrupt halt when a couple of shots reverberated through the gorge. She tried to convince herself it must be hunters shooting at dinner, or poachers ahead of rifle season. There couldn't be a whole lot of supervision out here. The alternative was unimaginable, pushed to a dark corner in the back of her mind. Stay positive, she told herself, as she cued Major for a canter, racing after Billy once again.

Nearly to the base of the mountain, TJ heard gunshots in the distance. Josephine gripped his arms. "Oh, TJ!" she shrieked.

"Could be anyone." TJ trotted to a good observation point and used his field glasses to scour the river basin below. "I don't see anyone. Let's go. We should catch up with our parents this afternoon."

When they reached the river, TJ noticed all the horse tracks immediately. "They crossed here," he pointed. "And, they're pretty fresh."

"It's pretty deep," said Josephine. "Maybe we should find a better place to cross."

"If they crossed here, so can we. We're so close, Jo; we can't lose ground now."

TJ kicked Cisco and, without hesitation, he jumped in, Bonanza following with a big splash. "Hold on, Jo!"

Josephine held tight around TJ's middle as Cisco lost his footing in belly-high water, then regained it. About halfway across, both horses slipped off a shelf into deeper water. Josephine screamed as Cisco struggled to carry them both across. TJ gripped her hands, fearing he might lose her off the back, but he was able to guide his horse onto the shelf again. But the big Buckskin, suddenly weighted down with wet sleeping bags and supplies, couldn't climb back up. TJ had to free the lead from his saddle horn, or they would have been pulled along as Bonanza was swept downstream.

"My Bo Bo!" she screamed hysterically.

TJ focused on getting them safely to shore. Once they were, Josephine jumped off the back and began to run downriver calling for her horse as Bonanza disappeared out of sight around the bend.

"Stop, Jo! We don't have time to go after him. We're so close to catching up!"

TJ trotted up to her and pulled her back on behind him. "Don't worry; he'll make his way to shore. His herd instincts will kick in and he'll come looking for Cisco."

"Oh TJ, I hope so. I hope he's okay!" she choked.

TJ could feel her chest heaving against him as she gulped breaths between sobs. "He'll be fine," he told her, squeezing her hands locked around his middle. "We'll find him, or he'll find us."

There is a sacredness in tears.
They are not the mark of weakness, but of power.
They speak more eloquently than ten thousand tongues.
They are the messengers of overwhelming grief,
of deep contrition, and of unspeakable love...

~ Washington Irving

Temper us in fire, and we grow stronger.
When we suffer, we survive...

~ Cassandra Clare

PART THREE

THE FIRE

21 – Meeting Place

Thursday

Passing the first creek he had pointed out to Katherine, Billy continued along the river until he could see the ridge, then he cut into the woods. He would need to cross the second creek, then circle to the backside of the ridge through the trees to climb it unnoticed.

A good distance from the meeting spot, he crossed Snake Canyon Creek and the trail leading to the highway. He guessed Ricky and his boys must be held up at one of many old hunting cabins scattered along the river north of there. They didn't seem like the camping type.

Billy found a good spot hidden from the trail to tie Red and began his ascent. He took his time placing every foot carefully and quietly up the rocky and steep backside of the ridge. When he neared the top, Billy looked for the odd vertical elongated rock he observed the previous day with his field glasses from the mountainside. It marked the spot with the best view of the creek and river below both directions. That's where he hoped to find one of the men staked out with a rifle.

Armed with only his knife, Billy peered over the odd rock. Sure enough there sat Kyle Schmitt, drawing a picture of a horse in the dirt with a stick, his rifle set aside. There wasn't much room on the rock shelf beside Kyle to land, so he would need to make an accurate seven-foot leap.

Cautiously, he climbed on top and silently slid his legs over the edge, decreasing the drop by a couple feet. Counting one, two, to himself, he jumped on three. Startling Kyle, he hit his spot, pushed the rifle away with his foot and held the knife to Kyle's throat.

"Not a peep," whispered Billy, nodding in the direction of the creek.

Kyle nodded and led the way down a much easier and more direct route to the creek. Billy followed, now armed with Kyle's rifle.

"Who else is on watch?" asked Billy, once they reached the bottom.

"Jake."

"Where?"

"In the bushes on the opposite side of the creek," pointed Kyle. "Where's Ricky and how many others are there?"

"He's at a cabin up river. There's no one else."

"You're doing good, Kyle. You're a smart fella. Okay, we're going to walk out together, real slow. Don't try anything. You know I'm not afraid to pull the trigger."

Again, Kyle just nodded.

When Katherine arrived at the creek, there was no sign of Billy or anyone else. She allowed Major to drink at the mouth of the creek as her mind flooded with questions. What happened? Where could Billy be? Was this the right spot?

Perhaps she had misunderstood him when he pointed it out to her on the way down the mountain. Then an idea niggled its way front and center. Since his plan all along was to leave her behind, he might have pointed out the wrong spot. Damn that Billy! She didn't get a good look at Ricky's map; Billy had immediately snatched it away from her. Then she recalled reading the word ridge on the map.

Katherine drew up her reins and rode as far as she could into a shallow portion of the river to get an unobstructed view around the trees further upstream. There it was! A rock-faced ridge bordering the east bank of the river. She guessed there must be another creek emptying into the river beside it.

Off they charged through the creek and northward along the river. Major covered the distance in no time. When she neared the ridge at the junction of the river and the next creek, she dismounted and led Major into the woods, hoping to approach the spot under the cover of the trees, undetected.

When she neared a small creek hidden in willows, she thought she heard voices. She tied Major so she could investigate.

Billy approached the spot in the willows holding Kyle as a screen in front of him with his arm twisted behind his back, his knife once again at Kyle's throat.

"Come out, Jake. I've got your brother," Billy yelled out. "Unarmed, hands in the air."

Unexpectedly, a horse whinnied to Red from the opposite side of the creek, and Red answered back. Billy heard a commotion and a yelp. "I thought you said Jake was alone!"

"He is; I don't know what's going on!" said Kyle in a panic.

Billy repeated his warning and instructions louder.

"Go ahead, slit his throat," Jake called back, still hidden in the willows. "I could care less."

Billy was at a loss. Two brothers having lived their whole lives together well into their fifties and he didn't care? Fear gripped Billy's chest as Katherine stepped out of the willows, followed by Jake with a shotgun aimed at her back.

"But I think you care about this one," said Jake. "Toss the knife away and lay on the ground with your hands behind your back."

For an instant, Billy considered letting his knife fly with trained precision, certain it would find his mark, but he didn't dare take the chance his knife wouldn't beat Jake's trigger finger.

"Let Kyle go and drop to the ground. Now!"

Billy pitched his knife toward Jake's feet and followed his orders. Immediately, Kyle ran to reclaim his rifle from where Billy had set it down. Jake kept his distance, knowing Billy had weapons beyond a gun or knife.

Jake pushed Katherine forward with the end of his shotgun. "Get down beside him." He picked up Billy's knife. "If either of them moves, shoot them," he told Kyle. Jake set his gun down and pulled two pieces of rope from his jacket pocket. Kyle nervously watched them, his rifle aimed at his back. When Jake bent down to tie him, Billy thought about turning on him and crushing his larynx, but did he dare test Kyle's nerve? Could he pull the trigger?

Lying face to face, Billy could see the terror in Katherine's eyes. For a moment anger consumed him, but within seconds the fear returned—fear for her life. He could understand why she felt she had to search him out. Unfortunately, she arrived at the worst possible moment. Or, was it the best possible moment, considering his predicament?

"Hold your hands still. We have a gun on the woman, so no funny kung-fu business," Jake told Billy. Jake no doubt recalled the night he took him and his brother out in seconds at Rudy's years ago. Once Jake tied their hands securely, he picked up his gun and stood guard while Kyle retrieved Major and Red.

Katherine had to remind herself to breathe and prayed she didn't pee her pants. Immediately, she recognized the Schmitt brothers—Jake, the bigger of the two, now carrying extra pounds settled around his waist, and Kyle who hadn't changed much, still taking orders from his brother. It was happening—

playing out just as they had imagined it would—that is, before Billy decided to go rogue.

"Help him on his horse," Jake told Kyle. Kyle held Red while Billy awkwardly mounted.

"Get up," Jake told her, grabbing her by the arm and shoving her toward Major. Kyle handed her horse over to Jake, who roughly grabbed a hold of Major's bridle. The Thoroughbred jerked back, eyes bulging, nearly pulling away from him.

"Easy boy," Katherine told him, stroking his neck. "It's okay."

"Shut up!" ordered Jake, looking Major over. "What are you doing out here with this fancy animal?" he asked, not expecting an answer. Major began nervously prancing in place.

"I'll hold him," offered Kyle, still holding onto Red.

Jake gave his brother a nod and grunted. The moment Jake handed Major over to Kyle, the horse settled down. Kyle slowly flipped Major's reins over his head, whispering to him as he stroked his neck, admiring his fine features.

Kyle certainly didn't look or act like a kidnapper or killer to Katherine, with his rifle casually slung over his shoulder. And the fact Major wasn't afraid of him, gave her some hope recalling something Betsy had told her as a child. "Animals are extraordinary judges of character," she had explained. Perhaps Kyle might be a sympathizer.

"His name is Major," she said.

Shocking her, Jake grabbed her arm so tight it would surely leave a bruise and then spun her around. "Shut up, bitch," he said, backhanding her across the face and looking to Billy for his reaction. Katherine tried to knee or kick him, but he held her out of reach of any prime targets.

Billy's face turned stone cold, his eyes full of hate as he locked his jaw, restraining himself. She guessed Billy knew nothing would be gained by a verbal confrontation with the brothers. He needed to silently wait for an opportunity to break free to take out Ricky when they reached him. She hoped the brothers were involved in Ricky's scheme primarily for compensation and once Ricky was out of the equation, they would just run with the loot.

"And you, stupid, help her get on her fancy horse," Jake said to Kyle, grabbing Red's reins.

Once she was onboard, Jake handed Red back to Kyle and instructed him to lead both horses ahead of him as he followed with his shotgun at their backs.

A short distance down the river, two horses stood tied and saddled. Jake held Red and Major, this time less forcibly, while Kyle fetched their horses. Jake kept a safe distance from Major who had his ears laid back flat. Katherine hoped he didn't try to take a chunk out of him, not knowing what Jake might do in retaliation.

As Kyle bridled and tightened each of their horse's cinches, she noticed he was especially gentle with the roan. Next, he untied Major's and Red's cavalry knots and handed Jake their leads while he mounted. Jake slung himself onto the back of the chestnut and instructed Kyle to, once again, lead both of their horses ahead of him as they continued north along the river.

Katherine could tell every step the brothers made had been well-orchestrated and rehearsed. She cursed to herself, knowing Billy might not get the opportunity to reach the hidden blade in the saddle unnoticed before they reached Ricky.

When a horse whinnied from behind their group, everyone spun around in their saddles. Katherine was mortified to see Bonanza trotting toward them!

Jake rode up behind Red, pointing his shotgun only inches

from Billy's head. "You not alone?"

"I don't know whose horse that is," said Billy. "We came alone."

Jake swiveled the barrel, now pressed against her ear. "We came alone, I swear!" she pleaded. Katherine's heart pounded nearly out of her chest, as much from recognizing her daughter's riderless horse as from the gun held to her head. Her mind raced with questions. What was Josephine doing out here? Where was she now? Had she taken a fall?"

"Maybe a hunter's horse got loose?" suggested Kyle.

"Pretty fancy saddle for an elk hunter, and strange it's being used as a pack horse," said Jake.

Kyle immediately noticed Bonanza's bare foot. "He threw a shoe, that's why. What should we do?"

Jake studied Katherine. She prayed her expression didn't give away her sheer panic. "Ricky's waiting. Let's get them to the cabin and locked up, then we'll come back and check things out." Jake clutched Bonanza by the halter, gathered the dangling lead rope and led him behind his horse, still bringing up the rear.

Katherine could read the disappointment in Billy's eyes, knowing he might not get the opportunity to work at the ropes. About twenty minutes later, they rode up to an old hunting cabin set back off the river in the woods.

Ricky came running out all smiles. "Ha, I told you they'd come," he said to Kyle, then noticed the extra horse. "What's this?"

"We found him loose by the river. Must have broken free from someone. They swear they came alone," said Jake. "I figured we'd lock them in the cellar and go back and check it out. We don't want some hunters riding in on us."

"Sounds good." Ricky approached Major. "Nice piece of horse flesh. Nearly as nice as this piece," he said, running his hand up her leg. Katherine's disgust was met with Billy's look of outrage. She turned her head away, dreading what might come next.

"Let's get them down," said Jake. Kyle led them around back of the cabin to a small corral, dismounted and helped Katherine down first. Immediately, she noticed what looked like dried blood splattered on a fence post beside a dark puddle on the ground and what looked like tracks from something being dragged into the cellar. Her heart began beating faster than she thought possible, causing her to feel dizzy.

Jake dismounted and opened the cellar doors, pulled Billy off Red and tied him to a support post snug against the back wall. "Keep her hands tied and hurry up; I want to get back to the river," he told Kyle.

Jake turned the saddled horses loose in the corral while Kyle led her into the dark cellar beside Billy. He whispered, "I'm sorry this is happening to you."

Kyle closed the doors and locked them in by sliding a large metal shank through two keepers on the outside.

Katherine listened to make sure they had left. "What is Bonanza doing here? Jo must have followed us, but how?"

"TJ. He must have called her after he found our vehicles. They're both out there," he said, solemnly.

"Oh my God, Billy, what if Jake finds them?"

"Can you get to the blade in my belt?" Billy turned as far away from the wall as possible.

Katherine backed in and slid his belt around as far as it would go and felt underneath. "It's not there! I can feel a piece of tape, but no blade."

"Damn it! It must have slid out. Let me see your hands." Katherine turned. "Strong knots, heavy rope. Shit! Look around, see any way out of here?"

"Did you hear Kyle?" she said to Billy. "He sounds sympathetic; maybe he'll help us."

"I wouldn't count on it."

Katherine surveyed their prison dimly lit by a gap between the cellar doors. There were no windows, only a musty and cobweb-laden room with dirt and rock walls and the cabin board floor as its ceiling. She could not find an escape hatch leading to the upstairs. Some shelves held canned goods in one corner and besides that, the floor was covered with trash. Panicking, she kicked the trash about looking for something she might be able to use to cut rope, even though she wasn't sure how she would be able to pick anything up or reach Billy's wrists with her hands tied behind her back.

Katherine came to a sudden stop. "Billy?"

"What?"

"There's a freshly dug-up area over here about six feet long."

"The blood on the fence."

"You noticed it, too?" She swallowed hard and dug her boot into the loose soil, uncovering a man's hand. Katherine gasped and jumped back. "Oh Billy, they've already killed someone!"

"Someone they didn't need any longer."

Katherine hesitantly covered the man's hand with dirt and backed as far as possible from the shallow grave. Her hands and shoulders that ached a moment ago now felt numb along with the rest of her body. Was she going into shock? The corpse… the kids… her imminent rape, the fire—it was all too much. She began shaking and crying.

"I need you to hold it together, Kat," said Billy, somberly, giving her a look that unmistakably said, "This is why I left you behind."

"I know. I'm good." Katherine took a deep breath. "I'm

sorry. I really messed things up, didn't I?"

"I wish you could have just let me go."

"Let you go die, you mean."

"I didn't come here to die, but if I do, I would have preferred to have done it alone."

Katherine walked up to Billy shackled in the shadows of their dark dungeon. "Oh Billy, what have I done?"

Billy shook his head. "Just rotten luck and timing. If Major hadn't called to Red… Hurry, keep looking."

Josephine looked back down river for Bonanza as they crossed another creek emptying into the river. She had already made the mistake of calling for him earlier, earning her a quick reprimand by TJ, explaining they needed to be as stealth as possible. She remained silent as TJ threw his leg over Cisco's neck and slid off in front of her. Josephine scooted up into the saddle and followed him as he studied the tracks along the river. There suddenly seemed to be so many of them.

"There are now five horses and Bonanza is one of them," said TJ.

"Oh no, Ricky has them!"

Suddenly, from around a bend in the river, two horses and riders appeared about fifty yards away. TJ ran to her, slipped his foot in the stirrup while grabbing the horn, kissed to Cisco, and flung himself behind her mid-lurch into a gallop.

"Duck down!" TJ screamed. Josephine bent over and grabbed ahold of the gelding's mane. TJ kicked and hollered as Cisco bolted into a dead run alongside the river. She could hear hoofbeats on the gravel behind them. If the Medicine Hat or markings had any protective powers, they needed them now.

As TJ reached around her for his shotgun, shots rang out.

"No!" screamed Josephine as TJ tumbled into the water.

It took several strides to bring Cisco down to a sliding halt. She spun him around on his haunches and sprinted back toward TJ, who lay face down in about a foot of water, streaks of red tainting the water as it flowed downstream.

"Stop right there, Missy!"

Josephine nearly lost her seat as a big red horse slammed into Cisco broadside. A large man grabbed ahold of the Paint's bridle. Josephine struggled to pull Cisco away from his grasp, striking and kicking the man. Then she felt a blow to her head, and everything went black.

Kyle rode up alongside his brother as he carried the young woman like a sack of potatoes over his shoulder, leading the Paint. Jake flung her down on shore.

"Please don't shoot her!" Kyle begged, taking ahold of their horse.

Jake flipped her hair off her face with his boot. "I'm not going to shoot anything that pretty. She looks just like the other redhead, but younger."

Kyle recognized the girl right away as Katherine's daughter from rodeos he had attended. He had cheered her on in barrel racing. "What are you going to do with her, Jake?"

"Keep her; she's mine. Ricky has his and I'll have mine. I'll show her what a real man is like."

"What about the boy's body?"

"Who's going to care about a dead Indian? C'mon, let's get back. Ricky is eager to get the party started."

Frightened out of her mind and nauseous after hearing two more gunshots, Katherine stood at attention when she heard footsteps at the cellar door.

"Stay back," Jake told her.

Katherine squinted as bright daylight split the dark cellar in two. At first all she could make out was the silhouette of a man carrying something in the ambient light. She feared it might be another body. Katherine gasped as Jake dropped her daughter onto the cellar floor. She had to silence herself, yet her daughter's name screamed in her head. She prayed she was alive.

"Found her down by the river. Know who she is?"

They both shook their heads "no."

The moment the doors slammed shut, Katherine rushed to Josephine's side and fell to her knees beside her. She could see her chest rise and fall. "She's alive!"

"Is she hurt?"

"I don't see any blood, but she has a bump on her head. "Josephine, wake up, sweetie; it's Mom. Can you hear me?"

When she glanced over to Billy, immediately she read the dread and horror in his eyes, having heard more shots. "Oh Billy… TJ," she whispered, on the verge of tears once again. "He must have gotten away."

"Not without Jo. I'm going to kill them all!" Billy began struggling to get free.

Katherine nudged Josephine with her shoulder and foot. "Wake up, Jo; please wake up!" She prayed she would have some good news about TJ. When she heard footsteps above, she hushed and listened. First the voices were soft, and she couldn't understand what they were saying. Then they became louder and heated, and she could identify Ricky and Jake's voices.

"I found her; she's mine," said Jake. "I want to take her with me."

"You have your fun, then she stays in the cabin with the others. We can't have any witnesses; you know that. We may not even have to start a fire with that forest fire heading our way. Can really smell the smoke today."

Katherine made eye contact with Billy and could feel his rage from across the room.

"I suppose you're right," said Jake. "I could see smoke to the north from the river. We better get things rolling."

"Damn straight."

"But I'd like to get some chow first," said Jake. "You rushed us out of here so damn fast this morning we didn't get much to eat. I'm starving."

Okay, I've waited nineteen years… guess I can wait a little longer."

Both men began hooting and hollering as their voices gradually faded.

"We don't have much time," said Billy. "Are her hands tied?"

"Yes, but in the front." Katherine continued to shake her daughter. Finally, she opened her eyes.

"TJ!" she screamed, then she focused on her. "Mom!"

"Jo, where's TJ?" she asked.

Josephine sat up, trembling, glancing at Billy and back to her. "Oh Mom, it was terrible. TJ…" she gasped.

"What happened, Jo?" she asked.

"He was shot… in the back!" she said, her voice breaking into sobs. "I loved him, Mom."

"Is there a chance he's alive?" asked Billy.

Josephine turned toward Billy and shook her head then locked eyes once again with her. "He… he was face down in the water…" Josephine choked, her body convulsing as she sobbed.

Billy's focus dropped to the floor, one grief-stricken moan escaping his parted lips. Katherine's eyes burned, unable to whip them free of her salty tears. TJ had been like the son she and Steven never got to raise and she ached for Billy. She couldn't imagine his anguish; having lost another son he would hold himself responsible for.

Katherine sat up and locked eyes with her daughter. "Oh sweetie, I need you to be strong. We need your help and we don't have much time. See if you can untie my rope." Katherine turned her back toward her daughter.

"I can't; it's really tight." Can you get up and search under the trash for something sharp on the floor, anything, a piece of glass or a sharp rock."

Her daughter whipped her face with her sleeve and began searching the cellar floor. "Can you tell us what happened, Jo? From the beginning?" she asked.

Between sniffles, as she frantically scoured the ground, Josephine explained how TJ had called her and how she had sneaked out and followed him.

"Here, will this work?" she asked, showing her a rock.

"Worth a try. Start on Billy's rope first."

There was little room between Billy and the wall to reach his wrists, but she squeezed her slender frame in and began working the sharpest edge across the rope.

"You can't cut me totally free, Jo, okay?" said Billy.

"I understand," she said. "You have to look like you're still tied."

"That's right," he said.

"Bonanza threw a shoe and we had to ride double," Josephine continued. "That night we got cold. It snowed." Her daughter glanced between her and Billy. "We slept together… to keep warm…" she trailed off and began focusing on the rope again.

Immediately, Katherine knew then what Josephine meant when she said she loved TJ. He was no longer just a friend, and she guessed Billy understood that, too, by the expression on his face.

"Then what happened, Jo?" he asked, tenderly.

Josephine worked at the rope harder. "We were at the river and TJ dismounted to study the tracks. Out of nowhere two men came charging toward us," she explained, her words racing to keep up with the events. "TJ hopped on behind me and we took off running. I heard shots and TJ fell into the water. I tried to go back for him, but a man caught Cisco and then I blacked out." Out of breath, Josephine turned to Billy. "I'm so sorry, Mr. Black Feather."

Billy just nodded.

Between outbursts of tears, her daughter continued working at the rope. Katherine's heart ached for her little girl, having felt what she was feeling now firsthand so many years ago. And, she couldn't imagine Billy's sorrow. It was every parent's nightmare, to outlive their child, and her daughter remained in grave danger. The very thing they were trying to avoid and protect their families from by carrying out this insane plan had come to fruition despite their efforts to prevent it. And now, the stakes were raised to save Josephine. Would Billy get the opportunity to break free in time?

She flinched as someone began unlatching the cellar doors. Josephine stepped away from Billy. It was Kyle.

"Hurry," he whispered, gesturing to her and Jo toward the door. 'The horses are still saddled."

Josephine ran to her side. "It's okay, sweetie; he wants to help us," she explained.

Kyle began to cut Josephine's hands free when Jake appeared outside the door. "What are you doing?"

"Leave the women alone, Jake! Let them go. Ricky's crazy. They never hurt him or his family."

Jake smacked Kyle so hard he fell to the ground. "You stupid fag! You never had a lick of sense or balls! Nearly fifty years old and I've never seen you touch a woman. I should have put you out of your misery long ago." Jake pointed his shotgun at Kyle.

Kyle raised his hand. "Please, Jake, I'm your brother."

"Don't remind me."

Kyle closed his eyes and Katherine cringed, expecting the worst. Instead, Jake hit him in the head with the butt of his gun, knocking him out cold. He pushed Josephine against the back wall, picked up Kyle's knife and grabbed her. Katherine struggled to free herself from his grip, kicking and screaming.

"I'll be right back for you!" Jake told Billy, then turned to Josephine. "And you, my little sweet tart, we have a date later."

Katherine fought his vice-like grip on her arm, as he pulled her around to the front of the cabin. Ricky was waiting under a big cottonwood tree. "Where's Kyle? We could use his help."

Jake shook his head. "I caught him trying to set them free. I locked him up in the cellar, too."

"That little weasel! I always told you he couldn't be trusted." Ricky sneered. "Put her there."

Jake threw Katherine to the ground and sat on her, straddling her middle. Barely able to breathe, his weight nearly crushing her, he held her down while Ricky tied her ankles and her wrists to stakes already pounded in the ground. She tried to resist, but she was no match for both men. "Let's get him and his horse," said Ricky.

While they were gone, Katherine tested her constraints, but the stakes held. Next, they would bring Billy to watch, but they said they were getting his horse, too. Why? His horse! She glanced over and sure enough a rope dangled from the cottonwood about twenty feet away. They were going to hang him Old Western movie-style, but not until they were done with her.

A gleam of hope entered her heart. Even if Josephine didn't weaken the ropes around Billy's wrists enough for him to break loose, he would get a second opportunity to reach the blade at the back of his saddle. Once his hands were free, he'd have access to the hidden knife.

Katherine imagined the most likely scenario playing out before her eyes. As soon as Ricky stood up and Jake began taking his turn, Billy's knife would find its mark in Ricky's heart and he would attack Jake. Fat old Jake with his pants around his ankles would be no match for Billy Black. She would just have to do her part until Billy broke free. She prayed Billy was close to breaking free and could constrain himself and wait until the time was right.

Ricky appeared around the corner of the cabin leading Red. Jake followed, dragging Billy along. "Get on your horse," he said.

With Jake's assistance, Billy mounted Red under the branch. "Bend down," said Ricky, slipping the noose around his neck. He then tied the loose end of the rope tight around the trunk of the tree. "Hope your horse stands well; I'd hate to have you miss all the fun!"

Katherine prayed harder.

22 – Revenge

Steven pushed Dandy as fast as the terrain would allow to catch up with Josephine and TJ. His big, strong gelding seemed to understand the urgency and responded willingly to the task—galloping straightaways, lunging up inclines, and trotting downhill, with the occasional rest at a walk down steep and rocky surfaces.

Disappointed he hadn't caught up with the kids yet, he guessed they must have gotten an early start and pushed their horses hard as well that day. When he reached the river, Steven noticed several tracks, some crossing immediately in deep and turbulent water and a set leading downstream to what appeared to be a shallower crossing point.

When shots resonated from upriver, Steven didn't hesitate and lunged into the deep turbulent water with Dandy, fighting the strong current to the opposite shore. He tried to convince himself it was a hunter, although rifle season didn't start for another two weeks. The alternative was unthinkable.

Having safely traversed the river, Steven asked Dandy for a steady canter heading north following well-defined tracks in the moist soil of the river bank. A distance ahead, he noticed a shape lying on shore, but he couldn't quite make out what it was. As he neared, his curiosity turned to shear panic, identifying the shape as a body. Steven kicked Dandy into a full run, skidding to a halt as he jumped from his mount.

It was TJ, and he was shot in the back! *Where was Jo?!*

Steven pulled him onto higher ground and checked for a pulse. To his relief he had one, but it was very shallow. He had lost a lot of blood and was unconscious. "TJ, TJ," he said, tapping his cheek, "Can you hear me? Where's Jo?"

There was no bringing him to. The ice-cold water may have kept him from bleeding out, but it appeared he was suffering from hypothermia. Steven came prepared for the worst with an extensive first-aid kit. He cleaned his wounds from a shotgun spray down his back, fortunately from a good distance.

He removed as many shots as possible, but a few were deep, which he hoped hadn't hit any vital organs. TJ's color was pale and his heart rate low. After Steven cleaned and dressed his wounds, he removed his wet clothing and dressed him in some of his extra clothes. He moved TJ into the sun for additional warmth, slipped his jacket onto him and wrapped him in a blanket. He knew TJ was in critical condition and needed to be flown to a hospital as soon as possible. His only hope would be flagging down Mike and the chopper.

At that moment he heard a helicopter groan in the distance.

Having returned to their search that afternoon after refueling, Mike scanned the dense forest below from behind Roy as the aircraft made another pass over the range between Billy's and the river, trying to gauge how far the kids might have ridden in two days.

"One more pass or do we move on?" asked Roy.

"They might have made it to the river today if they really pushed the horses," said Dane, seated in front.

"Okay, let's move onto the river basin and head north," said Mike. "We can't see shit with all this foliage anyway." As he feared, it would be a miracle to have spotted them in the woods. At least in the valley they would have a clear view and room to set the chopper down if necessary."

"Not sure how much farther we'll be able to go with the

fire's flume moving our way," said Roy.

Mike pulled away from his binoculars long enough to look to the north at the wall of smoke hovering over the horizon. When they first headed out that morning at a higher elevation, they could see amber and gold flames flickering within the flume in the distance. They knew the wind had shifted and the fire was no longer as contained and expected to spread south across the border that afternoon. Mike noticed the smell of smoke had become strikingly stronger.

"Hopefully, we'll find them soon," he said.

"Look, up there!" yelled Dane, pointing ahead to the right. "It's Steve!"

Mike switched sides and focused in on the shoreline on the east side of the river. Steven was waiving them down, motioning for them to land. "Is there room?"

"At that clearing up ahead." An open area where the river had changed course left a dry bed of river bottom.

Mike jumped from the chopper, followed by Dane. They ran to Steven who was struggling to hold his horse, spooking at the big, noisy, and windy bug.

"It's TJ; he's been shot. No sign of Jo, Kat or Billy," shouted Steven above the roar of the helicopter. "He's lost a lot of blood. You need to get him to a hospital asap."

"Okay. Now the Sheriff's Department will get involved," said Mike, "I'll radio your position."

"Their tracks lead north along the river," Steven added as he tied Dandy to a tree..

Mike nodded. "Let's get him loaded, then Dane and I will go in on foot from here."

"One of you will need to stay with TJ. He might need CPR," said Steven. "I can't leave."

"That will be me, then," said Mike. "Dane, you stay with Steve, but you wait for backup. Understood?"

"Yes, sir.".

Steven nodded. As he and Dane helped Mike carefully load TJ onto the helicopter, Roy was on the radio notifying St. Joseph's Hospital in Billings that they were on their way.

As soon as Roy signed off, Mike radioed the Sheriff's office and began explaining the situation.

Once they were in the air, Steven rushed back to Dandy who now stood calmly tied with the chopper gone.

Dane approached him. "I'm so sorry about all this. You must be going crazy."

Steven just nodded as he tightened Dandy's cinch. He couldn't trust himself not to break down if he tried to express how he was feeling. He didn't think Dane really expected an answer anyway.

"My dad will make sure to get word to Sarah."

"Good. I need to, you know," he said to Dane, nodding in the direction of the bushes. "Then I'll graze Dandy along the creek until help arrives. He's not too crazy about the choppers."

"Sure."

Steven wasn't about to wait for anyone or anything. His little girl was in danger and he tried not to think about what might have happened to his wife and Billy. He knew once Dane realized he hadn't just taken a piss and was gone, he wouldn't disobey a direct order and follow him. Dane needed to stay to flag down the county chopper and identify who they were searching for.

As soon as he was out of sight along the creek, Steven slung his leg over Dandy and rode into the woods along the river. When Dane was out of sight, he galloped north along shore following their tracks.

Chief turned onto the next trail head he came to in the long string of gravel roads heading west off Highway 89. He had found little activity up to this point, just hunting parties heading home due to the fire. When he reached the end of this road, he found recent tire tracks and horse manure and assumed the hunting party had left, until he noticed there were only horse tracks leading away from the parking.

A hunting party might have arranged to be dropped off, but following closer inspection, Chief found some suspicious tire tracks that inexplicably picked up a good distance from the parking area like they had been brushed away with a pine bow. Energized by his find, Chief quickly followed the tracks into a ravine. Under a pile of brush, he found the black Jeep!

Chief rushed back to his truck and radioed Mike.

"Found the Jeep," he told him out of breath. "And several horse tracks following a creek in the direction of the river."

"Steve found TJ shot," said Mike. "He's alive, but he's lost a lot of blood. No sign of the others."

Chief's worst fears had materialized. "Damn it!"

"We're flying TJ to Billings now. I radioed air support; they're on their way. Dane and Steve are waiting for them at the river."

"Deputize me, Mike. I'm going in. Radio land support, too." Chief gave him his location.

"Be careful."

"Will do."

Mike radioed the office to have someone contact Sarah and, then contacted the Flathead County Sheriff's Department. They assured him an Air and Rescue unit was on its way and that a ground unit would be deployed immediately, reaching the trail head in about an hour.

He had a feeling everything would go down sooner than

they could arrive, considering the fire moving south and the discovery of TJ. Ricky and his accomplices would be looking to finish their business and head across the border as soon as possible, either on horseback or in the Jeep. Regardless, an hour felt like an eternity.

"Your friend, Steven, must be going nuts," said Roy. "If that was my wife and daughter out there, I wouldn't be waiting for any chopper."

"I agree. He's probably already taken off, but I had to give the order just the same. Dane will wait."

"How fast do you think we can get back?"

Roy shook his head. "Not soon enough."

"That's what I'm thinking. This is going down now. Chief and Steven might be their only hope."

"I'm so sorry, Mike. I know these folks are like family to you. Chief filled me in on the whole story. Unbelievable, really." Roy turned and glanced at TJ stretched out on the floor behind them. "This reminds me of my 'Nam days, flying rescue missions."

"Chief hadn't mentioned you served."

It took Roy a moment to reply. "I don't talk about it much. It got pretty rough."

"I can imagine. Thank you for your service."

Roy nodded. "Thank you for yours. Is he going to make it?"

Mike stepped back beside TJ and checked his vitals. "He's weak, but Steve seems to think he stands a good chance. Lost a lot of blood, though."

"Our ETA to the hospital is about fifteen hundred," said Roy. "What's the daughter like?"

"She's beautiful; spitting image of her mother who is still a looker with long auburn hair, the deepest green eyes, and the face of an angel. She's supposed to be leaving for college the end of this week, UCLA—wants to be an actress."

"No kidding. Well, if this mess ends well, I'll see what I can do. I may have a part for her or know someone that might give her a chance."

"You're doing plenty already. The family will be very grateful for all your help, as we all are."

Roy nodded. "I called both of my girls last night. Thank God they're safe."

"Times like this we all count our blessings."

Billy watched Ricky and Jake's every move waiting for the opportunity to reach for the hidden box-cutter blade. Josephine had weakened one loop of the knot, but when he tested it while being dragged around the cabin, it still held tight. Just as he leaned back to reach the cantle, Ricky glanced over to him from Katherine.

"You look a little nervous up there, half-breed. All I have to do is send that horse of yours off at a gallop and…" Ricky contorted his face and stuck his tongue out to the side, resembling being strangled, and laughed. Then shocking the horse, Ricky pulled his pistol from his waistband and shot three rounds into the air. Red danced in place, but Billy managed to keep his hunting mount, accustomed to gunfire, from backing far enough to strangle him.

"Oops, I almost got ahead of myself," said Ricky. "I've been looking forward to having you as an audience."

"You sick son of a bitch!" said Billy. "She never did anything to you."

"She did plenty. She represents everything bad that has happened to me and my family. If it wasn't for her, Kurt and my Dad would still be alive. I wouldn't have spent the prime years of my life behind bars and I'd still have a home."

"That's all been you and your family's doing."

"You killed Kurt!" yelled Jake. "And you're going to pay."

"You're both going to pay!" said Ricky.

When Ricky and Jake turned their attention back to Katherine, Billy reached to carefully dig out the hidden blade. If he dropped it, all would be lost. He must stay focused even as he watched in horror as Ricky began his assault on Katherine with Jake cheering him on every step.

Ricky smiled at her fiendishly with his cigarette-stained teeth. Katherine cringed and looked desperately to Billy. She could see the panic on his face.

Ricky set his gun down. "Let's see what we have here," he said, leaning over her as he ripped open her blouse.

Katherine spit on his ugly face. In retribution, he backhanded her across the face. Hard. Her face burned, and she tasted blood, guessing he must have busted open her lip.

"I knew you'd be a feisty one," said Jake, now standing beside Ricky so he would have a front-row seat.

Ricky unzipped her jeans, watching for Billy's reaction. Billy grimaced but remained silent. She knew Billy didn't want to draw any attention to himself as he worked to free himself. *Please hurry, Billy!*

"She's a true redhead, just as I thought," said Ricky.

Jake laughed. "You're more like your brother than I thought."

Ricky gleamed. "Thank you. Now, let's settle the score for Kurt and Pa," he said.

"Hell, yes," yelped Jake. "I'm going to get us a couple beers from the creek and take a piss. Wait for me bro, okay?"

As soon as Jake disappeared into the bushes, Ricky leaned over Katherine. "We don't need to wait, do we, Red Locks? Just you and me and your heathen lover, just like I planned."

Katherine tried to think of ways to delay the inevitable,

hoping Billy would break free any second. She whispered back to her captor. "I'm glad Billy killed your brother for what he did to Sarah, and you're going to die for what you're about to do to me."

"Well, you're a bold bitch. So, exactly how do you think that's going to happen. Looks to me like I'm in control." Ricky picked up the Colt and held it to her head, then ran the cold barrel of the pistol down her chest.

Katherine winced. "It's called karma!"

Ricky glared at her. "What's karma?"

"It's paying for your sins in this world. Then you pay for them again in the next, in hell. You have a lot of paying to do."

Ricky paced back and forth. "Bullshit. What a bunch of nonsense. You're the one who's going to suffer for what you did to Kurt, Pa, and me. You're going to burn in this world and then burn in hell for cheating on your husband, with a dirty Injun no less." Ricky nodded his head toward Billy. "I was going to strangle you first, but now you're going to burn alive."

"You aren't going to live that long!" she spat at him.

"You're crazy! A crazy redhead, like my Pa always said. He offered you a fair price for your place when your uncle died, but oh no, you had to have your stupid school and your half-breed. And now look where it got you."

Ricky glanced over to Billy. Katherine drew his attention back to her. "So, what are you waiting for? Let's get this over with."

Ricky set the .45 caliber down to unzip his jeans and obviously took pleasure in seeing Billy squirm as he climbed on top of her, his foul breath in her face. "I've been waiting for this for nearly twenty years."

She tried to knee him in the groin, but they had her legs tied down too tight.

"Get off her!"

She recognized her husband's voice immediately. Ricky froze, hovering over her. She turned her head to see Steven walking toward them from the creek, rifle aimed at Ricky.

Billy yelled, "Look out, Steve!" but it was too late. Jake rushed Steven from behind, again using the butt of his shotgun, knocking Steven unconscious. Ricky got to his feet, pulled up his jeans and laughed hysterically. "Looky here, it's the pretty doctor. This is getting more fun by the second. Bring him to."

Jake poured an open beer on Steven's face, who came to, ready to fight until he turned and stared down the barrel of Jake's shotgun. "Stay on your knees," ordered Jake. "What if he's not alone?"

"I think we'd know that by now," said Ricky, turning back to Katherine. "Okay, Red Locks, who do you really love? You get to choose, which one dies, and which one lives, at least for a little while longer." Katherine's eyes welled up, looking between the two loves of her life. "Pretty Blondie here can have his head blown off, or your Injun bastard can dangle from this here tree—your choice." Ricky had his gun aimed at Red.

Jake laughed as he mimicked firing his shotgun at Steven's head, sound effects and all.

"No!" she screamed, tears rolling down her face. Katherine struggled to free herself.

"Guess I'll have to choose for you, then. Eeny, meeny, miny, moe… catch an Injun by the toe. If he hollers, let him go, eeny, meeny, miny, moe… Shoot him," he said to Jake, pointing to Steven.

Steven locked eyes with Katherine. "I'm so sorry," he said. She cried out, "I love you," between sobs. Was this how their story would end, all three of them murdered by a lunatic? Steven held his gaze with his wife as Jake raised his gun to his shoulder and took aim.

Suddenly, Billy was free of the ropes and noose and threw his knife, piercing Jake's heart. Jake crumbled to the ground beside him. After that it all played out in what seemed like slow motion. Before Ricky could react, Billy charged him on Red and just as Billy lunged from his mount to tackle Ricky, a single shot rang out, and the two men crashed to the ground in a heap.

Katherine was screaming hysterically as Steven tried to roll Jake's hefty body off his shotgun, then he located his rifle that Jake had tossed aside. By the time he raised it to shoot, Ricky was gone, and Billy lay still and broken on the ground.

"Billy!" shrieked Katherine. "Steven, is he okay?"

"He's been shot." Steven rushed to his friend and held him in his arms. He could see he was mortally wounded. "Thank you," said Steven, knowing he would be dead if it wasn't for his old rival.

Billy smiled and whispered between labored breaths, "Nothing happened, buddy... she's all yours… she always has been… she always will be."

"I found TJ. He's alive; he'll be fine," said Steven. "We'll take care of him and Sarah, I promise."

Billy eyes smiled for a moment then turned dark. Gasping to breath, he whispered, "Must… find… Ricky."

"There's support on the way. We'll find him."

"Thank you. Please… tell Sarah and TJ… I love them."

"Of course."

Then Billy turned his head toward Katherine who was struggling to free herself only feet away. Steven set Billy down to untie her.

Katherine could see the life draining from his face. "No, Billy, hold on!" she shrieked between sobs, crawling to his side. Katherine cradled his head in her lap and gently brushed his ebony hair from his face and kissed him on the forehead.

"Thank you," she whispered, acknowledging he had sacrificed himself to save Steven for her. She took the chiseled wooden heart from her pocket and slipped it into his hand. He grasped it and smiled his beautiful smile one last time as the light in his deep mahogany eyes faded. The heart fell to the ground.

Katherine shook her head in disbelief. "No!!" she screamed.

Steven knelt to hold her. "I'm so sorry, Kat. He's gone. There was nothing we could do."

"No, he was supposed to save us both!" She shook Billy's quiet remains, half expecting him to jump up, wearing one of his cocky grins, having pulled another gag on them pretending to be dead.

Steven reached over to close Billy's lifeless eyes.

As his body began to turn cold in her arms, her sorrow turned to rage. Just then Ricky galloped off from behind the cabin with all the horses running free behind him toward the river. Katherine set Billy's head down carefully, as if not to wake him, buttoned her blouse now covered in Billy's blood and zipped up her jeans. She stormed over to Jake's body, pulled Billy's knife from his chest and wiped it clean on the bastard's shirt.

"What are you doing?" shouted Steven.

Katherine stepped up to him and kissed him. "I love you."

"Now wait a minute!"

She slid the knife under her belt at the back of her jeans and pointed to the cabin. "Get Josephine; she's in the cellar."

"You can't catch him now."

"On Major I can."

"No! I won't let you. The authorities are on their way."

Katherine pushed past him and ran to the corral behind the cabin with Steven on her heels.

Josephine must have seen them through the crack in the cellar doors. "Dad! I'm in here!" she called. Steven swiftly acted to release her, holding his gun on Kyle.

Katherine whistled for Major. Like a good boy, he galloped up from the river and into the corral on cue. He still had his saddle on, but he must have stepped on his reins and busted his bridle off. With no time to spare, she closed the gate and grabbed two bale twines off the fence. With one, she made a noose and slipped it over his nose, running the rest behind his ears and back to the noose, tying it off. She used the other bale twine for reins, constructing a makeshift bit-less bridle.

By the time Josephine finished explaining to Steven how Kyle tried to help them, Katherine had mounted Major.

Steven turned. "No, Kat, don't!" He screamed, running to block off the gate of the corral.

"Move, Steven!" she yelled.

"Please, Kat, don't do this! This isn't your battle!"

"Yes, it is!"

Katherine kicked her warhorse, pushing Steven aside, and charged after Ricky.

23 – Backup

Steven couldn't believe his wife was chasing a murderer into a blazing fire, yet he could understand why. If there was a chance to end this now, she felt she had to take it. He just hoped Mike or the cops caught up with Ricky before she did. There was only one way to get to the border through the fire and that would be along the river. At least the chopper would be able to spot them easily.

Josephine ran to him. "Dad, what's going on? What is Mom doing?"

"Your mother is chasing down Ricky."

"What? Where's Mr. Black Feather? Why isn't he going after Ricky?"

Steven held his daughter by the shoulders. "He didn't make it, sweetie."

"What do you mean, he didn't make it?" Josephine shook her head in disbelief.

As he wrapped his arms around her, he could feel her shaking.

"I heard the gunshots," she whispered. "TJ, now Mr. Black Feather. When's it going to end?"

"Sweetie, I found TJ. He's alive and being flown to Saint Joe's."

Josephine broke away, staring into his eyes in disbelief. "Oh my God, he's alive? Is he going to be okay?"

Steven held her by her arms. "He's badly injured, sweetie, and he's lost a lot of blood, but he's young and strong."

"He has to make it, Daddy. We're in love." Josephine fell

back into his arms, sobbing.

Steven consoled his daughter. This news shouldn't have come as a surprise, considering what her and TJ must have gone through surviving two nights in the mountains together, but it did. "He'll be in good hands."

"What are we going to do?" she asked, wiping her tear-streaked face. "What about Mom?"

"There's a helicopter on the way and a ground unit." Steven turned around. "Where did Kyle go?"

"He went to find his horse, Strawberry. He's not a bad guy Dad. He really did try to help us. He was gentle with me and the horses. I hope he finds his horse and makes it to Canada," she said. "But I want the others caught."

"Kyle's brother is dead."

"Good," she spat. "They killed another man buried in the cellar. Kyle told me."

Steven quickly led Josephine to the cabin. When they turned the corner, Josephine shrieked seeing the bodies lying out front. Steven put his arm around her and rushed her inside. "You stay here in the cabin for now," he told her, as he grabbed a blanket off one of the cots. "I'm going after Mom."

"Okay, Daddy." Josephine sat down at the table. Halfway out the door, she asked, "Can I go look for Bonanza and Cisco?".

"No. They'll be fine. You stay put! The police will be here soon."

When Steven exited the cabin, he found Chief leaning over Billy's body checking for a pulse. Chief swung his shotgun around toward him, lowering it the moment he recognized him. "Steve, thank God you're okay," he said, out of breath. "I heard gunshots and came running."

"Are you alone?"

"Yes, but backup is right behind me," said Chief. "I'm so

sorry about Billy. What happened? Where's the others?"

"Jo and Kat are okay. Jo's in the cabin. TJ was shot."

"I heard, from Mike," said Chief. "I see the older brother is dead; that looks like Billy's work. Where's Kat, Ricky, and the younger Schmitt brother?"

"Kyle is nearby, looking for his horse," said Steven.

Chief raised his gun. "Is he armed?"

"I don't think so, but Jo said he tried to help them escape. He was locked up with Jo in the cellar when I arrived. He sneaked off when I was trying to stop Kat."

"Stop her from what?"

Steven shook his head. "Ricky rode off on horseback for the border and Kat took off after him on Major."

"What! Is Ricky armed?"

"Yes."

"Is Kat armed?"

"She took Billy's knife."

"How in blazes did this happen?" asked Chief, a couple octaves higher than his normal gruff caliber.

"I know. I've never seen her so determined. I tried to stop her, but she damn near ran me over. They'll be heading north along the river."

"Into the fire," said Chief, checking his watch. "We need to let them know. I have a radio in my truck, but it's too far up the creek. We don't have time. It'll be faster to head for the river and wait for the chopper."

Steven covered Billy with the blanket and picked up his rifle.

"What happened, Steve?"

"There's another body buried in the cellar behind the cabin. I'm guessing it's Ricky's friend with the Jeep. I'll tell you the rest later. You need to take Jo with you. Just follow the river south; you should run into Dane. I'm going after Kat."

"Of course," said Chief. "Good luck! I'll take care of Jo."

"Thanks!"

Steven found Dandy still tied where he left him. He slung his rifle into the scabbard, mounted and raced after Katherine.

When Steven didn't return, Dane knew he had gone after Jo. He couldn't blame him; he would have done the same if it was Jessie. As he waited to flag down the County Sheriff and Air and Rescue Team, he heard gunshots to the north. But he held his post and prayed his friends were okay and that they were the ones doing the shooting. A moment later another single shot rang out. "Shit, what's going on?"

Dane started upriver. When he nearly reached the next creek, a horse and rider barreled around the bend and headed up river. He couldn't identify the man. Dane raised his Browning .30-06, aiming for the rider's leg, but couldn't get a shot off before he disappeared behind the tree line. A few minutes later, another horse and rider followed. He immediately identified Kat on her big Thoroughbred and yelled to her to stop, but she didn't even look back.

"What the hell?"

Dane resisted the temptation to search for Steven and held his post hoping back up would arrive soon.

Kyle found Strawberry not far from the cabin along the creek, still saddled and bridled. He tossed the moneybag he took from the cabin over the horse's neck and carried the Jeep keys and his Canadian ID in his pocket. Kyle had mixed emotions about leaving his brother's body, but for the first time in his life he felt free.

He glanced up and downstream, figuring he had two choices: ride to the Jeep and attempt to drive to the border or escape on his girl into Canada. Each choice had its risks.

Would he be able to make it across the border before the cops shut it down? Or, would he be able to make it on horseback with the fire? Kyle patted his mare's neck. No, he couldn't leave Strawberry behind. They would make it out together or not at all. The smoke was getting worse; he must hurry!

"We can make it, girl. I know we can!"

Not long after Katherine raced past Dane, another man on horseback with two saddled riderless horses ran by on the same path. Dane recognized Kyle Schmitt, the younger brother Tammy was so concerned about. This time Dane had time to take a shot.

"Halt or I'll shoot!" he yelled, making eye contact. Dane hesitated, and Kyle darted into the woods.

Dane kicked a stone into the river out of frustration. Why hadn't he taken the shot? As he began hiking south back to the landing spot to flag down the chopper, he heard another horse running full out behind him. He turned in time to see Steven galloping up river. He just shook his head, cursing the Sheriff's Department for taking so long. Then he heard a helicopter in the distance.

As the chopper approached, Chief and Josephine appeared. "Thank God you're okay," he said. Dane gave the girl a hug, then turned to Chief. "What the hell is going on? I heard shots then a stream of riders came running by all heading north into the fire, including Katherine and Steve. I believe the other two were Ricky Werden and Kyle Schmitt."

"Ricky is heading for the border and Kat took off after him," said Chief.

"That's insane! I suppose Steve is trying to stop her?"

"Yes."

"Where's Billy?"

"He was shot." Chief shook his head. "He didn't make it."

"No!" Dane strode a few feet and bent over in grief. "Shit! I should have followed Steve."

"No, you did the right thing; you followed orders," said Chief.

It didn't make him feel any better. All he could think of was how he might have been able to save their friend.

As the chopper landed, Chief approached him and rested his hand on his shoulder. "I know what you're thinking and how you're feeling. I've been in your shoes more times than I care to remember," he said into his ear. "You didn't know everything then you know now, and even if you did, manning your post was the right thing to do. If that chopper had come sooner and you weren't here to flag them down, they would have turned back. And, we sure need them now."

Chief's words helped, but he couldn't help feeling like he had somehow failed.

The door opened on the aircraft. A sheriff identifying himself as Sergeant Peter Swanson greeted them. Dane, with Chief's help, explained the situation and urgency to the head officer. Onboard, the crew consisted of two Search and Rescue volunteers, the pilot and a medic, and one other Flathead County Sheriff in addition to Swanson.

The second officer, Larry Haas, got off the chopper to escort Chief and Josephine back to the cabin to wait for the land unit to arrive, in case Ricky circled back. Swanson had just radioed the ground unit. They were just leaving the parking area on four-wheelers down the trail toward the cabin.

"We need to lift off," said Dane. "They have at least a ten-minute lead on us." He boarded the helicopter with Swanson.

"Bring them back safe," said Chief.

Dane nodded. "Will do."

Shortly after Chief returned to the cabin with Josephine and

Haas, six officers circled the structure. Someone called out, "Anyone in the cabin? Come out with your hands on your head."

"It's me, Haas," the officer called out. They exited the cabin, Hass leading the way. Chief identified himself and the girl. "I'm retired Elkhead Police Chief Ken Taylor and this is Josephine Walker who was one of the captives."

A sheriff who Chief thought he recognized approached them.

"Hi, Chief Taylor," he said. "Captain David Brown. We met a few years ago at a state law enforcement event in Helena."

Chief recalled it was held at the capital the last year he served. "Sure, I remember."

The captain pointed to the bodies. "Can you identify the victims?" he asked.

Josephine turned away.

"Yes," said Chief. "Can the girl return to the cabin?"

"Negative. This building is now a crime scene and off-limits," said Brown. "She can wait for you over there." He pointed toward the creek. Officer Hass escorted Josephine to one of the vehicles parked at the trail.

"There's Bonanza, Cisco, and Red!" Josephine exclaimed.

"Is it okay if she secures the horses?" asked Chief.

"Sure," he said, turning to Josephine. "Officer Haas will assist you." Josephine eagerly started toward the horses, calling their names.

Chief led the Captain to the first body. "This is Jake Schmitt, a friend of Ricky Werden. He was one of the abductors. And, this is Billy Black Feather. He killed Jake before he was shot by Ricky Werden." Chief shook his head. "He was a good friend."

"I'm sorry," said Brown, placing his hand on his shoulder.

"We'll take good care of him."

"Thank you. And, you'll find one more body in a shallow grave in the cellar, back of the cabin. That should be Andy Ritter, the owner of the black Jeep and the cabin. He was an accomplice. I believe forensics will find the same handgun that killed Billy Black Feather also killed Andy Ritter. Hopefully, it can be traced to Ricky Werden."

"Where is Werden?

"He escaped on horseback."

"The only other man involved, Kyle Schmitt, rode off as well, but I've been told he tried to help the hostages. I don't believe he's armed or a threat."

"Where is the woman?"

"Katherine Walker. She rode off after Ricky."

"How did that happen?"

"That's what I said. The husband, Steven Walker, tried to stop her and took off after them. They're all on horseback."

"Great, we've got two civilians on a manhunt! Can our vehicles follow them?"

"No, I don't think so. The air unit is the best bet."

"Can't blame the husband, I suppose," he said. "I'd done the same. Hopefully our men will catch up with Werden before the wife and husband do."

24 – The Chase

Katherine heard Dane call to her, but there was no turning back now. As they galloped along the river bank, her emotions fluctuated with each of the Thoroughbred's long strides, from terrified to devastated to livid. At one point she had almost pulled Major up, doubting her reaction to risk her beloved horse and her own life to catch Ricky. That's what it had been—an emotional reaction, not a thought-out decision—but the thought of Billy lying breathless in her arms drove her onward.

"We've got to catch him, boy. End it once and for all—for Billy. Go!"

She leaned forward, pitching away her make-shift reins. Major responded, covering ground like a wolf on the hunt. She tried to clear her vision, her eyes watering from the mix of smoke and endless tears. She tried but couldn't shake the image of Billy's lifeless eyes.

"Focus on Major," she told herself. "Just ride your horse like you're on course again." My God, it had only been a few days since Billy cheered her on at the finish of their first cross-country course. It seemed ages ago.

Over the next rise the forest closed in on them, leaving little shoreline. Up ahead, low branches hung out over the water. They would have to enter the river! Katherine turned Major in a circle to slow him down before pressing him into the rushing water. Major balked for an instant, then sprang into the knee-deep rapids, his cleated shoes scrambling on the rocky floor of the river as it rushed under them.

Katherine leaned over, patting Major's neck. "Good boy!" Her emotions a jumbled mess, she began crying again, this time on account of her horse's unwavering trust in her and how hard he was trying to please her under the most frightening conditions. It was as if he could sense the urgency, unlike earlier that day at the river crossing. She wiped her eyes to clear her vision as she studied the surface of the water ahead, searching for telltale peaks, which forewarned of boulders hidden just below the surface.

She was able to maneuver Major with only the slightest pressure of her leg, only possible as a result of his schooling in dressage. Never could she have imagined his training playing such an imperative roll in their survival. One wrong step and they would go down. Her lessons with her students on the origins of dressage as military maneuvers came to mind for a fleeting second, disappearing the instant Ricky came into view over the next crest about a half mile ahead of them. They were gaining on him! Then just as quickly, he disappeared beyond the next hill.

Katherine couldn't guess how far the fire lay ahead, but smoke rose up to meet the clouds forming a solid wall of gray with the occasional red flare splitting the sheet of ash. She wondered if Ricky saw her and if he might try to lose her by turning away from the river, but he surely wouldn't leave the safety of the water with the fire so close. It appeared the burn was confined to east of the river, at least for now. But she knew all it would take is one tall burning tree to fall over a narrow portion of the river to spread the fire west.

Praying the woods would open again so they could return to shore to make better time, Katherine gasped when they topped the next crest. An old bald tree stretched across the now narrow river, glistening wet as water flowed over it like a dam. Katherine couldn't have dreamed of a more terrifying obstacle for her horse. Would she be able to keep Major moving forward to clear it?

She caught a glimpse of movement in the trees up ahead. It was Ricky maneuvering the black horse around fallen trees and low branches on land. He must have left the river to get around the log and now couldn't find a path back. If they could just clear the log, they would gain on him even more.

"C'mon, boy, go! We've got this!"

Katherine squeezed Major, holding him square between her legs, hoping he wouldn't suddenly spin away at the last second. The big bay braked once, twice, then lunged over the log barely clearing it. Next, she braced for the landing on unknown footing. The well-conditioned and athletic Thoroughbred slid with his front feet but gathered himself on his hind end to resume their pursuit.

No sooner than they recovered from jumping the log than she noticed a significant waterfall ahead to the left with a deep pool at its base. Their only route would be to jump up a series of smaller waterfalls to the right.

"Okay, boy, it's just bank jumps with water, that's all. You can do it!"

Again, Katherine rode him deep and strong, encouraging him and praising him over each tier.

With those obstacles behind them, Katherine was encouraged to see the woods open again so they could return to shore. Out of the corner of her eye she saw movement in the woods again, but it wasn't Ricky. It was Laddy, keeping pace with them. The dog's presence injected her with newfound confidence, knowing he had her back. He had forgiven her and must have been following her all day.

Out of nowhere, above the roar of the rapids, the rumble of a chopper closed in on them. Major began bending and twisting, trying to escape the frightening object approaching them overhead. Katherine had difficulty keeping him on track. Couldn't they see they were spooking him?! She waved them off, but instead they came in closer. Major began lunging and crow-hopping. Katherine held on and pushed him faster to get away from the aircraft. There was no sign of Ricky over the next rise. Where had he gone?

Katherine sat back and drew Major in, circling, as the helicopter flew past them. An old logging road crossed the river and she could see his tracks heading East. East! Into the fire? What was he thinking?

Then she realized he must have heard the chopper, too. The nearly grown-over road would give him cover, plus with the approaching fire and thick smoke, the aircraft would be forced to turn back. Katherine tore off a sleeve off her shirt and tied it around her nose and mouth. Down the two-track they raced!

She could feel Major's strides shortening. He was getting tired, but Ricky's horse had to be laboring more. She noticed she could no longer hear the helicopter and Laddy had disappeared. She wondered if they would try to land the chopper on the strip of open land where the road crossed the river.

Now, she could see the fire ahead; flames reaching over fifty feet in the air. The smoke was thick and blinding, turning day into night.

Suddenly, they were rammed!

Ricky had run his horse straight into Major's hindquarters. Both horses spun, legs becoming tangled, and the poor beasts crashed to the ground—Major in one direction, the black in the other. Katherine hit the ground hard with a thud, first her back, then her head. Major flailed, trying to get to his feet beside her. She heard snaps. Oh God, Major! In a daze, she tried to sit up to search for her horse in the smoke with blurred vision. Excruciating pain shot up her leg and her head began spinning. She passed out.

The ring of a single gunshot brought her to. "Major!" she screamed.

Where was her horse? Where was Ricky?! She couldn't move her right leg and couldn't see more than ten feet in front of her, but she managed to identify the black horse through the haze, lying still on the ground a couple yards away. She turned and found Ricky slipping its bridle onto Major. Thank God, Major was on his feet. Her boy was okay! But her relief didn't last long.

Ricky tied Major to a tree. "His leg was broken," he said, pointing to the black gelding lying motionless in a heap. "I put him out of his misery… just like I'm going to do to you."

"My horse won't let you ride him. He'll toss you in a second," she spat at him.

"He's too tired to put up a fuss."

He had a point as Major stood heaving and exhausted. Again, she tried to get up, but her leg was useless, the pain nearly making her pass out again. Then she felt something wet on her back. When she reached around, she felt a warm sticky substance. Billy's knife! It must have cut her when she fell. She frantically searched through the leaves behind her for it as Ricky moved some items from the dead horse to Major. She found it and laid it behind her out of sight, but how could she throw it accurately or with any strength from the ground? Her sudden adrenaline rush of hope burst into a million pieces.

Ricky approached her, gun in hand, wearing a stupid grin. "What a waste. Wish I had more time, Red Locks, to finish what we started, but I don't." He glanced toward the fire, then toward the river. "You should be thanking me for shooting you before the fire gets you."

"The police will find you quicker if you fire your gun." Katherine coughed. "And, you'll have a better chance of losing them on foot than on horseback."

Ricky laughed. "How stupid do you think I am? I killed your Injun for Kurt and now I'm going to kill you for Pa." Ricky raised his weapon.

Katherine closed her eyes, waiting for the inevitable end. The gun fired, but she wasn't shot! Ricky's scream startled her eyes open.

Laddy had a grip on Ricky's wrist holding the gun, dragging him away from her. With the gunshot and all the commotion, Major had broken free. Katherine whistled for him and he came to her, reins dragging. She struggled to pull herself to her feet with his reins just as Ricky broke free of Laddy's grip.

Another shot rang out. "No!" she screamed. Laddy lay sprawled out across the road. When Ricky turned the barrel toward her, she threw the knife just as he pulled the trigger, but his gun didn't fire. He had fired his last shot at Laddy.

"You bitch!" yelled Ricky with Billy's blade stuck in his thigh.

Katherine panicked, then remembered the knife under her saddle. She limped beside Major and felt for the butt of the knife, but she couldn't slide it out. It must have slid when Major fell and became lodged between the tree of the saddle and Major's back.

She turned. Ricky was bent over, cussing as he slowly pulled the blade from his leg. He limped toward her, his eyes wild.

Balanced on one leg, she loosened Major's girth and snatched the knife just as Ricky limped within reach. When Ricky lashed out at her with his knife, Katherine jerked back, hitting Major. The spooked horse swung away, his rump sending them both flying to the ground. When Ricky's knife went flying, he grabbed her wrist holding the only remaining weapon between them.

She fought him with all her might, but the knife slowly closed in on her throat as she weakened. Just as it began to dig into her skin, Laddy growled, having dragged himself within reach of Ricky's leg. With one final surge, he bit Ricky's ankle, distracting her assailant long enough for her to turn the blade on him.

Summoning strength she didn't know she possessed, she lunged the knife toward Ricky, stabbing him in the neck. Immediately, he fell away, rolling onto his back reaching for the blade. Within seconds his hands dropped limp to the ground as he bled out. Katherine turned away, shocked by what she had done.

She crawled to Laddy, lying motionless. "Oh Laddy," she said, stroking his soft head. He turned his yellow eyes to her, but he didn't move. The smoke had become so thick she couldn't see where he had been shot. "Please don't die, Laddy!" she cried, tears running down her flush face. She couldn't bare another loss. He had saved her life for a second time.

Her warhorse stretched down, smelling and nuzzling her head. "Thank you," she said, grabbing the reins. "I love you both so much. And, it's over now," she told her two heroes. She glanced at Ricky's lifeless body with Billy's knife planted in his neck. "We did it, Billy, together, like we said we would."

Startling her and Major, a large tree fell across the logging road about hundred yards away. The fire was closing in on them. She could feel the heat! She needed to think! If the cops were able to set the chopper down, they would be on their way to save her. But she couldn't count on them reaching her in time. She pulled her sleeve, now resting around her neck, back over her mouth and nose. Her mind raced, trying to think of a way out for all three of them. She knew if she set Major free, he could outrun the fire, but what about herself and Laddy? She couldn't carry her own weight, let alone a large dog.

Major was their only hope. She dragged herself to the dead black horse and quickly removed the cinch from his saddle and pulled out the saddle blanket. She noticed the bale twin Ricky had removed from Major laying on the ground and grabbed it. Next, she wrapped Laddy in the blanket and secured it with the twine, but would there be enough twin left to reach the saddle horn to drag Laddy to safety?

She pulled herself to her feet again with Major's help, focusing on her mission so she didn't faint again from the pain, and slid one ring of the cinch over the saddle horn and attached the twine to the other end giving her another two feet. But the tether remained too short. All she had left were the reins; she would have to get by with just one. That gave her what she needed. Now, to get herself in the saddle!

Katherine could put weight on her left leg, but her right appendage hung useless and jagged, obviously broken in at least two places. Between screams of agony, she guided Major into a drainage ditch running parallel to the road. With his back a foot or so lower, she gripped the horn and cantle of the saddle and managed to pull herself high enough to get her left foot in the stirrup. There was no way she could swing her bad leg over his back, so she had to balance on her tummy over the seat of the saddle.

She clucked to Major, asking for a walk. "Easy boy, nice and slow."

At first, Major was spooked a bit by the rope and Laddy dragging behind him, but with more coaxing, he settled down and they slowly moved down the road away from the flames. But, the heat of the fire was intensifying. Beads of sweat dripped down her face, unable to whip them away with both hands gripping the saddle to hold her precarious position. Above the roar of the inferno closing in on them, she could hear Laddy whimpering in pain.

Just as she considered going slower for Laddy's sake, Major began to tense up sensing the danger. "Easy, boy, take it easy," she begged, pulling slightly on the one rein, fearing he might bolt any second.

Katherine panicked as Major began turning in a circle, forcing her to quickly release the cinch ring from the saddle horn and let it drop. She feared Major would get tangled in the line and hurt Laddy worse. Another burning tree fell across the road behind them. They had run out of time! "I'm sorry Laddy!" she sobbed.

Tears streaming down her face, she clucked to Major. Laddy lifted his head for a moment, as if to say goodbye, then rested it back to the ground. As she and Major headed for the river, she heard a howl. Katherine turned. Laddy had dragged himself free of the sling and was trying to follow them. She had to get help!

Closing her eyes to the smoke, she held tight and cued Major into a trot. She gagged herself with her sleeve to silence her screams as her broken leg jostled alongside Major's barrel. They had to hurry! Her arms ached, the pain rivaling the pain of her leg, as she held tight with the dead weight of her right leg pulling her off center. She feared she wouldn't be able to hold on much longer.

"Help! Please someone, help!" she shrieked.

The moment Steven topped a rise in the logging road, he could vaguely see a riderless horse trotting toward him through the smoke. It was Major! But where was Katherine?!

Steven galloped toward Major, his heart in his throat, fearing the worst. As he neared, he thought he saw something jostling across his back. Katherine!

When he reached them, he grabbed Major's bridle slowing him to a walk. Steven pulled his bandana from his face. "Oh my God, what happened?" he asked, jumping off his horse to help her to the ground.

"My leg is broken," she sobbed. "Oh, Steven, I didn't think we were going to make it."

He held her at arm's length. "Where's Ricky?"

Katherine swallowed hard. "He's dead. I killed him. It's over," she said between labored breaths.

"Oh, baby." Steven held her tight.

"Is Jo okay?"

"Yes, and I found TJ. He's being flown to St. Joe's."

"Thank God!" Katherine pointed down the road. "Oh, Steven, you need to get Laddy. He's back there; he's shot."

"Laddy?"

"My dog," she managed between coughs.

Steven helped her mount and swing her injured leg over Major's back. "Head for the river; help is on the way. I'll get Laddy."

Katherine cantered off toward the river as he mounted Dandy and rode into the fire. He feared he was too late as he neared the motionless dog, but when he called his name, he lifted his head. Steven dismounted and approached the injured animal, afraid he might not let a stranger help him.

"Hey, boy, let's get you out of here. But you've gotta let me help you, okay?"

Laddy raised his head again and stared down the road, no doubt looking for Katherine. "It's just you and me, big fella. C'mon now and let me pick you up."

Steven retrieved the horse blanket and set it down next to Laddy. Tenderly he slipped his hindquarters onto the blanket. He could see he was shot in the shoulder, but it looked closed and no longer bleeding. But the fact he couldn't walk told him he must be in bad shape. Too weak to object, the dog allowed Steven to slide his arm under his front legs and swing him onto the blanket. Laddy whimpered in pain.

"I'm sorry, boy; only way out." The dog was heavier than he expected, and it took all his strength to lift and set him down gently across the saddle. Steven swung up behind the saddle and clucked for a trot, with the fire hot on their heels. By the time he reached the river, they had Katherine on a stretcher and were about to load her onto the chopper.

"Laddy!" she screamed. "Is he okay?"

Steven rode up beside her and dismounted "He's still with us."

Dane reached him first. "Thank God you found her—and who's this?" he asked, studying Laddy. "Is that a wolf?"

"Part, maybe. I need help getting him down."

Dane and one of the rescue team helped load the dog onto another stretcher.

"Where's Ricky Werden?" asked Swanson.

"He's dead, down the road," said Steven.

"We'll need a full statement from both of you later," said Swanson. "We don't have time to bring out the body. We'll have to come back for the remains later."

"We need to get in the air now!" yelled the pilot.

Steven nodded, grabbed his first-aid bag, and joined Katherine and Laddy in the aircraft.

"I'll get the horses back to the cabin," said Dane. "There's a horse trailer on the way."

Katherine tried to sit up. "Ride Dandy. Poor Major is exhausted."

"I was planning to," said Dane. "Meet up with you at the hospital. I'll make sure the horses get out safely."

"Thank you, Dane," she said.

As the chopper lifted, the medic put Katherine's leg in a brace as Steven worked on Laddy.

"Is he going to make it?" she asked.

"I don't know. We won't know until we get him X-rayed."

Once the medic finished with her leg and gave her some pain meds, he climbed up front beside the pilot.

Katherine reached to the stretcher beside her and stroked Laddy's ears. "Such a good boy," she cooed. The dog lifted his head in recognition, then rested it again.

"I gave him something for the pain," said Steven. "He shouldn't be too uncomfortable now."

"He saved my life… twice," she said. "He took the last bullet meant for me."

"He looks a lot like Shane," said Steven.

"He does, doesn't he? I want them to drop you and Laddy off at the clinic before they take me to the hospital."

Steven shook his head. "I don't think they'd go for that, sweetie," he said, nodding in the direction of the front of the helicopter. "And neither will I. They'll take him to a vet after they drop us off. They'll take good care of him."

"How bad is it?" she asked, glancing down at her leg.

"You're going to need surgery. I think you have two breaks.

"It was worth it. It's over." Her face turned cold. "I'm glad he's dead. I'm glad I killed him." Katherine took a deep breath and sighed. "Is that wrong?"

"No, honey, it was self-defense." Steven studied his broken wife. "Where did Laddy come from, Kat? Do you feel up to telling me the whole story?"

On route to the hospital, Katherine shared every detail starting with Ricky's letter clear through to Ricky's end.

"I did it for all of us, for Billy. Oh God, I can't believe he's gone, Steven. Poor Sarah and TJ. Perhaps if I hadn't followed him, stayed at camp this morning…"

"Don't, sweetie. Sounds like if you hadn't come along, Jake would have killed Billy on the spot at the river and perhaps his brother, too." Steven looked out the chopper window. "If anyone is responsible, it's me. I should have waited. I should have known Ricky wouldn't be alone. If Billy didn't have to use his knife on Jake to save me, he might have…"

"Stop, Steven. I'm glad you showed up when you did and so was Billy," said Katherine. "I just wish Billy knew Ricky was dead and that his knife ended it just as he planned." Katherine stared at her hand, her face drawn tight. "I don't even remember stabbing him."

"Maybe you had a little help."

"Maybe."

As they flew southeast, Steven held his wife's trembling hand and glanced back at the angry sky, a smoke flume now stretching across the northern horizon as far as the eye could see. The forest would eventually mend itself, but he wondered if his family and friends would ever recover.

25 – The Healing

Friday

Katherine opened her eyes in an unfamiliar dark room. "Billy!" she gasped. Had it all been just a bad dream? When she tried to spring up to a seated position, excruciating pain ran down her right leg as her head pounded, confirming it hadn't been—the nightmare was real. When she attempted to brush her hair from her face, tubes and wires limited her movement. The stuffy room smelled of ammonia and Band-Aids.

She was at St. Vincent Hospital in Billings and the last thing she remembered was going into surgery that morning. Steven guessed right, her leg had been broken in two places, and she had suffered a concussion. She searched for the button to raise the head of her bed and another to switch on the little overhead reading light. When her eyes adjusted to the dim light, she could make out a shape slumped in a chair across the room. It was Betsy, sound asleep.

When the door opened, a bright wedge of light split the dark room and a nurse entered. "I see you're awake. How are you feeling?"

"Okay, I guess. My leg and head hurt."

Betsy sat up. "Oh, sweetie, you're awake," she said to her before asking the nurse if everything was okay.

"She's doing fine," the nurse said to Betsy, opening the drapes. She turned to Katherine. "Your surgery went well. You now have a bionic leg," she said jokingly as she checked her IV, monitor, and vitals. Katherine studied her leg now in a cast from mid-thigh to her foot. "Would you like me to bring you a meal?"

"I'm not hungry, maybe later," she said, feeling a bit dizzy and nauseous.

"Sure, the anesthetic will do that to you. I'll be back with some pain meds and the doctor will be by later," she said on her way out the door.

"What time is it, Betz? It looks almost dark out."

"It's only around noon. It's been storming all morning."

"I hope it puts the fire out."

Betsy got up with her cane and hobbled across the room to sit beside her. When she reached out her hand, Katherine clasped it and gave it a squeeze. This was the first time seeing her dear friend following the horrific events of the preceding day. Katherine didn't know where to start. "Thank you for being here, Betz."

"Where else would I be? I got here as soon as I could. Steven drove me over early this morning while they were prepping you. He'll be happy to see you're awake."

"Where is Steven?"

"He just got back from checking in on the dog you found. He knew you'd want to know how he was doing."

"Laddy! Is he going to be okay?"

"His surgery went well, too. Steven said he's going to be just fine."

"Thank goodness. He saved my life, Betz… twice. He's an amazing animal, looks so much like Shane. I can't wait for you to meet him. Where's Steven now?"

"He's with Sarah in the chapel down the hall. He'd been waiting for an opportunity to see her in private. She's been with TJ since he came out of surgery."

"Poor Sarah. How is TJ? The last I heard he was in stable condition, but nothing more."

"He's out of ICU. He's in a room down the hall. Jo is with

him."

"Thank God he's okay."

Betsy went on to tell her about TJ's injuries—his collapsed lung, how close some of the wounds had come to his heart and main arteries, and how much blood he had lost. But Katherine barely heard her, her thoughts drifting back to the terrible events of the previous day. How could Billy be gone? They were laughing and teasing each just yesterday.

Betsy must have read the faraway look in her eyes and took a deep breath. "I'm so sorry about Billy."

Katherine tried, but couldn't hold back the tears any longer. She had stayed strong since they arrived at the hospital, but now in her weakened state, she gave into her sorrow. "It doesn't seem real. He seemed invincible."

Betsy patted her hand.

Katherine wiped her tears away. "I loved him every way possible—as a friend, a lover, a partner, and now as my hero. He saved Steven and me, Betz."

"I know, Steven told me. He's telling Sarah now how grateful you both are for her husband's sacrifice."

"It just hurts so bad. I feel a part of me has died, too."

"That's how I felt when Joseph passed. But gradually it gets easier. We must celebrate his life, not dwell on his death. He died a proud and brave warrior like our ancestors, and he will be welcomed with open arms into the spirt world."

Katherine nodded. "Yes, he was a brave warrior."

"And, so were you."

Katherine shrugged her shoulders. "I was consumed with anger and hate. I'd never felt like that before. It was like I turned into another person." She looked deeply into Betsy's eyes. "I killed a man. I never thought I could do that."

"I'm proud of you. Billy would be, too."

Katherine could feel her emotions building again. "I did

what I had to do. That's all. To end it… for us all… but mostly for Billy. I had to finish what he started. I didn't want him to have died in vain."

Betsy fiddled with her cane. "They found notes… written by Billy. He left them in his saddlebag. He must have known there was a good chance he wasn't going to make it out alive."

"To whom?"

"There's one to Sarah, TJ… and there's one to you. Steven's giving Sarah theirs now. He left yours with me to give you."

Katherine smiled. Only Steven could be so understanding. She wondered if he had read it and hoped there wasn't anything in it that would hurt or upset him.

Betsy reached inside her cardigan pocket. "They were written on the back of pork and beans labels."

The two women grinned.

"Billy always was resourceful," said Katherine, recalling how Billy etched his phone number onto a piece of bark he cut from a tree the first day they met. She reached out her hand.

Betsy handed the folded label to her. "You want me to step out?"

"No, you can stay." Katherine unfolded the note and read it to herself.

Dear Kat,
If you're reading this, you're alive and I'm not, so hopefully I did my job. I know you and you're going to feel responsible, please don't. Honor me by moving on with your life. Put this all behind you and be happy. Carry my heart in your pocket always.
Love, Billy

Katherine dropped her focus to her lap as her eyes welled

yet again. Would she ever be able to stop crying? How could she have lost track of Billy's token of his love for her? How could she ever put this all behind her and be happy again? She was alive, and Billy wasn't. Her world was no longer round; it was square and full of jagged edges of pain and sorrow. She couldn't even imagine how Sarah felt. How could she face her old friend again?

Once the floodgates of guilt opened, everything she might have done differently to prevent this outcome, from the beginning thirty-four years ago to yesterday's tragic end, swept through her like a tidal wave. Stripped of any logic or reason, she was left to drown in her remorse. If only she had taken Betsy's advice years ago.

"This has been all my fault," she sobbed. "It's happening all over again, but this time it's for real. Billy is gone forever!"

Betsy hugged her the best she could from her seat. "Sweetie, it was the Werdens' and only the Werdens' fault, then and now. You aren't to blame for their blind hatred."

Katherine tried to rein in her emotions. "That's what I told Billy when he said it was his fault," she sniffled.

"Then, heed your own words. You didn't do anything wrong. There's no sin in loving someone."

"But… Sarah?"

"That was Billy's doing. If it hadn't been with you, it would have been with someone else. He was always reaching for something just beyond his reach."

"Perhaps I had been as well," she whispered, considering what she had put Steven through. But those days were behind her now. She felt foolish for having taken so much for granted and for her folly. She had everything she had grown up longing for—a wonderful man who loved her beyond reason; two daughters she couldn't be prouder of; and she got to live her dream working with horses surrounded by the majesty of the

Rocky Mountains, at Two Ponies.

She would live as Billy had—in the present—and age gracefully as he never would have the opportunity to do. She lifted her chin, took a deep breath and in Billy fashion, moved on.

Folding the label once again, she handed it back to her friend for safekeeping. "Did you see Jo this morning? How is she doing?"

"She's doing well, considering," said Betsy.

Katherine recalled what her daughter had told her in the cellar about her and TJ and wondered if Steven had mentioned anything. "Did Steven tell you what we suspect happened between the kids?"

Betsy's eyes widened. "No…"

"They slept together. I think Steven is in denial. He still sees Jo as his baby girl. But, I'm pretty sure they had sex. Jo said they're in love."

"Well, it's no secret TJ's been crazy about her forever, but Jo—this comes as a bit of a surprise."

"I haven't had a chance to talk to her about it yet."

"How do you feel about it?" Betsy asked.

"Seeing her yesterday when she thought TJ was dead took me back to that night at the lake when I thought Billy had drowned, so young and so in love."

"Poor, dear," said Betsy.

"I don't know how to feel about it. I want to be happy for her, but I'm also afraid for her."

Betsy straightened her blanket. "She'll be leaving for school soon."

"Yeah, that's what Steven said."

"He told me you want pay for TJ's college education. Is that your strategy?"

"No. Well, maybe it crossed our mind. Either way, it's the

least we can do to help Sarah and TJ out any way we can. But, if they stay together, I can't help worrying."

"Times have changed. It's better than it was, especially in other places."

"I know; you're right. TJ is a great kid and we all know how much he cares about Jo. We couldn't ask for any better for our daughter. It's just hard to let go of the past, especially after all this."

"Best to see what they decide between the two of them, first."

"Of course. She is an adult now, which is still hard for me to wrap my head around sometimes. But it'll be difficult not to share my concern. Then, you know Jo… she'd be more likely to do something just to oppose me."

Betsy smiled. "She is the independent one. Reminds me of someone else I know."

Katherine chuckled. "Right, the apple never falls far from the tree."

"But she'll always be your little girl. You'll never stop wanting to protect her."

"Just like you haven't with me."

Betsy smiled and gave her hand another squeeze.

Sarah sat in a pew with her hands in her lap beside Steven. She had cried so much over the past twenty-four hours she felt certain her tears had run dry. She listened quietly as Steven explained every detail about how her husband had bravely fought and died, but still more tears streamed down her bronze cheeks. Steven's eyes moistened, too, as he shared how grateful he was for Billy's sacrifice, having saved him and his family. She welcomed Steven's lingering heartfelt hug, imagining his pain and guilt.

"I'm so sorry, Sarah. His last words to me were to tell you

and TJ he loved you."

"Thank you." Sarah wiped her face and offered a weak smile. "He used to joke that he'd never live to be an old man and that he wouldn't be any good at it anyway," she told him with a squeeze of his hand.

"Please let us know whatever we can do to help, with anything…"

Sarah nodded. The "us" and "we" brought Katherine to mind and allowed her animosity toward Katherine to resurface. She tried to fight her rage toward her old friend, but her face burned with anger at the thought of her. If it hadn't been for Katherine, her husband would still be alive, and her son wouldn't have nearly died. It wasn't enough she stole Billy from her for fourteen years; she had to take him from her forever. It might be irrational thinking, knowing it was Billy's decision and plan to confront Ricky himself, but her heartbreak would not allow reason, not yet anyway.

From the beginning, her relationship with Katherine had been a rocky one, with extreme highs and lows spanning over thirty years. But she had forgiven her, and they had become close again, raising their children side-by-side as neighbors and close friends for nearly two decades. They had rejoiced in each other's blessings and been there to comfort one another through their losses.

Then when Katherine began pulling Billy away from her a second time, it didn't take much to cut through the forgiveness to expose the jealousy and anger still lurking beneath. Ricky was just a consequence of Katherine's actions. Sure, Billy had played a major role, but he ended up paying the ultimate price, and she still had it all! How could she ever forgive her again, even for dear Steven's sake?

"… Including any funeral arrangements," Steven added, bringing her back from her thoughts.

"Thank you, Steve, but it'll be small—just our family and yours."

We'll hold something at Two Ponies. And, TJ's hospitalization. Just let us know when you start receiving bills."

"Oh, that's too generous, really. We have savings."

"And you're going to need them. Life insurance?"

"No. Billy wasn't much for planning for the future."

"That's what we thought. Kat and I already discussed this yesterday, and we insist on paying for a college education for TJ. He's been like a son to us and it's the least we can do."

"No, I couldn't accept such a gift," Sarah replied. She could see Steven was disappointed by her reaction. She wanted her husband back, and no one or any gift would bring him back! Why should she give Katherine the satisfaction of absolving her guilt so easily?

"Please, let us do this for you and TJ… for Billy."

Sarah stared out the foggy window. They had always wanted a college education for their son. Yes, for TJ, for Billy, and even for Steven, she would swallow her pride.

Sarah nodded. "Okay. TJ will be thrilled. It'll be a dream come true for him. But he'll work summers and we'll contribute as much as we can."

"Thank you for letting us do this, but we do have one favor to ask. We would like you to keep it a secret from TJ. Tell him that his father put the money away for him, or there was life insurance you weren't aware of. We don't want him to feel indebted to us or refuse our help.

"Okay, I won't tell him. I don't know how to thank you enough."

"No need. Just let us know which college he chooses. We won't say anything to Jo either," said Steven. "I need to go check in on Kat."

"Of course. Is she awake?

"She wasn't yet when I left her about thirty minutes ago."

Sarah could read the concern on his face. He was such a good man, far better than she deserved. "I hope the surgery was a success and that she has a full and speedy recovery."

"Thanks, Sarah. Kat's a fighter. I never knew how much until yesterday."

Sarah dismissed his comment. She was glad Ricky was dead but not ready to acknowledge Katherine's heroics.

Steven got up to leave and rested his hand on her shoulder. "Call us for any reason. I'm so glad TJ's going to be okay."

She just nodded, but she felt her emotions building again.

"Oh, I almost forgot," said Steven. "I have something for you."

Sarah turned. What else could he possibly offer or do for them?

"Letters were found in Billy's saddlebag." Steven pulled the notes from his pocket and handed them to her.

She had to smile. "Only Billy," she said, as she accepted the Campbell's Pork and Beans labels.

Steven smiled then left her to read Billy's goodbye in private. Sarah set aside the note to TJ and unfolded the one to her. She had to strain to read the small messy print in the dim light.

My Sarah,

If you're reading this, things didn't go according to plan. I just hope I took Ricky with me. I'm sorry I won't be there for TJ's wedding or for our grandchildren. I'm sorry about a lot of things. I'm sorry we parted on bad terms. You were right, and you were wrong about me and Kat. Yes, I still love her, but not as much as I love you. You have been my rock, the only one who never left my side no matter what stupid shit I did. Thank you. Find a nice guy, better than me, who will make you happy.

Love always, Billy

Sarah folded the label back up and stuck it in her purse along with TJ's. She knew her husband couldn't stop loving Katherine any more than she could stop loving him. The note gave her some peace, along with what Steven told her, knowing she was in his thoughts and heart near the end.

One more tear escaped. She brushed it away and headed down the hall to see her son. She couldn't wait to give him the news.

TJ opened his eyes to find Josephine sitting beside his bed watching over him.

"Hi there," she said. "How are you feeling?"

"A little dizzy and sore but better now that you're here." TJ smiled. This was the first he had gotten to see her. Josephine was wearing a pretty, sky-blue blouse with her auburn locks pulled back off her face with matching blue clips. She looked like an angel. "Can I get a kiss?" he whispered. It hurt to speak, but he didn't care.

Josephine stood up and studied him with a look of concern.

"You're not going to break me, Jo." TJ pointed to his lips.

She smiled and carefully leaned over him making sure not to touch any of the wires and tubes and delicately placed a kiss on his mouth. She sat down and held his hand. "I was so scared, but the doctors said you're out of danger now."

"All I thought about was lying next to you again, Jo. I've waited all my life to be with you; no way I'm going anywhere now."

"Seriously, though," she said, her brows narrowing. "They said it was a miracle nothing vital was hit."

"And, thanks to your dad finding me."

"I thought you were dead when they took me."

TJ squeezed her hand. "They didn't hurt you, did they, Jo?"

"No." Josephine felt her head. "Just a little bump."

"I'm sorry I didn't protect you better."

"But you did, if you hadn't jumped on Cisco behind me and told me to duck, I would have gotten shot too. We were both lucky to have lived through it all."

"It was Cisco," said TJ, smiling. "My Medicine Hat horse and his protective shield."

"Oh TJ, that's just an old wives tale."

"Well, I can believe it if I want to."

"Of course, you can. He's a very special horse."

TJ's mood turned somber, his brows creasing. "Remember my twelfth birthday?"

Josephine's eyes began to pool. She knew his dad would come up eventually. "Sure, I do, TJ."

"Cisco was the best gift my dad ever gave me. He helped me train him, you know."

The image of Mr. Black Feather lying in a puddle of blood outside the cabin nearly blinded her with tears. "Oh, TJ, I'm so sorry," she sniffled. "He was so brave. He saved all of us."

"I just wish he could have saved himself, too."

Feelings of guilt gripped Josephine's heart. "Me too," she said. TJ had every reason to blame her parents for the death of his father. She might, if the tables were turned.

"So, you all packed?" he asked. "It's nice of Jessie to fly out with you tomorrow to get you settled in."

Josephine scooted to the end of her chair. She couldn't wait to tell TJ her new plans. "I've been thinking, TJ… I just can't leave you and my mom like this. I'm going to tell my parents I'm not leaving tomorrow," she blurted out. "And, I'm not sure I want to go at all, now. I can't imagine being away from you that long."

TJ groaned in pain as he pushed the button to raise his head a little. "That's crazy! It's what you've always wanted, Jo—to be an actress. You need to go, I'll be fine. And I'll be here waiting for you when you return at Thanksgiving. It's only a couple of months away."

Josephine shook her head in disbelief. This was not the reaction she was counting on. She thought for sure he would be thrilled she didn't want to leave. This was so unlike the TJ she knew, who didn't want her to leave, ever.

"I could start in January then, after you're healed, and we could move to LA together. We could get an apartment close to school."

His face hardened. "Be realistic, Jo. You have to go now. Your parents have already paid your tuition. I'd do anything to have that opportunity."

"But, we're…" she began.

"No, Jo!" he interrupted. "I can't move to LA. It would never work anyway. You just need to go."

"But, TJ…"

He turned toward the wall, flinching in pain. "Go, now!"

Josephine broke out in tears and ran from the room.

Just as Sarah was about to enter her son's room, Josephine pushed through the door upset, and passed her without a word.

TJ looked distressed, too. "What happened?" she asked.

"Jo just doesn't understand."

"Understand, what?" Sarah sat in the still warm seat beside his bed.

"That she needs to leave for school, and I need to stay here!"

"Calm down, please. You shouldn't be getting so worked

up. Tell me what happened, slowly."

"First, she says she's not going to school, then she wants me to move to LA with her. I can't leave you alone. And, I can't support Jo and I, and I'm not going to allow her parents to support us. What would I do in a big city anyway?"

Steven's request of keeping the tuition a secret entered her mind. He was right; TJ was too proud like his father, he would never have accepted their gift.

"TJ, listen to me." She tenderly cradled his face in her hand, his father's eyes searching hers for answers. "I know what you're thinking. That you're not good enough, that you won't be able to compete with the college-educated white boys she'll be meeting, and she'll end up hurting you.

"Son, if you love her, and I know you do, give it a chance. Give Josephine a little credit. She isn't like most girls, that's why you love her like you do. Besides, you're both young and things might very well change for both of you in a year or two. But, if you give up on Jo now out of fear, you'll regret it the rest of your life. Don't let the color of your skin come between you and your happiness."

"Look what happened to dad because he loved a white girl."

That statement shocked Sarah, but it shouldn't have considering what he'd just gone through. And maybe he had a point, but she couldn't allow her fears to stand between her son and his dreams, and Jo was certainly one of them.

"Things are better now," she told him. "Ricky was just stuck in the past. You've loved Jo since you were old enough to walk and hold her hand."

"Now she hates me. I yelled at her."

"She doesn't hate you. You're going through a lot right now. Just tell her you're sorry, she'll understand. And, I agree with you—she should leave for school as planned. You both need to take it slow. If it's for real, the miles and time apart won't matter."

TJ smiled. "Thanks, Mom."

"Besides, as soon as you're healed, you'll be leaving for college, too."

TJ jerked his head up in obvious pain.

"Easy," she said, coaxing him to relax. "Your dad had set some money aside for your education and there was some life insurance I wasn't aware of. I know you've always wanted to be a veterinarian."

TJ shook his head in disbelief. "What are you saying? That we have the money for me to go to vet school?" TJ's eyes brightened, color returning to his face.

"You'll have to apply and get accepted, of course."

"Sure, and I'll have to take the GED test. But I know I can do it. I'll study hard and take it over and over until I get a good enough score."

"I'm sure Dr. Walker would be happy to write you a recommendation for all the summers you volunteered."

"I bet I'd be the first Blackfeet veterinarian ever!"

"Let's not get ahead of ourselves. If vet school doesn't work out, there are many other fields you'd enjoy, like ranching, livestock breeding or in the forestry service."

"I just can't believe it. But, what about you and the farm? How would you manage without me?"

"Don't worry about me. We'll need to sell most of the horses, not Cisco or Red, of course. I'll be fine."

"Wow, college. This is so exciting. I can't wait to tell Jo."

Sarah was so happy to see her son perk up. It would surely speed up his recovery. "Let's get you feeling better first, then we can start looking into schools and programs."

"I want to go to CSU where Dr. Walker attended. That way I can drive home for the holidays and summers."

"Okay, I'll contact them this week and get all the paperwork together. We can fill it out together."

TJ sat up. "I want to talk to my doctor to see when I can go home. I need to start studying. We need to find out when I can take the test."

"Whoa, slow down. You need to heal first. The doctor will be by sometime today. We can talk to him then. Would you like me to find Jo? She might be in with her mom. I can tell her you want to see her."

"Thanks, Mom."

"Then you need to get some rest."

Shortly after Betsy left Katherine's room to get lunch at the cafeteria, Josephine walked in obviously distraught about something. Katherine patted the arm of the chair beside her. "What's wrong, honey?"

Josephine sat down. "It's TJ. He's mad at me."

"About what?"

"I told him I didn't want to leave him or you right now, or maybe ever."

"Not attend UCLA?" Katherine couldn't believe her ears.

"I don't want to leave him. I love him and I'm afraid if I go, he'll meet someone else. He said he didn't want me to stay and he wouldn't move to LA with me."

"The last couple of days have been an emotional roller coaster for you both. I think you're overreacting. You can't put off school and not pursue your dreams out of fear of losing TJ. My God, the boy has loved you all his life. What makes you think that's going to change now?"

"It already has. He hates me."

"He doesn't hate you. He probably has the same fears you do, but he knows you need to go."

Josephine sighed. "You're right. He lost his dad and nearly

died. I'm the least of his problems."

"Don't say it like that. You know he still cares, or he wouldn't get so upset, right?"

Jo nodded and wiped her nose. "I'm sorry, Mom. I guess I am a bit of an emotional wreck. I haven't even asked how you're doing. Dad said the surgery went well."

"I'm waiting to meet with the doctor. You probably know more than I do."

"The doctor told Dad you should be able to go home in a few days, but the cast will be on for two to three months. Then there will be physical therapy for a while."

"See!" Katherine chuckled. "I'm sorry I won't be able to see you off to school tomorrow. Are you packed?"

"Mostly, I can finish tonight."

Katherine could see her daughter's reserve. "It'll be great. I can't wait to hear all about your classes. You've wanted to be an actress and writer since you were a little girl, always pretending to be someone famous, playing dress up, making up the most outlandish stories. You sure kept your father and I entertained." Katherine could see the old spark returning to her daughter's eyes. "TJ wants you to pursue your dreams, too."

"I know. It's just… I've never left like this about anyone before. I do love him, Mom. I think I always have; I was just afraid to admit it. You, Dad, my friends…"

"I'm sorry, Jo. We didn't mean to push you away from TJ, but now more than ever, I think you can understand why."

"I do."

Katherine had to ask. "When you said you slept together, what exactly did you mean? Did you have intercourse?"

Josephine blushed. "Isn't that pretty private, Mom? We're consenting adults, you know."

"That's true, and I'm going to take that as a yes. I just

wondered if you used any protection. I remember myself at your age. It's all so new and exciting, we sometimes don't think about such things."

"We were up in the mountains, Mom. But TJ did take the necessary precautions."

"That's not enough. We need to get you on birth control. Okay? We'll talk more about it after you get settled in at school."

"Okay. Thanks, Mom."

"Now go kiss and make up."

Just as Josephine left to see TJ, Steven entered her room. "Hi honey, I'm glad to see you're awake. How are you feeling?"

"I'm a little sore. How is Sarah?"

"Okay, considering. I told her everything. It was difficult reliving his final moments, but I think it will help her knowing."

"I hope so."

"Jo looked happy," he said. "Just passed her in the hall."

"She and TJ had their first spat. She going to make up with him."

"So, they're really a couple now, ha?"

"Yes, dear."

"This is going to take some getting used to."

Suddenly the hospital room door flung open.

"Hi, I finally made it!" Jessie entered the room balancing a colorful vase of flowers with a smiley face on a stick in one arm and a pile of magazines and books in the other.

Steven shot up to take the flowers before they ended up on the floor and set them down on the window sill. "Hi Jess," he said.

Katherine smiled and shook her head. Jessie was just what she needed, a little comic relief. She knew she wouldn't bring up Billy again unless she did. Jessie had given her condolences to her and Steven and the Black Feathers last night.

As soon as Jessie's hands were free, she gave her a hug. "I'm so happy you're okay… well, mostly, anyway. Bummer about the cast. Does it itch?"

Well it didn't until you just mentioned it!"

Steven snickered but didn't say a word.

Jessie panicked. "Oh no, I'm so sorry. I didn't…"

"I'm joking, Jess."

"Ha, you got me that time!"

"I get you every time," said Katherine.

"Hardly," said Jessie. "So, tell me more about Jo and TJ. You sort of left me hanging last night."

Steven shot her a look. "Well, like I said, they're a couple now," said Katherine.

"How hot of an item?" asked Jessie, earning an intense stare from Steven.

"They're intimate, if that's what you mean."

Steven rolled his eyes.

"I knew it," said Jessie. "I knew they'd end up together. How do you feel about it?" she asked, directing her question to both her and Steven.

"In light of the past week, at first, I was upset about it… more concerned really," said Katherine. "But, I'm taking it in stride. We all know how crazy TJ is about her."

Katherine glanced at Steven, who remained silent. "It's always harder on the fathers," she continued, smiling. "I'll make sure she gets on birth control before she returns home."

"Okay, I'm out of here!" said Steven, jumping out of his seat.

"Betsy's at the cafeteria," said Katherine. "Kimi and Luna were going to meet her for lunch and come up for a visit afterward."

"Great, I'll go join them," he said, grabbing his coat.

"We'll be talking horses anyway," said Jessie.

"Oh, I can't wait to see Major," said Katherine. "Wonder when I'll be able to ride again."

Steven paused at the door. "Major is in good hands with Jessie. He'll be waiting when you're ready, but only when the doctor says you're ready."

Katherine smiled. "And which doctor might that be?"

"This one, of course!" he laughed, on his way out the door.

As soon as Steven left the room, Katherine turned to Jessie. "How is Major doing? How do the nicks and straps look?"

"I put Fura-zone on the ones that are still open and Vaseline on the scrapes that are scabbed over. I don't think there will be any scars."

"Great, thanks! I sure miss him. We'd been working so close for so long. This is the longest we've been apart."

"I'm sure he misses you, too," said Jessie, as she stepped up to the vase and began arranging the flowers. She was happy to have her friend safely back into her life. It had been a rough week, not knowing day to day what was happening. Katherine had filled her in on all the details except for Billy's death and when she killed Ricky. She had only vaguely brushed over those events. Jessie couldn't blame her; she wouldn't want to relive those moments either. She knew Katherine would let her know when she felt ready. Jessie turned from the flowers and found Katherine gazing out the window.

"It looks cold and windy. Does Major have his blanket on?" asked Katherine.

"With the coat he grew over the past week, he didn't need his rug, but I put a medium-weight sheet on him."

"I'll bet he's happy to be home with his buddy, Cody."

"For sure, they're back to grooming each other and fighting over hay."

Katherine studied her injured leg. "I wonder if I'll be able to jump again. I don't think Major, or I, would be happy competing only in dressage. We both live for the excitement and challenge of cross-country and stadium."

"Don't worry about that now; just focus on healing." Jessie handed her one of the horse magazines she brought. "Here's some reading to help you pass the time."

Katherine stared at the pile of literature on her night stand, but her mind was apparently elsewhere. "Are you okay, Kat?" asked Jessie.

She turned her focus to her. "I guess so. I don't know. I'm grateful to be alive yet feel guilty I'm alive at the same time. Thankful Steven and Jo are okay, and TJ is on the mend, but I'm having trouble accepting Billy is gone. Don't know how I'll face Sarah again. I feel empty."

"That's understandable after what you've been through."

"I don't know if I even care about competing anymore. It doesn't seem as important now. I wanted to prove myself to the world. Now I just want to go home."

"You have nothing to prove, Kat. You have students to carry on your legacy, competing in all levels. There's Linda Carey who's tearing it up on the East Coast. She just earned her Silver. And that blonde in Kentucky, what's her name? She's planning to ride at Rolex this spring."

"Abbie Olsen. Yeah, if I had qualified, we probably would have competed against each other in Atlanta."

Jessie frowned. "So, you think this is it?"

"It would have been a miracle to qualify as it was, now… I can't see it happening."

"Let's get you feeling well enough to get you home. You just need a safe space to heal. Two Ponies has always been your sanctuary."

"Yes, Two Ponies has gotten me through tough times in the past."

Jessie studied her friend. Shadows ringed her normally bright green eyes; she looked exhausted. She had been through a lot and it would take time to heal physically and emotionally.

"You need some rest. I'm going to meet the others down in the cafeteria. Take a little nap and take advantage of the quiet. I'll hold everyone off for at least an hour."

By the time she picked up her purse and headed for the door, Katherine eyes were closed. Just before the door closed behind her, Jessie heard Katherine whisper, "Home…"

26 – Home

One week following the worst day of her life, Katherine sat bundled up on the front porch in one of the cozy chairs and ottomans Steven had dragged out from the library. Resting on the porch overlooking the lake and mountains had become the favorite part of her daily routine since she returned home. Her days consisted of Betsy waiting on her hand and foot, daily phone calls with Josephine, playing cards with Kimi and Luna, reading whatever she could get her hands on, and watching old movies, stirring away from anything with guns or that was too gloomy. Fun movies like "Man from Snowy River" and "The Black Stallion" that she used to watch with her girls helped cheer her up.

The sun warmed her face while she sat with her leg elevated in front of her. It was quiet; the geese and hummingbirds long gone. Another harsh Montana winter would soon be upon them. She took a deep breath, filling her senses with the aroma of pine and the earthly scent of fall. The fresh air was invigorating.

"This would be a beautiful day for a ride," she grumbled. Fall was her favorite time of the year to ride the trails and fields with Major, galloping through deep beds of leaves on a brisk morning. The doctors still couldn't tell her when the cast would come off or when she could return to riding, or to what capacity. Her body and mind had become accustomed to nearly daily rides over the past two years. She literally ached to ride her horse. Only when they removed the cast would they know if there would be any permanent damage or restrictions in her riding. She tried not to think about the later.

More than missing her daily rides, she simply missed being around horses. She would be happy to just get close enough to smell one, but the stairs and downhill hike to the barns had been deemed off-limits by Dr. Walker. The more Katherine thought about it, the more antsy she felt, trapped inside her bubble. She needed a horse fix—she needed to see Major!

Steven and Jessie were at the clinic and Betsy was taking her afternoon nap—this was the perfect opportunity for her steal away for just a few minutes. Katherine carefully got up on her crutches and hobbled to the side stairs. She grabbed the railing and slid her crutches down the stairs ahead of her and slowly sat down and slid on her bottom, one stair at a time. Picking up her crutches and getting back on her feet proved to be more of a challenge than she anticipated, but eventually she was on the drive heading toward the old stable. Just getting near her horses made her spirits soar.

Katherine stopped halfway down to rest and had to chuckle watching Major and Cody grooming each other in the paddock, in "if you scratch my back, I'll scratch yours" fashion. Major looked great, fuzzy, but he had gained most of his weight back. Jessie planned to work him twice a week to keep him in shape until she could ride again. The big gelding raised his head high, eyes alert and ears pricked forward, noticing her on the drive. She must have looked strange to him with two additional legs. He snorted and watched her cautiously, nostrils flaring as he attempted to identify the strange creature.

Opening the latch and getting herself and the crutches through the small inset barn door a foot off the ground was even more of a challenge than the stairs. Once she was through, she shuffled into the tack room and extracted a few sugar cubes from the yellow box on the shelf. Lumps in hand, she gimped to the stall door and whistled. She could hear Major snort again, then a moment later he appeared outside the run-in, his eyes rimmed in white.

"Major, it's me, boy," she called to him.

Major flicked his ears and looked away pretending not see or hear her. Katherine laughed. "Here boy, I have a treat for you." Katherine set her crutches against the outside of the stall, so he couldn't see them and hopped into the shelter on one foot and grabbed ahold of a support post.

She continued to call to him. Cautiously, Major approached her. Once he could clearly see in the shadows and smell her, he relaxed and walked up to her and nuzzled her hand. She extended her palm and he snatched up the treats. Major curiously smelled her cast, snorted, and stepped back a couple of steps.

"It's okay; it's still me. Come back, sweet boy."

Major walked closer again and as she stroked his neck and face, his eyes softened. "Your scrapes are all gone," she observed. "Wish I could heal as fast." Images from that afternoon flashed through her mind. "That was quite a ride, wasn't it, boy? You must have been as frightened as I was. But you charged through the river, jumped the scary log and waterfalls, and ran into the fire… just because I asked you to."

Katherine gave Major a hug then leaned against him so she could scratch his favorite spot on the top of his neck where he couldn't reach. "If you hadn't come to me and allowed me to pull myself up on your reins, who knows what might have happened." A cold chill ran down her spine at the thought of it. "Thank you for trusting me."

Unexpectedly, the crutches slid onto the floor with a clatter. "Major flinched, but Katherine calmed him with her soothing voice and touch, "Easy, boy, it's okay; it's just my dumb crutches." Thankfully, he didn't pull away or she surely would have ended up in a heap on the ground. "Soon I won't need them anymore and I'll be back riding you. Do you miss me, boy? I sure miss you."

Katherine stroked and scratched on him a while longer, Cody joining them for his share of pats. Then she hopped back out of the stall, threw them each a section of hay, and sat down on a hay bale outside the stall. She watched them with contentment as they carefully selected the most flavorful pieces, their eyes soft, ears relaxed. After exerting the most energy she had in a week, she needed to rest before heading back to the lodge. She closed the stall door and laid down on a bed of hay and closed her eyes, listening to the soothing sound of grinding hay. She smiled. Now she was home.

Katherine awoke to Steven's voice. "Kat. Wake up, sweetie," he whispered.

She opened her eyes, shocked to find herself still in the barn. She was certain Steven would give her a scolding.

"Betsy was a mess, worried you'd fallen. I caught her on her way out the door to search for you. I knew where to find you."

Katherine smiled and wiped the sleep from her eyes. "I just had to see Major."

"Well, it looks like you're still in one piece," he said, looking over her cast. "How about I drive you back to the lodge?"

Smiling, she reached out her arms for him to help her up. "Thanks, hon."

Steven handed Katherine her crutches. "I'll be right back."

Katherine shuffled into the tack room for a couple more sugar cubes. After grabbing a handful to give Major and Cody, she glanced down at the stump, recalling Billy's offerings to her as her secret admirer. Carefully, she leaned over and placed the Dots, one by one in the shape of a heart on top of the stump. Katherine smiled and hobbled out to the barn door to wait for Steven.

Steven opened the large barn door to make her exit easier. "I have a surprise for you."

Katherine imagined another book, but as they parked outside the side door, she noticed some movement on the front porch. It was Laddy! He sat tied to one of the posts and the moment he recognized her coming up the stairs, he began wagging his tail and scratching at the floor boards. She hadn't seen him since they stopped at the clinic on their way to her follow-up doctor's appointment a few days ago.

They had decided it was best to keep him at the clinic until his wound healed. At first, Steven hadn't been able to treat his injury or handle him without a muzzle, but with each day, Laddy came to trust him more. Besides the scar and shaved area on his shoulder, he looked great.

"How did he do on the leash?" she asked.

"Just fine, we've been practicing. He's definitely worn a collar before."

"Turn him loose, Steven," she said, taking a seat at the end of the picnic table.

"Are you sure? He might take off."

"I want him to stay only if he wants to."

"I'll need to take his collar off, then. If he runs off, we don't want him getting snagged on something in the woods. Besides, the wolves wouldn't take him back with a collar carrying the scent of humans."

"That's fine; take it off." Steven gently removed the collar and handed it to her. "It's Shane's old collar," she said, her eyes moistening.

"It's the only one we had that would fit him."

Laddy sat a moment, perhaps unaware he was free. "Come here, boy," she called, patting the side of her good leg.

Katherine was ecstatic when he came to her and placed his head in her lap, tail wagging. "Oh, Steven," she said, with happy tears as she ran her fingers through his beautiful coat. "I wonder if he's ever been indoors."

"Guess we're about to find out, aren't we?"

Katherine gleamed. "Get the door for us, she said." Into the side door she limped on one crutch then sat at the dining room table. "C'mon boy, it's okay. You're part of the family now."

Laddy smelled the doorway, then entered hesitantly. "Let's leave the door open for a bit."

"Good idea," said Steven, "In case he changes his mind, we wouldn't want him panicking and tearing up the place."

Betsy appeared at the doorway from the kitchen. "What was that all about… you going out to the barn?"

"Sorry, Betz. Just needed a Major fix."

"You might have fallen. If you want to ride again, you need to let that leg heal and follow the doctor's instructions." Betsy shook her head.

"Okay, you're right. Won't happen again."

"We'll bring him to you next time, okay?" she said, with a glint of a smile in her eyes.

"Perfect!"

"So, this must be Laddy."

Laddy smelled the floor and every object in the dining room then made his way back to Katherine's side and sat beside her. Katherine patted the top of his head.

"I'll take that as an 'I'm staying.'" Slowly she slipped Shane's old collar back on.

"We'll need to make him an ID tag and I have his rabies tag at the clinic," said Steven.

"Did you bring some dog food home?" asked Betsy.

"It's in the back of the truck. I'll go get it," said Steven.

Katherine turned to Betsy. "We have a dog again, Betz!"

"You have a dog again," she said. "This one looks as attached to you as the last one."

Katherine smiled and chuckled as Laddy nuzzled her hand to pet him. "I believe so."

"About time," said Betsy.

Katherine leaned over her hero. Brushing her face against his soft head, taking in his puppy-dog scent, and whispered in his ear, "You're home now, Laddy. We're home."

Following two weeks in the hospital, TJ was happy to be home. He sat studying for his GED test in the living room in front of a crackling fire. His mom had set him up with a lap desk and a cup of hot cocoa. Scheduled to take the test the following week at his high school proctored by one of his old teachers, TJ had done little else since his return home the day prior. He had been discharged from St. Joseph's earlier than planned to attend his father's funeral the next day but would remain under close supervision at a nearby medical center.

"How are you feeling today?" asked his mother when she brought him some soup.

"Better. My back still hurts when I move the wrong way and I can't lift anything with my left arm yet, but I can breathe easier."

"Take it slow, TJ. Allow yourself to mend," she said. "How's the studying going? Anything I can do?"

"Not really," he said, setting the study guide aside to eat his lunch. His mother sat across from him with a solemn expression. "Are you okay?" he asked. Neither of them had mentioned his dad since he got home.

"I will be… we will be," she said. "This kind of healing takes time, too."

She held out what looked like a folded can label. He set his spoon down. "What's that?"

"I note to you from your father. He wrote it the night before he died."

TJ stared at the label, shaking his head. "He knew?"

"He must have feared something might go wrong." His mother handed him the note and rose to her feet. "You know he went after Ricky for us, to keep us safe."

TJ nodded. "I know."

She quietly left him to read it in private.

Slowly, TJ unfolded the crumpled label and pulled the reading light closer.

Dear TJ,
I'm sorry you're having to read this, son. Be strong, and don't be sad. I lived a good life. You were the best part. I know you will take care of your mother. Pursue your dreams and don't be afraid to reach for the stars. I'm so proud of the man you have become and wish you much happiness and peace in your life.
Love you, Dad (Get a big buck for me this year.)

TJ traced the words "love you" with his finger. He couldn't recall the last time his dad had told him he loved him, not since he was a young boy. But he didn't need to hear it; he knew how he felt. He had to chuckle at his last comment. Going hunting together had become a tradition since he was old enough to pull a bow and raise the barrel of a rifle. He would miss those trips most, the one time every year they got to hang out, just the two of them getting caught up on school, sports, horses, girls —well, "girl" —because it was always about Josephine.

He was happy that Jo got the opportunity to tell his father about them and that he knew he was alive. TJ folded the label and slid it in his jean pocket. He knew the perfect place to keep it, in the old leather medicine bag decorated in beads and feathers that his father had given him on his tenth birthday. He had told him to fill it with items that represented the important things in life; love, happiness, pride, and honor. The note would join an acorn Josephine gave him when they were toddlers, a lock of tail hair from his first pony, a medal he won in wrestling, and a tooth knocked out in a fight defending one of his smaller Blackfeet friends.

He wondered what his father had in mind when he wrote "Pursue your dreams and don't be afraid to reach for the stars." He knew what they meant to him… his dream of becoming a vet and reaching for what he feared was an unattainable star, Josephine.

After a while his mother rejoined him. "He loved you dearly and was so proud of you, TJ, even though he never said it. I'm so glad he was able to express his feelings in his note. As you know, you were named after your grandfather. He was the same, kept his feelings to himself. It was their way; the way of Blackfeet men throughout history. I just wanted you to know that."

"I know, Mom."

She gave him a hug. "I'm so happy you're home."

27 – Goodbye

Dressed in black, Katherine was the last to exit the lodge on the cold and breezy Friday afternoon. She patted Laddy on the head as she balanced on one crutch at the door. "Be a good boy; we won't be gone long," she told him. Steven stood waiting on the porch to help her out the door and down the stairs.

Once out the door, Steven extended his hand. "I thought I had misplaced it, but I found it yesterday in the pocket of my hunting jacket." Steven placed Billy's carved heart in her hand.

Katherine caught her breath. She had forgotten Steven was beside her when she gave it to Billy. He had never mentioned it or questioned her about it. What an extraordinary man. "Thank you," she whispered, sliding the heart into her coat pocket.

Steven helped her down the stairs and to their SUV where Betsy and Josephine sat patiently.

"Sorry to keep you waiting," she said. Handing Steven her crutches, she slid into the front passenger seat.

"No hurry, dear," said Betsy.

Once seated, Katherine reached into her pocket and clasped the chiseled heart setting alongside the pearl white stone from Billy's first offering to her. That's what had delayed her, returning to her room to find it at the bottom of her disorganized jewelry box. Steven never knew that Billy had worshiped her from afar as a boy long before they ever met. That would remain their secret forever.

Katherine stared out at the appropriately dead landscape,

trees void of leaves and prairies turned brown, as they drove onto the reservation. No snow had fallen in their valley or east of the mountains yet, but several inches were expected that weekend. She looked forward to a brighter and more cheerful white world.

It had been a little over two weeks since Billy died. Normally held within a week's time, his burial had been delayed due to a dispute over his remains. The coroner's office wanted to conduct an autopsy as normally required involving a murder, but Sarah and her family insisted against it. Consistent with Blackfeet tradition and beliefs, a body needed to remain whole to enter the spirit world. Only after the Chief of the Blackfeet Nation got involved was it deemed unnecessary, since the accused was confirmed dead and there would be no trial.

Billy would be laid to rest in the same plot at the Blackfeet cemetery as his empty casket had been buried over thirty years earlier. His earlier marker, beside his first son's grave, had been removed some time ago. But until last week, no one had bothered to dig up the empty casket, containing only a few of Billy's personal belongings his parents had placed inside. There was no service or viewing as Katherine was accustomed to with a Catholic funeral.

The burial would be small, as Sarah envisioned, with just their two families, but the celebration of his life to be held the following day at Two Ponies had grown to include over fifty guests. Even a couple of the Thoroughbred breeders Billy worked for flew in from California to honor him. Katherine and Steven would have a full house of out-of-town guests, including Lisa and Daniel flying in that evening. Josephine arrived the day before.

It seemed surreal to Katherine to be standing in the same spot grieving for Billy again. It was heart-wrenching seeing

Sarah and TJ mourn, knowing very well that might have been her and her daughter mourning Steven's death if it hadn't been for Billy. Sarah had not visited her at the hospital, and this was the first time she had seen her since their return. Guilt once again flooded her heart. No matter how many people told her it wasn't her fault, she couldn't shake feeling somehow responsible, especially in the presence of Sarah and TJ.

She stood between Steven and Betsy as she had at her Uncle Joe's burial. Once again, they held hands as the casket was lowered. Just recently released from the hospital, TJ stood tall and brave beside his mother; one arm still in a sling. Sarah had asked Steven to say a few words, which he decided to keep short. He knew Billy would prefer it that way.

Following a traditional Blackfeet ceremony performed by one of the elders, Steven stepped forward.

"Everyone here loved Billy," he said, glancing from one tear-streaked face to the next. "We loved his smile, his jokes… his pride, his courage… his love of horses, but most of all we loved how alive we felt in his presence. His love of life was infectious. It is hard to imagine, still, that his bright light has been extinguished, well before its time. But he'll always shine on in our hearts. When I look to the night sky, I will imagine him up there riding one of those stars fast and furious."

Steven took a breath, but it didn't help keep his emotions in check. "He gave his life for mine and my family… and, I will forever be grateful," he said, his voice cracking. "So long, buddy, for now, until we meet again."

Steven wiped away his tears and threw a handful of frozen ground over the casket, followed by everyone present as they whispered their goodbye. Before they left for their vehicle, the Walkers gave Sarah and The Black Feathers a hug.

Katherine could feel Sarah stiffen as they embraced. She

wondered if they could ever be friends again.

It was a quiet ride home. Today they mourned their loss; tomorrow they would celebrate his life.

Katherine ran her finger over the smooth leather of Billy's saddle sitting on a saddle rack in the great room; his favorite Stetson resting over the horn. A portrait of Billy riding Red stood on an easel beside the tribute. She never knew a man who looked as comfortable in the saddle as Billy did—one of many things that had attracted her to him. Katherine couldn't help but grin back at that familiar, infectious smile as she passed through on her way to her bedroom with Laddy. The dog stopped to sniff Billy's hat.

"You remember Billy?" She asked. The canine wagged his tail for a moment. She could see Laddy wasn't comfortable with so many people in the house and decided to lock him up. "Stay, boy; it'll be a little quieter in here." Katherine ruffled his neck and ears. "I'll be by a little later to let you out."

As she hobbled into the library where the men were congregating, Steven rushed up to her. "You shouldn't be on your feet. You've done too much already today."

"I'm fine. I just wanted to let you know the food will be ready soon."

"Well, I hope you haven't been overdoing it in the kitchen."

"Kimi, Luna, and Jessie are doing most of the work under Betsy's direction. I just felt I needed to do something."

"Have a seat for a moment." Steven took her crutches and helped her into a comfortable chair.

Chief approached them. "Looks like you're getting around pretty well. You'll be back in the saddle in no time."

"I wish. The doctors say it's going to take months."

"Well, don't push yourself, then; let that leg heal," said

Chief, "Although, I can't imagine Betsy allowing you to do much of anything anyway."

"Ha, your right there. Between her and Steven, I'm lucky I get to brush my teeth myself."

Chief chuckled and gave her a lingering hug before rejoining Mike, Dane, and the rest of the men. "Go join them," she told Steven. "I'll rest a moment then we can all head to the dining room together. It's set up buffet-style, so you can return with your plates."

Steven gave her hand a gentle squeeze. From across the room she listened to stories about Billy, some of which she had heard, a few she had not. She overheard one fella from California recalling a time a colt had lain down on Billy twice before springing to his feet and bucking like a professional bronc without unseating him.

"It was as if he'd become a part of that animal," he said. "But hell, most of the youngsters never even fussed the first time he mounted them. He'd sweet-talk 'em and convince them there was no use putting up a fight."

Suddenly, she became unaware of the room full of loud voices and laughter behind her. Staring out the window, she recalled the fond memory of the first time she saw Billy, every detail vivid in her mind as if it happened yesterday. Down by the dam, she found him breaking a colt in the lake nearly naked, his bronze bare chest glistening in the sun with his long black hair falling over his broad shoulders. God, he was beautiful! That is how she would remember him—young and wild, like the horses he broke.

Startled, she jumped. "Hey, sweetie, you okay?" asked Steven, gently placing his hand on her shoulder.

Katherine turned and smiled. "I'm fine. We better lead the way before Betsy sends out a search party."

As Katherine slung her way through the great room, she

paused. Josephine sat beside TJ as he shared their harrowing experiences in the mountains with Kimi and Luna's boys and a few of his friends from school. As they sat gathered around the fireplace, light from the fire danced across their youthful faces. Katherine was pleased to see TJ in such good spirits, smiling and gesturing in an animated fashion while he described their crossing of the river. She was delighted to see him well on his way to a full recovery, physically anyway.

"Food is ready," she said to the teens.

"We'll be there in a minute," replied Josephine.

In the dining room, as the men filled their plates, she overheard a couple of Billy's local Blackfeet friends saying how shocked they were to learn of his death, agreeing they thought he would outlive them all. But they were not surprised by his acts of bravery and heroism.

"I can't count how many times he stood up for me, all of us," one man said.

"If there was a fight, Billy was always front and center," said another.

As she glanced around the room from her seat in the corner, Katherine felt Billy would be pleased by the turnout and how much everyone was enjoying the gathering. Billy couldn't have orchestrated it better himself—food, drink, and plenty of shared memories. After the men returned to the library, Jessie sat down beside her with a full plate.

"It's a nice gathering," she said. "Billy would be pleased."

"I was just thinking the same." Katherine picked at her food.

"Are you going to eat that," asked Jessie, looking at the last remaining chicken leg in her plate. "The men took all the dark meat."

"I don't know how you stay as thin as you do, girl. You eat like a horse—like Cody, to be precise."

Jessie laughed out loud. "Cody, really? That big piggy? Thanks!"

"How was your ride on Major yesterday?"

"Good. We did mostly flat work, but we jumped a little, too. He is so much fun."

"He isn't rushing the jumps, is he? We worked so hard to slow him down. Billy…" Katherine smiled. "Billy would set up the craziest gymnastics to back him off and force him to pace himself."

"Don't worry, he's hasn't even tried to pull me to a fence once. He learned well, and so did I."

"I'm sorry, Jess. I know he's in good hands. It's just so hard not being out there."

"I understand," said Jessie. "When's your next doctor's visit? When do you start physical therapy?"

"I go back Wednesday. I won't start PT until my cast is off, which we're hoping will be before Thanksgiving."

"That would be awesome. You'll be back in the saddle before you know it."

"Why does everyone keep saying that?"

"Could be 'cause that's all you ever talk about. Plus, it's written all over your face, moping around the place like a lost puppy."

Katherine laughed. "That obvious, ha?"

"We're all just trying to keep you positive."

"I know. Thanks, Jess. It's the uncertainty that drives me crazy. I've seen three different doctors and each one says something different. I'm hearing everything from I'll never ride again to being limited, whatever that means, to picking up where I left off. I don't know what to believe."

"You're a fighter. If anyone can make a comeback, it'll be you and Major."

Katherine shook her head. "I don't know, Jess. I still don't care if I ever compete again most days. What's up with that? I've been waiting for this opportunity for years, then to have a horse like Major fall in my lap."

"Maybe you're just trying to prepare yourself for the worst-case scenario." Jessie paused, then added, "Or, maybe it just won't be as much fun without Billy."

Katherine managed a weak smile. "I should know better than to expect anything short of the brutal truth from you."

"Someone has to keep it real."

"I love you, too."

When Jessie got up for dessert, Betsy took her seat. "About time you sat down," said Katherine.

"I haven't been on my feet that much. Dane pulled a chair into the kitchen for me."

"I'm glad," said Katherine. "Everything turned out great. Quite a crowd."

"Yes, it's nice so many people came. And, to have Lisa home. What a treat. Too bad, they could only make it for the weekend, but they'll be back for Thanksgiving."

"It's going to be a tough one."

"Yes, but we also have a lot to be thankful for," said Betsy. "Things could have turned out much worse."

"You're right. At least it's finally over, once and for all."

"That was a very brave thing you did," said Betsy.

"Funny, just a couple days before, Billy warned me there's a thin line between brave and stupid."

"It's bravery when you think of the safety of others before your own, remember that."

"Thanks, Betz. You always know what to say. I'm a lucky woman to have you by my side."

Betsy gave her a hug before leaving for the kitchen. "Time to start cleaning up."

Just as she was about to get up to see if she could help,

Sarah sat down beside her. Katherine held her breath.

"I wanted to thank you for today and for all you and Steven are doing for us," she said, void of any emotion.

"You're welcome. It's the least we can do." Katherine fiddled with a button on her blouse, then reached to take Sarah's hand, but she slowly retracted it.

"Thank you," she said again, before quickly getting up to help serve TJ some dessert.

Crushed, Katherine doubted they would ever be close again; their thirty-year relationship a casualty of love and war. Katherine shook her head, saddened, and left for the kitchen to assist.

Kimi took her plate. "We're doing just fine; you go rest. You look tired, sweetie."

"Maybe I am," said Katherine. "I'll say goodbye to our guests and call it a night."

She found most of the men circled around Billy's portrait with a drink in their hand. Steven raised his glass. "Here's one for you, friend. To Billy!" The men clanged their glasses with a mixed retort of "cheers" and "amen." Once their glasses were emptied, they filed out of the library. Those with wives stopped to collect them in the dining room on their way out.

Katherine and Steven thanked everyone for coming as they exited the side door, sending them off with a hug or a handshake, except for Sarah, who avoided her. She wished she had said more, but guilt and fear had taken hold. She prayed she would get the opportunity to apologize for her foolish behavior and let Sarah know nothing happened between her and her husband. She did have time on her side.

Katherine took a deep breath as the last couple left. Lisa and Daniel gave them a hug and kiss before they headed upstairs, followed by the fellas from California, all scheduled to leave the next day along with Josephine. Betsy had shoed

Kimi and Luna out of the kitchen, insisting they leave with their families, and retired for the night after finally agreeing to leave the rest of the cleanup for the morning.

Only Jessie and Dane remained. "See you tomorrow," said Dane, who planned to help chauffeur guests to the airport in the morning. "What time do you need me here?"

"Nine should be fine. Most of the flights are around noon," said Steven. "Thanks for helping out."

"I'll be by in the afternoon to get one more good ride in on Major before the snow hits," said Jessie, slipping on her coat.

"Thanks Jess."

Steven locked up and turned to her. "I'm ready for some quiet time, just the two of us."

After turning Laddy out, she found her husband on the couch and cuddled up next to him, resting her head on his shoulder. A few embers still cast a warm glow on the room.

Steven pulled her closer. "It was a nice goodbye."

"Yes, it was," she whispered.

28 – Surprise

October

At TJ's follow-up visit with his orthopedic surgeon, the doctor said the sling needed to stay on until the next evaluation in two weeks. Instructions to refrain from any lifting or straining of his left shoulder ruled out any riding.

Instead, TJ spent time grooming Cisco with his good arm as he studied his horse's muscle and bone structure. Even in freezing temperatures, he'd bundle up and trudge through the snow with his back pack full of books pertaining to the anatomy of the horse. He spent hours studying and comparing the illustrations and diagrams to Cisco and Red.

It had been nearly a month since he took his GED test, which he scored a 170. It wasn't a super score but along with his GPA of 3.5, he qualified to apply to CSU to its Animal Science Program only days before their deadline. Every afternoon TJ called Jenny Smith at the post office to see if there was an envelope from the board waiting for him. With every day that passed, the likelihood of being accepted for winter semester seemed bleaker.

On his way back from the barn one day, he noticed Dr. Walker's truck parked out front of their house. The horses were fine, and they had already received their fall worming and immunizations. TJ quickened his pace, curious to learn the reason for his visit.

After he pulled off his boots and hung up his coat, he found Dr. Walker sitting with his mother in the living room. "Hi, Dr. Walker."

"Hi TJ, I have a little news for you."

TJ looked to his mother, but she just sat there wearing a silly grin. He turned back to the doctor. "What news?"

Dr. Walker stood up and greeted him with a handshake. "Congratulations, you been accepted to CSU!"

"How, when?!" I thought we are supposed to be notified by mail."

"When your mom told me you were getting close to missing the deadline to start in January, I made some calls. I have a lot of connections still at the school and they were able to put a rush on things."

TJ gave Steven a hug. "Thank you!"

"It was close. Your grades and scores were a little lower than they typically accept into this program, but I spoke to the chair and sent him a letter of recommendation. Guess is worked. They called me this morning."

Nearly in tears, TJ hugged him again. "I can't thank you enough." He turned to his mother. "I'm in, Mom, I'm really in!"

Again, he turned his focus to Steven. "I'll make you proud, Doctor Walker. I'll work my ass off!"

"I know you will."

"I can't wait to tell Jo."

"Go call her now," said Steven, "She had a short day today."

"I hope I can reach her. Can I use your phone in the bedroom, mom?"

"Sure."

"Bye, Dr. Walker, thanks again for everything."

The dormitory phone rang several times before a mild and quiet voice answered—not his Jo. She put him on hold for what seemed like forever. Finally, a familiar warm voice answered.

"Hello."

"It's me, Jo… TJ.

"Oh hi, TJ, what a surprise. You normally call on the weekend."

"I have some great news! I got accepted to CSU!"

"That's wonderful!. So, you start in January?"

"Yes, I'm so excited. I have your dad to thank. He helped a lot."

"Sounds like Daddy. I'm so happy for you, TJ, but I have to run. I'm studying for a test with friends. I look forward to seeing you at Thanksgiving."

"Me too. I sure miss you."

"I miss you, too."

"I love you Jo," he said.

There was a pause. "Love you, too," she whispered. "Gotta go, bye."

"Bye, Jo.

TJ hung up the phone, disappointed by their short conversation. But that would be him soon, living at a dorm, busy studying—he couldn't wait. Before heading downstairs, TJ slipped into his room and pulled the medicine bag from his nightstand. This was how he spoke to his dad now.

"I made it, Dad. I'm going to vet school. Sure wish you were here to party with us. Love you."

TJ put the bag away and raced down the stairs to celebrate with his mom.

With Laddy curled at her feet, Katherine sat on the great room couch surveying piles of books, magazines, and videos stacked about the room. She had read or watched some of her favorites twice now, and nothing perked her interest. She stared out the window, feeling depressed. Darn leg! Her last X-rays showed one of the fractures healing well but the other was not doing as well. They had snow nearly every day now and it was piling up and the stairs were often icy, so more than ever, she was confined to the lodge.

Even her afternoons covered in blankets on the front porch didn't help lift her spirits any longer. Some days, as promised, Steven or Jessie brought Major to her for visits while she sat outdoors. The tall Thoroughbred would stretch his long neck over the porch rail for treats. But it only made her miss riding him all the more.

Startling her, Laddy sprang to his feet, listening and staring in the direction of the side door. "What is it, boy?" Katherine leaned as far as she could, trying to see out the side window overlooking the parking area, but all she could see was white. Laddy remained at attention.

"Betsy!" she called. "I think someone is here."

Normally, Betsy would be checking in on her every few minutes to offer her cookies or whatever she was fixing in the kitchen, which seemed to be endless. She had gained nearly ten pounds since she returned home. What could she be doing?

Katherine grabbed her crutches and thumped across the wood floor to the window with Laddy at her side. Huge, fluffy snowflakes nearly the size of cotton balls fell in slow motion, laying down a fresh, clean blanket over everything, making it hard to define anything beyond the side porch. Squinting from the brightness, she peered down the drive. Again, nothing but white. Something still held Laddy's focus outside. She considered there might be a wolf or coyote howling in the distance, beyond her hearing capabilities.

Concerned Betsy hadn't answered, Katherine called for her again and slung her way through the dining room into the kitchen, then realized it was her nap time. The old woman had become hard of hearing the past few years and was no doubt sound asleep, but Katherine checked in on her anyway. She lay resting on the top of her bed, covered with a throw. As she turned to leave, she banged one of her crutches against the wall, waking her.

"Are you okay?" she asked, startled. When she pushed herself up in the bed, her throw fell to the floor.

"I'm fine. Sorry I woke you."

"Do you need something, sweetie?"

"No, finish your nap. You need your rest, the way you've been fussing over me."

Betsy smiled groggily and settled back down on her pillow. Katherine hobbled up to her bed, picked up the throw and covered her frail body. It was hard to imagine she would be turning eighty soon. Her hair had grayed, her skin had thinned, but she was still as strong-willed as ever.

Katherine guessed her stubbornness was what kept her going, in addition to her need to take care of her. It would only be a matter of time before she would need to return the favor and care for her dear friend. The thought saddened her. Betsy was the closest to a loving and caring mother she'd ever have, always there when she needed her. Katherine rested her hand on Betsy's shoulder and left her to rest.

On her way back to the great room, she stopped in the kitchen to rummage through the refrigerator. Betsy had outdone herself baking again that morning. She passed on the brownies and grabbed a couple oatmeal cookies, hoping they would be a few less calories. She could barely stand to look at herself in the mirror these days.

As she maneuvered back down the hall, passing the side door where Laddy still stood at attention, she swore she heard sleigh bells! Straining to see out the frosted glass, she leaned one crutch against the wall and opened the door. To her amazement, Major stood in the drive, in harness and pulling a small sleigh! Steven stood just outside the door and Jessie grinned like a Cheshire cat in the driver's seat. "Surprise!" they yelled in unison.

"I was just about to come and get you," said Steven. "You beat me to it. Now you can get out of the house and spend time with Major, with our help, of course."

Katherine couldn't believe her eyes. Her beautiful bay looked so handsome dressed in the black harness with brass fittings. "How, when?" She was nearly shocked speechless.

"I purchased the cutter a couple of weeks ago and Jessie has been working with Major."

"I love it! I love you both! Thank you!" She leaned out the door and gave Steven a kiss.

"Don't I get a kiss?" said Jessie.

"You sure will, and I have one for Major, too. What a good boy; he never ceases to amaze me."

"Let's get you bundled up, so you can go for a ride," said Steven stepping inside.

"Really, now?" Katherine could hardly take her eyes off Major as Jessie circled him in the drive. "He's pulling a sleigh!" she said to Steven. Katherine had long-lined Major some but introducing him to pulling something must have been challenging. She would have loved to have witnessed that. She'd get all the details from Jessie later.

"One of my clients, Violet Mathews, advised Jessie over the phone. She hooked me up with the sleigh, too. Violet used to be a client of my dad's, but she's having to move to assisted living and her kids have no interest in horses. I dug out Wompa's old harness and had it cleaned and conditioned."

"Oh, Wompa, Lisa's old Appy. How she loved that horse. I remember her thirteenth birthday, when we gave her the harness and cart. You and Billy…" A lump formed in her throat. She swallowed hard and took a deep breath to keep her emotions in check. Would she ever be able to say his name without feeling a jab to her heart? "I remember you and Billy, putting the cart together the day before and hiding it behind the barn. Lisa was so surprised, she loved it... It seems like yesterday."

"Sit here at the table," Steven said. "I'll bring your coat and boots. I already cleared and salted the steps, but we better hurry. It won't take long for the snow to collect again."

"It sure is coming down. It's beautiful. I can't wait. I've been dying to get out, let alone with Major." Katherine's eyes moistened. It didn't take much these days for her to become emotional. How did Steven know she was nearly reaching her wits' end locked up indoors? This was exactly what she needed.

As Steven placed a warm cap on her head and wrapped a scarf around her neck, she reached up and cradled his face in her hands, causing him to pause as they looked into each other's eyes. Steven wiped a tear from her cheek.

"I love you," they said in unison, followed by the customary "Jinks." It had been years since they played their old childhood game.

"Let's get out there—Major is waiting!" she said.

"Do you want me to join you?" asked Jessie. The cutter was designed to carry a couple in the padded loveseat which hid a storage cabinet beneath it that opened to the rear.

"I'd like to go solo, if you don't mind. I'll be fine. I won't go far."

"Of course," said Jessie.

Steven smiled and nodded, not looking surprised as he helped her into the seat. The moment she took the driving lines from Jessie, Katherine felt whole again. She began talking to Major through the bit, a familiar conversation about whether it was time to go to work or not, then once the connection was made, off he went doing his job. It was just the two of them again, with the wind in their face, laying a track through the virgin snow, a different looking track, but still leaving their collective mark as one.

Katherine sat with her leg stretched out to the side, jostling a little over a few bumps, but she was amazed by how smooth the sleigh rode. She recalled how much she enjoyed her many rides sitting beside her Uncle Joe, driving Baldy along the two-track trails at Two Ponies as a child.

Following a lap down and back up the drive, Katherine pulled up to the side door. Betsy had joined Steven and Jessie on the porch, looking ready for a turn.

"Is it too early to sing Jingle Bells?" asked Betsy.

"Hell no!" said Jessie.

With some assistance, the old woman slid into the seat beside her and down the drive they went singing a Christmas carol in October, the happiest Katherine had felt in a long time. And, Major seemed happy too, enjoying yet another new job. She couldn't wait to tell Lisa and Josephine about her surprise gift and take them for a spin when they visited next month.

As she drove another lap up and down the drive, Katherine reflected on the past thirty days. For the first time since her world had been turned upside down, she felt truly hopeful. She had lost herself in a haze of grief, guilt, and pity. Getting outdoors had cleared her mind and soul of the clutter and she could see beyond the pain to a brighter day. It would be a bittersweet Thanksgiving that year, but like the Aspen surviving droughts and long winters as a grove, she prayed the strength of family and friends might someday mend the hole in all their hearts.

28 – Thanksgiving

Katherine opened her eyes to the early morning light peeking through the drapes. She wiggled her toes and stretched her arms and legs, smiling. Freedom! Her cast had finally come off. She still had to wear a brace out of bed, but after lugging that heavy cast around for over two months, the brace felt like nothing at all. She rolled over on her side, studying her handsome husband sound asleep beside her, his chest rising and falling to shallow breaths.

Their alarm would sound in a couple minutes, but she had always been able to set her mental clock to wake up just before the alarm went off. Betsy had taught her there were powers beyond comprehension that most people never learned to tap into.

Katherine gently brushed his straw-colored hair from his face and leaned over and kissed him. Steven turned to face her and opened his smiling eyes.

"Good morning," she said.

"How long you been watching me sleep?"

"Not long."

"You look beautiful… you look happy."

Katherine's smile broadened. "Our girls are home and we get to share the day with the people we love. We have a lot to be happy about."

"Yes, and be thankful for," he said, reaching to stroke her hair.

The alarm sounded, and Steven silenced it. "Guess we

better get moving… lots to do before the crowd arrives.

"It can wait," she said coyly, snuggling up to him.

Steven gave her a questioning look. "Your cast came off only two days ago."

"You're not going to break me. The doctor said we could so long as we're careful."

"You asked the doctor?"

"I sure did," she said, with a little attitude and a devilish grin.

"We have company upstairs and you know Betsy's up, probably for hours already getting the turkey in the oven."

"The kids would sleep to noon if we let them and Betsy's nearly deaf."

Steven sat up and laughed. "How about after everyone leaves Sunday?" He leaned in and kissed her sweetly on the cheek. "I want it to be special." It was true this would be the first time they would make love since she left for California. It seemed eons ago.

"Still the sappy romantic," she said.

Steven blushed. "Yep, that's me."

"Sounds wonderful. It's a date."

After their showers, they dressed for the day and found Betsy resting in the chair in the kitchen that had become a permanent fixture. It allowed her to keep an eye on her cooking and rest her knees.

"Happy Thanksgiving!" said Betsy, sitting at attention. She hadn't seen Betsy this full of vigor in a long time.

"I see you let Laddy out. Thanks," said Katherine. Betsy reached for her cane. "Stay put; what can I do?" she asked. "You've done enough already this morning."

"You can start on the pies," said Betsy.

"Great!" Katherine began pulling what she needed from the cupboards and refrigerator as Steven leaned over and gave

Betsy a kiss on her head.

"Happy Thanksgiving, Betz," he said.

"Okay, out with ya," she said, waving him away. "Women's work to be done."

Steven grabbed a hot biscuit off the stove and leaned over Katherine's shoulder to take the orange juice from the refrigerator.

"There's some hard-boiled eggs," said Betsy. "No room or time to cook a big breakfast this morning."

Steven nodded with a biscuit in his mouth, an egg in one hand and the orange juice container in the other as he exited the kitchen.

"When guests start coming downstairs, we'll set out a buffet and they can just help themselves," said Betsy. "I want to keep it light since we'll be eating early. We have fruit, toast, biscuits, oatmeal, cereal, juice, and coffee."

"Is that all!" Katherine teased.

Betsy shook off the comment, all business. "Once we get the pies in the oven we can start in on the sides. Kimi and Luna are bringing a ham."

"The girls can help with the table," said Katherine.

"Great idea!"

While Steven cleared the drive with the tractor and put up a few last-minute Christmas decorations, the women laid out the continental breakfast. Soon after, their house guests began filtering downstairs. Lisa and Daniel were the first to peek in the kitchen.

Katherine turned to face her deaf daughter and son-in-law so they could read her lips. "How did you sleep?"

Lisa swept by giving her and Betsy a kiss on the cheek.

"Great, but it's always weird being back in my old room," she said. "It's the same as when I was a kid."

Katherine had prayed the couple would be blessed with a

family, but Lisa never conceived even though they tried desperately for years, having just gave up recently. Lisa was heartbroken, and Katherine shared in her sadness, having lived through the disappointment herself. But her daughter seemed in good spirits, having accepted it just wasn't meant to be.

"Good morning, Mom, Betsy," signed Daniel. I always sleep well here. All the fresh air. Not New York."

Daniel wasn't much bigger than Lisa. She always felt they were a good match, both sensitive, loving people. Perhaps it was because they were both deaf, the silence giving them more time to reflect on what was important. She knew she did her best thinking and reflecting in the quiet of the woods or picking stalls.

"I suppose not," said Betsy, who could never understand why they stayed in the city following graduation. "Help yourselves in the dining room." The couple left them to their cooking.

When Katherine took a break from the pies and peeked in the dining room, Josephine had joined Lisa and Daniel. She could over hear Josephine telling her sister how they planned to ride out and cut a Christmas tree after breakfast, like they used to do when they were kids. Lisa and Josephine began reminiscing about Thanksgivings past.

About that time, Kimi and Luna arrived to help. The men and boys would drive over together later. Katherine was glad to see the new recruits. Her leg was beginning to ache, and she needed to get off her feet and rest it before their Christmas tree expedition. She glanced at Betsy who didn't look tired at all, enjoying all the activity and preparation. She lived for cooking for large groups. Katherine had to smile, watching her sitting on her throne, dishing out orders.

On her way to get something to eat for herself, she let

Laddy in the side door. Katherine took a seat between her girls as she spread some jelly over a biscuit and poured herself a glass of orange juice. Next to join the breakfast group was Roy and Sandy Higgins and their youngest daughter, April, who accepted their invitation and drove up from Helena the previous day. Immediately Josephine picked up where she and Roy left off last night, discussing his current film. Josephine had vaguely recognized him from a few of his earlier films and became intrigued when she learned he now directed as well.

The rest of their guests—Sarah and TJ, Jessie and Dane, Chief and his family, and Mike and his wife—would arrive around noon. In total they were expecting thirty-three, their largest Thanksgiving ever. The large group would require more seating than the formal dining room set provided, so the men brought in the two summer camp tables and benches from storage, forming one long table stretching the length of the large room for the adults and a separate kids' table.

When Jessie and Dane arrived a little before noon, Katherine sent Jessie out to the barn to prepare Major to hook up to the sleigh while Dane got the tractor and wagon ready for the tree-cutting party. Josephine directed traffic as vehicles began pulling in. On her way out, she let Laddy out to join the outdoor fun.

Katherine noticed Sarah and TJ pull in and waited by the side door. She hadn't seen or spoken to Sarah since their awkward exchange at the celebration of Billy's life. When she entered the lodge, Sarah handed her two loaves of Blackfeet bannock bread and some smoked trout, avoiding eye contact.

"Thank you, Sarah. The bread looks delicious and the trout is my favorite." After Katherine took her coat, she rested her hand on Sarah's arm. "Sarah, please join me in the library for a moment?"

Sarah gave her a questioning look.

"It won't take long."

TJ had already joined Josephine and the others gathered in the great room. "Okay," she said, hesitantly leading the way.

Katherine motioned for Sarah to take a seat and sat opposite her. She had rehearsed her words many times over the past two months. "Sarah, we used to be close; I hope we can be friends again," she began.

Sarah glanced up for a moment, her gaze returning to her lap in silence.

Katherine took a deep breath. This was more difficult than she had envisioned, but she must continue. She needed to get this off her chest. "I want you to know nothing happened between Billy and me on the coast or in the mountains. He loved you very much."

Sarah eyes met hers, her chin raised high. "I knew there was always a special bond between the two of you, and I accepted that, but when you pulled him away from me a second time, I…"

"I'm so sorry. It was wrong, but it wasn't what you think."

"What am I supposed to think when my husband won't touch me anymore?"

"I just enjoyed his attention. I didn't mean to lead him on, Sarah; I swear."

Sarah got up and walked to the window, gazing out into the white. "Do you know how difficult it's been always knowing he was with me only because he couldn't be with you? I know he loved me, but he loved you more."

Katherine joiner her. "No, not more, Sarah; just different. I represented something to Billy, something he had always craved and felt was beyond his reach — acceptance and equality. Funny thing was he had them all along but couldn't see it.

"I'll admit I loved Billy, very passionately at one time, but

I've learned he represented something I felt I needed, too. When we were kids, he was exciting, forbidden, and earning his love somehow validated my self-worth. I guess I needed that then."

Sarah turned to her. "And recently?"

"The way he looked at me, made me feel desirable, like a young woman again. The way I acted was unfair to both of you and Steven." Katherine turned away. "I called you in here to apologize so you might forgive me, but I don't deserve your friendship." She wiped the tear trickling down her cheek. "Thank you for even coming today."

Sarah placed her hand on her arm. "Thank you, Kat. I know that wasn't easy to admit, but I still don't understand why. You have the love and devotion of the purest hearted man I've ever known." Sarah shook her head, allowing a measured smile. "Are you crazy?"

Katherine faced her in tears. "Maybe I was. I've been such an idiot."

"Let's go enjoy this day of thanks, together as friends. Billy would have wanted it that way." Sarah squeezed her hand, smiled, and walked away.

Katherine took a deep breath and wiped her face. Admitting her foolishness had lifted a huge burden from her heavy heart. Perhaps now she could leave her guilt behind and truly enjoy the holiday.

By the time they had the Christmas tree group organized it was snowing heavily, a fresh blanket of white concealing any imperfections. The trees glistened and the world appeared shiny and new.

When Katherine slid in the seat of the cutter and took the lines from Jessie, Major looked as though someone had frosted him like a cake. Steven placed a saw in the storage cabinet beside a large thermos of hot cider and insulated cups, which Betsy had prepared for them, and started up the snowmobile that would drag their tree home. Betsy, Sarah, Kimi, and Luna stayed behind to have their feast ready by the time they returned.

Major soon became impatient, wanting to get moving.

"Hurry, Chief and Flo, hop in before we end up leaving without you!" The petite grandma and still fit grandpa slid in the seat beside her. It was a tight squeeze, but they would all keep warm.

Dane climbed onto the tractor already hitched to the hay wagon with straw bales as seats for their younger guests. After Lisa, Daniel, Josephine, TJ, and Violet, along with Chief's two sons and families, climbed onboard, Jessie handed out elk hides as lap warmers. The rest of the men chose to remain behind to watch the traditional Thanksgiving Day football game.

Finally, they were off with Major leading the way, sleigh bells jingling, and Laddy gleefully keeping pace alongside. The gelding happily trotted down the drive toward the trail leading to the back field where they had planted spruce and fir seedlings years ago when they first married, planning for Christmases to come.

"I hope we can find one that will fit in the great room," said Chief, above the chorus of "Rudolph the Red Nosed Raindeer" emanating from the wagon.

Flo laughed. "In fifty years, every tree he's brought home didn't fit our living room!"

"They don't look as big outdoors," explained Chief.

"Our stand has gotten big, but I think there are a few left that we can trim to fit. Of course, they're not as shapely as they used to be since we haven't trimmed them in a while."

"We'll make one work, even if it's a Charlie Brown tree," chuckled Chief.

"Yeah, we've had plenty of those over the years," giggled Flo. "We just added extra garland and decorations to fill in the holes."

For a good stretch down the drive, Chief and Flo shared more Christmas tree stories, including one about a hidden rodent, a tree destroyed by their cat and another peed on by their dog, as they laughed all the way.

When they reached the wooded trail leading to the back pasture, the beauty pulled her away from the laughter and singing, focusing only on Major's two-beat gait crunching through the snow. Her heart felt as light as the snowflakes collecting on her eyelashes—hopeful, but most of all thankful, as she rejoiced in the moment. She felt alive!

Like flicking a switch, she allowed the others back in and joined in the celebration. When they reached the back field, she glanced over to her loving husband pulling up beside her and smiled. She sang along to "Oh Christmas Tree" as they picked out the perfect, not-so-perfect blue spruce. Even Laddy howled along a few verses.

By the time they returned to the lodge with their prize tree, the game was nearly over. The Lions would lose again, this year to the Bears. Katherine headed for the kitchen to help with the last-minute preparations while Steven made room for the tree in the corner beside the staircase. With the help of a few of the men, they carried the huge tree in through the front door and secured it in the stand. It barely fit, requiring a little more trimming off the top and bottom to allow for the star. It didn't take long for the entire lodge to smell of evergreen.

"C'mon fella, think we'll put you in the bedroom again," Katherine told Laddy. The dog followed willingly, looking like he needed an escape from all the commotion.

Women scurried about the kitchen, nearly colliding as they took turns running dishes out to the tables with a goal of getting everything set out while it was hot. Betsy called all their guests to the dining room and quickly assigned seats. Once everyone was seated, one empty chair remained at the opposite end of the table from Steven. A familiar cowboy hat rested on the back of the chair.

In what had become a tradition in the Walker household, everyone held hands around the table. Katherine glanced around the room, taking in all the smiling faces. "First, I'd like to welcome our new guests, Roy and Sandy Higgins and their beautiful daughter, Violet. Roy so generously spent many hours and gallons of fuel to help total strangers in a time of need and, without a doubt, saved a life. Thank you."

TJ spoke up next, thanking Roy, followed by a collection of voices thanking him from around the room.

Roy blushed and shook his head. "No need to fuss," he said. "Glad me and my bird could help out."

Katherine looked down the table to the empty seat. The room became silent. "Thanks to the extraordinary sacrifice of our brave friend, my family is here today to share this joyous occasion. Let's all honor Billy by living this day and the rest of our days to the fullest as he did."

A murmur of amens and thank-yous followed.

Suddenly, Lisa stood up. "Daniel and I have an announcement to make." Katherine held her breath. Could it be? "We're expecting!"

As the table erupted in shouts and congratulations, Katherine rushed to hug the parents-to-be with tears of joy. "I'm so happy for you!"

Before Katherine could return to her seat, Jessie began tapping her fork on her water glass. "Dane and I want to congratulate Lisa and Daniel on their accomplishment." Everyone chuckled. "And we want to let them know how much we look forward to our kids playing together next

Thanksgiving."

Suddenly, the room became silent as everyone looked at each other with questioning expressions. Whispering could be heard. Katherine thought she heard Jessie right, but what if she hadn't? Did she dare congratulate them? Finally, Dane stood up. "We're having a baby, too!"

Again, the room burst into an uproar. Katherine couldn't believe it, two babies on the way. She rushed to Jessie with a hug. "Congratulations, Jess! Always the drama queen."

Katherine took her seat and rang her fork against her glass. "Any more announcements?" Silence. "Okay then, let's all give thanks for our health and happiness and for this wonderful meal prepared for us today with love." Katherine smiled across the table at Betsy.

"Let's eat!" Betsy shouted.

The room erupted into a frenzy of chatter and clatter as dishes were passed around the table. Then the room fell silent as everyone enjoyed their meal. She had never seen so much food disappear so fast. It must have been all the fresh air and trudging through the snow earlier.

After the tables were cleared and the leftovers stashed away, guests mingled throughout the lodge. Katherine insisted the dishes be left on the counter for the following day and had to drag Betsy from the kitchen to begin decorating the tree. Boxes of lights and ornaments, piled high against the wall, kept the adults busy while the kids strung popcorn, feeding the occasional piece to Laddy.

Bing Cosby singing "White Christmas" played in the background while a fire added warmth and a festive glow to the room as everyone took turns decorating the tree. Once the ornaments were perfectly placed, icicles were carefully strung bringing the tree to life as they reflected the fire and twinkle lights. For the final touch, Steven placed the antique O'Reilly angel, made of white feathers and lace trimmed in gold, on the top. Normally, Katherine did the honors, but this year she didn't dare try to balance on the stepladder with her weak leg. The star was all that remained of her great-grandfather's possessions, which accompanied him across the Atlantic from Ireland generations ago.

On cue, Betsy announced dessert was served. Guests moved from the great room back to the dining room where they had their choice of apple, cherry, and traditional pumpkin pie on one table and their choice of beverage on another, including coffee, tea, and hot cocoa.

"Josephine is dishing out vanilla ice cream and whipped cream in the kitchen," added Betsy, who said goodnight shortly after dessert. With all the hustle and bustle, she had missed her nap that day and ran out of steam.

Katherine and Steven stood on the porch with Laddy, hugging their day guests goodbye. It wasn't until nearly midnight before the last of the houseguests headed upstairs for the night. While Steven closed the fireplace and shut off the tree lights, Katherine collected strands of icicles strewn across the great room floor and rug before Laddy carried them throughout the lodge.

"Wow, what a day," she said, as she picked up the last strand. "I think everyone had a great time."

Steven walked up beside her. "It was perfect. We did good."

"Yes, we did. We're a good team."

"The best." Steven wrapped his arm around her and together they walked to their room, exhausted.

Friday afternoon, Josephine waited for TJ at the creek. She was so bundled up she had a difficult time mounting Bonanza. The thermometer read thirty-nine degrees on the porch on her way out to the barn. Even though she was freezing, she was glad they planned a ride together before she returned to school. They had not had an opportunity to be alone since their nights together in the mountains. She wasn't sure what to expect after TJ's outburst at the hospital. Sure, they had kissed and made up, but they hadn't discussed their relationship or future plans.

She had already been asked out several times at school and was tempted to accept out of curiosity and peer pressure. Her roommates were jealous of how much attention she was getting from the opposite sex and couldn't understand why she continued to decline. When asked if she had a boyfriend back home, she always avoided answering them, unclear of what she and TJ had. And besides, if she did tell them about TJ, they would ask her to share a photo like they had of their beaus, and she wondered how they would react to her Indian boyfriend.

She could hear the thin ice over the stream crackle as TJ approached. As soon as she saw him, off they went, Bonanza lounging through the creek and up the trail, snow flying. As always, she could hear Cisco closing in on them. Her goal at the end of the clearing became a blur, her eyes watering from the burning cold. But this time she easily entered the woods before TJ tapped her on the shoulder, clearly winning their little game.

"Whoa," she said, bringing Bonanza to a halt. "Did you just let me win?" she asked, bordering on angry if he had.

TJ rode up beside her and sweetly pulled her face to his and kissed her passionately. Any annoyance was lost in an instant. Her head swimming, she couldn't even remember what she was upset about. When he finally broke off their kiss, he just smiled and galloped off toward the cabin.

She nearly caught up with him, sliding to a halt at the

hitching post beside Cisco. TJ had just dismounted and was tying off his horse. "What was that?"

"That was how much I've been missing you and dying to kiss you."

Josephine quickly tied Bonanza and rushed to him. It felt like a summer day cradled in his arms, although their breath swelled into the frigid air like puffs of smoke from a peace pipe. TJ took her hand and led her to the stairs, where she located the key and opened the door.

"We need a fire," he said, rushing back out the door for some firewood stacked under the porch.

Josephine curled up on the couch and pulled the old quilt around her while she watched TJ start a fire in the potbelly stove. Once he got it going, he joined her on the couch, pulling her close to warm her.

"We need to talk," she said.

"No, we don't," he said, earning a questioning expression from her. TJ cradled her face in his hands and kissed her like he had never kissed her before, fearless and strong. She felt herself let go, yearning for more as he straddled her pressing every inch of his manhood against her.

TJ stood up and swooped her up in his arms, turning her so they would both fit through the bedroom door. "It's colder in here, but we'll warm it up."

Josephine giggled. "Go throw some more wood on the fire; I'll be waiting."

While TJ threw a couple more logs on the fire and set the damper, Josephine slipped out of her clothes and quickly climbed onto the bed, pulling the comforter only to her waist, her nipples standing at attention. The expression on TJ's face was worth her freezing for. He stripped off his clothes, flinging them about the room like a madman. Josephine slid under the covers, welcoming him to join her.

Unlike the times they made love in the mountains, TJ was confident and in control, positioning her differently each of the many times they made love that afternoon, every time more tenderly than the last. Any doubts about how she felt, or what they had together, vanished.

This had to be true love!

By the time they left for home, they had fully committed to one another, promising to be faithful always.

Saturday morning, Dane grabbed a full laundry basket from Jessie. Since they didn't have a washer and dryer, Jessie did their laundry at her parent's house. "You shouldn't be lifting anything that heavy."

"Geeze, sweetie, I'm only a couple of months along. I'm fine."

"Remember what the doctor said because of your age."

"Yes, dear, but a laundry basket is not a seventy-pound bale of hay."

Dane ran the basket out to her car. "Make sure your Dad helps you on their end."

"Okay, if it makes you feel better."

"Yes, it would."

The moment Jessie drove off, he heard their phone ring and rushed inside. "Hello?"

"Officer Collins?"

"Yes."

"This is Tammy Butler—Kyle Schmitt's sister."

"Yes, Mrs. Butler, what can I do for you?" Dane took a seat at their kitchen table to finish his morning coffee.

"We buried Jake a couple months ago."

Dane wasn't sure how to respond. Expressing his condolences wouldn't have been truthful, so he didn't say anything.

"I understand you saw Kyle up there."

"Yes, Ma'am, I did."

"I was told you had an opportunity to shoot him as he tried to escape, but you didn't get a shot off."

Dane thought he knew where she was going with her questioning. "We don't know where he is, Mrs. Butler. I was the last person to see him heading north toward the border and the fire east of Glacier. We don't know if he survived."

"That's not what I'm trying to find out."

"Ma'am?"

"I need to know if you didn't fire because you didn't have a clear shot or because you chose not to."

Dane remained silent. He could compromise his job if he told her the truth. "I hope your brother made it, Mrs. Butler, I don't believe he ever hurt anyone; he was just in with the wrong people. I later learned he tried to free the hostages."

"I think you answered my question the best you could. I needed to know before I told you something. Can this be off the record?"

Dane thought hard before answering. "Yes."

"I heard from Kyle. He's living in Alberta. He called me on Thanksgiving. He said he missed me. I was so happy to hear he made it."

"I am, too, Mrs. Butler."

"Call me Tammy, please." There was a pause. "He met someone. They have a small ranch with some cattle and horses. I'm going to visit them at Christmas. He sounded so happy."

Dane could hear her choking up. "Thank you for letting me know, Tammy. We never had this conversation." Dane truly was happy for him.

"Thank you for sparing his life."

"Happy Holidays to you and your family."

Thankfully, their call ended before Jessie returned between loads. He would have been torn between breaking his promise to Tammy or lying to his wife. Dane felt happy for this man he had never met, but felt he got to know through Tammy and what the Walkers had told him. He would take this secret to his grave.

Katherine took a deep breath and sighed, welcoming the quiet. It had been a fun four days with family and friends, but she was ready to spend some one-on-one time with her husband. Betsy was even gone for the night, having accepted an invitation to stay over for her twin brother's birthday.

After seeing Josephine, Lisa, and Daniel off at the airport that morning, Steven suggested Katherine take a relaxing bath while he watched a little football. They had plenty of leftovers, so she wouldn't need to cook.

Katherine sprinkled some lavender bath crystals in the hot water as she filled the deep, cast-iron, clawfoot tub. Then she lit a candle, turned off the lights and slipped into the silky water. Her quiet baths were normally a time of reflection, but that day she just wanted to clear her mind and enjoy the moment. Over the past couple of months, she had gradually become efficient at shutting out the noise in her head, focusing on the surrounding sights, sounds, and smells, to truly relax.

She was so relaxed she fell asleep and woke up to pruned fingers and cool water. She rinsed her hair, wrapped her head in a towel and slipped into her favorite robe and slippers, hoping Steven had started a fire. She didn't bother putting her brace on since she planned to just curl up on the couch, maybe watch a movie together.

The library and hallway were dark when she exited their room, but she was pleased to see the reflection of flames dancing off the walls of the great room ahead. A gentle fire burned in the stone fireplace beside the twinkling Christmas tree providing the only light in the room. As her eyes adjusted, she noticed the old bear rug back in front of the hearth. It had been replaced years ago by a runner to match the large Oriental rug centered in the room.

Upon closer inspection, she found two glasses of red wine sitting on the end table beside one long-stem rose. She smiled. *Where was Steven?*

Just as she was about to search for him in the kitchen, he entered from the dining room. "Close your eyes," he said.

"Steven, what are you doing? It isn't Christmas yet."

"Just close your eyes."

"Okay." When she closed her eyes, she heard something being slid across the floor. *What could it be?*

Steven turned her toward the corner of the room. "Open your eyes!"

Opposite the tree sat a lovely hand-painted Ethan Allen rocking chair with a big red bow. At first Katherine turned back to Steven, confused, then she smiled and shook her head in disbelief.

Steven approached her. "Grandmas need a rocking chair, right?"

Katherine gave him a big hug. "Yes, it's beautiful," she said running her hand over the smooth maple finish.

"Give it a test drive!"

She sat and rocked a moment, grinning ear-to-ear. "I love it!" For an instant, she imagined herself rocking her grandchild to sleep in her arms. It would be wonderful to have a baby in the house again.

"Now for my present," he said, taking her hand to lead her onto the bear rug. Suddenly, it clicked. The first time they made love was right here on this rug in front of a fire as teens.

Katherine smiled coyly. "You devil. Betsy staying over wasn't a coincidence, was it?"

"Nope. First, let's get rid of this," he said, removing the towel from her head, then running his fingers through her damp hair as he stroked her face with admiring eyes. Slowly, he untied her robe and pulled it off her shoulders, allowing it to drop to the floor. "Close your eyes."

"Again? Now what?"

"Be still."

Katherine shut her eyes. The smell of rose reached her senses followed by the tickle of the pedals tracing her mouth, neck, then down her chest to her tummy. Her body had come to life, tingling and ready for more.

She opened her eyes and broke the rose apart, sprinkling the rose petals over the rug.

"My turn," she said, as she began slowly undressing her man, tossing his garments to the side.

Steven reached for the two wine glasses and handed one to her. "To us," he said, "and to my girl." Wrapping around each other's arms, they drank from their glasses like she had seen in so many romance movies. Katherine felt sexy and desirable through the eyes of her hopeless romantic.

Steven framed her face in his strong hands and kissed her fervently. They hadn't kissed like that in years. She couldn't remember the last time she yearned to be ravished by Steven as she did that moment. Katherine pulled him down over her, onto the deep fur rug and fragrant rose petals. Once again, the firelight danced across their naked bodies as they made passionate yet tender love. This time there was no nervousness or awkwardness; they knew their way with the familiarity of a memorized puzzle, yet tonight it felt brand new.

As Katherine lay beside her best friend, lover, and soulmate, her body spent yet renewed, she gazed into the fire, allowing herself to reflect on the events that had changed all their lives in an instant. They had gone from fretting about everyday concerns to life-and-death choices and outcomes. Everyone but Billy survived, and life went on for the rest of them—some a little broken physically and all emotionally altered forever—but they were alive and thriving. They had pulled together to pick up the pieces and heal as a family and community, never quite as shiny and whole as before, but somehow more resilient.

Like the forest reborn after a fire, so were they, and stronger for it.

May the stars carry your sadness away,
May the flowers fill your heart with beauty,
May hope forever wipe away your tears,
And, above all, may silence make you strong.

~ Chief Dan George

Epilogue

Nine Months Later

Katherine halted and saluted finishing her dressage test, Major standing square beneath her. Smiling and patting her big bay's neck, she walked toward Jessie sitting in the judge's box at the end of the riding arena at Two Ponies. Her smile wilted as Jessie's unhappy expression emerged from the shadows.

"What? I thought it was good."

"No," she said, "It was great! Got ya!"

"Damn you, girl! You really think so?"

"You nailed the canter half-pass and flying lead changes!"

Katherine gave Major one more pat. She had shed a lot of sweat and tears all spring and summer getting herself and Major back in shape to compete back on the West Coast that fall. The canter posed their biggest challenge. Even so, she hoped to advance to the Intermediate Level by spring to qualify for some national events back East next year. The following year their would be to reach Advanced Level. If they did well, they would be on their way to qualifying for the 2000 Olympics in Sydney. They had five years to gain recognition and sponsors to get them there. Now they just had to stay sound and in one piece until then.

"Let's call it a day, short and sweet," she said, wanting to reward Major's efforts.

"Sounds good to me," said Jessie, stepping out of the judge's box. "Mom's taking Dad to a doctor's appointment this afternoon, so I need to pick up Cole by noon."

Katherine walked Major alongside of Jessie up the path to

the barn. "He's getting so big so fast. Three months now, right?"

"Yep, and he wasn't a lightweight when he was born… nearly split me in two."

"He takes after Dane, going to be a big boy," said Katherine, dismounting onto her left leg. Still, she didn't trust her bad leg, or perhaps it had just become habit. She had lost a few degrees in the turning radius of her right knee, but it didn't affect her riding much, thank goodness.

"How is little Beth doing?" asked Jessie.

"Still a tiny little thing like her mother. Lisa and Daniel plan to make it for Thanksgiving."

"Great! See you tonight, birthday girl," said Jessie, taking Major's saddle from her. "Looking forward to Betsy's chocolate cake. That's if it doesn't burn to a crisp first with all those candles!"

"She better not put all fifty-five on!" Katherine slipped off his bridle and pulled his halter over his ears. "I still can't believe Steven bought me a new jumping saddle for Valentine's Day."

"He knows the key to a horsewoman's heart."

Hand me that hoof pick on the wall. Thanks," she said, bending over to clean Major's feet. "He plans to fly out to visit a few times this fall. He's become my biggest fan,"

"I hope Dane can get away, too."

Katherine straightened her back. "Think we'll work out in the field tomorrow. We need better approaches and exits from our jumps—better angles to shave a few more seconds off our time."

"Sounds like a plan."

"Just set the girth and bridle down by the door; I'll clean them. You need to take off."

Katherine waved goodbye on her way to the wash rack

with Major. The sun felt good on her shoulders as she hosed off her horse and scraped the excess water away. She let Major graze loose outside the barn while he dried and she took her time cleaning his tack, enjoying the smell of leather and conditioner.

While she worked, she looked ahead to the fall. She would leave for the fall circuit down the West Coast again after Josephine and TJ returned to school. The kids had enjoyed a full summer of trail riding and camping together. They could hardly keep her out of the mountains now, exploring and fishing with TJ nearly every weekend between working their summer jobs during the week. It made her happy to see how in love they were. TJ seemed to be doing well and spoke of his father often. The healing had begun.

Soon one year would have passed since Billy's death. She still half-expected him to drive up in his Chevy truck and saunter up to her flashing that gorgeous smile. It still seemed unfathomable he could be gone. But he wasn't entirely. With every jump he had made for her and every training technique he had taught her that she applied daily, he was still with her.

Today she turned a year older. They would all celebrate her birthday at Two Ponies again that evening as they had so many years dating back to her tenth birthday. So many fond memories—the fun parties, Betsy's wonderfully decorated horse cakes, so many great gifts including her first saddle and the gold stirrup earrings from Steven on her sixteenth birthday, and the excitement of finding Billy's special offerings he left her on the stump each birthday.

In a nostalgic mood, she gathered Major's lead and led him to the old stable. Cody stood waiting for his friend at the gate.

"You were a good boy today," she said stroking Major's shoulder. The big bay nuzzled her hand. "You're right, I haven't given you a treat yet. You certainly deserve one."

Katherine turned him loose in his paddock where Cody gave him a friendly nip hello. Major watched her closely as she turned the corner of the barn. He came into sight just outside his run-in stall, checking to see if he might have a few sugar cubes coming his way. Katherine laughed and turned to enter the tack room.

She froze in the doorway. On the stump lay an eagle feather. She knelt to examine it closer. It could have blown in and just happened to rest center of the stump. Or, was this another birthday gift from Billy, letting her know he had earned his wings. She liked that idea. Tenderly, she picked up the black wing feather and twirled it between her fingers.

Katherine walked outside and glanced upward to the cobalt sky. The screech of an eagle sounded in the distance. She searched the skies above but couldn't locate the majestic bird circling somewhere above her. She closed her eyes and imagined it gliding above the earth, catching the slightest breeze to lift it higher and higher until it disappeared into the sun.

Katherine tucked the feather in her pocket. It would accompany the white stone and chiseled heart she now kept in a special box on her dresser—a hand-whittled and painted box with a woman admiring her horse carved into the lid. She knew its purpose the moment she spotted it while shopping on the reservation before Christmas.

Like the box, her heart would hold Billy's love forever.

Time is too slow for those who wait,
too swift for those who fear, too long for those who grieve,
too short for those who rejoice, but for those who love,
time is eternity…

~ Henry Van Dyke Chief

#

The third and final book of the

Two Ponies Trilogy

From the Darkness

to be released soon.

Follow the author's progress on Facebook
and on her website at www.susanabel.com.

If you enjoyed this story, a review on Amazon would be greatly appreciated. It's the best way to support any author you enjoy.

#

Made in the USA
Lexington, KY
26 November 2019

57700834R00233